THE MURDERER IN RUINS

CAY RADEMACHER was born in 1965 and studied Anglo-American history, ancient history and philosophy in Cologne and Washington. He has been an editor at *Geo* since 1999, and was instrumental in setting up renowned history magazine *Geo-Epoche*. *The Murderer in Ruins* is the first novel in the Inspector Stave series; Arcadia Books will publish parts 2 and 3 (*The Trafficker* and *The Forger*) in 2016 and 2017. He now lives in France with his wife and children, where his new crime series is set.

PETER MILLAR is an award-winning British journalist, author and translator, and has been a correspondent for Reuters, the *Sunday Times* and *Sunday Telegraph*. He has written a number of books, including *All Gone to Look for America* and *1989: The Berlin Wall, My Part in Its Downfall*. He has also translated, from German, Corinne Hofmann's best-selling *White Masai* series of memoirs and Martin Suter's *A Deal with the Devil*.

THE MURDERER IN RUINS

CAY RADEMACHER

Translated from the German by Peter Millar

A

Arcadia Books Ltd
139 Highlever Road
London W10 6PH

www.arcadiabooks.co.uk

First published in the United Kingdom 2015
Originally published as *Der Trümmermörder* by Dumont Buchverlag, 2011
Copyright © Cay Rademacher, 2011
English translation copyright © Peter Miller, 2015

The translation of this work was supported by a grant from the
Goethe-Institut, which is funded by the German Ministry of Foreign Affairs.

ISBN 978-1-910050-48-4

Typeset in Garamond by MacGuru Ltd
Printed and bound by CPI Group (UK) Ltd, Croydon CR0 4YY

Arcadia Books supports English PEN *www.englishpen.org* and
The Book Trade Charity *www.btbs.org*

ARCADIA BOOKS DISTRIBUTORS ARE AS FOLLOWS:

in the UK and elsewhere in Europe:
Macmillan Distribution Ltd
Brunel Road
Houndmills
Basingstoke
Hants RG21 6XS

in the USA and Canada:
Dufour Editions
PO Box 7
Chester Springs
PA, 19425

in Australia/New Zealand:
NewSouth Books
University of New South Wales
Sydney NSW 2052

Translator's Note

Our main character's name is Frank Stave. The surname is typical for the Schleswig-Holstein area of Germany between Hamburg and the Danish border, and is pronounced 'Stah-ve'.

As a major port, Hamburg was bombed on many occasions during the Second World War but the greatest attacks, signally known as Operation Gomorrah, took place towards the end of July 1943 with a series of massive air raids by the RAF and, to a lesser extent, USAF, with heavy bombs including air mines which created an immense firestorm with temperatures of up to 1,000 degrees Celsius.

Most of the city was destroyed. It is impossible to know for certain how many victims there were, but estimates of the dead range from 34,000 to 42,000 and the injured from 37,000 to 125,000

A Cold Awakening

Monday, 20 January 1947

Still half asleep, Chief Inspector Frank Stave reached an arm out across the bed towards his wife, then remembered that she had burned to death in a fire storm three and a half years ago. He balled his hand into a fist, hurled back the blanket and let the ice-cold air banish the last shades of his nightmare.

A grey dawn light filtered through the threadbare damask curtains he had salvaged from the rubble of the house next door. For the last five weeks he had secured them to the window frames every evening with a few drawing pins he got hold of on the black market. The windowpanes were as thin as newspaper and even encrusted with ice on the inside. Stave was afraid that one of these days the glass would crack under the weight of the ice. Even the thought was absurd: these windows had been shaken by the shock waves from countless exploding bombs without shattering.

The blanket was frozen against the wall in places. In the dim early morning light the layer of hoar frost on the walls was so thick they looked as if they were covered with a layer of calloused skin. All that remained underneath was a few strips of wallpaper that might have been fashionable in 1930, stained plaster and in places just the bare wall itself: black and red brickwork and pale grey mortar.

Slowly, Stave made his way to the tiny kitchen, its icy floor tiles freezing the soles of his feet despite two pairs of old socks. With stiff fingers he groped around in the little counter-top wood-burner until at last he got a fire glowing in its tiny barrel-shaped belly. There was a stench of burning furniture polish because the wood he had been feeding into it used to be a dark chest of drawers from the bedroom of the house next door which was hit by a bomb back in the summer of 1943.

Not just *a* bomb, *the* bomb, Stave thought to himself. The bomb that took his wife from him.

While he waited for the block of ice in the old Wehrmacht kettle on top of the stove to melt and at the same time bring a little warmth into the apartment, he pulled off the old wool pullover, the police tracksuit, two vests and the socks in which he had slept. Carefully, he set them down on the rickety chair next to his bed. With an allowance of just 1.95 kilowatts of electricity a month – precious energy reserved for the hotplate and his evening meal – he didn't switch on the light; he had taken care, as always, to lay out his clothes in the same order, so that he could put them on in the gloom.

Stave splashed glacial water on his face and body, the drops burning his skin, causing him to shiver involuntarily. Then he put on his shirt, suit, overcoat and shoes. He shaved slowly, carefully, in the half-light; he had no way of making lather and his razor blade was dull. New ones wouldn't be available on the ration coupons for a few weeks yet, if at all. He let the rest of the water continue to warm up on the stove.

Stave would have liked freshly ground coffee, like he used to drink before the war. But all he had was *ersatz* coffee, a powder that produced a pale, grey brew when he poured the lukewarm water on it. He stirred in a spoonful of ground acorn roasted a few days previously, so that it at least had a bitter taste. Add a couple of slices of dry crumbling bread. Breakfast.

Stave had traded in his last real coffee at the railway station yesterday, in exchange for a few crumbs of worthless information. He is a chief inspector of police, a rank introduced by the British occupation forces, and one that to Stave, who grew up with terms such as 'Criminal Inspector' or 'Master of the Watch', still sounds odd.

Last Saturday he arrested two murderers. Refugees from East Prussia, who'd got involved with the black market and had strangled a woman who owed them something and thrown her body into a canal, weighted down with lump of concrete from one of the ruins. They'd gone to the trouble of hacking a hole in the half-metre thick ice to dispose of their victim. It was their bad luck that they had no knowledge of the local tides, and when the water went out their victim lay there for all to see, lying in the sludge beneath the ice, as though under a magnifying glass.

Stave quickly identified the victim, found out who she had last been seen with, and arrested the killers within 24 hours of her death.

Then, as he did every weekend when he was not overwhelmed with work, he went down to the main railway station and mingled with the endless streams of people on the platforms and asked around amongst all the residents of Hamburg who had been on foraging trips in the surrounding countryside and all the soldiers still retiring home: asked them in a hesitant, whispering voice, if they might have heard anything of a certain Karl Stave.

Karl, the boy who in 1945, at the age of 17, had signed up as a schoolboy volunteer in a unit bound for the Eastern Front, which by then already ran through the suburbs of Berlin. Karl, who had lost his mother, despised his father as 'soft' and 'un-German'. Karl, who since the battle for the capital of the Reich had been missing, become a phantom in the no-man's-land between life and death, maybe fallen in battle, maybe taken by the Red Army as a prisoner-of-war, maybe on the run somewhere and using a false name. But if that had been the case, would he not, despite all their disagreements, have got in touch with his father?

Stave wandered around, spoke to emaciated figures in greatcoats far too big for them, men with the 'Russia face'. He showed them a grimy photo of his boy and was rewarded only by shaking heads, tired shrugs. Then, finally, someone who claimed to know something. Stave gave him the last of his coffee, and was told that there was a Karl Stave in Vorkuta, in a prisoner-of-war camp, or at least somebody who might once have looked like the boy in the photograph and whose name was Karl, maybe, and who was still behind bars there, maybe. Or maybe not.

Suddenly three knocks on the door jolted him out of his thoughts; to save a few milliwatts of power the chief inspector had pulled the fuse from the electric doorbell, For a split second he had the absurd hope it might be Karl, knocking on his door at this hour of the morning. Then Stave pulled himself together: don't start imagining things, he told himself.

Stave was in his early forties, lean, with grey-blue eyes, short blond hair with just the first hints of grey. He hurried over to the door. His left leg hurt, like it always did in winter. His ankle had been stiff ever since he was injured on *that* night, back in 1943. Stave had a slight limp as a result, but was in denial of his handicap to the extent that he forced himself to jog, to do stretching exercises and even – at least when the Schulzes downstairs were not at home – rope-skipping.

In the doorway stood a uniformed policeman, wearing the high cylindrical Shako helmet. That was all Stave could make out at first. The stairwell had been dark, ever since somebody stole all the light bulbs. The policeman must have had to feel his way up the four flights of stairs.

'Good morning, Chief Inspector,' he said. His voice sounded young, trembling with nervous excitement. 'We've found a body. You need to come right away.'

'Fine,' Stave answered, mechanically, before it hit him that the word was hardly appropriate in the circumstances.

Had he no feelings left? In the last years of the war he had seen far too many dead bodies – including that of his own wife – for news of a murdered human being to shock him. Did he feel excitement? Yes, the excitement of a hunter spotting a wild animal's tracks.

'What's your name?' he asked the young policeman, pulling on his heavy wool overcoat and reaching for his hat.

'Ruge, Police Constable Heinrich Ruge.'

Stave glanced at his blue uniform, the metal service badge with his number on the left side of his chest. Another innovation by the British who hated all German policemen: a four-figure number worn over the heart, a glittering target for any criminal with a gun.

The overcoat was much too big for this policeman, who was skinny and young, scarcely older than Stave's son.

When the British occupation force had taken over in May 1945, they had sacked hundreds of policemen – anyone who had been in the Gestapo, anyone who'd been in a position of power, anyone who'd been politically active. People like Stave, who under the old regime had been considered 'on the left' and been relegated to low-ranking unimportant jobs, were kept on. New people were brought in, boys like this Ruge, too young to know anything about life, let alone anything about police work. They were given eight weeks' training, a uniform and then sent out on to the street. These rookies had to learn on the job what it meant to be a policeman. They included poseurs, who were no sooner in uniform than they were snapping orders at their fellow citizens and striding through the ruins like members of the Prussian nobility. Shady characters too, the sort you'd have seen in police stations back in the days of the Kaiser and the Weimar Republic, except that then they were in the cells, not behind a desk.

'Cigarette?' Stave offered.

Ruge hesitated a second, then reached out and took the Lucky Strike. Smart enough not to ask where the chief inspector got an American cigarette.

'You'll have to light it yourself,' Stave added, apologetically. 'I've hardly any matches left.'

Ruge put the cigarette in his uniform pocket. Stave wondered if the lad would smoke it later or keep it to exchange for something else. What? He pulled himself together: he was starting to suspect the motives of everyone he met.

Ready at last, he turned towards the door, then reached for his shoulder holster. The boy in uniform stared and watched as Stave fastened the leather belt around him, with the FN 22, 7.65mm calibre pistol in it. Uniformed police carried 40cm truncheons on their belts, no firearms. The British had confiscated them all, even air rifles from funfairs. Only a select few in the serious crime department were allowed to carry guns.

Ruge seemed to be getting more nervous still. Maybe he had just realised that this was serious. Or maybe he'd just like a gun himself. Stave dismissed the thought.

'Let's go,' he said, feeling his way out into the dark stairwell. 'Watch out for the steps. I don't want you falling down them and leaving me with another corpse to deal with.'

The two men plodded downstairs. At one point Stave heard the young policeman curse quietly, but couldn't be sure if he had missed a step or stubbed his toe on something. Stave knew every creaking step and could make his way down even in total darkness by the feel of the banisters.

They emerged from the building. Stave's room was at the front, on the right on the top floor of the four-storey rental block in Ahrensburger Strasse: an art nouveau building, the walls painted white and pale lilac, although that was hardly obvious under the layers of dirt and grime; an ornamented façade, tall, white windows, each apartment with a balcony, a curved stone balustrade with wrought iron. Not a bad building at all. The next but one was similar, only with brighter paint. The one that used to be in-between was similar too, but all that remained was a couple of walls and heaps of bricks and rubble, charred beams, a stove pipe so tightly wedged into the ruins that no looter had managed to steal it yet.

That used to be Stave's house. He lived there, at number 91, for ten years until that night, the night the bombs fell and took the houses down with them: one here, one there. Leaving holes in rows of houses along the city's streets like missing teeth in a neglected mouth.

Why number 91, but not number 93 or number 89? There was no point in asking the question. And yet, every time he left the building where he now lived, Stave thought about it. Just as he thought back to pulling his wife's body out from under the rubble, or rather pulling out what remained of her body. A while later, somebody – he couldn't remember who now, he could hardly remember much at all from those weeks in the summer of 1943 – had offered him the flat in number 93. What had happened to the people who had previously lived there? Stave had forced himself not to ask that question either.

'Chief Inspector. Sir?'

Ruge's voice seemed to come from miles away. Then a surprise: there was a police car standing in front of him, one of just five functioning vehicles at the disposal of the Hamburg Police Department.

'Now that's what I call luxury,' he mumbled.

Ruge nodded. 'We need to hurry up before anyone gets wind of what's up.' He sounded particularly proud of himself, Stave thought.

Then he threw open the door of the 1939 Mercedes Benz. Ruge had made no move to open it for him. Instead he went round the box-like vehicle and climbed into the driver's seat.

He put his foot down, driving in a zigzag. Before the war Ahrensburger Strasse had been dead straight with four lanes, almost too wide, the houses on either side not quite big enough for such a grand boulevard. But now there were ruins in the road, house façades lying like dead soldiers who'd fallen on their faces, chimneys, indefinable heaps of rubble, bomb craters, potholes, tank tracks, two or three wrecked cars.

Ruge swerved round the obstacles, too fast for Stave's liking. But the boy was excited. The street lights, those that were still standing, no longer worked. The sky hung low above them; an icy north wind blowing down Ahrensburger Strasse. There had to be a crack in the old Daimler's rear windscreen, letting Siberian air into the car. Stave pulled his collar up, shivering. When was the last time he'd felt warm?

The headlights swept over the brown rubble. Despite the early hour and a temperature of minus 20°C, a few people were already wandering like zombies along either side of the street: gaunt men in dyed Wehrmacht greatcoats, skeletal figures with one leg wrapped in rags, women with wool scarves wrapped around their heads, covering their faces, laden down with baskets and tin cans. More women than men, many more.

Stave wondered where they were all going so early. The shops were only open between 9 a.m. and 3 p.m. in order to save electricity for lighting, and that's if they had anything to offer on the rations.

There were still nearly one and a half million people in Hamburg. Hundreds of thousands had died in the fighting or in the bombings; many more were evacuated to the countryside. But their place had been taken by refugees, and DPs, Displaced Persons, liberated concentration-camp inmates and prisoners-of-war, most of them Russians, Poles, Jews who either couldn't go back home or didn't want to. Officially they lived in the camps the British provided for them, but many of them preferred to struggle along in the devastated metropolis on the banks of the Elbe.

Stave looked out of the window and saw the jagged remains of a house, just walls, like those of some mediaeval ruin, only thinner. Behind them more walls, and then more, and yet more. It'll take centuries to rebuild, he thought to himself. Then he jumped, startled.

'One Peter, One Peter'. The Hamburg police call sign these days.[1] A tinny voice, but louder than the groaning eight-cylinder engine. The radio.

For the past year the British had allowed the police to use the old Telefunken boxes to transmit from their headquarters in the Stadthaus. However, the five radio-patrol cars could only receive and not send messages – none of them had a transmitter on board – so the people at headquarters had no idea if the messages got to them.

'One Peter,' the tinny voice continued. 'Please report in when you reach location.'

'Bloody bureaucrats,' Stave muttered. 'We're going to have to find a telephone when we get there. Where are we heading anyway?'

Ruge braked; a British jeep was coming towards them. He pulled to the side, letting it pass, acknowledging the soldier at the wheel, who ignored him and drove straight past leaving a cloud of dust in the dry air.

'Baustrasse, in Eilbek,' the uniform answered. 'It's…'

'…near Landwehr railway station. I know it.' Stave's mood was darkening. 'There's not a single house still standing in Eilbek. What are those idiots thinking? How do they expect us to report in? By carrier pigeon?'

Ruge cleared his throat. 'I regret to inform you, Chief Inspector, that we will not even be able to drive as far as Baustrasse.'

'We won't?'

'Too much rubble. We'll have to walk the last few hundred metres.'

'Great,' Stave muttered. 'Let's hope we don't tread on an unexploded bomb.'

'There have been lots of people hanging round the scene of the crime of late. There's nothing left to blow up there.'

'The scene of the crime?'

Ruge blushed. 'Where the body was found.'

'So, you mean the location of the body,' Stave corrected him, but trying to do so as gently as possible. All of a sudden he felt his mood lightening, forgetting the cold and the rubble and the ghostly figures drifting along the side of the road. 'Do you have any idea what we can expect to find?'

The young policeman nodded eagerly. 'I was there when the report came in. Children out playing – God knows what they were doing out playing at that time, although I have my suspicions there – but anyway these children came across the body. Female, young, and...' Ruge blushed again. 'Well, naked.'

'Naked? At minus 20 degrees. Is that what killed her?'

The policeman's face got darker in colour still. 'We don't know yet,' he mumbled.

A young woman, naked and dead – Stave had a creeping feeling he would be dealing with some dreadful crime. Since CID Chief Breuer put him in charge of a small investigation unit a few months back he'd had several murder cases. But this one seemed different from the usual stabbings amongst black marketeers or jealous scenes caused by soldiers returning from the war.

Ruge turned left into Landwehr Strasse, and eventually halted by the ruins of the train tracks running across the road. Stave got out and looked around. And shivered. 'St Mary's Hospital isn't far,' he said. 'They must have a telephone. We can report in there. After you've taken me to the location of the body.'

Ruge clicked his heels. A young woman dragging a mangled tree stump in a cart behind her gave them a suspicious glance. Stave could see that her fingers were swollen with the cold. When she noticed him looking, she grabbed hold of the cart and hurried off.

Stave and Ruge clambered over the railway tracks, the stone ballast frozen together in lumps, tracks jutting up like bizarre sculptures. Beyond lay Baustrasse, only recognisable as a boundary line of the gutted, roofless tenement houses, their black walls stretching for hundreds of metres. Even now, so many months on, it still reeked with the bitter stench of burnt wood and fabric.

Two uniformed policemen, stamping their feet and clapping their hands in the cold, were standing in front of a crooked wall, three storeys high and looking like the slightest cough would bring it tumbling down to crush the policemen.

Stave didn't call out to them, just lifted his hand in greeting, as he carefully made his way over the rubble. At least he didn't have to make an effort to conceal his limp. There was nowhere here that anyone could walk straight.

One of the two uniforms raised his right hand in a salute, pointing to one side with his left. 'The body is over there, next to the wall.'

Stave looked to where he was pointing. 'Nasty business,' he muttered.

The Corpse with No Name

A young woman. Stave put her at between 18 and 22 years of age, 1.60 metres, mid-blond, medium-length hair. Blue eyes staring into nothingness.

'Pretty,' murmured Ruge, who had come over to join him.

Stave stared at the policeman until he squirmed, then turned his gaze back to the corpse. No point in embarrassing his young colleague; the kid was only trying to hide his nerves.

'Go down to the hospital and report in,' he told him. Then Stave bent down beside the corpse, taking care not to touch it or the rubble on which she was lying, as if spread out on a bed.

It looks staged, Stave thought instinctively. And yet at the same time she'd been well hidden, behind the wall and a few higher piles of bricks. As far as he could tell, her body appeared to be unmarked, not even a scratch or a bruise, her hands spotless. She didn't put up a fight, he thought to himself. And those aren't worker's hands; this is no rubble clearer, no housemaid, no factory worker.

His gaze slowly moved down her body. Flat stomach, a line down the right side: an old, well-healed appendectomy scar. Stave pulled out his notebook and wrote it down. The only thing he could see was a mark around her neck, a dark red line on her pale skin, barely three millimetres wide, all the way round her neck at the level of the larynx, more noticeable on the left than the right.

'Looks like she's been strangled. Perhaps with a narrow cord,' Stave said to the two shivering uniforms, scribbling his observations down in his notebook. 'Take a look and see if you can find any wire lying around. Or a cable of some sort.'

The pair rummaged around sullenly amidst the ruins. At least they were out of his way. He didn't believe either of them would find anything. There were some dark lines in the hoar frost suggesting something might have been dragged along here, but unfortunately one of the slovenly uniforms had trodden all over them. The murderer probably killed his victim elsewhere and dragged her here.

'Pretty corpse,' somebody behind him said. The throaty voice of a chain smoker. Stave didn't need to turn round to know who was standing behind him.

'Good morning, Doctor Czrisini,' he said, getting to his feet. 'Good of you to come so quickly.'

Doctor Alfred Czrisini – small, bald, dark eyes large behind his round horn-rimmed spectacles – didn't bother to take the glowing British Woodbine cigarette from between his blue lips as he spoke. 'Looks like there wasn't much need for me to hurry,' he mumbled. 'A naked body in this cold – I could have taken another couple of hours.'

'Frozen stiff.'

'Better preserved than in the mortuary. It's not going to be easy to establish a time of death. Over the past six weeks the temperature has not risen above minus 10. She could have been lying here for days and still look as fresh as a daisy.'

'Fresh as a daisy isn't exactly how I'd describe her current condition,' Stave grumbled. He looked around. Baustrasse had once been a working-class district with dozens of tenement buildings, reddish-brown, brick-built, five storeys, well looked after, trees along the street. Artisans, manual workers, tradespeople had lived here. All gone now. Stave could see little more than a landscape of fallen walls, stumps of burnt trees, heaps of rubble. Only one building still stood, on the right, at the end of the street: the yellow-plastered building of the St Matthew Foundation, an orphanage. Preserved from the rain of bombs as if by a miracle.

'Two kids from the home found the body,' one of the uniforms said, nodding towards building.

Stave nodded back. 'Very well. I'll talk to them shortly. And that, doctor, makes your task in determining time of death a little bit easier. If she'd been lying here for any length of time, the lads from the home would have found her ages ago.'

He liked the pathologist. The man's name – pronounced 'Chisini' – had made him the brunt of jokes in the years after 1933, mostly threatening references to his Polish origins. Czrisini worked fast. He was a bachelor whose only two passions were corpses and cigarettes.

'Are you thinking the same as I am?' the doctor asked.

'Rape?'

Czrisini nodded. 'Young, pretty, naked and dead. It all fits.'

Stave shook his head from side to side. 'At minus 20 degrees even the craziest rapist might get a bit worried about his favourite tool. On the other hand, he could have done the deed somewhere warmer.' He nodded towards the drag marks. 'She's just been laid out here.'

'We'll only find out more when we've got her laid out on my dissection table,' the pathologist replied cheerfully.

'But not her name,' Stave muttered to himself. What if the killer didn't strip her out of murderous lust? But as a cold, calculated decision? A naked woman in the middle of ruins where nobody has lived for years: 'It's not going to be easy to identify her.'

Not long after, the crime-scene officer turned up. He was also the official police photographer; CID didn't have enough trained specialists. Stave pointed out the drag marks. The photographer bent down over the body. As his flash went off, Stave suddenly saw in his mind's eye anti-aircraft fire from the roads, the brightly lit, slowly falling parachute flares the first British aircraft used to mark targets for the bombers coming behind them. He forced his eyelids closed.

'Don't forget the drag marks,' he told the man again. The photographer nodded, silently; Stave had sounded angrier than he had intended.

Finally he had the police bring over the two young lads who had found the body: barely ten years old, pale, blue lips, shivering, and not just from the cold. Orphans. Stave wondered for a moment whether he should play the stern policeman, and quickly decided against it. He leaned down towards them, asked them their names in a friendly voice and told them there was no need to be frightened for being out on the streets so early.

Five minutes later he knew all there was to know about the case. The pair had lit out before breakfast to look for machine gun or flak cartridges. Every day there were kids out there finding live munition amidst the rubble, but there was no point in warning the two off. Stave could remember his own childhood. He would have done exactly the same thing. And what good would it have done if some adult had told him not to? Instead he asked them if they often came out her looking for things. They both said nothing for a bit, then shook their heads hesitantly: no, this was the first time. None of the other children had ever done it either. The St Matthew Foundation had only just started taking in children again. Stave took the two kids' names and then sent them back to the orphanage.

'Damn shame they've just moved here,' he said, looking at the pathologist who was watching two porters carry the body off on a stretcher.

'You mean you have nobody to prove that the body was left here only last night. You have to depend on me,' Dr Czrisini said matter-of-factly, though there was a note of self-satisfaction in his voice.

Stave shot a questioning look at the scene-of-crime man who was going over the ground in ever widening circles.

'Nothing,' he replied. 'No bits of clothing, not even a cigarette butt, no footprints, no fingerprints, and certainly no lengths of wire. But we'll go over the whole ruined block.'

At that moment Ruge came clambering over the rubble, a little out of breath. 'Those goddamn doctors in the hospital…' he began.

'Spare me the details,' Stave said, waving whatever the man had to say wearily away. 'Did you get through or not?'

'Yes, after some lengthy discussion,' the young policeman said, suppressed anger in his voice.

'And?'

The policeman looked at him for a moment as if he didn't know what he meant, then suddenly got it: 'We – you, I mean – have to report to Herr Breuer as soon as you're finished here.'

Stave didn't reply. Carl – 'Cuddel' – Breuer had been appointed CID chief the year before. He was 46 when the British appointed him, young for the job. In the 'brown days' under the Nazis, he had been considered a Social Democrat and as a result vanished for part of 1933 into Fuhlsbüttel concentration camp, though he was later left in peace. After his appointment he had cleaned out all the Nazis and insisted on precision and professionalism from all his officers. Stave wondered why Cuddel wanted to see him right at the beginning of an investigation. It wasn't like him. It must be something important, he thought. But what? Aloud he told Ruge, 'We're going to look around here for a bit yet. Then we'll drive back to headquarters.'

The chief inspector spun on his heel. Ruins, everywhere he could see. The only other thing, beyond the railway track, several hundred metres away, was the vast concrete cube of Eilbek bunker: a seven-storey-tall monolith with walls up to six metres thick. The Nazis had built nearly seven dozen such bunkers during the war. They had been the only shelter for tens of thousands of people throughout the incessant bombing. They were indestructible, windowless fortresses, emergency accommodation for those whose homes had been bombed, for refugees and others with nowhere to go. Nobody knew for sure how many people lived in them, crammed together in a foul atmosphere of noise, dirt and their own stench.

'Well, nobody will have seen anything from their windows, that's for sure,' the young policeman said, following Stave's glance.

'If I had to live in one of those shitholes,' the chief inspector growled, 'I'd only go there to sleep and would spend the rest of the time in the open air, even at these temperatures.'

Ruge realised what was on the chief inspector's mind. 'We could drive most of the way there,' he said, hardly thrilled by the idea.

'Good,' Stave said. 'Let's go and have a little chat with the bunker people.'

Back through the rubble, across the train tracks, then along the wasteland of road, driving carefully to avoid the obstacles. It took them nearly a quarter of an hour trundling over the cobbles of little Von-Hein-Strasse, which seemed to be squashed into the earth by the great bulk of the bunker. Stave climbed out of the Mercedes and looked around. Next to the bunker were just ruins, but opposite, miraculously preserved, were two great car repair shops: huge barracks, locked up at present since there were no cars to repair. Behind them was a small park by the side of a stream, thought most of the trees had been burnt down or chopped to stumps by people looking for wood.

The north-east wind blew in his face. A one-legged man who was swaying on crutches, walking into the wind, vanished into the bunker. Stave followed him. The entry was a little walled-in concrete hut by the side of the great concrete cube. The steel door still had a sign with air-raid warning instructions. Inside there was a steel spiral staircase, and air like that in a U-boat: heavy, muggy, damp. Water ran down the fissures in the concrete. It stank of sweat, disinfectant, damp clothing, coal and mildew.

The stairs led into the core of the bunker. Up one floor to where a Roman numeral in dirty oil paint on a steel door marked the first level. Stave looked at the scribbled paint line, the pale, melted paint that in the light of a naked 15-watt bulb looked like scarred human tissue. Beyond the door lay a labyrinth of walls made of rough wooden boards, with which the inhabitants separated off their tiny 'apartments', each of which housed four, six or even more people. There were jackets and wet raincoats hanging on nails. Somewhere in the distance a child cried inconsolably.

'I'll take this floor, you take the next one up,' he told Ruge. 'After that, we'll take it in turns until we've been through the whole bunker. Ask them all if they noticed anything near where the body was found. Anything, no matter how trivial. And don't ask them just about the past 24 hours; ask about the last few days. It's possible the body was lying there a while. If anybody refuses to talk, put pressure on them. A lot of these bunker people don't like talking to anyone, let alone the police.'

Ruge grinned, clicked his heels and put his right hand on his truncheon. Stave noticed, but didn't say anything. He was far too weary to start playing nursemaid to overzealous uniformed coppers.

Stave knocked on the wooden boards of the first of the 'apartments' that in reality were more like rabbit hutches. No reply. He pulled aside a dirty piece of cloth hung there to cover the entrance. Inside was a Wehrmacht stretcher that served as a bed, supported by two wooden fruit boxes; dirty clothing lay on the floor and on the wall was a school leaving certificate, the paper yellow and torn. On a sheet on the stretcher lay an emaciated young man, snoring. Stave shook his shoulder. The boy groaned and turned to face the wall, without opening his eyes. He stank of home-made hooch, obviously drunk. Stave gave him a punch on the shoulder but he didn't react. Just grunted. There was no point.

He tried the next hutch. Empty. Then the next. He rapped on the bare board.

'If you're looking for somewhere to kip, try next door,' a hoarse voice cried out. 'There's nobody in there any more. But don't let the warden catch you, and don't make any noise.'

'Police, crime squad,' Stave replied, and pulled aside an old heavy overcoat that covered the door. It was an oilskin, probably a sailor's.

Against the wall opposite stood a pair of rusty bunk beds without mattresses. On the lower bed was a rumpled blanket and an old rucksack obviously used as a pillow. The bed above was missing the metal webbing a mattress would normally lie on. Instead there were a couple of boards set across the frame as a sort of shelf, with an old seaman's duffel bag stuffed so full that at any moment Stave thought the board it lay on would give way and empty its contents on to the bed below. In front of the bunks stood an ancient armchair, ripped fabric of an indeterminate colour, the back covered in soot. Obviously looted from some bombed house.

On the armchair squatted a man whom Stave initially would have put at around 70 years old. Then he took a closer look and changed his mind: maybe 50. Iron-grey hair, unwashed for weeks. Greasy strands that reached down to his shoulders. A white halo of dandruff on his shoulders, like snow against his thick, navy-blue, woollen sailor's jumper. Dark trousers and heavy, iron-heeled working boots. A man who once must have been big and strong. His muscles, still impressive, could be seen beneath his slack wrinkled skin. He had blue eyes, bushy eyebrows and a scar as wide as a finger that ran from the left corner of his mouth across his cheek as far as his neck behind one ear. Despite the cold his sleeves were rolled up, revealing blue tattoos on his forearms: an anchor, a naked woman, a word that Stave couldn't read. A seaman run aground, the chief inspector thought. He put one hand on the grip of his gun while he pulled out his police ID with the other.

'Anton Thuman,' the man said, without getting up. There was nowhere else to sit, except on the lower bunk bed, which Stave did not fancy. So he stayed standing as he told the man that the naked body of a woman had been found nearby.

'What's that got to do with me?' Thuman interrupted him before he could finish.

'Were you out on Baustrasse during the past couple of days? Or near Landwehr Station? Did you see anything suspicious?'

'I hardly ever go out. Too cold. I'm sort of hibernating here in this bunker. As soon as the port is open and the English let proper ships come in again, I'm out of here. Until then I'm just squatting in this dump trying to move as little as possible.'

Stave described the victim as well as he could. 'Do you recognise her?'

Thuman gave a dirty laugh. 'I know lots of naked young women. Some cost more than others. Could be any one of them, from the way you describe her.'

The chief inspector took a deep breath, despite the foul air. 'Is there any young lady who's been living here who might meet that description? Mid-blond, medium-length hair, blue eyes, about 20 years old?'

He laughed, then shook his head. 'How would I know? I'm happy enough to have nothing to do with anybody else. Two doors along there's that young drunk, out of his head day and night. Next door there was somebody with tuberculosis coughing all the time. Then after him some family turned up, none of whom spoke German; French probably, maybe DPs from some camp or other. Never exchanged a word with them though I heard them whispering to one another from time to time. The walls are thin. Then one of your colleagues came along and took them away. Now it's vacant again, but sooner or later somebody will crawl their way into it. I couldn't care less. Every night some woman screams as if somebody's hacking her hand off. It's dreadful. But if you think I might know who is wandering around in here? No idea. And I've only been to any of the other floors the one time. What's the point? I don't know anybody here and don't go sniffing around anybody else, not even some young blond cutie. I just want a bit of peace. And that's hard enough to find.'

'Thank you for your help,' Stave said, and left without saying goodbye.

An hour later he met up with Officer Ruge at the entrance to the bunker. Stave took a breath of fresh air.

'Never thought I'd be glad of this goddamn Siberian storm,' he said, shaking his coat, as if he felt the stench of hopelessness would stick to his clothing.

Even Ruge looked pale, tired and sweaty. 'Bunker people!' he wheezed as if that explained everything.

The chief inspector nodded. The concrete caves were the last resort of outcasts, those who'd given up all hope, those who had nobody. Anyone who had a modicum of strength left escaped from them, built themselves a hut out of rubble and cardboard somewhere out in the ruins, rather than stay buried alive under six metres of reinforced concrete.

'I came across one old boy,' Stave said, 'who went into his sleeping neighbour's cubicle and tore down two pieces of paper from the wall: kids' drawings. When I asked him why he did it, he just said he hated everything that made the bunker nicer. Mad.'

'Nobody admits to having seen anything in the ruins opposite,' Ruge said. 'Nobody even admits being over there recently. Nobody noticed anything suspicious. Nobody knows any young woman. I'd have arrested the lot of them.'

'Why? They're already in a prison,' Stave said wearily, bashing one hand on the concrete wall. 'Nobody said anything sensible to me at all. I believe them. I think few of them ever go out.'

'It looks like we have no witnesses, Chief Inspector.'

By now it was nearly midday. Stave was hungry and tired. At least it's good I don't have to talk, he thought.

Ruge drove the Mercedes past more piles of rubble, the heavy vehicle bumping in and out of potholes. Stave had to hold on tight, so as not to be thrown out of his seat.

'Sorry,' the young policeman said, his brow creased in concentration. 'It'll get better in a bit.'

And indeed in the Old Town and New Town districts large areas of the main streets had been cleared. Stave leaned back in his seat and closed his eyes until they reached police headquarters.

The tall building on Karl-Muck-Platz was an 11-storey sandstone colossus built back in the 1920s: reddish-brown stone with white windows, modern, no chimneys. It used to be the seat of an insurance company until the police crime squad moved in after the war. Most of the officers didn't care much for the place, even though they appreciated the fact that it was mostly undamaged. Windows that closed properly were a rarity in Hamburg these days. Stave liked the building because it was the exact opposite of the great neo-baroque concert hall opposite – as if the crime squad wanted to demonstrate police strength and order in the face of light-hearted frivolity.

Stave said a curt goodbye to Ruge and climbed out of the

Mercedes. The building was fronted by a portico with ten mighty square columns. Blue, white and yellow lacquered tiles formed a pattern on the ceiling, a little hidden touch of colour in a grey city. The entrance hall was also decorated with coats of arms and allegorical figures in ceramic, including a three-metre-high bronze elephant that not even the Nazi raw-material requisitioners had dared touch. The crime squad lads nicknamed him 'Anton'. Above the door the figure of a young woman held a gold, brown, blue and white model of a cog, the famous flat-bottomed trading ship of Hamburg and the Hanseatic League. Some of the officers called her the 'Seaman's Bride', unless they were in a bad mood and she became the 'Harbour Whore'.

Stave had no idea what the figure had originally been meant to symbolise. He walked through the double doors of the headquarters, big enough for a sailing ship to pass through. Then he limped up the stairs with their red, brown and white pattern marked out in endless little tiles that, every time he walked up them, reminded him of the skin of some giant snake.

Eventually he reached the sixth floor, and room 602. His office.

In the anteroom, half hidden behind a great black typewriter, Erna Berg, his secretary, was sitting on a chair that looked as if it might collapse at any moment. Stave said hello to her, forcing himself to smile. No need to pass his bad humour to anybody else, just because he'd seen a naked corpse first thing in the morning. He liked Erna Berg. She was blond, blue-eyed, optimistic and slightly plump. God only knows how she keeps so much flesh on her ribs with the food rations, Stave thought.

She was always full of energy, despite being a war widow. Back in 1939 she had married one of the soldiers being rushed to the front; a son arrived soon after. Her husband had been missing since 1945 and comrades returning from the war had told her he had been killed in action. But as it had not been formally confirmed that she was a widow, she got no widows' pension. Stave knew that the bare minimum wage she got from the police wasn't enough to keep her and her son and that she had to deal on the black market from time to time. He turned a blind eye.

'The boss wants to see you,' she said with a wink. 'I heard about the body,' she added in a whisper.

'Word soon gets around,' Stave grunted. 'Open a new file. "Unknown murder victim, Baustrasse." I'll write up the report later. And put an autopsy request in to the public prosecutor's office. Dr Czrisini knows all about it.'

His secretary looked away. 'I'm afraid you're going to have to spell that for me,' she groaned. 'I can never remember his name.'

Stave wrote the pathologist's name down on a piece of paper and looked in vain for a free space on her tiny desk to set it down, eventually pinning it to the wall behind her desk. 'I'm with the boss if anybody asks,' he said, closing the door behind him.

A few minutes later he was standing in the office of the chief of Hamburg police. Cuddel Breuer was an average-sized man with a round face, thinning hair and a pleasant smile. He could have been taken for a genial, deferential post-office clerk from the provinces. And more than a few police officers – and criminals – had made that mistake on first meeting.

Breuer had sharp, quick eyes and shoulders far too wide for an ordinary person. While Stave admired his boss, he was wary of him.

'Sit down, Stave,' Breuer said, nodding at a wooden chair before his desk. Both of them still had their winter overcoats on; the temperature in the office was 10°C at most.

'Coffee?' the police chief asked. 'Just the usual *ersatz* stuff, but at least it's hot.'

Stave nodded gratefully, and warmed his hands on the enamel cup.

Breuer nodded at a piece of paper in a filing tray on his desk.

'Last year's figure,' he said. 'In 1946 there were 29 murders, 629 muggings, 21,569 serious thefts and 61,033 everyday thefts. To be more precise: those are the crimes that were reported. On top of that we have rapes, assaults and smuggling in every form. "Poverty crime figures," the public prosecutor calls it. And I fear he's right. I also fear 1947 will be no better, especially not with a winter like this.'

Stave nodded. A couple of days earlier a police patrol had run across two DPs with black market slaughterhouse meat. The culprits, two former Polish slave labourers, had immediately opened fire with guns. One of the policemen died and the other was still critically ill in hospital. The culprits had been arrested and a British military tribunal had sentenced them to death. They were now waiting for the sentence to be carried out.

'But a naked strangled woman is something we haven't had recently,' Breuer continued. He sounded friendly still but added, 'The word's going to get around, as if we didn't have enough to worry about. Freezing apartments, hardly any electricity, starvation rations, coal trains out there stuck in snowdrifts. Or looted the moment they arrive. British officers commandeering the best villa houses in the city and putting up notices saying, "Off limits for Germans!" Every day new refugees pouring into the city, from the eastern zone, from DP camps, freed prisoners-of-war. What are we to do with all of them? We can't build new houses; in this weather it's too cold even to stir cement. People are angry.'

'And if they can't vent that anger on anyone else, then they'll make it hot as hell for us if we don't catch the killer,' Stave finished the thought for him.

'You get my meaning,' Breuer nodded with satisfaction.

Stave gave his chief an outline of the case: the young unidentified victim, the lack of witnesses.

'Is Dr Czrisini going to do an autopsy?' Breuer asked.

'Today.'

Breuer leant back in his chair and crossed his hands behind his head. For minutes on end he said nothing, but Stave had learned not to be impatient. Eventually the police chief nodded to himself, lit up a Lucky Strike and inhaled the smoke with gusto.

'In Hamburg we have 700 police to deal with crime,' he said at last, letting the smoke drift from his mouth. 'Most of them are new to the job, because so many of our former colleagues had the wrong politics.'

Stave said nothing. Even before 1933 most of the police had been on the far right, and later, Hamburg Gestapo alone employed 200 men. When the British arrived, more than half of them were dismissed straight away. Without the political purge, Breuer would never have got behind the chief's desk. And Stave's career wouldn't have gone anywhere either. Those were facts that did not exactly endear them to their former colleagues, not least because the difference between getting a 'yes' or 'no' from the British was often a very close-run thing.

'A victim whose name we don't even know. A naked young woman. A criminal who even now in these difficult times commits an offence not out of necessity, but because he's driven by some evil urge. A murderer who leaves no traces. And a city that demands we sort it out and quick,' Breuer said, in an almost dreamy voice. 'It's a nasty case, this one, Stave. I can't put some raw recruits on it and none of the older men are up to it.

So you're giving it to me, because nobody likes me, Stave thought to himself. 'I'll take it on, boss.'

'Good. Now, do you speak any English?'

Stave suddenly sat up in his chair. 'A little, not much, I'm afraid.'

'Pity,' said Breuer, then added dismissively: 'Doesn't matter, from what I hear your man has excellent German.'

'My man?'

'The British want to second a liaison officer to the investigation.'

'Shit!' Stave blurted out.

'On account of the particular potential political and psychological influence on the population,' his boss continued without commenting. 'It's an official request. I'm also seconding an officer from the vice squad to work with you, under your command, obviously.'

'From the vice squad?'

'The victim was naked,' Breuer reminded him.

'Who?'

'Inspector Lothar Maschke. He immediately volunteered.'

'Not exactly my lucky day,' Stave grumbled.

Breuer smiled and called to his secretary, 'Please show the two gentlemen in.'

The first man was wearing the greenish-brown uniform of a lieutenant in the British army. Stave guessed him to be in his mid-twenties, though his bright, almost rosy countenance and short blond hair made him look even younger. Not very tall, wiry in build, with the sprightly step of a sportsman. Stave wondered what it was about the uniform, perfectly ironed but worn just a bit too casually, and the expression on the man's face, though friendly and obliging, that gave him the air of being ever so slightly blasé?

'Lieutenant James C. MacDonald of the British administration in Hamburg, Public Safety Branch,' was how Breuer introduced him.

The officer saluted briskly in greeting, leaving Stave, who had no idea of a military salute, not knowing what to do with his hand. MacDonald smiled for a second then reached out his right hand to shake Stave's. 'Pleased to meet you, Chief Inspector.'

He spoke German with just a slight British accent, but Stave suspected that the pronunciation was MacDonald's only weak point in the language. I wouldn't be surprised if he can write reports in German better than many of my colleagues, he thought. Aloud he just said, 'Welcome to CID, Lieutenant.'

The second man followed the Brit into the office rather hesitantly. Stave put him at around 30, tall, lanky, in a rather tatty civilian suit that was far too broad for him. He had reddish-blond hair and a thin little moustache. The second and third fingers of his right hand were yellow with nicotine and his movements were a little twitchy – a chain smoker who couldn't get his hands on enough cigarettes.

Stave nodded to him. Inspector Lothar from vice. He already knew him. Maschke was not long out of police academy, and he had already managed to fall out with most of the people in CID although nobody could quite say why. Stave reckoned he had grown the moustache to try to make himself look older. And he had joked about Maschke in private because he still lived at home with his mother. A policeman! And in the vice squad at that!

'Gentlemen,' Breuer said, rubbing his hands together. 'I can't wait to see your results.'

'Shall we go over to my office?' Stave suggested.

He nodded in farewell to his boss and directed the other two men down the corridor. Just what I needed, he thought to himself resignedly, lagging behind as they walked by the dim light of the 15-watt bulb.

Stave's own office was bright. The window looked out on to the Musikhalle, and the ruins beyond it. Stave's old wooden desk looked as if it was swept and dusted on a regular basis. He was particular about putting everything away in the desk drawers, and every case file was duly annotated and kept in a huge metal cabinet.

Erna Berg came in and gave him a large cardboard file with a sheet of paper in it: the new murder report.

The chief inspector introduced the two men to his secretary. Maschke just nodded but MacDonald reached over to shake her hand.

'Nice to meet you,' he said.

Stave was amazed to see his secretary blush.

'I'll bring in another chair,' she said, just a touch too quickly.

'Let me,' said MacDonald, springing to his feet and bringing in another chair from the outer office. Erna Berg smiled at him. Stave nodded at her, indicating she should leave them and shut the door behind her. Then he thought of Margarethe and how he had been when they first met: that mixture of enthusiasm and embarrassment. And suddenly he felt envious of the young British officer. Stuff and nonsense. He banished thoughts of all women, except for one: the naked corpse.

'Sit down,' he said formally. 'I'll give you an overview.'

The chief inspector methodically went over the basics of the case:

the naked body with an appendix scar, the strangulation marks on her throat, the spot where the corpse was found, the two street lads, the questioning of the bunker-dwellers and the overall lack of leads. When he had finished, MacDonald took out a packet of English cigarettes and offered them around. Stave and Maschke hesitated, as if each was waiting for the other to react first. Then the chief inspector shrugged, and gratefully accepted the cigarette. In reality he had given up smoking but it was clear that Maschke had been waiting to see if Stave, now his boss for the duration of this investigation, was willing to take a gift from a former enemy. The vice squad inspector lit up and sucked so greedily on it that MacDonald, with a smile that was sarcastic and polite at the same time, forced a second on him.

'So, what do we do now?' he asked. 'I'm a soldier, not a policeman,' MacDonald added. 'My experience is war, not murder investigations.'

Maschke coughed so loudly that a cloud of blue smoke poured from both his nose and mouth.

Stave forced himself to smile. 'The more we know about the victim, the more we find out about the killer,' he began. 'Often the murderer and victim know one another. So first of all we'll try to identify the victim. We'll cut her open.'

'We?' said MacDonald, no longer smiling.

'A pathologist will do it,' Stave reassured him, smiling genuinely for the first time himself. The shocked naivety of his question had all of a sudden made the young Brit seem more likeable. Some soldier you are if you're frightened of the dead. 'We'll just get the autopsy report. Then, hopefully, we'll know a bit more – ideally the time of death. But I doubt there's any pathologist in the world who could identify her.'

'Save for the doctor who performed the appendectomy,' Maschke interjected.

'Yes,' Stave said. 'That's a possibility. We'll order up some copies and send them out to Hamburg hospitals. Perhaps somebody will

identify her. On the other hand an appendix operation is routine
and it's not likely that any doctor or nurse would remember.'

'Especially as they've had rather a lot on their hands over the past
few years,' Maschke added. 'Insofar as the hospitals are still standing
and the doctors still alive.'

The chief inspector shot his colleague a warning glance. It was
irritating enough to have an officer from the occupation forces in the
investigation group. But there was no need to provoke him.

But MacDonald gave no indication he had even noticed. 'And
what if the doctors can't help us?'

'We'll bring out posters with photographs of the victim and put
them up around the city. Even if that might be a bit...' Stave hesitated, searching for the right word, '...indelicate,' he finished the
sentence rather lamely.

The Brit raised an eyebrow questioningly, so Stave explained:
'One way or another we need to do something to get some leads
from the population in general. It's possible that somebody knew
the victim; in fact it's highly likely. And I don't want the citizens of
Hamburg to find out by chance that there is a murderer out there.
That could cause unrest.'

'That's why I've been seconded to the investigation,' MacDonald
said with disarming openness. 'The British authorities are also keen
to see this investigation concluded as quickly and discreetly as
possible.'

'I understand,' Stave coughed, and put out the cigarette he had
only half smoked, something noted with amazement by Maschke
who had long since smoked his down to his fingertips. 'We don't
have a lot to go on,' he acknowledged, 'just some very basics.' He
was reassured to see that the British officer was sitting up straight in
his chair, paying keen attention. Maschke on the other hand just sat
staring at the glowing tip of Stave's cigarette lying in the ashtray. He
knows what's coming, Stave guessed.

'Well-kempt appearance, clean hands with no marks, good skin,
well enough fed – our victim is hardly working class, and I also

doubt if she's arrived with some column of refugees from the east over the past few weeks. Nor do I think she's a DP. Their bodies usually bear traces of their previous…' Once again he found himself looking for the right word. '…difficulties.'

'Difficulties?' MacDonald queried.

Stave sighed. There was no point beating about the bush. Not in a team of investigators, least of all when they were investigating a murder like this.

'No tattooed concentration camp number,' he explained. 'Apart from the scar from her operation, our victim bears no signs of having been beaten, kicked or severely undernourished. Obviously it's possible she could be Polish or Ukrainian brought into the Reich to work. Maybe she was allocated to some farmer somewhere in Schleswig-Holstein or Lower Saxony or to some factory. And then, come 1945, she decided it was better to remain here as a DP than to go back to a home in the hands of Uncle Joe Stalin. But as we've noted, her hands are not those of a worker.'

'The daughter of some well-to-do household,' MacDonald speculated. All of a sudden it seemed the officer was enjoying the investigation, Stave thought to himself.

'Possibly. But daughters who've disappeared from well-to-do households tend to be reported as missing fairly soon. Of course, it's perfectly possible that someone will report her missing in the next few hours. But if we don't receive such a report by tonight, then at least we won't have to make a painful trip out to some villa in Blankenese.'

'So who could the victim be?'

'A "nightingale of the street",' Maschke suggested, having finally given up his anguished concentration on Stave's smouldering cigarette.

'I'm afraid that's not an expression I know from my German lessons,' MacDonald admitted.

Maschke laughed out loud. 'A hooker. A whore. A woman of easy virtue. A pros-ti-tute. That's why I'm part of the team, isn't it?'

Stave nodded. He was coming to understand why so many officers didn't like Maschke. 'She could be taken for one, superficially,' the chief inspector reluctantly admitted. 'The circumstances of death too; there are certainly grounds enough to take Maschke's usual customers to task.'

'Sorry, what does that mean?'

'It means we're off to the Reeperbahn,' Stave said, with a sour smile.

MacDonald gave a gleeful grin. 'My colleagues down at the Officers' Club won't believe I got to do that in an official capacity.'

'Always worth winning a war,' Maschke said under his breath. Softly enough that Stave wasn't sure the Brit had understood him.

'I have to warn you, Lieutenant, that the gentlemen on the Reeperbahn won't exactly be delighted to see us. And, I'm afraid, nor will the ladies.'

Then he called his secretary in. 'We need copies of the photograph. Just the victim's head, enough to be recognisable. And not too grisly, if possible.'

'How many?' Erna Berg asked, looking at the British officer rather than Stave.

So much for my authority, Stave said to himself. 'A dozen for Inspector Müller of uniform. He should get a few officers together to send round the hospitals and stick the photo under the nose of every surgeon they can find. The vitamin had an appendectomy and maybe one of the gentlemen will recall performing the operation. Then one more copy for the print works. We need 1,000 posters,' he hesitated for a second, then changed his mind and said, 'no, make it just 500. I'll do the words later. Tell the relevant people on the beat police that we'll need their men to put up posters the day after tomorrow. And I'll need a further three copies for these two gentlemen and myself.'

'Consider it done, boss,' Erna Berg said and hurried out.

MacDonald watched her go and then, when he saw Stave was looking at him, made a show of looking all around the room. 'Nice place you've got here,' he said.

Stave gave him a long smile. Then he took a stub of pencil and a sheet of paper from his desk drawer and said, 'Right, I'm going to write the wording for the poster. We'll meet up outside the main entrance in half an hour. To take a stroll down the Reeperbahn.'

Exactly 29 minutes later Stave was standing in the entrance hall by the huge doors. He was hungry and cold, and there were a thousand things he would rather do than question a load of pimps and whores.

MacDonald was already waiting for him. Much to Stave's annoyance, Maschke came running down the steps two minutes late, his coat flapping behind him. He wondered what his colleague from the vice squad had been doing for the past half hour.

When they got outside, MacDonald turned to Stave and in astonishment asked, 'But where's your car?'

'Petrol is rationed for the police too, Lieutenant. We usually go on foot or take the tram. It's only a stroll from here to the Reeperbahn.'

'If I'd known, we could have used my jeep,' MacDonald said, clicking his tongue in sympathy.

'Oh yes? We'd have driven down the Reeperbahn from whorehouse to whorehouse in a British jeep,' Maschke grunted, 'with every British patrol saluting us.'

Stave shook his head in annoyance. Then he handed each of them a photograph of the victim, still reeking of chemicals.

'Let's go.'

He pulled up his coat collar. It was now early afternoon and he hadn't had anything to eat since his miserable little breakfast. An icy wind was still whistling through the ruins. Stave felt like he was being beaten up by it. MacDonald on the other hand, in his pressed uniform and rosy pink cheeks, looked as if was going out for a pleasant afternoon stroll – which, Stave supposed, he probably was. Maschke had his second English cigarette clamped between his lips and walked a few paces behind, as if he wasn't with them.

On the dirty wall of an apartment building were yellow posters, some as big as blankets. 'Military Government – Germany/Law

No. 15' Stave read as they walked past. Bilingual proclamations of the occupation. As a matter of routine, Stave scanned them. There was nothing new. Posters like these, a few handwritten notes, chalk scribbles on bare wall. These are the newspapers we've earned for ourselves, Stave thought. The actual local press appeared just once or twice a week, a few thin sheets; there wasn't enough paper for more. He'd heard that a German radio station was going to be allowed to start up in the coming weeks. The newsreels in the cinemas depended on film supplied by the British or the Americans.

How else could you reach ordinary citizens other than by putting things up on walls? The military government stuck their proclamations all over buildings or on the few *Plakatsäule* advertising columns that had survived: new rations, curfew extensions, new laws – no German could say he hadn't known And the Germans themselves, out of necessity, copied their new masters: posted notices up on the brick walls seeking information about missing relatives, swap offers, looking for accommodation. And we police join in, Stave thought, with our photos of criminals and murder victims on our 'wanted' posters.

They had got as far as Heiligengeistfeld, a vast, filthy square with no shelter from the freezing winds. Two giant bunkers stood out against the sky, massive heaps like temples of some ancient, extinct and dark religion. A makeshift sign indicated that the ground floor of the bunker housed the editorial of 'Northwest Magazines'. On the other bunker was another sign, only slightly larger, which read, 'Scala'. Underneath was the current programme: *1001 Women*. The bunker now housed a revue theatre, boasting a thousand seats and skimpily dressed girls in fantasy costumes made out of coloured cellophane. Stave found an establishment of the sort in a place like this particularly perverse. At the moment, however, it was totally deserted.

Even Hamburg's amusement mile was a ghost town at present. The light was fading but nobody had electricity for neon signs. Several of the bars and clubs had been bombed: the Panoptikum, the

Volksoper and the Café Menke all lay in ruins. Barkeepers had set up shacks made of planks of wood and salvaged tiles amidst the rubble, tawdry dens in which men who still hadn't had enough of shooting could practice their skills firing crossbows at wooden targets. But nobody was out to try their luck right at this moment.

There were, however, a lot of people about; men, women, children, washed-out coats strolling about apparently aimlessly on the street at the corner of Reeperbahn and Hamburger Berg, wandering around in circles, looking up at the sky. Black marketeers. As the three investigators approached, the crowd drifted away from them, as if they carried the plague. Stave cursed under his breath: it's that bloody British uniform. On his own he could have wandered around unnoticed. But under the circumstances he could only watch as bottles of schnapps or cartons of cigarettes disappeared beneath coats while women and children turned their backs and a few lads disappeared down the alleyways. The only ones who actually came up to them were two young girls, about 18, Stave reckoned, not even proper adults. Blond, polecat furs around their necks, easy smiles, only a few dozen metres away, coming straight towards them.

The chief inspector walked a few paces down the Reeperbahn, more out of sorts than ever. The David police station had survived unscathed, to the annoyance of Hamburg pimps. The Zillertal had survived the hail of bombs, as had a few other establishments, Onkel Hugos Speisrestaurant, the Alcazar and a few dozen metres further towards Talstrasse, the Kamsing, Hamburg's only Chinese restaurant, which even these days offered fiery soups and exotically spiced rice, though from God knows what ingredients. But the thought of the Kamsing made Stave feel hungry. He made a decision.

'There's no point in this,' he told the other two. 'The streetwalkers will come up and talk to us, but everybody else clears off.'

'Better than the other way round,' MacDonald said, smiling at the two girls.

I'm going to lose it with him here in broad daylight, if I don't take care, Stave thought.

'We'll split up,' he ordered. 'Lieutenant, you and I will go into the local establishments and quiz the clientele. Maschke, you stay out on the street and question the girls and their pimps. We'll meet up in two hours in the David police station.'

At least that way he was getting the British officer out of the lime-light. He was fed up with everybody staring at them. MacDonald would stick out just as much in the bars and strip clubs, but nobody can do a runner quite so easily there. Maschke could question the girls and pimps more inconspicuously by himself. It also meant he would have to spend a couple of hours freezing outside while Stave and the Englishman could at least warm themselves up, going round the bars and clubs. Stave smiled to himself for the first time in hours.

They nodded farewell to Maschke, then turned to walk away, before the two blondes got to them. One of the girls gave them a disappointed look, the other seemed as if she wanted to shout something a lot less friendly at them. But then both opened their eyes wide.

'*Bonjour mesdemoiselles*,' Maschke purred. '*Vous avez la bonne chance de trouver un vrai cavalier.*'

Stave realised the girl had recognised him as being from the vice squad. Too late, darling. And he wondered on the side where his colleague had learnt to speak such good French. He watched as Maschke pulled out his police ID and shoved it under the girls' noses. The he dragged MacDonald over to the door of the Zillertal and pushed it open.

The air was stale with the sour aroma of old, cold tobacco, cheap schnapps and cabbage soup. Most of the tables were empty. At one four old men with red faces sat with water glasses containing some clear liquid. Two tired-looking girls at the next table were pretend-ing not to hear the suggestive comments being made towards them, preferring to warm their skinny hands on steaming enamel bowls of cabbage soup. There were two young men at a table to the rear of the room, in expensive overcoats – from before the war certainly – and good shoes. They were smoking American cigarettes and glanced briefly at Stave and MacDonald, then turned away, whispering to one another. Black marketeers.

The landlord was at the bar. He wasn't old yet, but he had been fat once and now the skin of his cheeks sagged in folds. He quickly removed a few unmarked bottles from the counter, and hid them in a flash. The sale and distribution of alcohol was strictly regulated, but everybody knew that the barkeepers of St Pauli offered smuggled or home-made schnapps as 'mineral water'.

Not my problem, Stave told himself, and went up to the landlord, who was looking even paler than he had done when they came in.

He pulled out his ID, then held the photo of the dead girl in front of his face: 'Ever seen her before?'

The man looked at him, then at the ID, and then MacDonald, as if he hoped the latter might save him. But the Brit was no longer smiling; he was staring back at the man coldly, Stave realised. Like a hangman, he thought to himself, and suddenly wondered if it wasn't just because of MacDonald's good German that he had been delegated to the investigation. Perhaps he had other skills. Eventually the landlord gave up hoping and turned his concentration to the photo, looking slightly ill, then shook his head.

'Don't know her. Who is she?'

'Thank you,' Stave said, turning away.

'Let's ask the lads with the cigarettes,' he whispered to MacDonald. 'But keep an eye on the two ladies supping away at their soup. We don't want them to do a runner on us.'

'What if they go to the ladies'?'

'You go with them.'

Stave had reached the table at the back of the room. The two black marketeers still had their backs to him, even though they had obviously noticed him long ago.

Stave pulled up a chair without asking them and sat down. Mac-Donald stayed standing a few steps behind him.

Eventually the chief inspector looked the two lads in the eyes: they were clean-shaven, well fed, with hard eyes and sarcastic smiles on their faces. Lads barely 20 years old, but they had already seen everything thanks to the war. Murderous brats. Stave had to suppress the urge to arrest them then and there. Instead he just pulled out, as before, his ID and the photo, showing both to the pair of them.

'Do you know this young lady?' he asked politely.

For a second or two, the pair were so taken aback that the grins fell from their faces. They expected different questions from a policeman: about cigarettes, money, medicines; the usual interrogation faced by black marketeers. Stave watched them visibly relax.

'No,' the taller one said, adding, 'sorry.'

His companion took a few seconds longer, but he too then shook his head. 'Not one of the girls on the Reeperbahn, that's for sure, Chief Inspector.'

'A customer, perhaps?' He didn't need to add, on the black market.

The two of them quickly exchanged glances, then decided they would answer the question properly: 'It's not all that easy to remember faces, if you know what I mean,' the taller one said. 'So I can't be 100 per cent certain, but I don't think I've seen her.'

'She was certainly pretty,' the other one remarked, as if that had anything to do with it.

Stave closed his eyes. He believed the two black marketeers, and also the landlord – this wasn't going well. 'Thanks,' he said amicably. As he got to his feet he realised how tired he was. He would have preferred to stay there, drinking a round or two with the two of them. Absurd.

'We'll ask the girls, then we're out of here,' he told MacDonald.

'What about the boozers over there?'

'Fine, you go talk to four heroes. I'll talk to the girls.'

'I'd have preferred it the other way around,' whispered MacDonald, but he gave a little smile and walked over to the men with the glasses of 'water'.

'What's up then, Master of the Watch?' the older of the two asked as Stave came over.

She's been watching me, he thought, and knows I'm no punter.

Smart girl. He studied the girls for a moment or two. The older girl grinned cheekily back at him, the younger looked embarrassed. They were early or mid-twenties. About the same age as the murder victim.

'Your colleague there looks keen,' the older one said, pointing towards the window.

Stave followed her gaze and spotted Mashcke towering over some elderly miserable-looking prostitute.

'I recognise your man with the red hair. He stops every woman who might be wearing a trace of lipstick because he can't tell the difference between an elegant young lady and a streetwalker. One of these days he's going to arrest the mayor's daughter. But I don't know you, nor your English companion.'

Stave didn't bother showing them his ID, or telling them his name, but just pulled out the photograph. The older girl was moved, but the younger one went pale and held up a hand to her mouth in shock.

'What bastard did that?' the older one asked. Her accent was broad, and she drawled. From East Prussia, Stave reckoned.

'That's what I'd like to know,' he replied. 'But I'd also like to know who the victim is.'

'Never seen her.'

'What about you?' Stave asked handing the younger girl the photo.

'I feel sick,' she groaned. 'I feel like throwing up. Take that away from me.'

Stave didn't move. 'You can throw up if you like, but only after you've told me whether or not you've ever seen this young woman.'

'No,' she almost screamed, then got to her feet and ran, bent over, to a grubby door to the rear of the room.

MacDonald leapt to his feet. To his horror Stave saw that the Brit had pulled a gun. Damned quick on the draw, he thought to himself, waving at the man to put it away. The lieutenant sat down again with the men, who'd all gone pale and were staring at him in terror.

'Hildegard's only been on the game a week,' the older girl whispered, almost apologetically. 'Where she comes from, they don't see stuff like that every day.'

'But you do?'

She gave a harsh laugh. 'I came here in a refugee column from Breslau. I've seen so many corpses that a photo has no effect on me. Do you think she was a streetwalker?'

Stave had been about to answer gruffly that it was none of her business. But he could hear a kernel of fear underlying the cheekiness in her voice: the fear every street girl had that the next punter will want more than just a quickie round the corner.

'What's your name?' he asked instead.

She hesitated a second, then whispered, 'Ingrid Domin. As far as most of my customers are concerned, I'm Véronique. It sounds more erotic. French, you know?' She made a scornful expression.

Stave thought back to the way Maschke had addressed the two street girls earlier. Then he dismissed the thought, tore a leaf from his notebook and scribbled on it: Tel 34 10 00. Extensions 8451–8454, and then his name.

'Do me a favour: if you hear anything call me. Or come by the office.' He added the number of his office. 'Whatever, no matter how hysterical or crazy it might seem, just tell me. Promise?'

She agreed and quickly shoved the piece of paper into her handbag.

The chief inspector got to his feet. 'I have no idea whether or not this woman was...' he found himself looking for a suitable word, '...whether or not this lady belonged to your trade. Up until a few minutes ago, I had assumed so, but now I'm not so sure, which doesn't mean that I'm ruling it out. So keep a look out. And talk it over with the other girls.'

'I'm a tough girl, I can look out for myself,' she said quietly. And smiled at him again

'Looks like you're lucky with the ladies,' MacDonald said as he came over.

The corner of Stave's mouth twitched. 'One of them ran straight out of the room to throw up,' he reminded the lieutenant.

'But the other one was a lot nicer to you than the four old boozers over there were to me.'

'So that was a waste of time too.'

'Absolutely. Never seen her, though, that said, at least one of them was so drunk he wouldn't have recognised his own mother.'

'Happens more often than you might think – that children don't recognise the corpses of their own mothers,' Stave replied.

'What now?'

'We hit the next joint. Then the one after that, then the one after that…'

'Good job there aren't so many left then,' MacDonald said. 'Never thought I'd be so grateful to our Air Force comrades for their bombing raids.'

Stave said nothing, just pushed open the door.

An hour and a half later the pair of them walked through the door of Kamsing, the last venue on their list, with nothing to show. They had questioned half a dozen landlords, a few guests, at least 20 street girls, as many pimps and a few black marketeers. But not one of them admitted to knowing the dead woman.

'Let me buy you one of these dreadful Chinese soups,' MacDonald said. 'They probably serve up monkey brains and rats' tails.'

'As long as it's hot,' Stave muttered gratefully and plonked himself down on a wobbly chair next to a little round table. Then he took a look around.

The restaurant was full, or at least fuller than the other places they'd gone round. Eight well-dressed young men were playing cards – poker – at a large table in an alcove. The notes on the table in front of them were thousand Reichsmark notes.

Bastards, Stave thought to himself, though he was only too well aware that his indignation was mainly fired by envy. Black marketeers gaming away their nights, gold watches on their wrists. His colleague called them the black marketeers' Iron Cross and had told Stave that they hid ration cards under the collars of their overcoats, and traded jewellery and medicine over the tables, wrapped in newspaper. But not yet, it was too early for that. Anyway, it wasn't his problem. He slurped at his soup.

'No idea what they use to spice this,' MacDonald said between spoonfuls. 'But it's at least as warming as a single malt whisky.'

Stave didn't bother telling the lieutenant that it had been years since he'd tasted even a drop of whisky. 'Indeed,' he muttered. At least he felt warm for the first time all day. His mouth was burning and numbed by exotic spices. He felt as if every muscle in his body was unwinding. If I don't get to my feet, I'm going to fall asleep here and now in front of MacDonald, he thought as he forced himself to stand up.

'Time to take the field. You do one half of the customers,' he indicated a rough line through the middle of the room, 'and I'll deal with the rest. Meet you at the door.'

A few minutes later they were done at Kamsing, no wiser than when they had entered. They wandered back down the Reeperbahn to the David police station where Maschke was already waiting for them. His breath hung in front of him in small white clouds, his nose was blue from the cold and he was rubbing his hands together. Stave suddenly felt sorry for him.

'Not one person on the Reeperbahn ever laid eyes on our victim. She must have been quite a girl,' he said.

Maschke's cynicism irritated Stave. Was he really such a hard case?

Or was there something else at play? The shyness of a grown man still living at home with his mother? Or, like many of his other colleagues who worked on the vice squad, had Maschke developed a protective attitude towards his little 'street swallows', as they called them? Was it relief he was hearing in the man's voice? Relief that the victim wasn't one of the Reeperbahn girls?

'Right, it's back to the office to talk through what we have or haven't found, then home to Mum for us all,' the chief inspector said.

Stave looked out of the office window at Hamburg spread out beneath him, as dark as during the wartime blackout. There were only a few lights here and there to be seen, probably from houses the British had commandeered. Other than that he could make out flickering flames from wood stoves, dangerous enough in themselves in the half-bombed semi-ruin, and the glow of candles. Even his own office in the grey evening gloom was lit by no more than a single dim bulb. Stave looked up at it with some concern: if it were to blow, he had no idea when he'd get a replacement. Probably not until the spring. He sighed and looked at the other two waiting in front of his desk.

Erna Berg was long gone. She'd left Inspector Müller's report on his desk. Stave flicked through it silently. 'No surgeon recognises the body,' he said at length. He was exhausted. 'Obviously one afternoon wasn't enough for them to go round all the relevant doctors in the city. They'll start again tomorrow. It looks as if the victim's appendix scar isn't going to give us a lead either, for the moment at least. Nor have we had any missing person reports over the past 24 hours.'

Maschke was drumming on the desk with his nicotine-stained fingers. 'It would also appear that none of the street girls has gone missing,' he said.

'Maybe she was new in Hamburg?' MacDonald suggested.

'The ice on the Elbe is a metre thick, the port is closed,' Stave interjected. 'Most of the railway lines are covered in ice, the points frozen, snowdrifts everywhere.'

'The bridges have been bombed, the stations destroyed,' Maschke snapped. MacDonald paid him no attention.

'Most of the trains that get through are carrying coal or potatoes, not people, and on the few passenger trains that do get through, returning prisoners-of-war are given priority. It's not impossible that some woman from somewhere else arrived in the city over the past few days, but it's extremely unlikely. Particularly a woman in such rude health as our victim.'

'Maybe somebody drove her here in a car?' MacDonald mused.

Stave was amazed at the lieutenant's honesty; he had wondered the same thing himself, but not dared to say it. 'Indeed,' he replied. 'Fuel is rationed, Germans have to carry a book in which they note every journey, and longer trips need special permission. Apart from anything else there are next to no cars or trucks still in working order. That makes it extremely unlikely that any German could have given her a lift. On the other hand it would have been no problem for someone British.'

'Good point,' Maschke said.

MacDonald looked unperturbed. 'I have a photograph of the victim. I'll pass it round my fellow officers.'

Stave smiled. 'Thank you. I'm glad to say that what we'll call the "British angle" isn't all we have. Let's assume that our victim is neither a streetwalker, nor a missing daughter of some respectable family, nor a working-class girl, nor a new arrival – then there are only a few alternatives remaining. Perhaps she was a little known secretary working for the city authorities, the occupation forces or in one of the few firms that have reopened for business?'

'Or she might be a shop assistant in one of the clothing shops,' Maschke suggested. 'C&A on Mönckeberg Strasse is open again.'

The chief inspector nodded. 'What else? Our unknown victim was earning honest money, at least enough to keep her well fed. Then she goes missing but nobody reports the fact to the police. Does that mean she has no friends or relatives here?' He thought of Erna Berg. 'Maybe she's a war widow? Or a refugee who arrived in Hamburg a year or so ago?' He got to his feet and began pacing up and down. Suddenly he no longer felt so tired. 'The other possibility is that she has a boyfriend or some other relative who doesn't want us to come across him, because he himself is the murderer. In most cases murderers and victims already know one another. Maybe we should look for a fiancé? Or an uncle? That's possible too.'

'So, what do you suggest?' MacDonald asked.

Stave gave him a cool smile. 'I suggest we meet up here again tomorrow. Good evening.'

An hour later Stave was standing in his freezing apartment, trying to light the fire. He had fetched three potatoes from his meagre rations in the cellar. They had been frozen and were exuding a sweet-sour slime as they thawed out. He cooked them on his cast-iron stove, along with his last white cabbage. Then he put it all through the mincer, formed the mush into a long loaf-like shape, added salt and fried it. 'Poor man's sausage,' the neighbour who had given him the recipe called it. Even though it took more than an hour to cook on the little stove, Stave didn't mind. It gave him the illusion at least of eating something nourishing. The other advantage was that cooking stopped him thinking.

Eventually it was time for bed. He lay down on the bed in his pullover and jogging pants, pulled the blankets up and stared at the window where the moonlight cast greenish patterns on the sheet ice.

Stave wanted to think about the dead woman, to weigh up the pros and cons of all the possible theories, to see if there were any leads they had missed. But the image of the unknown victim only brought to mind the image of his own dead wife. And that took him back to that night four years ago, amidst the hail of bombs.

If only I had schnapps, he thought to himself. Then at least I could drink myself to sleep.

Frozen Earth

Tuesday, 21 January 1947

He faced a wall of flames, red, white and blue, a burning heat on his face, his every breath agonising. All around him beams collapsed, tiles fell from the walls, a thunder louder than machine-gun fire, a stench of burning hair and scorched flesh. Stave was running through rubble, fire all around him, running and running, but stumbling because of his goddamn leg, painfully slow, even though he knew Margarethe was only a few steps away. He could hear her screams. She was calling out to him. And he was stuck somewhere else, amidst scorched walls, and smouldering wood, trying to call out her name, but only coughing and choking from the smoke that forced its way down his throat. And all of a sudden there was no sound from Margarethe, just a terrifying silence.

Stave jerked upright in bed, cold sweat all over his body. Utter darkness, ice on the window panes – yet he could still feel the burning, the fierce glare of the fires, a blaze as high as the apartment building. Goddamn nightmares, he told himself, and wiped his eyes. In reality he had been on duty on the other side of Hamburg that terrible night. He had been trapped in a collapsing building, his limp a perpetual reminder. But it was only several hours after the hail of bombs had stopped that, wounded and in shock from fear, he discovered the ruins of his own house. He had never heard Margarethe's screams.

There were others who were haunted every night by events they had actually experienced: the fear of death on the front line, in a submarine, cowering in a cellar, sitting in a Gestapo cell. There were ways of dealing with that, Stave reckoned – maybe now that the war was over, maybe revisiting the scene of the horror. But how could anyone break free of a nightmare based on something they had never witnessed?

Self-pity was no help either, he reflected, clambering out of bed. The sheets crackled as the frost on them broke. I need to get more fuel, he said to himself as he kindled fire in the wood burner.

A short while later he set out on the long walk to CID headquarters; there was no fuel for the buses. A few tram lines had been patched up and were working again, but only for a few hours each day. I could get used to having Ruge's taxi service, Stave thought to himself.

But secretly he was grateful for the hour's walk. He was used to the sight of the rubble, the yellowing posters, the chalk graffiti, the cowed figures on the streets; none of that got him down any more. He enjoyed keeping up a brisk pace. It warmed him up, while at the same time the icy wind kept his head clear. Nothing to worry about, nothing to trouble him – for a whole hour.

By the time he reached the tall building on Karl-Muck-Strasse he was in a good mood. Erna Berg was already waiting for him, a smile on her face, maybe even a little more cheerful than normal.

'The Herr Lieutenant is waiting for you in your office.'

Maschke was there too, but his secretary had either forgotten that or deliberately not mentioned him. The chief inspector said hello to both of them and sat down, preferring to keep his overcoat on. Erna Berg hurried over, set two mimeographed sheets down in front of him, gave MacDonald a shy glance and disappeared.

'Doctor Czrisini's report,' Stave said. The other two were silent for a moment while he studied it. 'A few things at least are clear. The date of death was between the eighteenth and twentieth of January, most probably towards the latter. So we may as well take the twentieth as a starting point. Cause of death: strangulation. It seems likely the murderer used a piece of wire. And highly likely he approached his victim from behind and slung the wire around her neck. It doesn't look as if she tried to defend herself. Apart from that no other marks or evidence either on or inside the body.'

'No sign of sexual intercourse?' Maschke asked.

Stave shook his head. 'No indication of rape. Nor any traces of sperm or other suggestions of consensual sexual activity shortly before death. Although obviously that possibility cannot be totally excluded.'

MacDonald coughed, clearly embarrassed. 'How do you mean?'

Maschke gave a wan smile. 'In the case of consensual sexual intercourse there would be no obvious wounds. Down there, I mean. And if the lucky lad she'd last let do the business was wearing a French letter, there'd be no trace of sperm either.'

'That's one way of putting it,' Stave muttered. 'But it is also clear that she'd been lying there for two days at most, meaning the killer hasn't had that much time to vanish into the woodwork.'

The lieutenant smiled: 'Given that no ships and only a few trains have left the city, that means he must still be in Hamburg.'

'Not exactly reassuring for the good folk of our city,' Maschke added.

'But it makes our work a bit easier, I hope,' Stave said, before turning to MacDonald: 'Have you asked around amongst your fellow officers?'

'They all took a look when I showed the photo of the strangled woman around at the club,' the lieutenant replied. 'But nobody recognised her. The officers have promised to ask their men, but I fear we won't get much of a response there.'

Maschke snorted dismissively, but said nothing, catching Stave's warning glance.

'Keep at it,' the chief inspector muttered. 'It's like surgeons and appendectomies; you can't be 100 per cent sure of anything until you've eliminated all possible alternatives.'

The lieutenant nodded, and smiled again: 'My pleasure.'

For him this investigation is just a bit of sport, like fox-hunting, Stave thought to himself, but then maybe that's not such a bad comparison. He sighed wearily, 'I need to go and file a report to the public prosecutor. Lieutenant, will you please be so good as to ask around a bit more amongst your comrades-in-arms? At the moment, British soldiers are the only ones who can easily leave Hamburg. And time is pressing.'

MacDonald nodded.

'And Maschke, perhaps you can make enquiries amongst the street crime department. It might have been a mugging, somebody taking the girl for everything she had on her. These days even underwear fetches a price on the black market. See if they have anything on their files.'

Maschke cleared his throat, embarrassed all of a sudden. 'You know, Chief Inspector, the files aren't...'

Stave cursed under his breath. On 20 April 1945, with the British at the gates of the city, the Gestapo had burned all their files, some of them in the crematorium of the Neuengamme concentration camp. In doing so they had not only destroyed the evidence of their own crimes but also documentation relating to large numbers of ordinary criminals. If, prior to 1945, there had been reports of a mugger who was happy to murder using a piece of wire like a garrotte and taking every item from his victim including their underwear, then like as not there would no longer be a file on him.

'Give it a go, even so,' he said.

Maschke got to his feet and left, nodding to Stave but ignoring the lieutenant.

MacDonald however had got to his feet too, and casually asked Stave, 'Which public prosecutor is responsible for this case?'

'Doctor Ehrlich,' Stave replied. 'I've not dealt with him before.'

'I know him – from England.' The lieutenant gave him a look that was part sympathetic, part amused. 'You should take care. He's a tougher nut than he looks and he might not be the greatest fan of the Hamburg police.'

Stave slumped back down on his seat and suggested MacDonald sit down again too: 'I would be grateful if you could fill me in.'

MacDonald smiled: 'Just between the two of us?'

'But of course.'

'Herr Ehrlich,' the lieutenant said in a measured tone, 'joined the Hamburg public prosecutor's office in 1929. He's a very cultivated man, well-educated and gifted in music, a collector of modern art, above all the Expressionist movement. And, unfortunately, Jewish.'

The chief inspector closed his eyes. He knew what was coming.

'In 1933, of course, he was immediately dismissed,' MacDonald continued in the same dispassionate tone. 'He got a job as a copy editor for a legal publishing house thanks to his wife – who by the way was Aryan enough to be a Wagnerian opera star. Both their sons were sent to private school in England, to get them out of the line of fire. Then came *Reichskristallnacht.*'

Stave nodded. He remembered the night. When the first reports of arson came in he was in the police station at Wandsbek, about to rush out to the nearest synagogue. Then came the order to remain in the building. A very clear order. And he complied. Not exactly the most heroic moment in his life. He had never spoken of it to anyone, not even Margarethe.

'Ehrlich was arrested on the night of 1 November 1938 and taken to Neuengamme. I can imagine it wasn't much fun, even though he almost never mentions it. A few weeks later he was released; friends in London had got a British visa for him. He sold off his art collection – for a song, I imagine. He managed to scrape together just enough money to buy his passage to England. His wife was not allowed to go with him; the visa was for him alone. Then war broke out.'

MacDonald shrugged almost apologetically. 'The woman was on her own, desperate, abandoned by her husband and sons. The neighbours avoided her. She couldn't even give piano lessons any more because nobody wanted to be seen in her company. Back in London Ehrlich was like a caged tiger pacing up and down: he tried everything to bring her over – via Switzerland, the USA, Spain, Portugal. There was no way. Eventually in 1941 he received a message from the

Red Cross that his wife had taken her own life with an overdose of sleeping tablets.

'By then I had already got to know him. He had found lodgings in Oxford and was lecturing on Roman law. It would be exaggerating to say we had become friends. Nonetheless it was me who got him the job at the public prosecutor's office here, a few months ago.'

'You?' Stave almost blurted out.

MacDonald gave him an ironic smile, and Stave found himself wondering just how much power this young officer wielded.

'Ehrlich was keen to return to Germany – to help with the reconstruction, to build a democracy, as he put it. So I asked around amongst our people and came up with this. There is a shortage of legal personnel with a clean slate and we're grateful for every non-Nazi we can find. Not just in the prosecutor's office but in the police too.'

Stave vaguely recognised it as a compliment. 'But why on earth Hamburg? Ehrlich must have a lot of scores to settle here. Not exactly the best qualification for a public prosecutor.'

'On the contrary, an excellent qualification,' MacDonald replied. 'Herr Ehrlich is one of the plaintiffs in the Curio House case.'

Stave didn't need any explanation. Since 5 December 1946 the house on Rothenbaumchaussee had been the setting for the trial of nine men and seven women who as guards at the female concentration camp at Ravensbrück were charged with responsibility for the deaths of thousands.

'Does he have the time to take on a new case?'

'He asked to be put in charge of it. Herr Ehrlich is a hard worker.'

After the lieutenant left the room, Stave sat there for a moment, thinking. Why Ehrlich? The Curio House case would give him opportunity enough to bring particularly nasty Nazis to the scaffold. Why would a politically motivated public prosecutor like him be interested in the naked corpse of an unknown woman? It looked like a hard case, for sure, but in no way political. Was it?

In the end he gave up, and got to his feet with a sigh. Maybe what attracted the prosecutor to the case was nothing personal at all, but just the very mystery attached to it. Then again, maybe he wanted to be in charge of a case the police fell down on, giving him the chance to cashier a few CID men who might have worked rather too closely with the Gestapo but got away without being sacked in 1945.

He was likely to find out soon enough. And Ehrlich was equally likely to find out what Stave had done in 1938 when the synagogues were being plundered. Absolutely nothing.

Hamburg Palace of Justice was a huge Renaissance palace with a bright red façade of light golden sandstone and tall white windows, some of them flanked by twisted columns: a great big nineteenth-century shoebox which, incredibly, managed to escape being hit by a single bomb in two world wars. It was in this fortress that the public prosecutor's department had their offices.

Stave walked into the building. It was only a few paces across the square from the CID building, past the concert hall and through a neglected little park.

A few minutes later he was sitting on an uncomfortable visitor's chair. Nervous, feeling like a schoolboy called in to see the headmaster, angry with himself for the way he felt but unable to do anything about it. He glanced around surreptitiously while the man sitting opposite leafed through documents in front of him.

Doctor Albert Ehrlich was a small, bald-headed man, with eyes swimming behind the thick lenses of old-fashioned horn-rimmed spectacles. He was in collar and tie with an English tweed jacket and razor-sharp pressed trousers. There were no photos of his wife or sons, nothing at all of a personal nature, just filing cabinets and sheets of paper and on a little table next to him a big black typewriter. Stave glanced furtively at Ehrlich's short, chubby fingers covered with a light down and noticed he wore no wedding ring.

He no longer wore a wedding ring himself. One night in the summer of 1943 he had thrown it into the Elbe down by the harbour. The water was seductively close and dark ... But he had turned on his heel and gone home, if that's what you could call the ruins he inhabited. He closed his eyes for a moment.

'I'm very sorry to have kept you waiting,' Ehrlich said at last, closing the file in front of him. 'Can I offer you tea?' he said, in a quiet, cultivated voice.

Stave gave a timid smile. 'Thank you, yes.' And he opened his eyes wide to see a secretary come in with a steaming teapot that smelled wonderful. Real tea, Stave realised, Earl Grey even, rather than nettles with some hot water poured over them.

Ehrlich poured the tea. 'I used to drink coffee,' he piped up, 'I only got used to tea during my time in England. It is a lot easier to get hold of, especially here in the British occupation zone.'

'Is that why you came back to Hamburg, the chief port in the British zone?'

'Ah, I can see Lieutenant MacDonald has already put you in the picture,' Ehrlich replied with an amused smile. Stave thought there was something striking about his oversized owl-like eyes, something furtive.

You idiot, he told himself, typical CID attitude, ready to break into the conversation, take the man by surprise: not exactly the right way to deal with a public prosecutor.

'Thank you for agreeing so readily to our request for an autopsy,' he said, to change the subject.

Ehrlich sat back, relaxed: 'Tell me about the case. I'm all ears.'

Stave told him what they had found out including the various theories about the victim and her possible attacker.

'A difficult one,' Ehrlich said at last when the chief inspector had finished.

'The first thing is to find out who the victim is. Otherwise we're never going to get anywhere,' Stave admitted.

'So you don't think it was a robbery-motivated murder, despite sending Maschke off to find files on such incidents even though you know as well as I do that they've been burnt in a certain oven.'

He's a wily one, thought Stave in surprise. In a mugging, the identity of the victim doesn't necessarily lead to the perpetrator, as criminals often attack people they don't know. Ehrlich must have decided that the victim and her attacker were acquainted and that Stave had an idea.

'I'm simply trying to be efficient,' he replied.

'Ah, efficiency – a very German characteristic,' the prosecutor replied, with just the slightest hint of irony.

'A characteristic in criminal work everywhere,' Stave shot back, regretting that they had got into this game of cat-and-mouse. 'But you're right,' he added, in a conciliatory tone. Maybe he had suddenly come to trust Ehrlich, or maybe it was just the effect of the hot tea. Contrary to his normal habit of presenting prosecutors with no more than hard facts and the most plausible theories, Stave decided that this time he would mention something that was little more than the vaguest suspicion. 'This crime was not just brutal,' he ventured, hesitantly, 'but also particularly efficient. Lethal force, resulting in immediate death. Then the thorough stripping of the body.'

'Cold blooded,' Ehrlich interjected.

'Indeed. Carefully planned and perfectly executed. Someone capable of that has either had every sense of morality blunted – or is mentally ill but at the same time capable of logical reasoning.'

'After this war and the 12 years of that regime there are more than enough people running around Germany whose underdeveloped conscience hasn't the slightest problem with one death more or less. And we would see most of them as ordinary honest citizens.'

'Even so, it's not every day here in Hamburg that a young woman gets garrotted, stripped and left lying in the rubble.'

The prosecutor nodded: '*Touché*. So, what do you really think happened, Chief Inspector?'

'I reckon it was somebody mentally deranged. Somebody who knew the victim or at least had been surreptitiously watching her. Somebody who planned the deed over weeks or even months, and chose the moment to strike.'

'What evidence do you have?'

'Apart from the brutal nature of the attack, none at all.' Stave didn't see the point in trying to make the prosecutor think he knew more than he did. 'In our line of work we often have to deal with mentally unsound people. I'm no expert in this field. If people like that – as I've heard said – have a particular modus operandi, there's none obvious here. But then it's a bit too early for that.'

The two of them sat in silence for a while. There was no need to say what both Stave and Ehrlich were thinking: there would be more such murders.

'So what do you intend to do now?' the prosecutor finally asked, pouring them both more tea.

The chief inspector nodded in thanks and warmed his hands on the cup, inhaled the aroma, and smiled. Then he pulled out of his coat pocket a roll of paper that still smelled of fresh printer's ink.

'This is the first copy of a reward poster we intend to put up,' he said, handing it over the table.

'"A reward of one thousand Reichsmarks",' Ehrlich read out in a quiet voice. '"Robbery and murder. On Monday, 20 January 1947, an as yet unidentified woman was found dead in Baustrasse, Hamburg. Violent robbery suspected." Well, you're not exactly a poet, Chief Inspector.' Ehrlich examined the photograph of the deceased and read the description.

'One minute you tell me you don't suspect it was violent robbery,' he said. 'And yet here I am reading it in black and white.'

'I don't want to get people worried,' Stave said in justification. 'And in any case, I don't think suggesting it might be a mentally disturbed individual is exactly going to help.'

'What do you mean?'

'If we say we're looking for a lunatic then hundreds of witnesses will turn up accusing their neighbours, colleagues or anybody who's got up their noses. That will mean a waste of time and effort, and cause more problems than it solves.'

'You may well be right.'

'We're going to put up these posters all over town, and wait until somebody who knows the victim turns up.'

'And what do you intend to do in the meantime?'

'I intend to go to the cemetery,' Stave replied. 'They're burying the victim this afternoon in Öjendorf. I'll stay in the background and see if any mourners turn up.'

Stave didn't return directly to his office after the interview. Instead he wandered aimlessly around town. He needed to get his thoughts in order, and that was something he did best while walking. He went through every detail of the case again in his head: what did he know about the victim? Nothing. About the perpetrator? Even less. What else could he do but wait? Wait for a witness to turn up, or at least somebody who could identify the victim from the photograph on the poster. But what if nobody turned up? Maybe he had missed a trick? But if he had, what was it?

Stave felt under pressure, and he didn't like that. Under pressure from Cuddel Breuer, and from Ehrlich. He preferred to work on his own. He liked to bring in experts only when necessary: photographers, forensics, pathologists. But what was he supposed to do with Maschke? Not to mention MacDonald. Neither of them were CID people; they were amateurs not professionals. On the other hand, maybe an outsider's opinion might be useful: it was possible the Brit might notice something he had missed. He seemed bright enough, and he had influence.

Stave dragged himself away from his thoughts. He was back at Eppendorfer Baum, a long way from Karl-Muck-Platz. A snack bar had been set up in a half-ruined building. The upper stories had been hit by a bomb and the remainder of the building stood like a half-eviscerated corpse. Only the ground floor seemed undamaged and somebody had put up a board with the childishly scrawled words 'Fresh meals'.

Stave walked into the brightly lit but sadly unheated room and sat down at a table. He did his best to ignore the throbbing in his left ankle. He cast a casual glance around. It was midday and there were a few workers, a few office people, a mother with two children, and sitting on his own in a corner a man with a 'Russia face' in an undyed Wehrmacht greatcoat, the empty left sleeve sewn up to the front of it.

Stave ordered the dish of the day, which cost one Reichsmark: a pickled herring with two thin slices of gherkin and a spoonful of some murky vegetables with no taste. He gobbled it down, only to feel hungrier than before. If only they had coffee. He sighed deeply, paid and left.

Back at the office MacDonald was waiting for him. Or at least that's what he said. Stave had the impression that it was not so much the murder investigation that had brought the lieutenant to Karl-Muck-Platz as the chance for a chat with Erna Berg.

'Anything new from the ranks of the British army?' Stave asked.

MacDonald gave an apologetic shrug that for a moment made him look like a little boy. 'Everybody stares wide-eyed when they see the photograph, but there's no indication that anybody recognises her.'

'Have you got your jeep here?'

The lieutenant nodded. 'Are we going on a car chase? Like in the American movies? Should I get us Tommy guns?'

Reluctantly Stave found himself smiling: 'We can hide the hardware in a black coffin. We're going to the cemetery.'

The chief inspector was relieved that he didn't have to travel by tram and on foot all the way out to the east of Hamburg. MacDonald drove him there in his boxlike, mud-coloured jeep, parking it right by the main entrance. When they set off the wind was blowing so hard the collapsible windscreen rattled back and forth and cold draughts blew through rips in the canvas top, while the suspension was so hard, every time they bounced over a pothole it was like a blow to the solar plexus. But Stave didn't mind. He closed his eyes for a moment, massaging the thigh of his bad leg. He had cramp and was in pain.

'An old war wound?' MacDonald was driving carefully, keeping his eyes on the road, but he must have spotted him out of the corner of his eye.

Stave felt he'd been somehow caught out. 'A ceiling beam fell on me; I didn't get out of the way in time,' he told him curtly.

The lieutenant just nodded.

'How is it you speak such good German?' Stave asked him, trying to steer the conversation away from himself, and because he couldn't think of anything else to ask. He had to repeat it, louder, to make himself heard over the noise of the engine.

'I learned it at university, Oriel College, Oxford. I was actually studying history but my special subject was Prussia. I did my master's degree on Bismarck's attitude towards Great Britain in the years prior to 1870. I even came to Berlin to study some documents.'

'You did all of that before the outbreak of the war? How old are you then?'

MacDonald laughed. 'I was a Christmas baby, born on 24 December 1920. I was in Berlin during my first year at university, aged just 18. That was the summer of 1939. I had intended to stay for a few months, but in August it was becoming ever more clear that war was likely, so I upped sticks and left. There are probably a few books of mine gathering dust in a rented room somewhere. Unless, of course, the rented room has been burnt to the ground.'

'Why did you settle on the history of Prussia? A pretty esoteric subject in Oxford, I'd imagine.'

'Esoteric subjects are what Oxford is all about,' MacDonald replied with a nostalgic smile. Then all of a sudden he turned serious.

'Do you have any idea what it's like living in a society based on class, Chief Inspector? Earls and dukes, exclusive private schools, London clubs, stiff upper lips, ancestors who came over with William the Conqueror?'

Stave shook his head, and then, to his own surprise, nodded. 'Here we had party members, German blood or non-Aryan; you didn't need to have aristocratic ancestors, but it helped in a big way if you'd been on the 1923 demonstration at the Feldherrnhalle in Munich or at least had joined the party before 1933.'

'But you didn't join in any of that.'

'I had German blood, nothing I could do about that, but the party? No thanks.'

MacDonald stared silently ahead. On either side of the street lay slabs of concrete, piles of fallen roof tiles and twisted piping like some surreal sculpture. One four-storey façade stood on its own, with torn curtains flapping in the wind like flags. Then came an area completely cleared of rubble with two dozen Nissen huts standing on it, like corrugated iron pipes cut down the middle: barracks put up by the Brits as emergency housing for the homeless.

'I wasn't born with a stiff upper lip,' the lieutenant said eventually. 'My parents have a junk shop in Lockerbie, a little town in the south of Scotland. But I didn't want to spend my life in a nowhere. I studied hard and won a scholarship to Oxford. Then I chose German history because I was sure that sooner or later we'd be at war with you again. It was obvious that after the First World War you still held a grudge against us. I said to myself: know your enemy, that way you can be useful to your country.'

'Seems to have worked all right,' Stave muttered.

MacDonald smiled. 'At first I wondered if maybe I shouldn't have stayed in Berlin that summer of 1939. Hitler looked certain to win. But things worked out differently and so here I am, in Hamburg. You might not believe me, Chief Inspector, but even in the state it's in now, I prefer this city to the dump I grew up in.'

'You're right; I don't believe you,' Stave replied wearily. 'Straight ahead, on your right. We're nearly there. At least I imagine our cemetery is bigger than Lockerbie's.'

They stopped by the low, wide entrance gate. Before the war the cemetery had been a big, beautiful park with roads running through it, and even bus stops. Now nearly all the trees and shrubbery had been hacked to the ground for firewood, and many of the graves had gone to ruin because nobody had the strength or energy to look after them, or often because there just wasn't anybody left.

Stave and MacDonald strolled along a straight path that led to the centre of Öjendorf Cemetery. There were a lot of fresh graves, the chief inspector noted. Then he noticed a grove, like a little garden within the cemetery, for cremation urns with flowers next to them. There were no recent ones; these days nobody was about to waste expensive fuel on burning dead bodies. In the midst of the garden was a bronze statue of a female mourner, seated. Amazing that hasn't been stolen yet, Stave thought.

The statue suddenly made him think of Margarethe, even though there was no facial resemblance to his late wife. He turned away so the lieutenant wouldn't notice him struggling to maintain his composure. Margarethe was buried in Öjendorf Cemetery but Stave couldn't face going to visit her grave with the lieutenant. He said nothing and just quickened his pace.

They arrived in time to see a tired pastor, two coffin bearers, and an open grave. The ground all around was frozen to about a metre below the surface. Stave wondered how they'd managed to dig a hole; with pickaxes rather than spades in all likelihood.

The pastor mumbled a prayer, holding a black bible in hands that were blue with cold. He was in a hurry. Stave couldn't make out a word he said. He and the lieutenant remained in the background, discreetly glancing around them. There was nobody else to be seen. The pall-bearers dragged the coffin over to the graveside and laid it on two planks. Then they opened it and the body wrapped in a grey cloth tumbled out as if falling through a trap door and hit the earth with a dull thump. In the silence it was frighteningly loud. The two men put the lid back on the re-usable coffin and carried it off. They would need it again; that saved wood too. The pastor nodded to Stave and MacDonald and walked off.

'We needn't have bothered,' the lieutenant murmured, clapping his hands together.

'It was worth a try,' Stave said. But his voice was muted.

An Old Man

Saturday, 25 January 1947

Stave was sitting in the twilight in his flat, warming his hands on a cup of steaming *ersatz* coffee, slowly sipping at the bitter liquid. He should really have been up and out long ago, walking the platforms of the main station from early morning, asking for news of his son.

Karl was their only child. They would have liked more, Margarethe and he, but there had just been the one; the doctors never found out why. Karl would be 19 now, Stave thought to himself. If he was still alive, that was.

He wished they hadn't argued back then when Karl volunteered for the front. Youthful idealism. Bravery. Or just because he despised his father? He had to try to find him.

But on the other hand, Stave was tired. True, he had got out of bed early enough, out of habit, but he'd rearranged the furniture a bit, and chewed on some dry bread with a bit of thin yoghurt. Breakfast and lunch all together. By now it was already past two o'clock in the afternoon and he still hadn't left the house. He was afraid he would spend yet another weekend searching in vain for his son, afraid of stopping one shabby figure after another to ask in vain if they might know or have seen him, afraid of the empty looks, the shrugs of indifference.

And then the past week at work had got to him. Nothing. Nothing at all. Nobody had responded to the poster offering a reward, not even the usual crazies who as a rule never missed a chance. It had probably been too cold, even for a nutcase, to go out to the nearest police station. But was it really possible, that a young woman could go missing in the middle of Hamburg without anyone noticing? Even if she had no family, no friends, surely there was a neighbour who would recognise her. Stave knew what it was like in the Hoch-bunker and the other places where people took refuge. If anyone left, their place was taken immediately, as if they'd never been there. But surely the photograph on the poster would have driven even the most hardened bunker-dweller to go to the police.

Breuer and Ehrlich had left him to it, but the chief inspector knew they expected him to turn something up. But what? He had no idea. He felt at his wits' end, frozen cold and most of all would have liked to just curl up under the blanket on his bed.

So he was almost relieved when there was a knock at the door. He would have to get up to answer it, whoever it was.

When he opened the door to Ruge, Stave knew he could no longer hide away from the real world. The young beat policemen stood up straight and took a deep breath, but the chief inspector interrupted whatever he was about to say.

'If you've come to report the discovery of another corpse, then come in before you say anything,' he said quietly. 'No need to announce it to all and sundry in the stairwell.'

The young man gave an embarrassed smile, entered the narrow hallway and removed his cap. 'I'm sorry, Chief Inspector, it always seems to happen when I'm on duty. I hope that doesn't start to make me a suspect.'

'Don't count your chickens,' Stave growled, grabbing his gun, coat, hat and scarf, managing at the same time to offer Ruge a cigarette.

This time he didn't hesitate and took it with a nod of thanks.

'Where is it?'

'Lappenbergs Allee, Eimsbüttel.'

'That's way over in the west. Why do I have to attend?'

'The victim is naked, Chief Inspector. And it looks like he's been strangled. But this time it's an old man.'

'That's a bit different,' Stave muttered, pushing open the apartment door. 'Have Maschke and MacDonald already been informed?'

'Word's on the way to them now. Herr Breuer wants them all to turn up at the scene. He's going to be there too.'

That'll be fun, Stave thought. By the time they got to the scene, on the far side of the Alster, it would be dark; not exactly the best time of day to carry out a search, not least when the boss is watching.

Within a few minutes they were on their way, once more in the old Mercedes with the clunking engine. Stave stared out of the window, trying to find a connection between the killings: both were naked, both had been strangled. But why a young woman and then an old man? What was the link? He suddenly felt ill. It was just hunger and the stale air in the car, he told himself, but he realised there was something else: the ghost of fear.

It was more then 11 kilometres from Wandsbek to Eimsbüttel. Even though Ruge was pushing the Mercedes to the limit, bouncing over potholes and swerving around huge bomb craters, it still took them nearly half an hour. When they finally stopped, Stave was relieved to open the door and climb out. He took deep breaths to get rid of the feeling of nausea in the pit of his stomach, then looked around; this was another working-class district, heavily bombed in the war. The trees along Lappenbergs Allee had either been burnt to the ground or chopped down for firewood. Behind them had been four-storey sandstone apartment blocks, all now destroyed. The previous summer work gangs had gone round pulling down the remaining walls and façades because they were in danger of collapse. Now the area was a bizarre wasteland of rubble and roofing tiles in piles three, five or even ten metres high, with bits of guttering, tangled wiring and ceiling beams protruding from them. Trampled footpaths led here and there between them. The nearest buildings still standing, as far as Stave could make out, were some 150 yards away.

A jeep screeched to a halt almost immediately behind the Mercedes, so close that for a moment Stave imagined it was going to crash into it. MacDonald climbed out and nodded to them. Better than a military salute, Stave thought.

'Have you ever seen a murder victim before, Lieutenant?' Stave asked. He wanted to prepare the man in case he keeled over at the sight.

But MacDonald seemed unflustered. 'I suppose you could say so: I buried enough bodies during the war. But then again, no, insofar as soldiers obviously see things differently to the way the police do.'

Stave gave a mirthless smile and nodded in the direction of the pool of light created by two generator-powered spotlights set up between the piles of rubble. They could hear the hum of the generator. 'I guess it's over there.'

They followed a track that led from Lappenbergs Allee around a huge heap of ruins. After barely a dozen paces the track was already out of sight of the main road. They passed another couple of piles of rubble and then a bomb crater about one and a half metres deep filled with ice and a dented petrol canister lying in it.

The body lay next to it.

Two uniformed policemen were standing in the flickering glare of the spotlights; another was bending over the generator, while a photographer was setting up his kit. Maschke was walking up and down a little further away, smoking. Doctor Czrisini was taking off his suede gloves and replacing them with long rubber ones.

'Definitely not a sex crime anyway,' he said, nodding to Stave and at the body.

'Maybe I should recommend you for my job if I get tired of it,' the chief inspector replied.

'Yeah, we could swap!' Czrisini said with a laugh.

They bent down to take a look at the body. It was an old man, 65 to 70 years old, Stave reckoned. A short man, about 1.60 metres, slim, but not undernourished. His hands were not those of a working man. He was lying on his back, as if taking a rest, feet close together, his left hand to one side, open, the other behind his rear end. The body was frozen solid and covered with a fine layer of snow, as if dusted with icing sugar. The pale flesh beneath already showing signs of blood settlement.

The pathologist looked at the man's head. He had a full, grey, bushy beard, a large, slightly hooked nose. The eyes were closed. When Stave looked closer he realised they were swollen, as if after a fight.

'There's blood in both ears,' Crzisini said in a calm voice. 'A small wound to the chin, eyes and forehead swollen from blows. The man was beaten either with a blunt object or with fists.'

'Beaten to death?'

The pathologist shook his head. 'I'll only know for sure after the autopsy, but I reckon the beating was just to waken him. He may have been knocked down, might have lost consciousness.' He indicated the body's left hand. 'Abrasions. It would seem he tried to defend himself, at first at least. Then he gave up. Do you see the fine line around his throat? He's been strangled, with a wire loop, I'd say.'

Stave closed his eyes. 'The man was attacked either front on or from one side, beaten to the ground with a hail of blows and then when he could no longer defend himself, strangled. He had probably lost consciousness by then.'

Crzisini pointed to a rectangular iron bar as long as his forearm, lying in the dirt near the head of the corpse. 'The dark colour on that iron bar is probably blood.'

'The murder weapon, then?'

'Maybe. But it might just have been lying there and blood spattered on it when he fell.'

Stave wished it were still daylight. Apart from anything the flickering of the spotlight was hurting his eyes; there were shadows dancing everywhere amidst the ruins, and the drone of the generator made his head ache.

They waited until the photographer had taken the first few pictures, then Czrisini bent down and touched the body carefully, opening his eyelids. 'Blue eyes,' he noted. Using both hands he pulled the man's lower jaw down. 'No teeth. I assume he had dentures.'

Systematically, he examined the rest of the body from head to toe. 'Small wart on the left hip,' he noted. 'Signs of a hernia, enlarged scrotum. Normally that would require a truss, and it would still cause problems walking.'

Stave looked silently over at the edge of the bomb crater. There was a dark-brown polished bamboo walking stick lying there, with a carved handle, covered in a layer of snow as fine as that covering the body.

'That might have been his walking stick,' he mumbled.

The flickering light briefly caught a metal button lying next to the body. When they finally got the corpse on to a stretcher, they found a leather strap under the body, like that of a rucksack.

Then Stave noticed something small and shiny on the ground just about where the dead man's shoulder had been. He bent down and picked it up. It was a medallion, made of silver, no bigger than a tiny coin, on a thin, broken chain, also made of silver.

'The killer must have missed that when he stripped him,' Czrisini suggested.

Stave stared at the tiny circle in his gloved fist, took it closer to the spotlight, silently cursing the flicker. The reverse of the medallion was plain, polished smooth by long contact with the wearer's skin. But the front bore a cross, standing on a sort of jagged hill, maybe a cliff even, and at an angle on either side two other objects that Stave thought at first might also be crosses.

The pathologist came over, pointed to the two objects and said, 'Those are daggers.'

'Are you sure?'

'Longer than a knife, shorter than a sword. Classic, elongated, slightly oval blade shape.'

'That means the blades of both daggers are pointed towards the cross.'

'Curious, isn't it? Never seen anything like it.'

Stave stared at the medallion. Czrisini was right, he thought to himself. Daggers and a cross. What was that all about? He slid the object into a paper bag. A clue, he thought. Finally, a first clue. The only question was, what did it mean? 'How long do you reckon he's been lying here?'

The pathologist shrugged. 'At least a day, going by the settlement of blood in the body, maybe longer. It's hard to be certain with these Siberian temperatures.'

'The same length of time as the body found in Baustrasse?'

Czrisini looked him in the eyes for a moment and said, 'It is possible that they may have been killed around the same time.'

'What do you think, Lieutenant?' Stave asked, as Czrisini made a pained face, removing his clammy rubber gloves.

MacDonald had been watching them silently from a discreet distance. 'The poor sod's making his way through the ruins, where the murderer is lurking in wait for him. He comes out, beats him to the ground, strangles him and strips him.'

Stave scratched his head. 'Would an old man wearing a truss and using a walking stick take an uneven path like this?'

The lieutenant smiled in acknowledgement of Stave's point. 'In his position I would feel safer on the cleared streets. So you reckon he was going down Lappenbergs Allee, his attacker beat him to the ground there, then dragged the defenceless man over here, where nobody would see him, to finish him off?'

'Maybe,' Stave replied bluntly. He was thinking of the young woman they had found on Baustrasse. 'Let's imagine for a moment that we're dealing with the same killer as in the case earlier in the week. Just supposing, for now, because certain things suggest otherwise; a young woman in one case, an old man in the other. In the first case there was no indication she put up any resistance; in the latter everything points to the victim fighting back. What links them is the thin strangulation mark around the neck.'

Maschke came over and added, 'Plus the fact that they were both found amidst the rubble. Naked. In both cases in a former working-class district that had been flattened by bombing. Maybe the killer knows his way around these parts.'

Stave nodded. 'Maybe, but one case in the east of the city, the other in the west. They're more than ten kilometres apart. You think he might have lived for a bit in Eilbek, and also in Eimsbüttel? It's not impossible. But it's also possible that he chose these ruined, uninhabited districts because he knows there are unlikely to be any witnesses. It's also possible that he kills his victims somewhere else altogether and just dumps the bodies in places he's unlikely to be seen.'

'Don't the walking stick, button, medallion and leather strap suggest that the man was robbed and murdered here?' MacDonald asked.

'Sure, they suggest that,' Stave replied, 'but they don't prove it. They might just have been lying here next to the body. These bombed districts are full of bits and pieces of people's belongings lying all over the place. But you're right: these objects may well be clues. Perhaps somebody will come forward to identify them. I'll have photos taken of the medallion. We'll put Inspector Müller on to it, maybe he can find out what the cross and daggers is all about.'

'And I volunteer,' Maschke said with a trace of resignation, 'to go round dozens of white coats, all the dentists we can find that is, to stick the photos under their noses and see if anyone remembers fitting him out with dentures.'

'Good idea,' said Stave, impressed, with a tired smile. 'Right now I need to talk to the lad who came across the corpse.'

'It's not a lad, Chief Inspector, it's a lady. A lady looter to be exact.'

The uniformed policeman brought over a figure who had all this time been waiting behind one of the heaps of rubble, under guard, apparently, since another policeman Stave had not noticed before was with her. Stave took a good look at her when she came into the circle of light surrounding the body. She was slim, almost as tall as him. She pushed back the hood of a heavy English wool coat, which once upon a time had cost somebody a lot of money, but was now so threadbare it looked as if you could pull it apart with your fingers.

Stave saw a thin, almost almond-shaped face, dark eyes, long black hair. Early thirties, he guessed, and would have been well-to-do at some stage. Her hands were not those of a manual labourer.

'What's your name?' he asked her.

'Anna von Veckinhausen.'

She had a gentle voice, Stave thought to himself. But it was a voice filled with the self-confidence that only comes with having had social status and money from earliest childhood. It sounded like a violin slightly out of tune playing in a grand orchestra, a wrong note, the sound of nervousness. Or fear.

'You found the body?'

'Yes.'

Stave cleared his throat. He could feel Maschke, MacDonald, the doctor and the uniformed police watching him. This could be tough.

He decided to take a friendly tone. He introduced himself, took a step to one side, her following him, so as to be a little further from the others.

'Please tell me exactly how it happened,' he asked her.

Anna von Veckinhausen hesitated for a minute. Stave waited, thinking to himself, she's trying to decide what to tell me.

'I was on Collau Strasse and used the path through the ruins as a short cut to get to Lappenbergs Allee.'

Stave got his notebook out of his pocket, awkwardly, taking time over it, time for the witness to think her story through, but time for him too, time to think what to make of her. She was a looter, according to one of the uniforms. It was hard for the police to judge figures wandering around in the ruins. They might be former inhabitants looking for things they had lost. Or workmen tearing down dangerous walls or gathering valuable metal for the city. Or just passersby taking a shortcut. Or indeed looters, looking for wood, metal, bits of furniture, anything that might be of use. Nearly everyone in Hamburg had 'sorted out their own way' of getting hold of the things they might need from time to time. Stave only had to think of the wood he used in his little stove. But if you were caught you went straight to a British tribunal: an English judge, an interpreter, a stenographer, a few cold questions, a quick sentence and then it was on to the next one. Forty cigarettes from Allied stock would get you 21 days behind bars. A worker who took three pigs' feet thrown away as unusable from a cold store could get 30 days. Looters found rummaging around in the rubble could get between 50 and 60 days.

He decided not to press the looting charge at the moment. 'Then what happened?' he asked.

The witness gave him a brief smile of relief. Then she looked serious and rubbed her elegant hands together, as if she were washing them with soap. Like a nurse disinfecting her hands, Stave thought. Or perhaps a doctor.

She hesitated, looking for the right words: 'I came across the body by accident. I immediately hurried to Lappenbergs Allee and asked my way to the nearest police station.'

'Asked your way?'

'Yes.' Anna von Veckinhausen stared at him. 'I asked one person after another until I found someone who could tell me how to get to the nearest police station.'

Stave still couldn't get used to the new self-confidence women had these days. A few years ago it would have been unthinkable for a woman – a lady like this in particular – to come across a dead body and react the way she had. In the old days a woman would have screamed or fainted. It was probably because the war had turned women into the family breadwinners; trading on the black market, foraging, manual labour – women could do it all just as well as men. Better even. But they paid a high price, and not just tiredness and exhaustion. Many marriages broke up when the men came back from the war, sometimes after years of absence, to find their wives could get by in this new world of ruins and black markets better than they could. Stave shot a discreet glance again at Anna von Veckinhausen's hands: she wasn't wearing a wedding ring.

'That would have been Station 22,' Stave said. 'If you didn't know it, I guess that means you don't live around here.'

The witness hesitated for a few second. 'No,' she admitted. 'I live in one of the Nissen huts along the Eilbek canal.'

Stave made a note of the address. A looter who had decided to check out a new area, he decided. But he said nothing. He found Anna von Veckinhausen imposing, even a little intimidating. Such self-assurance. She came from another world. There was just the trace of an accent in her voice, but where did it come from? Obviously not from Hamburg or the north of the country. Maybe somewhere in the east? 'So, you found the body, ran down Lappenbergs Allee to the police station. Have you witnesses to that?'

She gave him a confused look and said nothing.

'The people you asked for directions to the police station – do you know who they were? Did you take a note of their names?'

'What do you mean?' she said indignantly, but still in a quiet voice. 'Are you treating me as a suspect?'

Stave smiled, though he knew that right now the grimace on his face would be taken the wrong way. 'Just routine,' he said.

She threw her head back and looked him in the eye. Challengingly. 'They were just anonymous figures. Men with hats and their collars turned up, women with headscarves and hats. All of them hurrying along in the cold. I didn't get any names and couldn't even tell you what they looked like.'

Stave made another note in his book. 'And what about before, when you found the body? Did you touch it?'

'What sort of questions are you asking me? I come across a naked man's body, what do you think I might have touched?'

'You knew straight away he was dead?'

'I've seen a few corpses lying in the snow, if that's what you mean. I could tell immediately…'

Stave didn't ask when and where she'd seen corpses lying in the snow. 'Do you know how he died?'

Anna von Veckinhausen shook her head. 'No? How did he?'

The chief inspector ignored her question, just made another note. His fingers had turned to ice. He found it hard to write, the words barely legible. He knew that he was making the witness nervous. But then she should be nervous, he told himself. 'Did you notice anything else? Anything about the body? Anything lying near it?'

She shook her head. She's bitterly cold too, Stave thought.

'And what about immediately before you found it? When you didn't know what you were about to come across in the ruins? Did you see anything suspicious, anything along the path? A person? A noise?'

'No. Nothing.'

Quick answer. Too quick. Suddenly Stave was certain there was something she was hiding from him. Should he take her into head office for questioning? Maybe threaten her with a looting charge? He hesitated. His experience was that most of the time witnesses told what they knew. Sometimes you just had to give them a bit of time and they would turn up at the police station and add to their statement. And if it turned out that Anna von Veckinhausen wasn't one of those he could always interrogate her again. That meant see her again.

That's all you need, making a fool of yourself, Stave told himself, immediately banishing the thought. 'You can go,' he told her. He gave Anna von Veckinhausen a piece of paper with his office telephone number scribbled on it. 'If anything else should come to mind, ring me.'

'Thanks,' she said, folding the piece of paper carefully and putting it in the pocket of her coat. She suddenly looked drained.

Once upon a time Stave would have ordered a patrol car to take the witness home. But not nowadays with the shortage of vehicles and fuel rationing. 'G'bye,' he said to her. He intended it to be friendly but the way it came out it sounded more like a threat.

'Why did you let her go?' Maschke asked as they watched Anna von Veckinhausen disappear behind another heap of rubble. He and MacDonald had come over to Stave who had given them a brief rundown of his conversation.

'There's no reason to suspect her,' he said defensively.

'She was in the vicinity of the second murder,' Maschke came back at him, 'And she lives in the Nissen huts up by the Eilbek canal, not all that far from where the first victim was found.'

Stave sighed. He had thought of that too, but didn't want to mention it. 'In the case of the first murder, she's just one of thousands living in the area. And today she reported it to the police herself.'

'I can't say I see her as someone used to strangling people with a garrotte,' MacDonald interjected.

'I can,' Maschke said.

'Let's leave our colleagues here to clear up,' Stave said wearily. 'Czrisini will want the corpse. We should go back to headquarters and think this through.'

'Not so fast, gentlemen, give me five minutes.'

The massive figure in the long dark overcoat, big hat and black leather gloves was Cuddel Breuer. Stave hadn't seen him arrive.

'Sorry I couldn't get here earlier,' their boss said, 'but I had a meeting with the mayor. Goddamn this cold,' he muttered, though he didn't exactly look as if he was freezing.

'I'll have the spot guarded,' said Stave, after giving his report. 'One of the uniformed officers will stay here overnight. I hope he doesn't freeze to death. Tomorrow when it's light we'll do a proper search of the area.'

The chief nodded, then looked up at the three detectives. 'So, what do you think? Is it the same killer?'

It was the question Stave had been dreading. He thought carefully before answering. 'We will keep all avenues of investigation open,' he began. 'There are some indications that it is the same killer – or killers, we haven't ruled out that possibility. But a few of the clues don't quite fit the first murder.'

Breuer said nothing, just stood there looking at him.

'It just isn't possible that in a city like Hamburg two people can be murdered without anybody missing them,' Stave said defensively. 'It would help us if we could find the link between the murderer and his victims.'

'What if there isn't one?'

'Then it's going to be difficult,' he admitted. 'If we're really dealing with a killer who chooses his victims at random, then his modus operandi is unpredictable. In the one case he kills a young woman, in the other an old man. One attack in the east of the city, one in the west. In the one case the victim does nothing to defend herself, in the other he has to beat the old man up first.'

'So what do I tell the mayor in the morning?' Cuddel Breuer could have been inviting Stave to a picnic.

'Ask him not to come to any hasty conclusions. It's a difficult case. We're going to need some time.'

Breuer scratched his head and sighed. 'I know, I know. But Hamburg is blocked in by the ice. Coal supplies will only last another few days. We have very little food left. People are freezing to death every day. It's not easy for the mayor to keep control of the city. Time is the one thing he doesn't have.'

'In that case the most important thing is to maintain public order,' Stave blurted out.

Breuer smiled. 'Indeed. Nobody wants to shout this thing from the rooftops. I shall advise the mayor simply to ignore it. For the moment.'

He touched the brim of his hat, turned round and was gone.

'Fuck!' Maschke muttered, as soon as the chief was out of hearing range.

But he wasn't fooling Stave. He could sense an undertone in Maschke's voice, an undertone he didn't like: *Schadenfreude*.

They trundled back to headquarters in MacDonald's jeep without speaking. The dim yellow light of the headlamps made the building façades and piles of rubble seem like the stage set for an Expressionist silent movie. Stave wouldn't have been surprised if from the corner of his eye he'd seen the bat shape of Nosferatu perched on some ruin, pointing at him with an outstretched claw-like finger. Pull yourself together, man, he told himself. It wasn't a vampire he was looking for, but a normal-looking human being with a garrotte or piece of wire in his pocket. Someone who felt no compunction about killing a young woman or an old man.

At the end of Karoline Strasse a frozen policeman was directing traffic with sharp, abrupt gestures: jeeps, British lorries, two hardy civilians battling their way against the icy wind blowing down the street. MacDonald drove slightly nervously towards him. Then a misfire from the undercarriage caused the policeman to jump. MacDonald, spying his reaction in the rear-view mirror, gave a smile of satisfaction. Three minutes later they had arrived.

Stave was astonished to find Erna Berg already waiting for them in his office with something resembling tea poured out. He picked up the warm cup gratefully and inhaled the aroma. Nettles, he guessed. But at least it was hot.

'What are you doing in here?' he asked her.

'Herr Breuer told me there would be work for me today,' she said. 'I can take a day off in lieu, sometime when it's quieter.'

You'll be waiting a long time, Stave thought to himself grimly. 'Okay then,' he said, when they'd all found seats in his little room. 'So who exactly are we looking for?'

'Not a sex killer, anyhow,' MacDonald said.

'Well then, that just leaves some 900,000 possible suspects in Hamburg.' Stave leant back and stared at the ceiling as if imagining a 'wanted' poster materialising.

'Let's start from the beginning again,' he said, sounding as if he was talking to himself rather than to the others. 'We have no real clues. What possible connection could there be between a young woman in Eilbek and an old man in Eimsbüttel? A lady of the night and her pimp? Our friends from the Reeperbahn don't recognise the girl so there's nothing to indicate that that's the case. What else could link them? Some place they met? Some common history?'

Nobody said anything. They all knew Stave wanted to answer his own question.

'The black market, obviously,' he eventually announced.

It was illegal but omnipresent. Men and women standing around on street corners or in city squares, wandering up and down, faces hidden beneath hats and collars pulled up high. Whispers, gestures. Where else could you get stuff that wasn't on the ration cards – a radio maybe, a pair of women's shoes, a pound of butter, home-brewed hooch? In exchange for a wad of 100-Reichsmark notes or some cigarettes. There were raids all the time, but there was nothing to be done about the black market. In the previous year alone the police had confiscated more than 1,000 tons of food, 10,000 litres of wine and 4,800 doses of morphine from army stockpiles, stolen penicillin, even horses and cars.

For many citizens of Hamburg there was something sleazy, something degrading about it all. Standing around on street corners like a hooker. Getting paid next to nothing for some family heirloom salvaged from the rubble, just a few cigarettes for a valuable antique, but 1,000 Reichsmarks for a couple of pounds of butter. Touts and fences were called 'crust stealers', just as their like had been back when the Nazis were in charge. But then again, when your shoes fell apart and you couldn't find another pair anywhere on the rations, what else was there to do but hang out with the shady street corner characters?

Everybody in Hamburg ended up on the black market one way or another, rich and poor, old and young. Any piece of merchandise might be swapped for any other; any link between two people was possible, however absurd it might otherwise seem. And there was big money too to be paid for lost treasures or things people simply couldn't get by without. There were things worth killing for, not least because nobody dealing on the black market would go to the police.

'It might well be something to do with the black market,' Mac-Donald agreed.

'Every damn crime in Hamburg is something to do with the black market,' Maschke retorted. 'But we have nothing else to go on. Maybe they were both looters, and one became competition for the other vying for the best patch of rubble to loot. It could be as simple as that.'

Stave nodded. 'It's a possibility. But there are others. We have hundreds of missing person cases in town. It would seem that not one of them corresponds to the young woman, and we won't know about the old man until tomorrow at the earliest. Perhaps we'll find some sort of common factor amongst the missing person cases.'

MacDonald raised an eyebrow. He obviously wasn't following Stave's line of thought. 'What sort of common factor?' he asked.

The chief inspector shrugged. 'I've no idea. Maybe we'll find out that lots of young women have gone missing recently. Or lots of old men. Or that one of our missing person cases was related to a young woman and an old man. What do I know?'

'Sounds like a pretty vague line of inquiry to me,' the lieutenant said.

Stave paid him no attention, but he knew he was right. 'And then there are the DPs, people with no roots here,' he added. 'People with nothing more to lose. People who remain unidentified even to the Allied command, people whose movements go unchecked because nobody is interested in them or their business. Maybe we shouldn't be surprised that nobody from Hamburg recognised the picture on the poster?'

'But we put the posters up in the DP camps,' Maschke said. 'People there live cheek by jowl. Somebody would have recognised the victim. And even if none of the DPs wanted to speak up, either because they are afraid or don't trust the German authorities, a British overseer would surely have recognised her.'

Maschke hauled himself to his feet and began pacing up and down. He's not happy, Stave thought to himself, probably because he's realised we haven't a single decent lead, and the only thing we can be relatively certain of is that sex isn't involved. That means the investigation might have no need of someone from vice and we'll send him back to his pimps, Stave reckoned, almost feeling sorry for Maschke.

'Right then,' he said aloud, just for the sake of it, 'let's admit we don't really have a clue, literally, for now at least. Therefore we should take every theory seriously, no matter now vague. I'll organise a major raid on the black market dealers. This coming Monday. We'll grab a few dealers off the streets and see what we come up with – maybe a rucksack with one strap missing. Or another medallion with a cross and two daggers. Or a spare truss.'

The other two laughed.

'You, Lieutenant, will look through the missing persons files. Maybe you'll find some sort of pattern. Don't be afraid to come forward with anything that strikes you, no matter how improbable it might seem. You never know. And you, Maschke, go round the dentists. And check in with the Street Clearance and Rebuilding Department up at Heiligengeistfeld; the people there are in charge of everything concerned with clearing the rubble and getting rebuilding under way. If anybody's heard about turf wars amongst the looters, it'll be the rubble boys.'

I may not like you, but I'm keeping you on board, Stave thought inwardly. Maschke gave a smile of relief.

'Good idea,' the vice squad man said.

Maschke and MacDonald left the room. Stave nodded to his secretary before closing the door after them and said apologetically, 'I'm afraid I'm going to need you in a minute.'

He sat down behind his desk. Time for the bloody paperwork. He opened a new file, for the second murder, and wrote out by hand the details of the corpse's discovery, then the text for a new poster asking for information. And finally the autopsy request.

When he finally got to his feet to take the pile of papers out to his secretary, he stopped dead in the doorway. MacDonald was still there, chatting away to Erna Berg. They both fell silent mid-sentence at the sight of him, red with embarrassment, just like a pair of teenagers. This could be entertaining, Stave thought. But at the same time he felt something not unlike a pang of jealousy. Only a pinprick, not a dagger plunged into his heart. But even so. Absurd, he told himself.

Stave handed his secretary the documents to be typed up, grabbed his hat and coat, muttered a few meaningless phrases and left the room. The minute he closed the door behind him he could hear the conversation resume, as if someone had dropped a record player needle back in the same spinning groove in the vinyl.

It was Saturday evening. Once upon a time he would have been on his way home with Margarethe and the boy after a paddle steamer trip up the Alster or a long walk along the banks of the Elbe. They would have sent Karl off to bed – knowing perfectly well that as soon as his parents had left the room he would have turned the light back on and immersed himself in some crime novel. Then Margarethe and he would have gone out, to a restaurant maybe, or the cinema. And then later…

What a load of sentimental nonsense, Stave told himself. I must be getting old. Or I've got maudlin from seeing too many dead bodies of late. He wandered around town at random, through Rotherbaum and Harvestehude, districts that had hardly been scratched, pleasant urban villas, peaceful and calm. There were some streets where you wouldn't even have believed there had ever been a war – that was, if you ignored the British jeeps parked in the driveways. The driveways of villas that had been commandeered.

Still, the thought suddenly struck him that the rich had it good. Then he told himself there was no point in replacing one daft line of thought with another.

He must have been wandering about like that for half an hour or so before he found himself on Hoheluft Chaussee with his back to the partly demolished elevated railway station, though there had been no trains running for months now.

Stave shivered. The Hoheluft Chausee was a four-lane dual carriageway but the buildings on either side were not particularly striking. Stave picked up speed along the pavement. He had a goal now. The Capitol. It was a cinema he and Margarethe used to go to.

It had survived undamaged and had re-opened. There was no electricity for the elevated railway, but there was for the cinema. People had to prioritise.

He almost ran the 300 metres from the stop to the Capitol. There was no neon lighting, just a poster he could hardly make out in the dark. But the cashier's office was lit up. He bought a ticket and went in without even asking what film was showing. Who cares; all that mattered was that inside he could warm up. And kill time.

First up was *The World in Film*: the weekly news, pictures from Moscow and London. Stave let them wash over him. A British warship in some port or other, India maybe, Stalin in uniform. Stave was gradually thawing out. Suddenly, right at the end, there were images of children, nameless unidentified refugee children who had been picked up in Hamburg. The authorities put their photos on the screen in the hope of getting in touch with their parents or other relatives. Four different unidentified children every day. What must it be like to nip into some cinema and suddenly find a photo up on the big screen of your own child, a child you'd maybe long ago given up for dead? A chill ran down Stave's spine. And at the same time he found himself absurdly wishing Karl might appear on the screen.

The main film was *17 Grosse Freiheit*, a 1944 musical set on the street of the same name in Hamburg. Starring Hans Albers and Ilse Werner. Just like in the old days. Stave dozed off.

It was late by the time the lights went up again, flickering as ever. Most people were in a hurry to get out. Stave glanced at his watch: it was just before 11 p.m. It would be midnight soon, after which nobody was allowed to leave their home before 4.30 a.m. The English word 'curfew' had entered current usage in German.

Purely out of routine Stave fumbled in his jacket pocket to check he had his papers, including the police ID that allowed him to be out on the streets during the hours of curfew. They were all there. They always were. So he had no need to hurry. He slowly put on his overcoat, wrapped his scarf around his neck and pulled his collar up high, then put on his hat, pulling the brim low on his forehead, and finally his tight leather gloves. He had a long walk ahead of him to the other side of the Alster. But he could take his time.

He wondered if the lieutenant had had a pleasant evening. With Erna Berg perhaps? He liked MacDonald. There were people in Hamburg, young lads, some of them fresh out of POW camps, who would mug British soldiers on dark street corners, out of 'national pride' as they called it. But they didn't dare do anything worse.

Stave didn't hate the occupying army, even though it had been an English bomb that had taken his wife from him. He felt more ashamed of the crimes committed by the Nazi regime and in a perverse sort of way was relieved that both his city and his life lay in ruins. It was just punishment of a sort. And now maybe it was time for a fresh start.

As he strode briskly down the road to keep warm, his thoughts turned from MacDonald to Maschke. He knew no more about him than he did about the British lieutenant. And he found him a lot less likeable. Why though? Stave didn't like the vice squad man's attitude: his cynicism, his sarcasm, his sour grapes, his lack of respect for other people. Maybe that was the way you turned out when you had to deal with prostitutes, pimps and madams every day, he thought to himself. And when you still lived at home with your mother.

If things go on like this, the thought suddenly struck Stave, who knows where they'll transfer me to? Immediately he revisited his instinctive disdain for the vice squad man. He had two murders and not one lead. Everybody was expecting him to deliver results: Ehrlich, Breuer, the mayor even. He was expecting it of himself, goddamnit. I'm no rookie in this business, he told himself.

And there was one other thing nagging at him: what if this was just the beginning of something? If it proved to be a genuine serial killer at work? If again and again they kept finding out there in the ruins the naked bodies of strangled nameless people? If the murders continued until the killer finally made a mistake and they found him? But what if he didn't make a mistake? Ever? What do I do next, Stave asked himself.

His thoughts turned to Anna von Veckinhausen. What had she been holding back from him? If she was holding anything back at all, that was. Did she have something to do with the murders? Had she seen something? Stave decided to interview her again, and soon. And that had nothing at all to do with the fact that she was pretty and secretive or that it was Saturday evening and he was on his way home from the cinema.

On his own.

All of a sudden he spun round. There was nobody to be seen. Obviously. It was almost midnight. He shivered: it was minus 20°C at least and freezing gusts of wind blew into his face, shredding his skin. A yellow half-moon shone down from a clear starry sky. The street lights were out, the streets themselves gloomy canyons, the mountains of rubble in total darkness, moonlight peeping through the empty windows of bombed-out buildings. Side streets blocked off with temporary barriers because at any moment a bombed-out building could collapse. It was silent. No sound of distant traffic, no human voices, no crackling radio, no late evening birdsong. Nothing. Nix.

Stave stopped for a moment and cocked his ear. Somewhere in the ruins he heard a soft crunch. A sigh. A stone rattling to the ground. The rhythmic creaking of a door to an empty building swinging in the wind, backwards and forwards, backwards and forwards. The quiet patter of rats' feet as they darted amongst the fallen timber, squeaking to one another.

I'm getting paranoid, Stave thought to himself, but picked up speed, walking down the middle of the road now, as far as possible from the darkness and ruins on either side. He felt in his pocket for his FN22, the cold, oily feel of the metal suddenly reassuring.

When he finally got home he flopped on to the bed, too exhausted even to take off his clothes, too exhausted to be hungry. Too exhausted to think of Margarethe, or their son.

The Black Market

Minus 36 degrees Celsius. The moment Stave walked out of the building the wind hit him in the face like a fist. He pulled his woollen scarf up over his face, and with his left hand in its thick glove rubbed his nose to stop it freezing. The air was so dry every breath hurt.

Before even going to the office Stave hurried down to the Food Ration Card Distribution Centre. Even the name was demeaning. He had to pick up his own coupons for the coming month, then hurry off to the shops to see what he could get with them. Soap would be a result. Each adult was only allowed 250 grams for four weeks. But as it was too cold and heating fuel was too expensive to take a bath or a shower, most of Hamburg's residents stank like soldiers returning from the front: of sweat, dirt, old clothing and dry skin. Stave hated feeling dirty and both used the soap and took a shower whenever he could, even if he had to stand there shivering. He wouldn't turn his nose up at coffee either, but there was not much chance of that.

Stave joined the queue outside the distribution centre. It moved quickly. Most food and clothing had only been available on rations since 1939. The Brits simply changed the name of the Reich Ministry for Nutrition and told the officials who worked there to get on with it. And like most officials they took the bureaucratic procedure to extremes. There were currently 67 different food ration coupons in circulation: two for milk, two for flour, one for eggs, three daily-use coupons, 14 entitlement coupons, two coupons for potatoes, 21 coupons for use by different classes of consumers and 22 supplementary coupons. That was not counting the special coupons. If you needed to get your shoes re-heeled, you had to have a shoe repair coupon.

If only I could eat the coupons, at least then I wouldn't be hungry,

Stave thought to himself as he grabbed hold of his grey sheet of
perforated paper. He was classed as a normal consumer with no supplementary entitlements. His coupons allowed him to claim 1.7kg
of grey bread that tasted of sawdust, seven-eighths of a litre of milk
that looked like blue-white dishwater, 2.5kg of turnips (because
there were no more potatoes), 15g of a yellowy substance that was
supposed to be cheese, 100g fat, 200g sugar, 100g sticky *ersatz* jam,
125g soya flakes. And that was his lot.

Come to think of it, it was a miracle that more people had not
thought of strangling the next person they met in the street and
stealing every last stitch from their backs.

Then it was time for the next queue: outside a half bombed-out
house with a ground-floor shop, above the door of which someone
had scribbled 'Dairy Goods' with chalk on the cracked walls. When
he finally got to the front the shop owner – surprisingly fat for the
times – handed him the miserable slices of cheese on a piece of
grubby paper.

'Milk's gone already,' she told him curtly.

'When's the next delivery?' Stave asked wearily.

'Tomorrow maybe. Or maybe the next day.'

Stave left the shop without saying goodbye. That's one ration for
the birds, he thought to himself. Thank God I don't have any kids in
the house any more. And then he realised what he had almost said
and hurried away, as if somebody might have heard him.

When he had done the rest of his errands and taken his scanty haul
back home, Stave went to the office. There was no rush; on the last
Monday of the month everybody was busy getting their ration entitlements. Erna Berg was the only one there already. Stave wondered
if she'd managed to get milk for her kid, but didn't dare ask.

Inspector Müller had left a note for him. 'No luck with the
symbol on the medallion. Still working on it.'

Stave wondered if he was, or whether he had just chucked the
photo of the medallion into the bin.

The post-mortem report was on his desk. There was almost nothing new in Dr Czrisini's report except that on the left wrist of the corpse he had found traces of fine red lines, like that around the neck, and also that the old man was circumcised.

A few minutes later Maschke and MacDonald came into the office. Maschke's face was red and there was a thin layer of hoar frost and snow on his overcoat.

'I went back out to where the body was found yesterday,' he said. 'A couple of uniforms had been there at dawn and searched through the rubble, but they didn't find anything more than we did the night before.'

Stave showed them the report and told them about the red lines around one wrist, and the fact that the man was circumcised.

'A Jew?' MacDonald asked.

'With a medallion around his neck with a cross on it?' Stave shook his head. 'Doesn't seem likely.'

'I doubt it too,' Maschke agreed. 'Over at the vice squad whenever we raid a brothel, we usually have to haul a few punters out of the beds; you wouldn't believe how many blokes I've seen in their birthday suits nor how many of them are circumcised. Good churchgoers and probably even one or two party members.'

'My thinking is,' Stave resumed, 'that the old boy was just walking along Collau Strasse, slowly – he was lame after all. The street is narrow because of all the rubble heaps which spread out across the pavement on to the road. The killer is lying in wait where the footpath between the rubble meets Collau Strasse. He knocks his victim to the ground, slings the wire around the unconscious man's throat and drags him off the street into the ruins.'

'A bit like certain species of spiders,' MacDonald interjected.

Maschke gave him an irritated glance. Stave ignored both of them.

'So, attacked from behind, felled, dragged off – all of that in just a few seconds. Then amidst the piles of rubble where the killer can be fairly sure that nobody is going to surprise him he has more time to do the deed. He strangles the old man with the piece of wire, then strips him naked, but misses the walking stick, the piece of leather and the medallion.'

'We didn't find any tracks on the path to indicate the body being dragged,' Maschke said.

'The gravel is frozen solid as if it were covered in concrete; the layer of snow is no thicker than a sheet of newspaper. The body might have been lying there for a day or two. In that time dozens of people could have walked along that path and their footsteps would have erased any drag marks,' Stave replied.

'And none of them spotted the corpse?' MacDonald queried.

'It was lying in a bomb crater, off to one side. Couldn't be seen from the path.'

'If the old boy was really walking along Collau Strasse and was very lame, then that might mean he lived nearby. The lads from the lab did good work and made dozens of copies of the police photo,' Maschke said. 'This morning we went out and asked the local residents. It was easy enough as they were all queuing up at the nearby ration card distribution centre. I can't say we asked each and every local resident, but most of them must have been there and I'm afraid not one of them said they had ever seen the old man. It did ruin the appetite of a few of them, though.'

'So if he didn't live there,' Stave asked, 'how did he end up there?'

'Because somebody dumped him there,' Maschke suggested. 'Only the killer knows how he got those red marks on his wrist, but maybe he tied him up before killing him. Maybe he even dragged him by the wrist after he was dead. He might have strangled him, stripped him and then secretly dragged him amidst the rubble. Job done.'

'Don't forget the stick,' MacDonald added. 'Assuming it actually belonged to the victim, that would suggest that the old man got to the spot where we found him of his own accord. Whether he was attacked on Collau Strasse or anywhere else, why would the murderer have taken his stick too and left it lying beside him? Despite robbing him of almost everything else? I reckon he was attacked right there on the footpath, strangled and then stripped, but the murderer simply overlooked the walking stick, otherwise he'd have taken it too. Another hint that the attack took place at night, although that's hardly surprising in any case.'

'So how do you explain the marks on his wrist?' asked Maschke. 'If our killer did him in then and there, no need for him to tie him up or drag him anywhere.'

MacDonald smiled and shrugged. 'Not the faintest idea, old boy.'

For him all this is just an intellectual puzzle, Stave thought, but he couldn't bring himself to get angry with the young officer. Yet another reason for winding this case up as soon as possible.

'We're not getting anywhere like this,' he told them. 'It's not making sense. We'll print off 1,000 posters. Stick them up everywhere, particularly at the ration card centres in the area. Find out who didn't collect his coupons today. Rattle the doors of the local doctors. Maybe somebody was treating him for his leg. Meanwhile I'll write up a basic report for the files, and then we'll hit the black market.'

A short while later Stave was sitting alone at his desk, bashing away at the typewriter with two fingers, quick then slow, like a machine gun with an autoloader problem. He glanced over what he had written: 'The darkness gives a character all of its own to these rubble-strewn districts.' Stave sat back in surprise. That wasn't the sort of language he usually used in official reports.

I'm getting emotional, he thought to himself, and wondered what Cuddel Breuer or Chief Public Prosecutor Ehrlich would make of it. Should he change the wording, retype it? Nonsense, if they wanted to consider him some daft romantic, that was up to them. He sighed and slid the report into the registry file.

Then the office began to fill up again. MacDonald was the first to arrive, followed by Maschke who announced that he'd come across a couple of people turning up later at the ration card office, but that none of them recognised the victim either.

There was a knock on the door, a few muttered words of greeting, and the atmosphere in the room began to thicken as first a colleague from the criminal operations team came in, along with another from the missing persons and lost property office, one from the youth liaison department, a representative of the female police, and obviously a man from Department S, which had been set up specially to combat the black market.

Stave gave them a quick briefing about the murders, but noticed almost immediately that word had got around amongst the operations teams. It would be nice if people would share a bit more. 'If we're lucky the raid will throw up something that belonged to one of the victims,' he said. 'That at least would give us a lead.'

The search team lad, a young, pale-faced man with tired rings around his eyes, gave him a sceptical look. 'We have no idea who the victims are. We don't know what might have been stolen off them. Obviously a raid is going to throw up lots of stuff but how are we to know if anything we confiscate might have belonged to an unknown person?'

Stave lifted his hands. 'People handle all sorts of stuff on the black market. Maybe somebody's got a set of false teeth for sale? Or a truss? If so, we'd like have a chat with him or her. Maybe we'll find a few pushers of American cigarettes or homemade hooch. They might have nothing to do with the murderers, but sit them down in the interrogation room and you never know what they might suddenly recall. Maybe they'll remember somebody else touting the clothes of a young woman one day and those of an old man the next? Maybe they'll have heard of a medallion with a cross and two daggers on it? I grant you it's a slim chance, but we need to pick up any lead we can.'

'Who cares? The black market is the black market. A raid is always worthwhile.' The head of Department S – once a chubby character, but now shrunken to a shadow of his former self, shivering in a suit too big for him – rubbed his hands with glee. 'We haven't done a big job since Christmas. It's high time we pushed the gentlemen spivs in the hot seat again. Good training for my lads. I suggest we hit Hansaplatz Square. That's where you find most customers and more stuff for sale than anywhere else.'

Nobody contradicted him.

Stave nodded. If there was one place absolutely made for the black market then it was the Hansaplatz, once a tranquil spot in the St Georg district surrounded by four-storey middle-class apartment blocks. As if by a miracle the buildings had survived the hail of bombs undamaged and the square was only a short walk from the main station. The smugglers and pushers brought their goods from all the occupation zones and even abroad to the station first and foremost. The spivs would hide their stocks of penicillin, cigarettes, coffee and hard spirits in the cheap hotels or rented apartments around the square. On a few occasions the lads from Department S had discovered what were effectively warehouses full of contraband. Piece by piece this contraband would make its way down to the Hansaplatz where every day the good citizens of Hamburg would turn up in search of something or other that was not available on the ration cards.

Nobody who lived in St Georg would ever grass on one of the dealers or their customers, because they lived on the crumbs from the illegal trade: a pound of butter in monthly rent perhaps for somebody who would let a room in their apartment without asking too many questions, a case of Lucky Strikes for a couple of lads who would keep watch, a discount on illicit hooch…

'When do we start?' Stave asked.

'Now, today,' the man from Department S said. 'Before anybody gets wind of it. Just give me the time to get my people together. We'll need about 100 in uniform, a couple of British lorries so we can get our people to St Georg without being noticed. Let's say, 5 p.m. this afternoon. That's when you've got people coming out of offices and shops, the square will be full and the spivs will all have stocked up. Also it'll be dusk and they won't notice us coming until it's too late.'

'Good,' the chief inspector said. 'I'll be at the Hansaplatz at 4.30 p.m. to take a look around. Nobody there will notice me. Maybe I'll spot someone suspicious. Then at 5 p.m. we bag the lot of them and ship them to the police station. I want everyone we grab to be interrogated before the end of the day. And a complete inventory of every article seized.'

Stave's colleagues filed out of his office, smiles on their faces, whispering to one another. Adrenalin flowing. Eager for the hunt.

It took barely half an hour to walk from the CID HQ to the Hansaplatz. Stave walked across the Lombard Bridge with his coat collar pulled up high and his head down. The Outer Alster on his left was a great blue-white expanse of ice, tinted pink by the pale afternoon sun. Two children were skating in squiggly patterns over the ice, a few couples walking over it uncertainly. Stave made a face. Icy surfaces were always a good excuse to slip and grab hold of one's partner for support. A certain romance, even when it was 20 degrees below.

The quickest way would have been to go straight to the station, and then turn left towards Hansaplatz, but Stave decided to take a different route. It was true that nobody in the St Georg black market knew him, but he regularly hung around the station, asking about his son. So he took the back streets through St Georg until he came to Brenner Strasse, which would lead him into the Hansaplatz on the opposite side from the station. He passed by the Würzburger Hof hotel where the lads from Department S last autumn had unearthed several barrels of preserving alcohol stolen from the State Institute for Zoology. The thieves had also taken the glass jars complete with their content: tapeworms, lizards and snakes. The preserving alcohol was palmed off on the black market as home-made 'double caraway schnapps' at 500 Reichsmarks per litre. By the time the authorities had got the tip-off and managed to raid the store, almost half of it had gone down the throats of unsuspecting drinkers: 10,000 litres of tapeworm happiness.

At the end of Brenner Strasse two teenage layabouts were hanging around, keeping watch. They gave him no more than a bored passing glance. Stave was hardly the only one heading for Hansaplatz. Men in long overcoats and flat caps; old women with wicker baskets; a one-legged veteran scouring the ground for cigarette butts and almost falling on his face every time he bent down to pick one up; workers from the port; men with bulging worn briefcases; two Chinese standing by the entrance to the Lenz bar.

Stave wandered amongst the throng. Slowly he began to make out a pattern, like waves on an ocean, like the ripples created by a stone tossed into the water. There would be quiet whisperings and then suddenly off would come an overcoat or a briefcase lid would be opened, cigarettes and Reichsmarks would pass from hand to hand, each exchange done quickly, inconspicuously.

In the entrance to an apartment block a young woman was offering a pair of men's shoes: '400 Reichsmarks,' she whispered, a flurry of motion and the shoes went to an elderly man with a briefcase who handed her something in return, then both walked off in opposite directions. An old man was offering bread coupons to three women standing round him clearly outraged by the price. The old boy looked round nervously, obviously an old soldier, with boots too big for him, in a dyed Wehrmacht greatcoat held together with safety pins, and pulled out a tin can from his pocket: 'Butter two nine.' 290 Reichmarks for one pound. Some smugglers must have brought a big load through the control points, otherwise it wouldn't be anywhere near so cheap. Either that or it's not the real thing. Two men were whispering together in a doorway and then suddenly there was an aroma of coffee in the air, before the banknotes changed hands, lots of banknotes. An old, careworn woman disappeared with one of the Chinese into the bar. A boy, barely 14 years old, was heedlessly calling out 'Flints', 'Flints for cigarette lighters, just 18 Reichsmarks!' Another teenager was peddling Lucky Strikes, seven Reichsmarks each. Stave opened his ears and let the prices roll over him: 'Wehrmacht cutlery, rust-free, four-piece, very useful for refugees – 23 Reichsmarks. A ball of yarn – 18 Reichsmarks. A pound of sugar – 80 Reichsmarks. A month's food rations – 1,000 Reichsmarks.'

We must have a word with the man selling the ration card, thought Stave to himself. Most workers and office employees earned no more than 50 Reichsmarks a week. If you had to keep your nose to the grindstone for six weeks to buy a pound of butter, then you really were poor – and ready to deal yourself on the black market. Or to take risks.

Watches, gold coins, dollar bills in shoe polish tins. Two metres of zinc guttering. Three freshly caught trout. A clean false identity card to get through the denazification process. Blank passports. A tiny Persian rug. Penicillin from Allied supplies. A leather suitcase. A woman's blouse.

But no false teeth, no truss, no medallion.

Damn it, thought Stave, the boy from the search team was right; how on earth could you link any of the objects for sale here to one of the victims? Could the blouse have belonged to the young woman? Did the old man pull the piece of guttering out of the rubble and get himself killed for it?

'Police!'

The word resounded across the square, like the warning cry of some Stone Age caveman.

Police helmets, green overcoats, truncheons cut down the side streets, screaming women, obscenely cursing boys. People pushing, shoving, clanking everywhere as tin cans, Wehrmacht cutlery, spectacle frames, work tools land on the cobbles along with cigarettes, false identity cards and bundles of Reichsmarks.

The experienced dealers realise straight away that they're caught and immediately dispose of the evidence. It's gone for good one way or another but if they don't find anything on you the penalty is less severe.

However their customers are novices. They clutch their booty and run for it, into an alleyway, into the next doorway, into a bar. But the police are suddenly everywhere, staring at them fiercely or maybe just laughing maliciously at them, even raising their hefty truncheons. But they don't need to use them; it's enough to bark out orders, then march towards the mass of people, crowding them ever closer together.

Stave cursed, pushing his way through the crowd, pushing and kicking his way through towards the man who had the ration card to sell. The man is not making a fuss, the ration card has almost certainly been dropped on the cobbles somewhere. He's young, pale, dark hair shaved to a millimetre length, a horrible scar on his left cheek as if he'd been struck by lightning.

A former soldier, Stave reckoned. He had to be careful.

The chief inspector pushed an old woman to one side and found himself next to the man, took out his police ID and held it under his nose.

'CID!' he shouted at him.

There was more he wanted to say, read the man his rights for example, but all of a sudden a fist hit him in the face. It went black before his eyes and he could taste the salt of his own blood. Not very good manners, Stave thought to himself as the pain in his head diminished.

The younger man had turned, trying to flee. But he faced a wall of bodies. He pushed the old woman Stave had already shoved out of the way brusquely to the ground. But one foot got caught in her shopping basket, leaving him jumping up and down, swearing and kicking at the wickerwork.

Stave was on him in a split second, forcing his arm up behind his back and throwing him down on the cobbles so that the man cried out. The crack of ribs breaking. With the taste of his own blood still in his mouth, Stave leapt on him, both knees on his breastbone, and heard the crack of another. The dark-haired man didn't cry out any more, just gurgled.

'Nice move!' somebody called.

Stave turned around and recognised the kid from the search team who had somehow fought his way through the crowd.

'Judo,' he replied, coughing, as he got to his feet and smoothed his hair. Eugene Hölzel, an average-sized man with yellow horn-rimmed glasses had turned up at the Hamburg Criminal Police department a year ago. He turned out to have been German judo champion several times over. The Brits had banned him from indulging in his sport other than to train the police. Stave, rather naïvely, imagined the training might help him overcome his limp. Now he thought to himself with no little satisfaction, at last Hölzel's torture had been worth it, as he watched two uniformed policeman lead away the man, who was still bent double.

'I'll interrogate him first,' Stave told the uniforms.

Men, women and a few children were all lined up against the wall of a big grimy apartment block. The Hansaplatz was covered with a thick layer of snow, as well as tins, boxes, paper rustling in the icy wind and a few things that were unidentifiable at a distance. A few of the policemen were chasing after Reichsmarks whirling in the air.

Stave wondered idly how many of the notes would ever be handed in. His burst lip was no longer bleeding but it had swollen up. I just hope I don't dribble like a drunk during the interrogations, he thought. The dark-haired character would go down for six months. That's if he wasn't linked to the killings, in which case he'd be for the noose.

The uniformed police were dragging the prisoners two by two on to the backs of trucks that had come down Brenner Strasse. One or two women were crying, a few men were cursing the police, but most were calm. They were tired. Resigned to their fate.

Stave's mind went back to other prisoners, thrown on to the back of a truck by the police in broad daylight, in the middle of town. It was only a few years back. Would it all never end? And who was to say that this was more justified than what happened back then? He had to force himself to think of the two strangulation victims, and that their murderer might be amongst those being loaded on to the back of these trucks.

'Back to HQ,' he ordered the teams. 'It's going to be a long night. I wouldn't mind if somebody brought a pound of the coffee lying around here with them so we could all have a decent cup.' But of course, nobody touched the confiscated goods. They were all honest German officials. And besides, there were a couple of British occupation troops watching them.

Back at head office Stave, Maschke and a couple of the other CID men took charge of the interrogation rooms. The uniformed police would bring the prisoners from the overcrowded holding cells.

'Bring me the dark-haired guy first,' Stave said again.

However a few minutes later Stave would find himself in the situation of a poker player who has overestimated the strength of his hand. By a long shot.

The suspect, sitting bent over and pale on the chair in front of him, had a perfect alibi. He had been 'organising' food supplies in another city in the British occupation zone to bring them to Hamburg where people were prepared to pay much higher prices. But he had been spotted and arrested. The police had only found half his wares, but for that he was given two weeks behind bars. One call to his colleagues in Lüneburg told Stave that on the probable night of the murder, the twentieth of January, the man in front of him had indeed been sitting in a nice clean cell, 60 kilometres away from the ruins of Hamburg. Stave had the man led away, and wrote a report for the British judge who would take over the next day.

'Next!' he called to the policeman waiting outside, despondency clearly audible in his voice.

Next was a pale student, father reported missing at Stalingrad, mother killed by a bomb. He had 80 cigarettes and 17.40 in Reichsmarks on him. Next: a practised black marketeer with a record as a pimp, with 3,000 Reichsmarks but no contraband. Next: a housewife with a pound of butter. Next: a boy with no contraband, no cigarettes, no money. Stave sent him straight home. Next: an old man trying to palm off two old watches.

By two in the morning Stave felt as if somebody had driven a Sherman tank over him. Erna Berg brought him a cup of tea, but the world went black again when the hot tea touched his burst lip.

His eyes watered as during each interrogation he flicked through the CID records of known criminals: their description, fingerprints, distinguishing marks, last known address, front and side-profile photos.

He was hungry, cold. He felt a great temptation to smash the skull of the next person dragged into the room. It turned out to be Anna von Veckinhausen.

One look in her dark eyes and he realised she was as angry as him. This could get tricky, the chief inspector thought to himself.

He decided to be polite, offered her a seat without mentioning that it was not the first time that he had questioned her. Maybe she hoped he wouldn't recognise her amongst the dozens of others? She, likewise, gave no indication that they had ever met. Impressive self-control, thought Stave, a possible indication of a cold heart.

He leafed through the record book. No mention of her. Then he glanced at a piece of paper with her details that one of the uniformed police had handed him. Born 1 March 1915, Königsberg. No further information as to her family or when she moved to Hamburg. At least now he understood her accent.

'What were you dealing on the black market?' he asked her.

'I wasn't dealing,' she said angrily. 'I was just leaving the station and crossing the Hansaplatz when your…'

'Raid,' Stave genially supplied the word.

'…your "action" began,' she continued. 'I already told the officer who arrested me that it was a mistake. But he wouldn't even listen. Just like the Gestapo.'

The chief inspector ignored the deliberate provocation, although Anna von Veckinhausen wasn't totally wrong. He looked down at his documents. 'We found 537 Reichsmarks on your person,' he said calmly. 'Can you tell me what you hoped to buy on the black market with a sum like that?'

'I don't have to tell you anything at all. My money is my money.'

'I was just wondering if you had sold something just before the raid. Maybe something that a couple of days ago had belonged to a man of about 70?'

Anna von Veckinhausen looked as if she were about to jump to her feet. But instead she closed her eyes and took a deep breath. 'I thought you might have forgotten me,' she mumbled.

Stave allowed himself a brief smile. 'I wouldn't be in this job if I had.'

'I didn't sell anything on the black market. I really was on my way from the station. You arrested everybody on the Hansaplatz. Ask any one of them.'

'With 537 Reichsmarks on you?'

'With 537 Reichsmarks on me.'

'And you refuse to tell me where you got so much money from or what you intended to do with it?'

'Neither one nor the other has anything whatsoever to do with you.'

Stave looked down at the paperwork again. It was hard to disprove her story. But on the other hand, just the circumstances of her arrest would be enough for a British judge to lock her up for a couple of days. And what good would that do?

'We didn't carry out this raid to arrest housewives out to buy a few matches. We did it in the hope of laying our hands on something that might have belonged to the murder victim – the murder victim whose body you found.'

'And have you?'

Stave chose to ignore the question, even though he realised Anna von Veckinhausen wasn't being sarcastic but really wanted to know, either because she was genuinely interested – or genuinely worried.

'Let me take you back to the afternoon when you found the body. You had been walking down Lappenbergs Allee. You then turned off and walked along the footpath through the ruins to get to Collau Strasse. That was where you found the body, amongst the ruins.'

'Yes,' she sighed, wearily.

Stave made a note.

'How long were you with the corpse?' he asked.

She gave him a surprised look. 'You think I said a prayer for the dead or something?'

'I'm asking if you just looked down, realised what you were looking at and immediately ran off. Or if you took a good look around?'

Anna von Veckinhausen put her right hand on her left shoulder, so that her arm lay across her upper body. Stave wondered if it was out of embarrassment or an instinctive desire for protection.

'I … don't know,' she admitted hesitantly. 'Maybe a few seconds. I saw the body but it took me a bit to realise what I was actually looking at. Then I left. I didn't run. There was no need to hurry.'

'So you took a long look at the body, but didn't notice anything in particular about the place where it had been left?' Stave pressed her.

'I guess you could say that.'

Stave stared down at his desk. He had a difficult decision to make. But it was the middle of the night and he was hungry, cold and exhausted. His head hurt. Should he keep Anna von Veckinhausen in custody? The 537 Reichsmarks was evidence enough. Or should he let her go? Show lenience, but keep her under observation.

'You can go,' he said at last, and then to his own surprise, added: 'Sorry for the inconvenience.'

She stared at him for a second in disbelief. Then she smiled, said, 'Thank you,' and got to her feet. When she reached the door she turned back to him and asked, 'What happened to your lip?'

'I slipped on the ice,' Stave replied.

When the door closed behind her he looked down at his notebook. On the evening when she found the body, Anna von Veckinhausen had claimed she used the footpath to cross from Collau Strasse to Lappenbergs Allee. When Stave had gone over her story, he had deliberately reversed the names. And she had confirmed that she had been going from Lappenbergs Allee to Collau Strasse.

It was an old Gestapo trick. Maybe she had just been tired. Or so upset by being arrested that she hadn't been paying attention. But it was also possible that she had told a lie first time and could no longer remember exactly what she had said.

'Next!' he called to the uniformed policeman outside.

Two hours later it was finally all over. His back aching, the chief inspector got up from his chair and walked up and down in his office to get the circulation in his injured leg going. Eventually he had worked off the worst of his limp. Then he called in the other officers. The Department S chief looked as fit and fresh as if he had had a good ten hours' sleep. According to him the raid had revealed a tank of schnapps and half a tonne of penicillin. Also the CID search guy was pleased: they had caught a major racketeer.

Maschke and the rest, however, looked tired and unhappy. The only one who still seemed optimistic was MacDonald, and he hadn't taken part in the raid or sat in on any of the interrogations.

Why didn't he just go home hours ago, Stave wondered. 'Thanks to you all, gentlemen,' he said, and got to his feet.

Not one of the items they had confiscated, not one thing any of those arrested had said, had been of the slightest help to the murder investigation. Nothing, zero, zilch! What might we have simply missed, the chief inspector asked himself. He waited until they had all left, then sat back down at his desk and began once more going through his notes and the interrogation reports, one by one, for nearly another hour. If it had been summer at least it would have been light by now, he thought. His eyes hurt. Nothing, except for the one potentially important, but also potentially laughable, contradiction in the statements by Anna von Veckinhausen.

Stave wondered if he should just put his head down on his desk for an hour or two. But when he considered the possibility that he might fall into a deep sleep and his colleagues, fresh from a night's sleep, would find him curled up in a ball on the floor, he decided it was better to go home. He made his way slowly to the main entrance. Then stopped dead.

A shadow.

Stave held his breath and gazed at a massive column in the outer hallway. There was a man crouched down on the other side of it. All Stave could see at first was a leg and a shoulder. He kept still. The unknown figure gradually got to its feet, obviously not having noticed him. Maybe it was just a drunk, sleeping it off accidentally right in front of the CID building. The man staggered a step or two away from the column and walked out on to the square, yellow moonlight falling on his face.

Stave recognised him as one of the young men they had arrested a few hours earlier. He wondered who had interrogated him and let him go. Then he realised something else: the man was not drunk; he had been beaten up. His eye was swollen, his lip cut open, and he was walking with the crippled gait of someone who had been beaten and kicked in the stomach and lower body. A vile thought immediately came to mind: Gestapo. The man had been beaten up during his interrogation. Then he was released purely so that no other officer or British summary court judge would see his injuries. But he had been hurt so badly that he could hardly make it out of the building. It was only now that he had gathered strength enough to stagger away.

Stave followed him, as discreetly as he could.

The unknown man staggered down Holstenwall, then turned right at Millerntor, finally getting as far as the warren of tiny streets north of the Reeperbahn, to a half-destroyed rental block, with bits of cardboard next to the doorbells giving the names and birth dates of recently moved-in homeless. The man stopped, still bent over, then leaned down and scraped a handful of snow together to wipe his face. Trying to make himself presentable before his mother sees him, Stave thought to himself. The young man fumbled in the pocket of an overcoat that was way too big for him, his hands numb with cold and possibly also with bruises. When eventually he managed to find the key, Stave quickly approached him.

'CID,' he said in a low voice. No need to wake the neighbours.

The man turned round, an expression of horror on his face. 'What do you want now?'

He was barely 20 years old, Stave reckoned. Undernourished. Perhaps this was the first time in his life he had been badly beaten. On the other hand: who knew what he might have done in the war?

'Who did this to you?' Stave asked, indicating his swollen eyelid. He was too tired to beat about the bush. Also he was counting on the young man being afraid. Ask a simple question and he might get a simple answer.

'A policeman,' the lad said. 'While I was being interrogated.'

Stave closed his eyes and cursed under his breath. 'Which one?'

'Inspector Maschke.'

Why am I not surprised? Stave asked himself angrily.

'Why did he treat you like that?'

The young man stared at him as if he'd asked a stupid question. 'Maybe your colleague learnt his trade with the Gestapo,' he said at last.

Stave offered the lad a cigarette. A few more questions and he had got the basic facts. His name was Karl Trotzauer, 19, resident in St Pauli district, unemployed and caught on the black market with a bottle of schnapps and an oil painting of a farmhouse in a gold-painted frame. But you didn't beat people up for being in possession of a bottle of schnapps and a piece of kitsch. Apparently Maschke had also asked where he had been on the night of the twentieth of January. And Trotzauer, with no idea what he was on about, had told him he had been over at his aunt's house in Eimsbüttel and had then come home via Lappenbergs Allee.

'That's when he started hitting me,' he said, pointing to his swollen eye. 'No warning, no shouting, just laying into me with his fists and kicking me. I thought I was going to die.'

'Then what happened?'

'When I came to my senses he asked me how I had killed the old man.'

'The old man?'

'I had no idea what he was talking about. It was only after he had beaten me some more that I realised he was on about a murder victim. Gradually it dawned on me that he wanted me to confess to killing some old man.'

'And did you?'

Trotzauer glowered at him. 'It hurt like hell but I'm not stupid. Obviously I didn't confess because there was nothing to confess to. I didn't kill any old man. I told Maschke that, again and again. In between his blows. Eventually he let me go, promising that he would get me in the end.'

'Off you go,' Stave said.

On the long way back the chief inspector had plenty of time to reflect. On one occasion he had to stop to show his CID pass to a British patrol. Other than that, he saw nobody. It was as if Hamburg was deserted, the streets ruined and ripped apart, the shops stripped bare, the bombed-out railway stations all abandoned by the inhabitants, all of them gone somewhere else to build a new and better city.

Had Maschke been in the Gestapo? He was supposed to be relatively fresh out of police training college, so he couldn't have been there since before 1945. Nor could Stave imagine his big, gawky, chain-smoking colleague who still lived with his mother getting up at five in the morning to kick down the door of some Jew or other.

But even if Maschke had been in the Gestapo: why would he want to beat up some low-life black marketeer? Over-enthusiasm? Just because somebody had been in the area around the supposed time of the murder was no reason to beat him up. Why would Maschke want to make a suspect of a 19-year-old on practically no evidence? Why would he want to beat a confession out of him when he almost certainly had nothing to do with the real murderer?

The truth is I know nothing at all about Maschke, Stave thought to himself when he finally reached his own front door. Maybe it's time I looked into that. Tomorrow. After a few hours' sleep.

The following afternoon Stave had the first opportunity to find the answers to a few questions – and almost completely screwed up.

They were discussing the case in his office. He was staring at the snowflake patterns on the ice on his window, glinting like cold stars, while MacDonald was going over their next steps. The lieutenant was leafing through yellow pages looking at names, descriptions and dates of birth. Hundreds of them as far as Stave could see.

'This is a copy of the Hamburg missing persons list,' MacDonald said. 'I've gone through all the names – and there is no one there who fits either of our two victims. There are, of course, young women and old men, but their descriptions do not match either of the two. Nor can I find any pattern in the lists. Missing men, women and children. People unaccounted for since the bombings, people lost amongst the stream of refugees fleeing the east, or just gone missing because that is the way things are after a war. There are cases of husbands or wives reported missing, relatives and friends, employees reported missing by their firms or offices. If any of them should have ended up amidst the rubble with strangulation marks on their throat, I have no idea how we should find out their names from what we have here.' MacDonald folded the list up and put it in his uniform jacket pocket. Then he raised his hands in apology.

'Same thing here,' said Maschke, his tone of voice sounding as if it made him furious not to have found something the Brit had missed. 'No dentist ever examined this old boy's choppers, and no doctor ever examined him down below.'

MacDonald gave him a querying look and he smirked.

'I mean his rupture was never treated by any hospital or dear old family doctor in Hamburg, that's pretty much for certain.'

'Maybe he was treated by a doctor who didn't survive the war?' Stave suggested.

'I went round to the Street Clearance and Rebuilding office too,' Maschke continued, flicking open a grubby notebook. 'Did you know that in Hamburg more than 250,000 apartments and houses were destroyed by bombs? As well as 3,500 offices, 277 schools, 24 hospitals, 58 churches, and that altogether there are 43 million cubic metres of rubble. The rubble boys are pretty proud of their statistics department.'

'That'll keep them in work for the next 20 years,' Stave said morosely. 'But what's it got to do with looters?'

'It just shows that there's a lot of opportunity. But the rubble boys say there are no turf wars between gangs looting treasures from the ruins. At least not at the moment. Since it's been so cold, the stones, concrete slabs and all the dirt around have been frozen solid so that it's hardly worth it for the professionals to go out hunting for booty. They're waiting for the thaw. At present there are only amateurs out there amongst the ruins, looking for a metre of stovepipe, an oven plate or firewood. Too few of them to get into each other's way. Fewer looters out there than there were a couple of months ago, and almost no incidents of fighting between looters. Whatever happened to the girl and the old man, it almost certainly had nothing to do with looting.'

'Great,' said Stave, before he realised what a stupid thing it was to say. He sighed and rubbed his forehead. He could do with an aspirin, he thought, but you had to go to the black market to get those.

MacDonald finished up for the day. Stave held back his vice squad colleague under the pretext that he wanted further details about what he had found at the Clearance and Rebuilding office.

'What else is there to say?' Maschke asked, when the Brit had left the room.

'Just routine,' Stave replied – the phrase that put the wind up every criminal – and not a few police too.

'Is something wrong?'

Stave could have kicked himself. He forced a smile and then quickly carried on. 'I'll get straight to the point, Mashcke. This sort of investigation isn't exactly your speciality. And you haven't been at the job all that long.'

Maschke nodded, only partly mollified.

Stave pretended to examine Maschke's notes, but obviously there was nothing of any interest. 'You graduated from the police academy in 1946?' he asked, trying to sound as if he was just making small talk. 'When you were training did you do a stint with each of the city departments? In my day that was compulsory, although obviously we didn't have the Street Clearance and Rebuilding department back then.'

Maschke tried to nod and shake his head at the same time, then gave up and said, 'Yes, I graduated in '46, but no, I have never seen inside most of the city departments. But I'm not sure it's any great loss.'

'What did you do before police training college?' Stave asked, handing him his notebook back. It was a harmless enough question, he thought. But Maschke flinched, as if Stave had made him some immoral proposition. He blushed and there was a nervous tick in his right eye.

Stave caught his breath. He'd been too direct.

But a second later Maschke smiled, as if embarrassed, waved his hand in the air and mumbled, 'What did I do? I was in the armed forces, the navy, on the U-boats. In France. Sent straight to France in 1940, to the U-boat bases on the Atlantic. Out of France in 1944. But in between, trips out of Brest on the U-boat and a month's leave every now and then. *Un temps pas mal, même pour un boche comme moi.* At least I managed to polish my school French. I got to know my red wines too, not that that's much good at the moment.' He laughed.

Stave squeezed out a smile. 'Good work,' he said, nodding at the notebook. 'See you soon.'

He had heard his share of U-boat stories: damp in the close confines of a steel hull, endless patrols in the icy Atlantic. Depth charges that shook the subs from tail to stern. Floating coffins. Most U-boat sailors never came home. All of a sudden he looked at Maschke through different eyes: his constant, nervous smoking. The typical beard of a U-boat man with no means of shaving for weeks on end. His brutal impatience during the interrogation the night before. His superficial cynicism. Living at home with his mother – a sense of security.

After Maschke left, the chief inspector nonetheless made a call to an old friend in the personnel department, who owed him a favour. At least now he had concrete details about Maschke to go on.

Five minutes later he slammed down the receiver: it was quite clear that not only had Maschke never been in the Gestapo, he had never worked for any branch of the Hamburg police prior to 1945. He had applied to CID after the war and been signed up for police training college as he said. And, yes, in the papers submitted with his application there was a CV and documents to confirm his service on the U-boats in France. No Gestapo history, no time spent with the 'special units' in the east, no hidden years as a concentration camp guard. Maschke was clean.

On Friday Dr Ehrlich called him in. 'The raid saw us catch a good few fish in the net,' the public prosecutor began, politely, sitting back in his chair and putting his hands together over his stomach.

'Unfortunately not the ones we were fishing for,' the chief inspector replied. Stave wasn't interested in metaphors; it was time to tackle the main topic.

'I have to say I have no ideas,' Ehrlich admitted. 'If I were in your position, Stave, I would have done the same. And I wouldn't have a clue what to do now.'

Just what I wanted to hear, the chief inspector thought. 'We're following up a couple of leads,' he said.

'Glad to hear it. I thought you might be waiting for the next murder to see if anything might turn up.'

'We don't even know for sure if both murders were committed by the same killer.'

'But you're working on that assumption?'

Stave said nothing.

Ehrlich waved a hand wearily towards the window. He had long-fingered hands, Stave noticed, pianists' hands.

'I suspect that the perpetrator you are looking for is 30 or younger,' the prosecutor said.

'In that case you know more than I do.'

Ehrlich took his horn-rimmed glasses off, and began cleaning them. He probably can't recognise me without them, Stave thought.

'A 30-year-old,' the prosecutor began, 'would have been born in the turnip winter of 1916/17, the year of serious famine in the last war. That was followed by revolution and then counter-revolution. The failed right-wing putsch in Berlin; hyperinflation with your thousand Reichsmark notes being carried around in laundry baskets; the unemployment of the 1929 Depression; the street fighting between the Storm Troops and the Red Front from 1930 onwards; the Nazi terror; the war; bomber raids; concentration camps; occupation, and now this winter. What you and I still think of as normality hasn't existed for the last 30 years. Normality has become violence, suffering, death. That is why I think someone who can strangle a young woman and an old man with apparently methodical indifference has to be someone who has never known anything but violence in his life. That makes him 30 years old, or younger.'

'I can't exactly subpoena every young person in Hamburg,' Stave mumbled. 'And not every 30-year-old is a killer.'

'If you include soldiers, Gestapo men, party functionaries, concentration camp guards and senior officials in the old regime in that group, then I'm afraid I must contradict you. Seen like that most young people are guilty.'

'And a lot of older people too. That is hardly a help.'

'Are you aware of my oath of office?' Ehrlich asked him.

Stave shook his head, confused.

'I swear, by God the Almighty, to apply and carry out the law of Germany with justice and mercy towards everyone irrespective of religion, race, urging or political conviction, to the advantage of none and disadvantage of none; that I shall follow the laws of Germany and the legislation of the military government according to the word and intent, and that I shall at all times do my best to respect the equality of all before the law. So help me, God.

'The equality of all before the law, Stave. Have you any idea how many officials the British-controlled Committee for Denazification scrutinised in Hamburg alone? More than 66,000. And how many were dismissed because of their Nazi past? 8,800. Do you know where Jews who survived the concentration camps have to sign up when, in their weakened state, they are entitled to apply for larger rations?'

'At the police station.'

'Exactly. At the police station, sometimes in the same building, even in the exact same offices where the Gestapo used to sit. And who do you think is sometimes still sitting in those offices?'

The prosecutor paused for a moment, then said: 'The police separates concentration camp survivors into three groups. Group 1A: party political offenders. In other words, Social Democrats and Communists. Interesting, isn't it, that the police still use the term "offenders"? Then there is Group 1B: other political offenders. And finally 1C: criminals and anti-social elements. Which group, would you suggest, do the Jews come under?

'Anyone who can survive all this humiliation gets a special ration from the Red Cross: a loaf of bread, a tin of meat, five Reichsmarks for a meal in a public canteen, and eight weeks of extra coupons on their ration cards. That's it. Because the doctors of Hamburg's Medical Council have decreed, and I quote, that "the general state of health and nourishment of a concentration camp inmate is satisfactory".'

Ehrlich's face had gone red, his hand was no longer waving out the window but clasped around his teacup, his knuckles so white that Stave was afraid the porcelain might shatter at any moment.

'Even so,' the prosecutor continued, 'I shall do everything to ensure the "equality of all before the law". And do you know why? Because I do not want revenge, I want justice. Because only justice will let us build a better state. Because only justice will banish fear.

Because only justice will allow us to raise a generation for whom "normality" will actually be normal again.'

'Two strangled bodies isn't exactly normal,' Stave muttered.

'Two strangled bodies is not normal; it is tragic, but it is hardly threatening. However, what if two becomes three? Or four? People will start to become afraid. And frightened people look towards a strong man, someone who will clean things up without worrying about collateral damage. And that, Stave, is absolutely the last thing we need. That would sabotage everything I work for here on a daily basis.'

'It's what I work for too,' Stave said wearily.

Ehrlich smiled for the first time. 'I know that. That's why I'm speaking openly with you. I don't want to put pressure on you.'

'But that's what you're doing.'

'That's what I'm doing. The circumstances are doing it. We absolutely have to stop these killings. If only it were summer, if the homeless were just starving but not freezing and squatting out there in the darkness at the same time, then murders like this would horrify us but that might be all. But right now, in this miserable, long, destructive winter, the city is on the brink of total collapse. Nothing works properly any more, absolutely nothing. You experience it every day. The camel's back is already overloaded, if I can put it that way.'

'And these murders might be the last straw.'

'That's what I mean. So as far as I am concerned you have per-mission to interrogate every single citizen of Hamburg, up to and including the mayor if you have to! Turn over every single stone in the mountains of rubble until you find a lead. Tell me your most absurd suspicions, the most implausible ideas. I have your back, inspector. But find me the killer!'

Stave thought over what the prosecutor had said on his short walk back to HQ. He had the backing of Ehrlich, a public prosecutor with the best of contacts amongst the British. A public prosecutor set on hunting down former secret concentration camp guards and who in most cases demanded the death penalty, which the judges usually passed. You could have worse allies, he thought.

So anxious was he to get back to work that the chief inspector ran down the hallway, barely noticing his limp. He threw open the door to the anteroom without knocking.

'Frau Berg, please call Inspector Maschke and Lieutenant Mac-Donald and tell them to come to my office,' he said, hoping his voice sounded normal.

A few minutes later the two were in his room. Stave gave them a rough summary of his meeting with Dr Ehrlich. 'We can do whatever we want and we have his full support,' he said in conclusion.

'Full support for what precisely?' Maschke asked.

Stave had been thinking about that for the past two days, ever since the raid on the Hansaplatz. Both the lines of enquiry he now wanted to follow were frankly a pain. One of them was politically delicate to say the least. The second would involve them treading on toes, toes that belonged to important people whose private lives they would need to look into.

'We're going to take on the Displaced Persons files, every single one of them.' He turned to MacDonald and added, 'Obviously that means we are going to need the agreement of the British authorities.' That was the politically delicate part. 'And we are going to investigate every single missing person in Hamburg,' this to Maschke. 'That means not just going through the lists of names and ages. We are going to burrow around in each and every case.' That would mean digging into private lives. Either our two victims are DPs, in which case we will find a link to them in the camps. Or they are natives of Hamburg, in which case somebody somewhere must have realised they're missing – maybe just one person, and maybe that person has a reason for not coming forward. One way or another we are going to find out who they are.'

MacDonald looked confused. Maschke's face had gone the same colour of grey that army recruits used to go when they got their orders for the eastern front a few years back.

The Girl with No Name

Saturday, 2 February 1947

His left leg hurt. Since early morning Stave had been plodding up and down the station platforms like a nervous sheepdog. It was now coming up to midday. Every half-hour a train would arrive, pulled by battered steam locomotives belching black sooty clouds, with a whistle and screech of iron wheels on iron rails.

Most of them were either carrying potatoes in from the countryside, open-topped freight trains or standing-room-only trains, former third-class carriages with the seats ripped out in order to squeeze more people in. Men in suits or overalls piled out, young women so weak they could hardly walk, in headscarves, or just old curtains wrapped around their heads and necks to protect them against the lethal wind that blew through the carriages. You could only see their eyes. Some were carrying cardboard boxes in their hands or net shopping bags, ripped rucksacks or bags cobbled together out of strips of torn canvas, people who'd been out foraging in Lüneburg or Holstein, buying potatoes. The farmers out there were getting rich. People would offer their last valuables, the family silver, gold coins, stamp collections, old paintings, smuggled Wehrmacht weaponry. They would even beg.

Most came back with just a few pounds of potatoes, some with nothing at all. Several of them were bleeding from ragged wounds to their arms, thighs or buttocks, visible beneath their ripped clothing: some of the farmers got so fed up with the begging, they set dogs on them.

'Hamsters' was the popular name for them, but to the police it was officially 'direct producer-consumer trade', and it was illegal. It went against the rules of the emergency economy, sabotaged the ration system. British military police and uniformed German police kept watch at stations outside the city, and would occasionally close down the main station to carry out a raid. More than one 'hamster' who'd spent two days begging in the countryside and in the end handed over his gold watch for four pounds of potatoes would find himself robbed of them when he got back and thrown into jail.

Stave wasn't interested in the 'hamsters'; they weren't why he was here. He was watching the emaciated figures in Wehrmacht great-coats. Could his son have become one of these wraiths? Would he even recognise him? The chief inspector watched the returning veterans as they stood there on the platform, still confused, getting their bearings once again. Then he would go up to them, speak to some of them, offer them cigarettes. It was the same ritual every time, the same brief surge of hope, like the effect of a glass of schnapps in the bloodstream. And then the same empty faces, the mumbled regrets, sometimes confused, even crazy, answers. Karl Stave? Never heard of him.

'Can I help warm you up?'

Stave spun round in surprise. A girl, just 12 years old, Stave reck-oned, though her emaciated figure might be deceptive; she might be 14. He shook his head, about to turn round again, then hesitated, put his hand in his pocket and gave the kid two cigarettes.

'Maybe these'll do you some good. Keep you out of the hands of a pimp.'

The girl snatched the cigarettes, shouted, 'Don't be so fucking sentimental,' and vanished.

The next train was on platform four, from the Ruhr, not from the east, but Stave didn't want to miss any of them. There were two former soldiers on the wooden walkway from the platform, and in front of them two British military policemen. With trembling hands the two ex-POWs showed them their release papers. Stave waited until they had been checked.

A hand on his sleeve.

The chief inspector spun round, expecting to see the skinny girl again. But it was Maschke.

'At last,' the vice squad officer said, before a smoker's cough wracked him. 'I've been looking for you for an hour,' he managed to croak out.

Stave closed his eyes wearily. 'Not another murder?'

'Maybe.'

'What do you mean, *maybe*? Is it a murder or isn't it?'

'It's a murder but it's not clear if it's the killer we're after.'

'Why not?' asked Stave, glancing back at the two ex-POWs, then following Maschke who was already striding forcefully towards the main exit.

'In this case too, the victim was strangled by a thin wire,' his colleague said, hesitatingly, 'but this time it's a child.'

The patrol car was standing outside the former Deutsches Schauspielhaus theatre, now renamed the Garrison Theatre and reserved for the British. Maschke carefully settled back in the driver's seat, turned round, glanced in the mirror and then edged the old Mercedes ever so carefully away from the curb. When he saw how nervous Stave looked, he smiled apologetically.

'I learnt to drive in the Wehrmacht, in one of the VW *Kübelwagen* bucket-seat jeeps on the broad French *allées*. They were a lot more basic than this grand old lady. I don't want to get any dents.'

'We're in no hurry,' Stave replied.

Maschke coughed. 'We're going to Hammerbrook. It's not far. Bill Strasse.'

Stave closed his eyes. In the east of the city again, another working-class district that had been heavily bombed, razed to the ground more than any other part of the city.

'Nobody lives there any more,' he muttered.

'The body was found in the lift shaft of a former mattress factory, 103 Bill Strasse, out by the mouth of the Northern Elbe, at the end of the port.'

'Who found it?'

'A ship's watchman, who'd been walking along the canal. Probably looking for coal. You sometimes find bits dropped from a load. Said he was just taking a walk. The report came in about 10.30 a.m.'

'Have you already checked him out?'

Maschke shrugged. 'Says he was in Lübeck with his mother up until yesterday. We're checking that out. If it's true he can't be a suspect. If it's not true then he's got a problem.'

Maschke drove the heavy old car carefully down the empty streets, making wide detours around the heaps of rubble, but swerved to the side of the road when faced with oncoming British jeeps, avoiding them as if they were tanks. It was about five kilometres from the station to the spot in Hammerbrook where the body had been found, Stave reckoned. It would have been faster walking than with Maschke driving. But at least he didn't have to face the icy wind.

They passed endless rows of charred façades with no windows, like stage sets in some gigantic burnt-out theatre. The steel structures of the elevated railway, its tracks and bridges, bore the scars of bomb impacts; collapsed in places, bent into grotesque sculptures or reduced to tiny red-black lumps by the ocean of flames that had engulfed them.

The Mercedes rumbled a kilometre or so along Bill Strasse to where a façade that had collapsed on to the street blocked their way. Maschke parked next to the rubble behind a British jeep and the crime scene team's vehicle.

As Stave stepped out of the car he almost trod on a wooden cross at the foot of the heap of rubble, nailed together at an angle and with the words 'To our Mother Meta Krüger 27/28.7.1943'. He imagined she was still lying under the rubble, and turned his face away.

They had some 200 metres to walk through the rubble, the meter-thick ice on the Bille canal glistening to their right. Somewhere or other the wind was being sucked through a burst stovepipe, making a noise like an eerie organ. There was nothing living visible anywhere, not even a rat or a crow. Stave had climbed around a partially intact wall before he came across signs of life: uniformed police and figures in long overcoats with caps pulled down low over their eyes. British military.

'This is it,' said Maschke, somewhat superfluously.

'Narrow strangulation marks on the throat,' Dr Czrisini whispered, 'the lower right arm has an old scar, about two centimetres long. Teeth complete, no signs of undernourishment, about 1.10 metres tall. I would guess six to eight years old.'

'Time of death?' Stave muttered, trying to keep hold of himself.

'I'll have a better idea after the autopsy, but she's been dead at least 12 hours. In this cold she might have lain here even longer.'

'In this cold,' muttered Stave. 'Any signs of abuse? Any other harm?'

'Not as far as we can see at present. But we'll soon know more.'

'And as ever, no means of identification?'

The photographer and crime scene man came up with something in a bag. 'We found this next to the body. It might have belonged to her, but it might also just have been lying there.'

It was a red braided cord about half the length of a finger. The chief inspector shook his head. 'What is it?'

'You obviously don't have daughters,' the photographer said with a weak smile. 'It may have come from a Spencer, a type of traditional short jacket. The sort of thing a girl her age would be likely to wear.'

Stave waved one of the uniforms over. 'Go the nearest police station and call the head of Department S. He needs to send people out to all the black market areas of the city, immediately, and tell them to take into custody any of them selling a traditional girl's jacket with red cord braid.'

The officer saluted and clambered off over the rubble.

Stave looked around him. 'The girl can't have lived round here. The closest even half-inhabitable buildings are hundreds of metres away.'

'Which means the killer brought her here,' Maschke concluded for him.

'Or the kid was here gathering coal and bumped into our killer,' MacDonald suggested. 'She wouldn't be the only child out doing that, it seems.'

The two detectives gave him a quizzical look. He explained, 'When the first policemen got here after the body was reported, they grabbed a boy who said he was here looking for coal. No idea whether or not he'd seen the body.'

Stave nodded. 'Right, well let's ask the ship's watchman the usual questions. And then we need to talk to the boy.'

The watchman's name was Walter Dreimann, 35 years old, thin with a face that suggested he suffered from stomach ulcers. Or maybe he just hadn't got over the sight of the dead child.

'You were out looking for coal?' the chief inspector asked.

'I was just taking a walk,' Dreimann replied, in a whiny voice that suggested he was insulted by the idea.

'Do that often, do you?'

'Every day. Apart from the last two weeks when I was up in Lübeck visiting my mother. But I already told your colleague that.'

'But before you went to visit your mother you took a walk along here every day?' Stave asked, flicking through his notebook.

Dreimann nodded.

'Right here, in this patch of rubble?'

The watchman replied without thinking about it. 'It's part of my usual route.'

'And when were you last here, before you went off to Lübeck?'

'Must have been the eighteenth or nineteenth of January.'

'And the lift shaft was empty that day?'

'Obviously!' Dreimann gave him a shocked look. 'You don't think I'd have found the body of a dead girl and said nothing!'

'Did you know the girl?'

'No.'

'Are you certain of that? Do you want to take another look at the body?'

Dreimann's face turned green. 'I've already seen enough.'

Stave forced the ghost of a smile and said, 'You can go.'

The chief inspector looked around the devastated landscape. The photographer was packing up. Two porters in dark overcoats lifted the thin little frozen body from the lift shaft and laid it on a stretcher. Just like during the war, Stave reflected, particularly in the weeks following each bombing raid when they kept pulling little bodies out of the ruins. But this was supposed to be peacetime, for Christ's sake.

He flinched. Something glinted on the grimy oil-covered floor of the lift shaft, something that must have been uncovered from the oil by the shoes of one of the porters. Something silver.

'Dig that out,' he said to one of the crime scene men, nodding at the object.

A minute later the chief inspector was holding in his hand an oily silver medallion. About the size of a small coin, one side smooth and plain. And on the other a cross and two daggers.

'Our murderer makes mistakes,' he thought to himself.

'People normally wear medallions round their necks,' MacDonald mused. 'It would seem that in the case of the last two victims the medallion was ripped off while the murderer was throwing his garrotte around their necks. He took everything from his victims but seems to have missed the little silver medallions.'

'Or placed them there,' Maschke suggested, 'as a sort of visiting card.'

'Some sort of nutcase, planting clues for us?' Stave wiped his brow with his right hand. He was tired. He didn't want to go along with Maschke's theory, not least because the last thing he wanted to do was to get inside the head of some deranged killer in an attempt to imagine his next moves. But he reminded himself that he was supposed to be a professional. 'In that case why didn't we find a medallion next to the first victim?'

'Maybe the killer is developing his style,' Maschke replied. 'Or maybe he did leave a medallion there, and we were just too stupid to find it?'

Another accusation, Stave thought to himself. If you keep on like this, I'll have you moved to traffic duty, if it's the last thing I do!

'I think MacDonald's suggestion is the more likely,' he said. 'At least in that case there would be a link between the old man and the child. The two of them were wearing the same medallion. Maybe they belonged to the same family.'

'So what about the young woman?' Czrisini asked.

'Maybe she was wearing a medallion too but in her case the murderer spotted it and stole it. Or maybe we really were too dim and didn't find it. I'll send somebody over to Baustrasse again to search the rubble.'

'If the medallions were ripped off at the time of the attack,' MacDonald developed his train of thought, 'then that means the victims were murdered where we found them, or else the medallions wouldn't have been next to the bodies.'

'But if they've deliberately been left by the killer,' Maschke interjected, 'it means nothing. He might have strangled them anywhere, and afterwards just sought out somewhere in the rubble he could dump the corpses, and leave them with his parting gift.'

'But he hasn't left any two bodies in the same place. Each time he has chosen a new lot of ruins,' Stave said. 'You were down at the Street Clearance department. Just how many lots of ruins are there to choose from to hide a corpse?'

The vice squad man shrugged: 'Hundreds, maybe thousands. There are a couple of posh areas like Blankenese that we can exclude – too little bomb damage – and then there are a few areas like the port: badly bombed but cordoned off by the British, where nobody would get in without being noticed. Apart from that, take your pick in what is the greatest ruined cityscape in Europe.'

'Maybe the killer wants us to find his victims,' MacDonald suggested. 'Maybe he's challenging us? Trying to provoke us?'

Stave waved the idea away. 'No point in coming to premature conclusions. Wherever the killer might hide the bodies they're going to be found sooner or later. How's he going to make a corpse simply disappear? Weight it down with a couple of concrete blocks and throw it into the water? Even out on the Elbe the ice is a couple of metres thick. The Alster and the Fleete are frozen solid. Bury it? The ground is frozen hard as iron. Burn it? There's next to no petrol and or coal in Hamburg, hardly even any wood. In one respect at least this winter is the policeman's friend – there's no way for a killer to simply dispose of his victim.' Stave stretched. 'Any more witnesses?'

The lieutenant gave a wry smile. 'Maybe. I have the boy in a car with one of our military police. It's not quite so cold in the car and there was no need for the lad to see this.' He nodded towards the stretcher with the body being carried off between a couple of broken walls.

'Maybe he should,' Stave muttered, and made a sign to the two men in dark coats to put the stretcher on the ground.

MacDonald barked something in English and a military police-man brought over a skinny boy, almost invisible inside a grown-up's overcoat that was far too big for him: unkempt brown hair, probably lice-infested, a scabby rash on his neck, missing one of his front teeth.

'What's your name?' Stave asked him, indicating to the British soldier that the boy shouldn't come too close.

'Jim Mainke.'

'Jim?'

'Wilhelm.'

'Age?'

'Sixteen.'

'Try again. Age?'

'Fourteen. That is, I'll be fourteen this summer.'

'Where do you live?'

Wilhelm Mainke waved a hand somewhere across the ruins.

'With your parents.'

'No, thank God,' the boy replied with a smile. 'If I did, I'd be in Öjendorf Cemetery.'

The cheeky answer irritated the chief inspector but he kept calm.

'Do I have to drag everything out of you? Or can you string more than a couple of words together at a time?'

Maine averted his eyes. 'My father worked at Blohm & Voss,[2] my mother was a housewife. They were both killed by a bombing raid in 1943. I was staying with my grandmother out in the country at the time. I live in a cellar in Rothenburgsort, with a few friends.'

That was more or less what Stave had guessed. There were more than a thousand vagabond orphans on the streets of Hamburg, some whose parents had been killed in the bombing raids, some refugees who'd got separated from their parents. A few of them had joined gangs and were literally fighting for their existence; many survived by collecting lumps of coal, looting amongst the ruins, working for the black marketeers – or sold themselves on the station platforms.'

'You come here a lot?'

'Of course. I know my way around the port area. I used to be able to visit my father at the shipyard. I come here looking for coal.'

'Other kids do the same thing?'

Mains shrugged. 'You get a few hanging around. Thirty, maybe forty. Not so many right now. Too cold.'

'And you were out and about here this morning?'

'Yeah. Until the patrol nabbed me.'

'Did you see the girl?'

Mainke quickly shook his head. 'When I got here, the cops were already on the scene. They wouldn't let me get any closer.'

'But you know why the police are here?'

The boy nodded. 'One of the military police told me.'

'Were you here yesterday too?'

'No, had to find myself a bite to eat. It's two, maybe three days since I was last here.'

'Do you think the girl could have been lying in the lift shaft then and you wouldn't have noticed her?'

The boy moved his head from side to side indifferently. 'She could have been there for years and I wouldn't have noticed her. I usually keep to the riverbank. That's where you find lumps of coal, if you're lucky. As soon as I find a couple, I'm out of here. Not worth staying around any longer. Not worth wandering around in the ruins, nothing left there.'

'Apart from a dead girl.'

Jim Mainke went silent.

Stave sighed. 'I'm sorry about this, but I have to ask you to come with me.'

'Are you arresting me?'

'You could say that, but it's not exactly what I mean at the moment.'

The chief inspector led the boy over to the stretcher, where the two porters were standing having a smoke. The military policeman gave Stave a dirty look and glanced at MacDonald, but dropped it when the lieutenant gave an imperceptible nod.

Stave pulled the blanket back from the head end of the stretcher. 'Do you recognise this girl?'

Mainke didn't throw up, didn't even go pale, just stood there looking at the body. Eventually the chief inspector had had enough and pulled the blanket back over the victim's unseeing eyes.

'Never seen her before,' the boy said.

Stave nodded to the porters for them to take the stretcher away.

'What're you going to do with me now?' Mainke asked. 'Can I go back to looking for coal?'

'You're too young. I can't just let you loose around here. The policemen will take you to Rauhes House.' It was a charitable institution where all the orphans picked up by the police were taken in. A former locksmith was in charge and a few volunteers; Christian idealists looked after the boys and girls, delousing them and washing them, patched up scratches and dealt with other minor illnesses, gave them hot soup and a clean bed. Even so, most of the children did a runner within a day or two.

Mainke turned round and walked off behind the military policeman.

'Where did you get the name Jim from?' Stave shouted after him.

Maine turned and gave him a real boyish grin. 'I have an uncle in America. Honest. In New York. I'm going to go to him as soon as big ships start docking in the port again.'

'Good luck,' Stave murmured, but Mainke was already too far away to hear him.

'A witness?'

Stave turned round on hearing his boss's voice: Cuddel Breuer was standing there facing him.

'I don't think so. The boy only got here after the police were already on the scene.'

'So, anything else?'

Stave almost said, 'Just the usual,' but stopped himself in time. He quickly went over what they had found.

'Do you think the killer is the same?' Breuer asked.

Stave paused, took a deep breath, then nodded: 'Yes. Victims two and three have something to do with each other. Members of the same family, I suspect, even though we have no proof as yet. The circumstances are remarkably similar: both strangled with a thin wire, stripped naked, left amidst the rubble. It is even possible the little girl was murdered at the same time as the other two.'

'A killer wiping out an entire family?' Breuer looked around. 'Anything else to do here?'

'The crime scene man will go over everything again. But there's nothing more for us to do.'

'Good. Let's go back to head office. I'll give you a lift.'

Stave followed his boss to his old Mercedes. Breuer drove himself. He was a relaxed, self-confident, fast driver. They soon left Maschke in the old patrol car far behind.

'So, we have a serial killer,' said Breuer, looking dead ahead through the windscreen.

'I'm afraid it seems so.'

'We're not going to be able to keep this under wraps much longer. The type of killing, the appeals for identification of the victims

– sooner or later some journalist will put two and two together and get a story.'

'And we can't control what he might write.'

'Not these days, thank God. That is one of the prices of democracy, made in Great Britain. One way or another we've done well, you and me, Stave. But even so, in this one particular case, I almost long for the old days when you could simply tell them what they could print, and what they couldn't.'

'Even that wouldn't help. People talk. There'll be rumours. I'd prefer a piece in the newspaper, so at least we know where we are.'

'And where are you?'

Stave shrugged. 'They can't write any more than we know. And that's precious little.'

Breuer, for the first time, turned and looked at him, even though they were turning fast into the square outside headquarters. 'We have a serial killer, one who attacks people in the ruins, amidst the rubble, or at least that is what people are going to think. But nearly all of Hamburg is in ruins. Worse: the victims are a young woman, an old man and a child. What are people going to make of that? That they're all members of one unfortunate family? Victims of some domestic drama? Hardly. They are going to believe that anybody is likely to be murdered. That men and women are in danger, and even children. That the killer is someone who can strike almost any citizen in almost any part of the city. *That* is what they're going to make of it.'

'And they might be right,' Stave mumbled.

'That doesn't exactly make the job any easier. Your job, I might add. Enjoy your Sunday, Chief Inspector.'

Stave climbed out, nodded, closed the heavy Mercedes door and watched as the car moved off.

'Enjoy your Sunday,' he muttered, than went into the office. It didn't look as if he was going to have time today to hang out at the station looking for his son.

He didn't even manage to get as far as his office without being stopped. A shadow emerged from between the columns by the doorway to the building: a young man, freshly shaven, bright, with notebook and pencil in hands that were still blue from the cold.

'Ludwig Kleensch, from *Die Zeit*,' he introduced himself. 'Can I have a word?'

Stave had to make up his mind quickly. Should he just ignore the journalist? Or would he speak to him. The British had allowed daily and weekly newspapers to start up. Most were run by political parties and were local Hamburg-only papers. *Die Welt* was unaffiliated to any party and was available throughout the British zone, as was *Die Zeit*, the weekly that was the first to be licensed by the British authorities. But in this winter even the daily newspapers only had four to six pages and were published just twice a week. There was too little paper, even the yellowish, unrefined stuff reminiscent of old cheap drawing paper for children, but thinner.

The chief inspector did his calculations. Today was Sunday; between now and Thursday when *Die Zeit* came out he would be left in peace, at least as long as Kleensch was the only journalist already in on the story.

'Very well,' he said, trying in vain to manage a smile as he held the door open for the journalist. 'At least in my office your hands won't drop off from the cold.'

Kleensch nodded, grateful and surprised to be treated so cordially.

'I want to talk to you about the rubble murderer,' Kleensch said when they were upstairs.

'The "rubble murderer"?'

'That's what I intend to call him. It has a ring to it. Or would you prefer the Hamburg Strangler?'

Stave didn't bother to answer, nor did he bother to ask how the journalist already knew so much, even the fact that he was the one running the case. He thought about the crammed newspaper pages, which had to carry official notices, wedding and death notices and news from all round the world. Kleensch wouldn't have much space.

Maybe the readers wouldn't even notice his story. After 12 years of Nazi censorship nobody believed anything they read in the newspapers any more.

As if he'd read Stave's mind, Kleensch leaned towards him and said, in a rather threatening tone of voice, 'I've already told the editor it's a big story.'

The chief inspector nodded resignedly, then gave the journalist a straightforward account of the case, handed him copies of the posters requesting information about the victims and told him what the CID had done so far. He only kept to himself what he planned to do next. He felt it might sound a bit pathetic.

'Will there be more murders?' Kleensch asked, scribbling so intensely he didn't even look up from his notepad.

What a stupid question, Stave thought to himself and then realised that it was a trap. If he said, 'We can't exclude that possibility,' the journalist would quote him on it, and that wouldn't sound good. Instead he said, 'We hope to have our hands on the killer within the next few days.'

Kleensch smiled, half in disappointment, half in recognition of what the inspector had done. He left Stave a card, printed on the same grubby paper as the newspapers themselves. 'If anything should turn up, I'd be grateful if you'd give me a call. I don't want to get anything wrong.'

The journalist shook his hand, opened the door and nearly walked straight into Dr Crzisini. He stared at him curiously, as if about to ask a question, then thought the better of it and left.

The pathologist came in, followed a few moments later by Maschke. Stave wondered if he'd been lurking somewhere out of sight until the journalist had gone down the stairs. Then behind him MacDonald and Erna Berg appeared. Stave wondered who had asked her, but said nothing.

'I'll make tea,' she said with a smile.

Stave rummaged around in his desk until he found his large-scale city map and unfolded it carefully. It was a post-war version, hatched grey and red where the bombed areas were. And there were a lot of them. Stave used tacks to put the map up on one wall of the office, then stuck three red-topped pins into the bombed areas, marking the places where the bodies had been found.

The others watched him in silence. Maschke was smoking, Czrisini gave the impression of somebody following an interesting operation and MacDonald looked like a soldier. Erna Berg, a steaming teapot in her hands, had stopped in the doorway and was looking at the map with horror.

'He's attacking people everywhere,' she mumbled.

'Three times is not yet everywhere,' Stave contradicted her. 'In what way could the victims be related?' he asked, looking at Czrisini.

The pathologist nodded thoughtfully. 'A grandfather, daughter and her daughter? Possible. It could actually fit with their ages. If we put the first victim, the young woman, at the upper end of the likely age spectrum; I would put her as at most 22. And we put the child at the youngest age, probably six. That would make her a very young mother, with a very old father because he had to be around 70. It is also possible that the first and third victims were actually sisters, two girls about ten years apart. The old man could have been their grandfather. I reckon that is more likely, although not very probable either. But how can you prove it? Up until now I've found no distinguishing features, such as birthmarks or the like.'

'But nor is there anything to suggest they were not related?'

'No.'

'Apart from where the bodies were found,' Maschke intervened, pointing the glowing end of his cigarette at the map. 'The bodies were found very far apart. If they had been one family, wouldn't they all have lived together? The child at least would have lived with its mother – or the two sisters would have lived together, if they were sisters, that is.'

'Or they lived with their grandfather,' MacDonald said. 'Like that little Mainke who was taken in by his grandmother.'

'We can't exclude any possibility,' Stave said again, scratching his head. 'Let us assume it is a family. Let us assume they were all killed in the same place. Remember: there is nothing to say they were killed where they were found. Might it not even be possible they were all killed at the same time? And that the murderer deposited the bodies in difference places afterwards. To cover up any clues.'

Czrisini looked thoughtful. 'It's so incredibly cold,' he murmured. 'It's hard to make exact estimates to compare with one another. The same time of death is indeed a possibility, and we just found them at different times. I can say that for certain about the old man and young woman. And I'll soon know more in the case of the child.'

Stave found himself imagining the little body lying on the dissecting table and forced himself to look out of the window instead. Some things just didn't bear thinking about.

MacDonald sighed. 'That might mean there are still more bodies lying around somewhere, that we just haven't found yet. The father, grandmother, brothers or sisters to the child…'

'I still think it's more likely that they have nothing to do with one another,' said Maschke, twirling his lit cigarette dangerously close to the map. 'They were all out there in the ruins, maybe looking for something, maybe just taking a shortcut. The murderer was lying in wait for them. Where they were found is where they were killed. The medallion is the calling card of a madman.'

'That would mean that the victims come from three different families and lived in three different places. Then surely somebody would have come forward to identify at least one of them,' Stave said quietly. 'It's simply not possible for so many people to be murdered in the middle of Hamburg without anyone missing any of them.'

'We don't know about the child yet,' Dr Czrisini reminded him.

'Quite,' the chief inspector said, nodding. 'We need to get a new poster printed. You deal with that, Maschke. Get as many printed as possible and include a photo of the medallion on it. Get in touch with the authorities in all the big cites, including those in the east. I want our posters up even in the Soviet zone.'

A telephone in the outer office rang, causing them all to flinch. Erna Berg went to answer it, said a few words and put the receiver down.

'That was the police in Lübeck,' she called out to the chief inspector. 'The mother of the ship watchman has confirmed that her son was staying with her the past two weeks. One of her neighbours saw him too.'

'Well, I guess that would have been too easy,' Stave said, and crossed out a line in his notebook.

'What next?' MacDonald asked.

'We still have three hypotheses,' Stave said. 'If the killer is a looter who murders people amongst the ruins to steal everything from them, then sooner or later an item will turn up on the black market that we can link to one of the victims. Maybe somebody will finally see a suspicious character lurking in the ruins. Or some spiv or pimp will hear something. It could be that in the next day or two we manage to identify one of the victims. And you never know, we might even catch him in the act. Sooner or later we'll get him.

'Hypothesis two: some madman is killing people and leaving this strange medallion as a calling card. In which case, does anyone have any idea how we might get a lead on him?'

'We urgently need to find out what this cross and two daggers is all about,' Dr Czrisini replied.

'If it is a madman, then he won't necessarily stop killing. Sooner or later we'll catch him at it,' Maschke said hopefully.

'Somebody will catch him,' Stave replied. 'But will it be us, or those who've taken our jobs?' He quickly tried to banish that note of pessimism, standing up straight and announcing: 'Hypothesis three: somebody wiped out a whole family. In that case, there may be no more victims, no more objects and no witnesses. Or we find the bodies of more people who were killed at the same time as our current victims. So we should be looking not for a murderer who has vanished without trace, but for a family that nobody has reported as missing.'

'Refugees from the east or Displaced Persons,' MacDonald murmured.

'Let's start with the child,' Stave told them. 'Maybe we'll have more luck than with the other two. Perhaps there are carers, teachers, playmates who'll recognise her. She must have gone to school somewhere. Let's knock on the doors of schools and homes that house the children of refugees and DPs.'

The phone rang again. Stave, who hadn't had a call in days, stared in irritation at the black object. His secretary nodded, said something politely and hung up.

'Department S,' she said. 'They've sent out plainclothes people to all the black market areas. None of them have come across a Spencer. But they promise to keep their eyes open.'

'Good,' Stave replied, even though he was suddenly quite certain that they were never going to find relevant items of clothing popping up on the black market. Somebody was systematically covering their tracks.

'I'll get on with the poster then,' said Maschke, and vanished.

'I have work to do in the pathology department,' Dr Czrisini said. 'The body will need to thaw first. Not that I expect examination of the girl's body to reveal anything I don't already know.' He gave a low bow and left the room.

'You should just go home,' Stave said to MacDonald and Erna Berg. 'There's nothing more to be done here today.' He stood there and watched the pair of them until the door to the outer office closed behind them.

The public prosecutor was scratching his bald head when Stave walked in. The office was almost warm. The chief inspector inhaled gratefully the aroma of freshly brewed tea. It felt more like a living room than an office, Stave thought to himself, and wondered if Ehrlich spent every Sunday here.

'Sorry I had to drag you away from the station,' Ehrlich said, nodding towards the guest chair. 'You were looking for your son?'

The chief inspector stared at the prosecutor dumbstruck, as if he'd been caught doing something embarrassing.

Ehrlich waved his arms to say it was of no importance. 'I was just guessing. I had heard your boy was unaccounted for.'

'I don't like that term,' Stave replied.

'And yet there is a trace more hope in it than in "missing". Or just "gone". Don't you think?'

'You also have sons,' Stave said. The prosecutor might as well know he knew things about other people's private lives too.

Ehrlich nodded calmly. 'Two boys. They're at boarding school. Back there.'

Stave took a second to realise that Ehrlich meant England.

'They're teenagers. It's a difficult age. And the last few years haven't been easy. I was in exile. They had to endure humiliation here, and then the passing of my wife.'

'Unaccounted for' instead of 'missing', 'passing' instead of 'suicide'. Stave had read some of the indictments Ehrlich had written and been impressed by his precise, crisp style. But obviously he kept that for indictments, a weapon best kept concealed when dealing with friends. He changed the subject, not wanting any more details of Ehrlich's personal tragedies, and certainly not willing to give any further details of his own. He gave him a quick rundown on the latest murder.

'Does this give the case a new dimension?' Ehrlich asked.

Stave sat staring at the prosecutor in silence, not knowing what to say.

Ehrlich passed the time cleaning his glasses, then said: 'Men and women being killed is horrible, but it happens all the time. A child, however? Isn't that the last taboo? A total abnegation of the slightest morality?'

'If you mean, are we looking for a murderer who is capable of absolutely anything, then the answer is *yes*, in my opinion. A man devoid of any scruples,' Stave agreed.

'Most killers who do away with children are driven by

uncontrollable emotions, either sexual lust or despairing mothers lashing out in a fit of anger or revenge. But in this case the murder is so...'

'...methodical,' Stave completed the sentence for him. 'The deed is simply carried out in cold blood, using – if you'll forgive the expression – a tried and tested formula. Then afterwards all traces are erased.'

'Remind you of something?' Ehrlich asked in a quiet voice.

'The concentration camps,' Stave answered immediately. 'The Gestapo. Special Units, SS. Men who killed irrespective of the age or gender of their victims. Systematic murderers who carried out their killings methodically, the corpses either dumped in mass graves or gone up in smoke. Documents that simply disappeared, camps that were emptied before the Allies arrived.'

'Well, that's not exactly a lead in itself,' Ehrlich said pensively, 'but it just might be the beginning of a lead.'

'The concentration camp guards are already on trial,' Stave reminded him, somewhat unnecessarily.

The prosecutor gave him a glance that was part sympathetic, part insulted. 'A few of them. The ones we caught. Most of the guards who were at Auschwitz even are still running around free. The same goes for most of the Gestapo hit men. And that's without even mentioning all the former members of the SS.'

'You think we might be looking for some Nazi thug who's stayed true to his murderous ideology even after the collapse of the regime and is waging some sort of one-man war?'

'Maybe. Or someone who wants to dispose of inconvenient witnesses to deeds committed in the past.'

Stave thought for a moment. 'But how does that help me? I can't go through the history of everyone in Hamburg to find out what they might have been up to prior to 1945. And even if I could, and unearthed every misdeed, how am I to link that with the murders being committed now? We don't even know the identity of the victims!' Stave shook his head. 'The only way we're going to find the killer is by finding the names of his victims. When we know who they are, then we can start looking for connections. It may well be that they lead to the death squads of the past. My biggest hope at present is the little girl. She must have gone to school somewhere. There have to be teachers or schoolmates who can identify her. The two adults might have been recluses, but a child is always out and about.'

'Good thinking,' said Ehrlich, taking out an embossed sheet of paper with his name at the top, unscrewing the top of a weighty Montblanc fountain pen and writing a few lines on it. Stave watched in silence as he fluidly scrolled his signature beneath.

'This is a letter of recommendation,' Ehrlich told him, handing it over. 'In case the girl might come from a family of DPs or persecuted Jews, then you should first check out Warburg Children's Health Home in Blankenese. This letter should make it easier for you to gain access. But you will still need a permit from the British.'

'A children's home?'

'A very special children's home.'

Stave didn't ask any further questions, nodded, folded the brief carefully in two and put it in his overcoat pocket, regretting that he'd sent MacDonald home early.

'I'll go to the lieutenant,' he announced, 'while it's still light. Maybe I can get the necessary paper straight away. Then I can start asking questions at Warburg tomorrow morning.'

He got up and went to the door. As he opened it, the prosecutor called him back.

'Happy birthday, by the way. I noticed the date in your file.'

'Thanks,' Stave murmured, somewhat taken aback. Ehrlich was the first person to congratulate him. On his forty-third birthday.

MacDonald lived in a requisitioned villa in Innocentia Strasse in Harvestehude, 'Zone A', an almost undamaged part of the city. The British and American bombing raids had been intended primarily to kill workers, and most of the leafy, well-to-do areas had been unharmed. Probably also, Stave thought to himself, because they realised that after they had won the war they would need somewhere nice for their officers to live.

On his way to Harvestehude the chief inspector found himself walking through Planten un Blomen, once the city's finest park. As late as 1944 they had been planting rose bushes which ever since had erupted into a blaze of red every summer. In the meantime they had ploughed up the strips of land between the pathways and the rose bushes to sow potatoes. Now the transformed former park was covered with a partial layer of snow, dirty brown here and there, dirty white elsewhere; abandoned.

There were signs on the side streets: 'Out of Bounds for German Civilians!', 'For British Forces Only!'. Freezing British military police stared past him indifferently. The grand villas were perfectly cared for, except for the few make-do stovepipes that occasionally jutted out. The trees along the streets were undamaged. There were tin bins outside the gates. It was calm between the villas, the houses and trees offering shelter from the freezing gusts of wind. Occasionally a military patrol jeep would trundle by over the cobblestones. A few figures sloped from bin to bin, one-legged war veterans, a man with a rucksack holding the hand of a girl of about ten, old people, women with headscarves wrapped tight so that nobody could see their faces and see their shame. They opened the lids of the bins, and rummaged inside for bit of rotten potato, wilted lettuce leaves, apple cores. A young cigarette-butt collector was picking up trodden ends of English cigarettes from the pavement. Nobody spoke, nobody looked up. The military police left them alone.

Colonial masters, Stave thought to himself. The English live here the way they do in India or Africa, and we're their new coolies. Except that neither the Africans nor the Indians set half the world on fire and had only themselves to blame for their humiliation.

Innocentia Strasse: bare branches of young oak trees, jeeps parked at the side of the road, behind them rows of white, four-storied villas, maybe 50 or 60 years old. There was jazz coming from the window of one of them, the BBC maybe, or perhaps a record playing on a requisitioned gramophone.

House number 28. The chief inspector showed his police ID to a soldier standing guard at the gate and asked for MacDonald.

'Third floor, second left,' the Brit answered, in English of course.

He's about the same age as my son, Stave reckoned, and at that moment he would have preferred to simply turn round and run away from there, out from under the oak trees back down to the railway station. But instead he simply nodded and climbed the grand staircase, trying to conceal his limp from the sentry's eyes.

Stave knocked on the door. No answer. He knocked again. Maybe the lieutenant had gone out? He was about to turn away when he heard a noise behind the door. So he waited. Eventually MacDonald opened the door, barefoot, wearing just a shirt and trousers. The villa was heated but it was hardly warm enough for that.

MacDonald was out of breath, but he pulled himself together, and forced a smile. 'What can I do for you?'

Stave, noticing that the lieutenant was blocking the doorway, took a step backwards and gave a gentle cough. He explained as quickly as he could about his visit to Ehrlich and the Warburg Children's Health Home and the British permit he needed to go there. But even as he was speaking he glimpsed a shadow, a movement behind MacDonald's shoulders.

Erna Berg.

Stave continued talking as if he hadn't noticed. MacDonald glanced nervously over his shoulder, then looked at the chief inspector as if wondering whether or not to admit he had been caught out. Then he gave a brief smile and made an oblique, vaguely apologetic gesture.

'I'll sort it out,' he promised. 'We can go there together in the morning. It'll be quicker in my jeep. And I'm curious too to see if we can find out anything there. I'll pick you up from the CID headquarters. If you want, we can take Maschke too.'

'Thank you,' Stave said. 'Enjoy the rest of your Sunday.'

'You too,' MacDonald called after him, but Stave had already turned away. He was in a hurry to get out of the house.

Survivors and Missing

Monday, 3 February 1947

They drove in silence, MacDonald at the wheel, Stave in the front passenger seat, Maschke on the hard bench behind. The vice squad man had to hold on tight to the jeep's metal frame to avoid being sent flying every time they went over a pothole. He looked as if he was being driven to the dentist. The lieutenant stared straight ahead as they thundered down the Elbe embankment. The chief inspector watched him from the corner of his eye.

Nobody had said anything about their encounter the previous day. Erna Berg came into the office, as merry as ever. Either she had no idea I spotted her yesterday, thought Stave, or is so thick-skinned that she couldn't care less if I caught her out. The fact was that Stave's secretary was married, although her husband was on the 'unaccounted for' list. Theoretically she was committing adultery. But what has that to do with me, Stave told himself, and tried to concentrate on the interrogation ahead.

Interrogation was probably the wrong word. They were going to a children's home. He had a police photo of a murdered girl in his coat pocket. Should he even show it to the children? Children whose parents had been gassed, or their school friends shot dead, or their houses bombed? Should he just show it to the warden? But did he know all his charges well enough to recognise one of them from a police photo?

He looked around. To their left the thick ice on the Elbe sparkled in the morning light, as rough and flat as a slab of concrete. A few small ships, freighters and fishing boats were frozen in alongside the ruined piers. The superstructures of two sunk steamers reared out of the ice. Cranes leant low, half toppled over. Two men, bent double and wrapped in overcoats and blankets, crossed the ice from the Hamburg side walking into the brutal wind.

'Why do I need a British permit to visit a children's home?' Stave asked, partly out of curiosity, partly just to break the awkward silence.

MacDonald was quick to answer, obviously pleased to have something to talk about. 'The home's official name is the Warburg Children's Health Home, in English. It is located in a villa belonging to Eric Warburg, the man who founded it.'

Stave nodded. 'The banker? The one who emigrated?'

'To the USA. In 1938. After the war he came back, and it now belongs to him again. Its main purpose is to help Jewish children, mostly concentration camp survivors. Many lost more or less their entire families. They come from various countries. Here in Blankenese they are nursed, given decent food and schooling. The institution is under the particular care of the Occupation Authorities.'

'Have you spoken to any of the people there?'

'On the telephone, this morning. I let them know why we were coming, but not in too much detail. The female teacher I spoke to had in any case heard that a child had been murdered. Things like that get around town fast. She'd already seen the police posters of the two previous victims. They're all over the place. But in Blankenese no child of that age has gone missing.'

'Why are we even bothering to go out there, then?' Maschke said.

'If the murdered girl had ever been in a concentration camp then we might find somebody who knew her,' Stave explained.

They turned into Kösterberg Strasse, a narrow, cobbled lane leading uphill, bordered on either side with hedges, behind which they could see villa roofs sparkling with frost. At the top of the hill was a huge, yellow-painted castle with tall windows in the midst of a meadow. It turned out to be just the city water works, a relic of long-gone days of extravagance and plenty, when they even built stately homes for pumping machinery.

The entrance to house number 60 was opposite. High hedges and wrought-iron gates that hung on yellow-painted pillars. A young man opened one of the heavy gates when he saw the jeep. The drive was raked gravel. Behind a huge bare oak tree stood a villa from the wealthy mid-nineteenth century, with windows round as bullseyes in the upper storeys.

Children peering out from behind the windows with inquisitive looks. A woman at the door, aged about 30, with short black hair, in a grey woollen overcoat, welcomed Stave and Maschke as if they were tabby cats.

'I'd prefer it if you don't pull out your ID cards,' she said to Stave. 'It can bring back unfortunate memories.'

Strange choice of words, Stave thought. Odd accent too. He considered and then dismissed shaking her hand, and gave her a slight bow instead. MacDonald gave her a casual wave.

'My name is Thérèse Dubois. I was the one you spoke with this morning, Lieutenant. I've been given instructions to help as much as I can with your business.'

Camp inmate, Stave guessed. Probably French. Maybe Alsace. Lots of French – mainly Jews or resistance fighters – were taken to Bergen-Belsen. Or Ravensbrück. He recalled the trial going on in the Curio House. Ehrlich probably knows her. He didn't bother to ask who had given her 'instructions'.

'I'm sorry to have to turn up here under such unpleasant circumstances,' he said at last. 'I will try to keep our visit as brief as possible.'

'Please come in,' Thérèse Dubois told them, leading them through to a glassed-in, heated veranda, with wicker chairs and rubber plants in big ceramic pots. Stave had to stop himself staring – it had been years since he'd seen houseplants.

He explained why he was there, mentioning the other two murders also. Then he cleared his throat and took out the photo.

The teacher looked at it. Her face turned paler, but she studied it attentively. Then she shook her head. 'I've never come across this poor creature. I'm quite sure of it. She's not one of ours.'

Stave was silent for a few moments, drumming nervously with his fingers on the arm of the wicker chair, then realised what he was doing and folded his hands. 'Do you think any of your children might have known her? Perhaps gone to school with her?'

'You want to show this photo to the children?'

'If it helps me to find whoever murdered this one, then yes.'

Thérèse Dubois leaned back in her chair and thought. 'We currently have 30 children in the home,' she said quietly. 'Some of them are just two years old. They never leave here. Those of school age are taught here, not in German schools.' The tone of her voice suggested those schools were prison camps.

'At present we do have two children who are allowed to go out, to do errands, go on trips or just to play, although of course it's been too cold for that of late. I'll call them.'

'And may I show them the photo?'

'They've both seen more dead children than you have, Chief Inspector.'

She left the room and came back shortly with a girl and a boy, both of whom Stave guessed to be about 15.

Thérèse Dubois introduced them as Leonore and Jules. The pair stood shyly in the middle of the room.

Stave smiled, MacDonald nodded encouragingly, Maschke coughed and got to his feet.

'I'd like to smoke if you don't mind,' he said.

Stave nodded and Maschke disappeared out into the park. Before long the bare oak trees were being treated to the smoke from an English cigarette. Stave had no problems with that: the fewer adults these children had to face, the better. And Maschke's cynical comments were the last thing he needed right now.

He calmly explained to the children why he was here. Thérèse Dubois translated for the boy, whispering in French. The girl seemed to understand him.

Then Stave showed them the photo.

Leonore and Jules stared at it. There was pity written all over the girl's face, clinical interest on the boy's. But even before they said anything, the chief inspector knew what their answer would be.

'I've never seen this girl,' Leonore said, quite certain. Her accent was thick, from way out in the east, Stave guessed. Galicia maybe.[3]

'*Non, je n'ai jamais vu cette fille,*' Jules mumbled. Nobody needed a translation.

Stave put the photo back into his coat pocket, disappointed on the one hand that once again he had had no luck, relieved on the other that he no longer had to hold the photo beneath the children's noses.

'Has either of you ever been down to that part of the port, the Bille canal, to gather coal?' Stave asked them.

'Our children have no need to go looking for coal,' Thérèse Dubois said under her breath, clearly shocked. Stave ignored her.

Leonore smiled uncertainly and, Stave thought, a bit enviously. 'Never been there, it's too far.'

The teacher sighed and translated the question into French, drumming in irritation with her fingers. Jules smiled the smile of a boy who'd been out of the home a lot more than the grown-ups knew. But he shook his head too.

Stave got to his feet. 'That's all, then,' he said.

'Will you find whoever did this?' Leonore asked.

The chief inspector was taken aback for a moment. Then he saw the urgent look in the girl's big, earnest eyes.

'Yes,' he replied. 'I will.'

'What happens then?'

'Then the murderer will go to court and be sentenced. There's no getting away with things like that these days,' and he indicated his coat pocket with the photo in it.

The girl reached out her hand and said, 'Good luck.'

Thérèse Dubois smiled for the first time since they had arrived and led them back to the entrance,

'What will happen to the children?' Stave asked, his hand already on the door handle. MacDonald was behind him, and Maschke was striding up and down outside like a caged tiger, watched curiously by a group of boys and girls who had come out of the guest house and were standing under an oak.

'When they're healthy enough we're going to organise transport to Palestine, to their new homeland. It's easier to fix from here in the British-occupied zone of Germany than anywhere else, because the controls are more lax. One of the ironies of history?'

MacDonald looked as if he'd just choked on a peppercorn.

Stave remembered hearing somewhere that the British had occupied Palestine ever since the end of the First World War. He'd also heard about the fighting between Arabs and Jews and that the British were not allowing any more Jews from Europe to travel to the Middle East. But the Jews, those who'd survived the mass murder, wanted out and would do anything to smuggle themselves on board ships to Palestine. No wonder that the lieutenant looks so uncomfortable, he thought to himself with just a hint of *Schadenfreude*.

'Should you come across anything, please let me know.' He pulled a page from his notebook and gave her his name and telephone number.

'It must be hard to get things back to normal,' she said, folding the piece of paper carefully.

The chief inspector wasn't sure if he'd quite understood her meaning and gave her an inquisitive look.

'After so many catastrophes,' she explained. 'There's so much to clean up – and I don't just mean the rubble in the cities. And there aren't many men like Herr Ehrlich and you.'

'You know the public prosecutor?'

'I was a witness in the Curio House trial.'

'Ehrlich is in charge of this case too.'

'As if he didn't have enough on his hands. A man with a mission!'

She accompanied her guests to the jeep. Maschke joined them, smelling of smoke. As he climbed into the jeep Stave noticed that one of the girls standing under the tree was saying something to her companion, nodding at the vice squad man. Then she brought her hand up to her throat and made the quick slashing gesture of some-body cutting a throat.

She knows Maschke, Stave realised with a shock, and not as a friend.

Rather more awkwardly than necessary, he went to the jeep and took Thérèse Dubois discreetly to one side.

'Who is that girl?' he whispered, a fleeting gesture with his right hand indicating the little girl, not worrying whether or not the question would worry the teacher. He had only seconds before Maschke noticed.

She realised that it was important. Hardly moving her lips she whispered, 'Anouk Magaldi, eight years old, arrived a few weeks ago.'

'From a camp?'

'No. She'd been living in France, near Limoges. Her parents, both Jews, were murdered there. We're also bringing orphans like her to Hamburg because, as I said, it's easier to organise transport to Palestine from here.'

'Goodbye then,' Stave said out loud. 'Many thanks for all your help.' And with that he climbed into the jeep.

On the way back Stave stared silently out of the window, uncertain as to whether he knew more than he had known this morning or not. The dead girl was clearly not from the home, and probably not a Jew from one of the camps. So did that mean she was from Hamburg, or a German refugee, or a DP? Which non-Jewish DPs were still living in Germany 19 months after the end of the war? Primarily Russians and Poles who were afraid of the communists and therefore didn't want to go home. Should he send pictures of the bodies to the Polish and Russian police? How would you do that? And would the former enemies even be bothered about looking for people who preferred to hang about in the ruins of the Reich rather than return home?

I still don't know anything, he thought. Nothing at all.

Or do I?

Two observations kept coming back to him, dragging him away from the hunt for the triple murderer he was supposed to be pursuing. What was that gesture aimed at Maschke? How did the little girl from the home know the vice squad man? Maybe under the cover of his job he was molesting little girls?

He tried discreetly to glance in the rear-view mirror for a glimpse of his colleague's face. But the jeep was bouncing along and the mirror shaking; he'd get a distorted view for a second or two and then it was gone.

What about Ehrlich? Thérèse Dubois called him a 'man with a mission'. Why was the prosecutor so keen on this case? Maybe it wasn't anything at all to do with rebuilding democracy, like he said? Maybe this man whose wife had been driven to suicide had some other issue: revenge? Revenge on her old regime tormentors. Maybe this enigmatic case was just a way for him to get back at some National Socialist or other. But how?

'What now?'

MacDonald's question gave Stave a start. He hadn't even noticed they were back at headquarters.

'Wait,' he said. 'We're sending out the posters with the photo of the girl and medallion today. Wait and see if this time somebody turns up. Maschke, go back and have another look at the last location, maybe you'll find some witnesses. Maybe you'll come across something we missed. Maybe our colleagues from Department S will turn up something on the black market. Maybe Dr Czrisini will come across a lead in the course of the autopsy.'

He took his leave of both men, climbed wearily up the stairs to his office and opened the door to the anteroom. For some reason it annoyed him to see Erna Berg – he knew her secret, would never betray it, but it annoyed him to see her.

Sitting there alone at his desk, he went over everything. Then he came to a decision. He would continue the search as normal. But he would also make a point of checking up on Ehrlich and Maschke. You never knew.

The next morning Stave's colleague from Department S rushed into the office, stopped in the doorway and called to him: 'Nothing to report – no girl's coat, no truss, no false teeth – we've not found anything we can link to the victims. If you want you can come and look at a few dozen winter coats, pairs of stockings or worn-out shoes that we've confiscated in raids over the last 48 hours. I have no idea how we might link any of them to one of the victims. We're still at it. The next raid is going ahead this morning.'

'Thanks,' the chief inspector muttered wearily, but by then the door had already closed.

The posters got no response from the public. It seemed nobody knew who the girl was. Nobody recognised the medallion.

Stave nodded awkwardly to Erna Berg, grabbed his coat and said, 'I'm going over to the Search Office.'

She looked at him in amazement. 'Lieutenant MacDonald is already there.'

'I want to hear what they have to say for myself.'

'Search Office' was another one of those terms you had to learn to live with. The Red Cross and both churches had merged their documentation and expertise to create perhaps the world's largest institution dedicated to finding people. They collected every bit of information: record cards, police reports, old Wehrmacht order papers, official registration notices, prisoner lists from the occupying forces and thousands of other documents that might provide information on unaccounted-for soldiers and missing refugees. The number of Wehrmacht soldiers alone, sought after by families who had no idea whether they were living or dead, was three and a half million. Added to that there were 15 million refugees. That amounted to 18.5 million record cards in rows of cardboard boxes that stretched for kilometres, each card with a name, date of birth, last address, last known sighting, and any other potentially relevant information.

One of those cards bore the name of his son.

Stave knew how to get there. He'd been often enough. Down Feld Strasse, then across smaller footpaths through the rubble of city districts that had been all but wiped out, with not a single house intact, not even a piece of wall in most cases. Where there was a wall, it was covered with posters and pieces of paper, requests for information, orders from the military government, the latest police 'wanted' posters. Some of it was his work, but already half ripped down by the gusting icy winds. A burnt-out bus lay in the middle of the ruins with a banner on its roof, declaring 'Leather Goods'. Stave wondered who on earth would buy something here.

Eventually he got to number 91 Altona Allee on the right-hand side: the local courthouse. It was somehow inevitable that it had survived; a typical palace of justice from the first Kaiser's day with light-coloured stonework, columns, figureheads and statues along the façade. Undoubtedly they were allegorical figures, but Stave saw them as carved images of missing persons.

The judges had been thrown out. Now it was the workspace for 600 men and women, pale, discreet, hard-working and long since immune to the tragedies of others; 600 trying to discover the fate of 18.5 million.

Outside the imposing building was one of the fat round advertising columns with a huge poster on it, black and white with a red cross in the middle, and many photos of children. Above it the heading: 'How do I search for and find my nearest and dearest?' Posters like this kept appearing all over Hamburg, the same every week, but also different: the photos were new. There were 40,000 orphans in Hamburg, many so young they didn't even know their surnames, let alone their addresses. Their faces, some shy at having their photo taken, some indifferent, cheeky or frightened, seem to stare down at Stave as he walked up the steps and pushed open the heavy door.

The long, dimly lit hallways were narrowed by shelves on both sides filled with wooden drawers filled with record cards. The offices were packed with big tables covered in books: bound lists with dates and photographs, primarily those of soldiers. The tomes of the missing.

The chief inspector resisted the temptation to go over to the row of drawers marked 'S' and get out the record card for 'Stave, Karl'. What was the point? He went to the office of Andreas Brems, one of the researchers he knew from earlier visits.

Brems looked up and shook his head with a sympathetic expression that was part of the job. Just like an undertaker, Stave thought.

'Nothing new on your son, Chief Inspector.'

'I'm here professionally,' Stave replied, sounding more unpleasant than he had intended.

Brems nodded, neither insulted nor curious, and sat there waiting for the question.

Stave told him about the murders. He gave a thin smile.

'An Englishman was already here about that. Your men have also brought us the "information wanted" posters,' he said patiently. 'Nobody here can remember ever seeing any of the persons on the photos. And without names, there's nothing more we can do.'

'What about a date?'

Brems gave him a confused look. 'We sort our card indexes by first and last names of the missing person. It's not easy if we don't have a name. In the case of little children who don't know their own surname, obviously we use different criteria: estimated age, place they were found, et cetera. One of my colleagues looked through all that material using the details of the murdered girl, but nothing came to light.'

'Can you tell when somebody made a request for information?'

'That's noted on every index card – including when the first request was made. But the cards aren't sorted chronologically.'

Stave rubbed his neck. 'Have there been many requests in the last few weeks? I'm only interested in the time frame from the week before the first murder up until today. The 35 days from the beginning of January until now.'

The researcher shook his head in amazement. 'New missing person reports come to you, not us. The war has been over for nearly two years. Anyone looking for somebody missing from then would have reported the case to us long ago. There are basically two groups of people who still make new requests, the first being refugees who've only just reached the western zones. But as there haven't been any trains for the past few weeks because of the cold, there have definitely been no new arrivals from the east. On the other hand, we have those who are worried or despairing but who, if you'll excuse me, don't trust the police. They turn to us because our requests for information via the Red Cross and the churches can more easily extend beyond the occupation zones. Wives of men who have reason to believe, for example, that their husbands have got to Sweden, or even America.'

'If somebody these days turns to the Search Office as well as the police, that means the missing person has left either no trace or highly enigmatic traces: that the indications are so few and far between that their family don't believe the police will ever find them. That means that in those circles there's a chance that I might get some clue as to the identity of our victims if I just work at it hard enough. Or – something I'm not hoping for – I come across the names of other potential victims whose bodies may be still lying out there in the rubble undiscovered. Maybe I'll find some sort of pattern.' Stave gave him a meagre smile.

Brems nodded slowly, but then it was as if somebody had turned a light switch on in his head, and all of a sudden he was interested. 'A colleague of mine works on new requests of that sort. There can't have been many in the past few weeks. I'll ask her.'

He rushed out of the room and came back ten minutes later. 'Just one,' he said. 'On the thirteenth of January.'

'One week before we found the first body.'

Stave took the card from him. Dr Marin Hellinger, born 13 March 1895 in Hamburg-Barmbek, an industrialist, address in Hamburg-Marienthal, reported missing by his wife Hertha. There was a photo, apparently from an old passport: thinning hair, probably grey, nickel-framed glasses, pudgy cheeks, neck bulging out over his collar.

'Definitely not a refugee or a soldier. Why did you even bother to include him?'

Brems coughed: 'My colleague was bored and she was sympathetic to Frau Hellinger. So she opened a file and sent out enquiries. To England.'

'England? Anywhere else?'

'America too, but why just those two I don't now. Frau Hellinger suggested her husband might be there. Kidnapped possibly.'

'So why didn't she go to the police?'

Brems coughed again, but said nothing.

Stave made a note of all the information on the card. Marienthal was a suburb near where he lived. It would do no harm to knock on her door.

'Thanks,' he grunted.

'See you soon, Chief Inspector. We'll let you know if we hear anything. About your son, I mean.'

Back at the office he met with Maschke and MacDonald. Stave let them give their reports first. The vice squad man reported that no ration card had been left unclaimed at any of the distribution offices. MacDonald had had no luck either; the murdered girl had not been registered at any Hamburg school, or at least no teacher recognised her.

'We need to print yet more posters,' Stave said wearily. 'We need to warn people not to go anywhere with strangers. And not to buy any suspicious article of clothing.'

'What constitutes a "suspicious article of clothing"?' Maschke asked.

'No idea. The first bit is a warning to the populace. The second is intended for the killer, to make him nervous, worried about selling his loot, if that is the motive for his murders.'

'If...'

The two men turned to go. Stave opened his notebook and mentioned his little detour to the Search Office and read them the few details concerning Dr Martin Hellinger.

'I'm going to pay a visit to his wife.'

Maschke turned and stared at him blankly. 'I can's see how that's going to help us,' he said.

MacDonald had reddened. For a moment Stave thought the missing man's name had meant something to him. But then he noticed that the Brit had already opened his office door a fraction and was glancing at Erna Berg, who was standing with her back to them sorting out folders on a shelf. Happy and in love, Stave thought, feeling the needle of envy prick his heart. 'I shall drop by Hellinger's wife in the morning,' he told them.

'Will you need me with you?' Maschke asked dismissively, making quite clear what he thought of the idea.

'No,' the chief inspector answered, not exactly devastated. 'What about you, Lieutenant?'

MacDonald was still blushing. 'I'm afraid I have a meeting tomorrow morning.'

A 'meeting' with Erna Berg, my secretary and a married woman, Stave thought, but he forced a smile.

'Very well then. I shall go on my own. Just to dot the "i"s and cross the "t"s.'

A Witness and a Piece of Paper

Wednesday, 5 February 1947

Stave stared out through the iced-up windows of his apartment. It was early morning. There was no point in going into the office, only to come all the way back to Marienthal to speak with the missing man's wife. On the other hand he could hardly ring her doorbell at 6 a.m. the way the Gestapo used to do. So instead he sat there counting the crystals on the thick ice in the middle of his windowpane, then breathed on it, trying in vain to ignore the cold and the pain in his leg.

Gradually the grey day dawned. At long last he got to his feet. If he walked slowly he wouldn't be there before 8 a.m. – and in this weather nobody was still asleep by then.

Marienthal was a Shangri-la, a district of villas in the east of Hamburg only a few hundred paces from the rental block Stave lived in. The Allies had never attacked Marienthal; only the rare stray bomb had landed there.

Stave wondered along Ahrensburg Strasse towards the centre of the district. Grey light, passers-by who avoided one another. Nobody glanced at anybody else. Nobody walked next to the ruins even though they sometimes provided shelter from the icy wind.

He stopped by an advertising column to examine his department's handiwork: a 'wanted' poster, put up early that morning. '5,000 Reichsmarks Reward!' And the photos of the three victims. The words beneath read: 'A murderer is at large. A monster in human form.' Then there was a description of the victims and where they were found. 'Has nobody missed any of these people? Can people simply disappear in this city without family, friends or acquaintances caring?' Did I really write that, Stave wondered. I must have been tired.

There was a tiny park by the edge of the road, scarcely bigger than a domestic garden: cobblestoned paths, trees and bushes hacked down to stumps, the skeletons of two benches, their wooden seats long since stolen.

Stave turned into Eichtal Strasse, townhouses on other side, two stories, with a loft and a gable wall facing the street. Every house was that little bit different: some faced in red brick, others with white or yellow plasterwork, or covered with ivy. Chestnut trees and beeches grew from amongst the cobbles, some chopped down, some still standing. His footsteps sounded loud on the stone. Five hundred metres away, Margarethe had been burned to death. And yet here everything was still as it ever was.

A small untended front garden under a layer of dirty hoar frost. Behind it a villa. A few dirty streaks on the white plaster, one window knocked askew. Otherwise in good condition. A thin, blackish grey trail of smoke from the chimney, the bitter but oh-so-sweet stink of glowing coal. All of a sudden Stave was in a hurry to get indoors.

The doorbell made no sound, so he knocked. It took a while, but eventually the door opened. A wave of warm air washed out, causing the chief inspector to shiver involuntarily. A woman in her fifties, grey streaks in her long dark hair, a soft face, brown doe eyes, in an elegant if somewhat worn housecoat.

Stave presented his ID, gave her his name.

Frau Hellinger hesitated for a moment, then gave a shy smile and invited him in. Parquet floors, antique dressers, blank spaces on the four walls where once pictures must have hung. Stave realised how the Hellingers had paid for their coal. His host led him to the rear of the house, to a room with a bay window looking out on to a quiet garden. She offered him a wicker chair.

'Would you like a cup of tea?' she asked. Stave nodded gratefully.

'I hadn't reckoned on the police calling by,' she said.

Stave gave a thin smile. 'Why's that?'

'I originally reported my husband as missing at the nearest police station. An officer there took down my details on a form. And I had the impression that that was that.'

'Which is why you went to the Search Office?'

She nodded, sipping at her tea, her hands shaking ever so slightly.

'Tell me something about your husband,' Stave brought out his notebook.

'My husband is primarily a builder and engineer,' Frau Hellinger said, with another shy smile. 'He founded his own company as a young man. Nothing big, you know, but solid. A company that made specialist machines.'

'What sort of machinery?'

'Trigonometric calculators. Primarily for U-boats.'

She noticed Stave staring at her blankly, and held up a hand apologetically.

'It was his own invention. As far as I understand it, U-boat captains have to make complicated calculations before firing a torpedo. They have to work out their own course, and that of the ship they intend to attack, the speed of the ships, the speed of the torpedo, currents, all that sort of thing. My man made calculators that could help them work it all out. The officer would put in some data, turn a few wheels – and there was the result. It was a bit like a calculating machine you get in offices, my husband used to say, but more complicated. He delivered the devices to Blohm & Voss and the shipyards installed them in every U-boat that left the port here.'

'A good business to be in, I imagine,' said Stave. 'At least up until May 1945.'

She gave him a pained look. 'After the...' she struggled to find a suitable word, '...collapse, despite the great problems, my husband managed to keep the firm together.'

'Most of the ships sunk by U-boats were English. I can't imagine that the new masters of our city were particularly interested in the welfare of a company that sent half their fleet to the bottom of the ocean.'

Frau Hellinger coughed. 'Obviously my husband immediately

stopped production. Machinery was machinery. That's what he said. He didn't care much what he produced – as long as it was complicated enough to keep him interested.'

'What does the firm make nowadays?'

'Precision timepieces, time clocks for offices and factories. Timers for automated machinery.'

'There's a market for those again?'

'Of course, lots of firms are trying to get production up and running again, despite all the problems. You'll even find our clocks hanging on the walls of the British barracks and clubs.'

That's what it's like to be a winner, thought Stave, and felt suddenly as if there were a wet leather overcoat weighing down his arms and shoulders. No matter who wins wars: winners do business. They have the bread, literally. They live in villas. The only difference here is that normally they do not vanish without trace.

'What happened on the thirteenth of January?'

'I don't know exactly. The night before we were late going to bed. My husband has always been an early riser; he's never needed much sleep. He got up at his normal time; I remember that even though I was still half asleep. Then I fell back into a deep sleep and when I woke up it was about 10 a.m. and he was gone.'

'Gone?'

Frau Hellinger blushed slightly. 'My husband and I have been married for 30 years, we know each other very well – he often gets up before me, but he never ever leaves the house without saying goodbye. And if he's going to visit a customer instead of the office, he always tells me.'

'But on this occasion the house was empty when you got up?'

'Yes, he had just gone.'

'Had he taken anything with him? Money, for example?'

Now she was blushing deeply. 'Not as far as I know. We don't keep a lot of cash in the house. And no, there are no valuable items missing. At least none that weren't missing beforehand, if you know what I mean.'

Stave glanced at the bare patches on the walls and nodded, then glanced down at his notebook to read the notes he had made at the Search Office.

'You stated that he was wearing his winter coat. Navy-blue wool, hat, gloves and scarf.'

'That was what was missing from the cloakroom. That was what he normally wore in winter.'

'And his briefcase was missing too.'

'He took it with him to work every morning.'

'What did he keep in it?'

Frau Hellinger shrugged her shoulders. 'Documents, I imagine. I never looked.'

'Diagrams? Contracts?'

'I really have no idea.'

Stave wondered if someone involved in the production of trigonometric calculators and complex timepieces had call to use thin lengths of wire. Wire loops. 'Was the house door locked that morning, when you noticed your husband was missing?'

Frau Hellinger looked surprised. 'It was closed, but not locked.'

'Thank you,' said Stave and closed his notebook.

'There's something else.'

He looked up.

She hesitated, taking a deep breath. 'When I started looking around I found a screwed-up piece of paper on the floor in the cloakroom where his overcoat normally hung. I didn't notice it at first; I thought it was just something the cleaning lady had missed. But later, when my husband was nowhere to be found and I began to look for clues as to what had happened, I picked it up.'

She opened the drawer of a commode and took out a piece of paper the size of a hand. Squared paper, torn down one side, clearly hastily torn out of a notebook, Stave reckoned. The sort of notebook used by engineers or technicians for doing calculations or drawing sketches.

He took it from her and examined it. The innumerable creases like a net across the hatched page showed how scrunched up it had been. One side was blank, on the other, a single word, scrawled in pencil, in English: 'Bottleneck.'

She stared at him uncomprehendingly. 'I can't speak any English but a friend translated it for me.'

'The neck of a bottle.'

'It was obviously thrown aside in haste, but it is definitely my husband's writing. What on earth does it mean?'

'I'm wondering that myself,' Stave said.

The chief inspector took his leave, slowly and in a hurry at the same time. It would have been nice to stay a little longer. Every fibre of his being had enjoyed the warmth inside the villa, the opportunity to take his coat off, sit down and drink some hot tea. He would have liked to close his eyes, fall asleep. On the other hand, he was intrigued by this new discovery. He needed to talk it over with his colleagues, exchange ideas, test the plausibility of crazy theories.

He walked quickly, limping, but not even noticing it. Bottleneck. Bottle. Neck. Coincidence. What could it mean? Is Hellinger the killer? But why leave the note? Why an English word? Or was the industry boss just the killer's accomplice? Or maybe a witness?

All of a sudden Stave stopped. If Hellinger wanted to disappear that morning, would he have dropped the note by accident? Unlikely. But if, as his wife believed, he had scribbled the word in haste, crumpled the note up and dropped it when he was putting his coat on, surely that meant he only had a few moments? And that he wasn't alone? So who had been with Hellinger in the villa that morning? And did the magnate go willingly with whoever it was? Or was he abducted? That was what his wife seemed to believe. But who would want to abduct him?

By the time he got to his office Stave was still lost in thought. He sat down at his desk and looked again at the piece of paper that he had managed to persuade Frau Hellinger to give him, though she had been reluctant to do so. Perhaps she thought it might be the last link she would have with her husband, the chief inspector reflected. She might well be right.

'Drum up MacDonald and Maschke for me,' he shouted to his secretary through the closed door.

He caught the smell of cold tobacco before the door even opened. Maschke came in. A few minutes later MacDonald also arrived.

He gave both men a quick summary of what he had been up to. Maschke thought long and hard and then nodded appreciatively. MacDonald just stared at him attentively. Stave returned the look.

'Bottleneck,' he said at last. 'That's what's on the piece of paper. Just that.' He showed it to him.

The lieutenant looked pale. 'What could it mean?' he whispered.

The chief inspector held up his hands. 'It means you're going to have to ask around amongst your colleagues again. It might have something to do with our murderer. Then again maybe not, but in any case the disappearance of Hellinger is odd. And this is the only lead we have. An English lead.'

MacDonald let his head drop so that they could no longer see his face. Difficult to make out what it meant, Stave thought to himself. Was he ashamed because the clue pointed to one of his compatriots? Or was it anger at a German policeman accusing an Englishman?

MacDonald looked up, his face expressing agreement. 'You're right, Chief Inspector. An English lead. I'll get on to it.'

The Briton was just getting to his feet when there was a knock on the door. It was Erna Berg, who gave him a quick smile before turning to Stave.

'There's a lady here who wants to speak to you.'

'Who is it?'

'An Anna von Veckinhausen. She says you know her.'

Stave ignored the curious glances from MacDonald and Maschke and nodded goodbye to them. The vice squad man squeezed past the dark-haired woman outside without saying a word. MacDonald was more polite, waited for her to come in, greeted her and then closed the door behind him.

At last, thought Stave. He indicated the chair on the other side of his desk. Involuntarily he glanced at her hands and noticed a bare patch on the ring finger of her right hand. A missing wedding ring? Divorced? Widowed? Or was it nothing to do with a ring at all? Maybe it was a healed wound made by a loop of wire she'd been holding in her hands? I'm getting paranoid, the inspector realised.

Her almond-shaped eyes were watching him carefully. Maybe she regrets having come here, Stave wondered. He let her take her time.

Anna von Veckinhausen sat down on the chair opposite him, her right arm folded diagonally across her chest, her hand on her left shoulder. The same defensive pose. Then she forced a smile.

'You know why I'm here.'

'I have my suspicions.'

'I didn't tell you everything.'

'When I first questioned you, you told me you took the path through the rubble to get from Collau Strasse to Lappenbergs Allee. The second time you told me you had been going along Lappenbergs Allee and took the path to get to Collau Strasse, the opposite of what you said the first time.'

'I shan't underestimate you again,' she murmured.

Stave suppressed a smile. 'So what were you really doing out there in the ruins on the night of the twenty-fifth of January? And what did you see?'

'I didn't see anything in the rubble on the evening of the twenty-fifth of January. In fact, I wasn't even there.'

Stave opened his notebook and leafed through this scribbles. 'But you reported the murder on the twenty-fifth? At the nearest police station.'

'But that wasn't when I found the body.'

'So when did you find it?'

'Five days earlier, on the twentieth of January. I was coming along the footpath in the rubble, from Collau Strasse as it happens, though that hardly matters now. I saw the body, but didn't report it to the police.'

'Why not?'

'I was afraid. I didn't want any trouble. I've never had anything to do with the police in my life. I'm not from Hamburg. I don't know anyone here who would help me if things got difficult. I thought I could just leave it to somebody else. There was nothing anybody could have done for the dead man anyhow.'

'But nobody else reported it.'

'It was unbelievable. I read the newspapers, expecting each day to see a report about a naked corpse. Nothing. Eventually I realised that the body still hadn't been discovered. It wasn't really that surprising. Probably very few people used that path. And even if anyone did, they wouldn't necessarily spot the body. It was lying in a bomb crater, a bit to one side of the path. I started feeling guilty. After five days I could take it no longer. I reported it to the police and let on that I had just discovered it. Ever since I've been thinking about the lie and wondering if it might somehow have hindered the search for the murderer. So I came here to tell you everything, I just hope it's not too late.'

The chief inspector sat there silently for a while. Then he said, 'If it wasn't easy to spot the body from the path, how did you come across it?'

'I was looting,' she said. 'I had left the path and was searching the rubble.'

Stave didn't react.

Anna von Veckinhausen gave a sad smile. 'I wasn't looking for what you might think,' she continued. 'I come from Königsberg, as you can probably guess from my name. A noble family. The usual estate, the usual education. The usual hasty flight.'

'When did you arrive in Hamburg?'

'I fled in January 1945. On the *Wilhelm Gustloff*.[4] When it sank, I was picked up by a minesweeper and taken to Mecklenburg. From there I made my way onward as best I could and got here in May 1945.'

'On your own?'

'On my own,' she answered quickly, decisively.

Stave stared down at the pale line on her finger. He would have liked to know if she had been alone when she boarded the *Wilhelm Gustloff*. And if she had got to the west before the Red Army reached the east.

'And ever since you have lived in a Nissen hut on the Elbe canal?'

'Yes.'

'That's a long way from Lappenbergs Allee.'

'I was a specialist looter. Most people are after wood or bits of metal or electrical goods. I was looking for antiques.'

The chief inspector couldn't believe his ears. 'In the bomb wreckage of ordinary people's rental apartments?'

'Obviously they weren't villas with art collections hanging on the walls. But almost every family has one inherited piece of some sort in their apartment. And each block of ruins once housed hundreds of apartments. You wouldn't believe what you can find, if you have a trained eye. Medals from the Kaiser's time, silver coffee spoons, grandfather's pocket watch.'

'And you have a trained eye?'

'I grew up amongst valuable antiques. And over the past few years, I have trained myself to spot things like that, often bent, grimy, inconspicuous, lying amidst bricks and tiles.'

'Then what?'

'I clean them up, write on a piece of paper what I know about them: age, origin, et cetera – and then I sell them to British officers. Or to Hamburg business people who've come through the war okay.'

The word 'bottleneck' flashed across Stave's mind. 'Do you sell valuable bottles? Old glass? Perfume bottles or stuff like that?'

She gave him a surprised look. 'No. You don't normally find stuff like that in these ruins. At least not undamaged items.'

'Do you know a Dr Martin Hellinger? An industrialist from Hamburg-Marienthal? Maybe a customer of yours?' He showed her the man's photograph.

'Never seen him. Never heard the name either. Why do you ask?'

'It was just a passing thought. Had you just sold something on the black market when we arrested you? You were carrying 500 Reichsmarks.'

'I'd just met a British officer outside the Garrison Theatre next to the station, and sold him an oil painting. A piece of colourful kitsch, German pine trees, treetop view, you know the sort of thing. But he liked it. I was on the way home when I got caught up in your raid. It was pure chance.'

Stave made a note; MacDonald needed to look into it. 'So on the evening of the twentieth of January you were looking for kitsch paintings and old pocket watches in the ruins off Lappenbergs Allee?'

'You have to survive somehow. It was the first time I had been there. It's a long way from the Elbe canal, but I hoped to find something that would make the trip worthwhile.'

'And did you?'

'Didn't have time. As soon as I got there I saw this shadow move on a wall.'

'Shadow?'

'A shape. It was dusk already. I'd underestimated the distance and got there later than I intended. It wasn't exactly a person I saw, more a movement. Do you know what I mean? Something threatening, glimpsed out of the corner of my eye. I hid behind a pile of rubble.'

'Why?'

'I was new to the area. I was looting. That's reason enough, don't you think?'

'Then what happened?'

'I waited for a bit until I thought there was no more sign of movement. Then I got to my feet, walked on and came across the naked corpse. You know the rest.'

'Can you remember anything about this shape you saw? What it was wearing? Was it big, small, fat, thin? A man? A child?'

'It wasn't a child, that's for sure. Not especially big, not tiny either.

More like large and thin. At the time I thought it was a man. But it might also have been a woman. Whoever it was had a coat on.'

'A wool overcoat? A man's coat? A Wehrmacht greatcoat?'

'A long, dark coat. Black or dark brown.'

'Or dark blue?'

'Possibly. There was a scarf around the face, or a headscarf. Or maybe even a cap with cloth wrapped around it.'

'Do you remember anything else? Shoes for example? Hands? Was the person wearing gloves?'

'I didn't notice.'

'Did you hear anything? Any sound at all?'

'Sound?'

'Like someone calling out or being beaten, cries for help. Perhaps muffled?'

Anna von Veckinhausen shook her head. 'On the contrary, now that you mention it. It was quiet, unnaturally quiet. I think it was this weird silence that made me nervous. That was why I was scared, even though I could hardly see the figure.'

Stave closed his eyes and thought hard. Anna von Veckinhausen had arrived at the ruins relatively late. It was getting dark already, the light would have been bad, visibility poor. Perhaps that was the best time of day for looters, just light enough for a trained eye to spot something in the rubble, but dark enough for people not to notice you.'

She sees the murderer, at least in outline. Then she finds the body. She doesn't report it to the police – maybe because she's afraid to, like she said. Also because she doesn't want to invite awkward questions that would reveal her to be a looter.

Stave believed her story. It all fitted together. If the shape she had seen was the murderer, then Anna von Veckinhausen must have happened along just after the crime had been committed. The old man was already dead, and probably had already been stripped. That meant it had still been daylight when the old man set out, maybe indeed crossing the ruins on the footpath. Or he had been killed somewhere else and carried there by the killer. But would the murderer try something like that before it was dark?'

'Did this unknown figure see you?'

She hesitated, put her arm across her body again. 'I had hidden quickly. I moved into cover, as a soldier would say. I had the impression that the figure did the same. But I can't be sure.'

Shit, Stave thought. If that's true, not only was Anna von Veckinhausen the only witness to the murder, but the murderer knew there had been a witness.

'Anything else come back to you?'

She thought for a minute. 'There was a smell in the air,' she said eventually. 'In this cold air, it doesn't pay to breathe in too deeply, but even so I got the impression that there was a smell of tobacco in the ruins.'

'The unknown figure was a smoker?'

'Not necessarily, I mean, I didn't see a cigarette, no glow, but there was just this smell of tobacco. And then it went away.'

A carton of cigarettes, Stave pondered. Maybe the old man had a load of cigarettes and that's why he was killed. Maybe it was a mugging, for goods to sell on the black market.'

'I'm going to type up your statement. If you would wait and read it through and then sign it for me, unless you have anything more to add or changes to make.'

She nodded, then said, hesitantly, 'What about my looting? Will you have to mention that?'

Stave managed a smile. 'I think we can just say you were walking along the path.'

He took her to the door and pointed to a seat in the anteroom, ignoring Erna Berg's inquisitive look. Then he typed up the statement with one hand, pulled the sheet of paper out of the typewriter and read through the text. It wasn't much, not the type of witness statement that could send someone to the gallows. But then the murderer didn't know that.

She's bait, Stave thought to himself, realising as he did that it weighed on his conscience. Nonetheless, he would ring the journalist and tell him this new development. No names, obviously. No details about her age, or where and what she had seen. Simply that the police had a witness. That would be enough to make the killer nervous. And then he might make a mistake.

He lifted the receiver and asked to be connected to the editorial section of *Die Zeit*. He asked the operator at the other end to put him through to Kleensch. There was a click on the line. Seconds ticked by. Hurry up, Stave thought.

Eventually Kleensch came to the phone.

'There's been a new development in the rubble murderer case.'

'I see you're not one for small talk, are you, Chief Inspector,' the journalist said, laughing so loud that the line echoed.

But Stave could hear in his voice something that he wanted to hear: the call of the hunt. He could imagine the man reaching for his notebook and pencil, hungry for a news story.

'We are now certain that there is just one killer. A witness saw a figure near one of the crime scenes. A figure in a long coat with its head covered. More details may follow.'

'At which of the crime scenes was this?'

Stave hesitated. Would he be putting Anna von Veckinhausen in danger if he told him? On the other hand, there was always the possibility that the killer would return to the scene of the crime to eradicate any traces. Hardly a good idea, but sometimes murderers did so. He didn't have enough men to have all three crime scenes watched, but he could manage one.

'The ruins near Lappenbergs Allee. Where the old man was found.'

'So who is your mysterious witness?'

'I'm afraid I can't release any further details.'

'I understand.' Silence, save for the crackling of the telephone line.

Was there somebody else on the line, Stave suddenly wondered. Then he pulled himself together. Nonsense.

'I'm afraid that's all I can tell you for now.'

'Can I rely on you to keep me posted?'

'Yes.'

Stave put the receiver down. Let's wait and see what happens, he thought. Then he looked up at the closed door to his office, and called Anna von Veckinhausen in. His only witness. His bait.

She read through the statement carefully, the corner of her lip twitching once or twice.

'You're not exactly a poet, but it's surprisingly good prose for a policeman.'

'The public prosecutor says the same thing,' Stave grumbled. 'Do you recognise your own words?'

Her answer was a fluid signature at the bottom of the page, followed by the date.

'Can I go now?' she asked.

'May I accompany you?'

Stave was surprised by his own words. They had just popped out without him thinking.

Anna von Veckinhausen gave him a look of astonishment.

'We go the same way,' he added quickly. 'I've just got a bit further to go, as far as Wandsbek.'

She smiled briefly. 'If we hurry we can just catch the last tram,' she replied.

Stave got to his feet, grabbed his coat and hat, and held the door open for her. Erna Berg was staring at him in confusion.

'Send someone for me if anything important crops up,' he told her.

That was all the explanation he gave her. Stave felt a spring in his step he hadn't felt for years, even though he knew he was behaving like an idiot and looked like one too.

They both broke into a quick pace as they left the building. They had to get to Rathaus Platz, where the trams left from, in time to catch the last one. They only ran for a few hours each morning and afternoon, to save electricity. Stave and Anna leaned forwards into the wind, her scarf and headscarf wrapped tight, his collar pulled up high and his hat low over his eyes. There was no time for them to talk. Stave didn't mind. He was busy enough concentrating on walking without his limp showing.

Don't go falling in love, he told himself; don't make a fool of yourself. She's your only witness. Bait, without even knowing it, for an unscrupulous killer, bait that you yourself laid. Or maybe she could even be the murderer herself? You can't rule that out. You know nothing about her, not even whether or not she's married. Maybe there's a husband and children waiting for her in her Nissen hut. Children! What would Karl think, if he ever came back? His home in ruins, his mother dead – and the father he'd fallen out with before the war living with another woman? It was unthinkable.

They almost ran across the windy Rathaus Platz, Anna's cheeks red from the cold and the effort of walking so fast. Delicious, thought Stave to himself, then turned his eyes to the ground.

The three tramlines intersected in front of the city hall. The lines had been repaired and cleared of debris. The carriages were battered, people everywhere pushing and shoving. Black marketeers with their lackeys pushing their way in with huge, heavy crates of coal or carrots. Weary postmen laden with packages. At least there was no rubbish on board. In the mornings the trams were used for carrying waste out to the dumps on the edge of the city. How else was anyone to get rid of it?

And in between the crates and boxes were the people: black marketeers, office workers, shop workers, all of them going home at the same time because of the electricity cut-off.

Stave clumsily tried to forge a way through for Anna von Veckinhausen, to help her up the step on to the tram. But she was better at it on her own; she did it more often. The carriage was stuffed, stank of wet overcoats, old shoes, sweat, bad breath, cheap tobacco.

The people piling in after them shoved Stave and Anna von Veckinhausen against the window on the far side of the carriage. The chief inspector fought back with his elbows, without turning round, then gave up and allowed himself to be pushed up against the woman who was going to help him catch the rubble murderer. He gave her an embarrassed smile.

'Just a couple of stops and then we'll be back in the fresh air,' she said.

A shunt, the screech of steel wheels on tracks and a lurch as the tram turned a corner. Blows to the shoulders, the stomach, the weight of the man next to you swaying, a pain in the hand when somebody reached out to grab the same handhold as you. Muttered imprecations, growing louder. Nobody apologised, nobody looked at anybody else.

Stave said nothing. Every word could be dangerous. Nobody knew what the person next to you did in the war. There were cases of people cursing under their breath, then being stabbed by former veterans from the Russian front. Teenagers, who at the age of 15 were enlisted into the Hitler Youth and sent to the front for beating to death somebody who accidentally insulted them. Our society is a wasteland, the chief inspector thinks to himself. We detectives are just clearing up the rubble.

Stave couldn't bring himself to say anything in the obscene crush. Anything he said would be overheard. You either cursed or shut up. In any case, what would I say to her, he thought to himself.

Fortunately the tram began to empty after the third and fourth stops – both unmarked amidst a wilderness of ruins, dozens of people clambering out. Where were they going, Stave wondered. Only now, when finally it was possible to move, a sweating conductor made his way across to them. Stave handed him a multiple journey ticket he had bought two weeks ago and to date had only used for one journey. Single tickets were no longer being sold: there was not enough paper. Stave rarely used the tram; he used the cash he saved to buy cigarettes he could exchange at the station for information from returning veterans. In any case walking strengthened his bad leg.

'Two,' he said to the conductor.

'Generous,' Anna von Veckinhausen said.

Good that she hadn't used his title. If she'd said, 'Chief Inspector,' then everyone would have turned to look at him. And that wasn't a pleasant feeling if you were in a carriage where at least half of those present had been trading on the black market.

'Do you take the tram often?' Stave asked needlessly, when there was finally enough space around them that he felt comfortable talking normally.

'I've got used to it since I came to Hamburg.'

'How did you get around before that?'

She gave him an attentive, slightly amused look. 'Is that an official question?'

'Private. You're not obliged to answer.'

'In a car. Or a carriage. Preferably on a horse.'

'The home of a well-to-do family.'

'A well-to-do home. I know what you're thinking.'

'What am I thinking?'

'You think I come from some landed Junker family east of the Elbe. That it's people like me who ruined Germany.'

'Did you?'

She exhaled angrily. 'We were nationalists, conservatives. But we never voted for Herr Hitler.'

The chief inspector wondered what she meant by 'we', but didn't ask.

'I get out here,' Anna von Veckinhausen said, as with screeching brakes the tram came to a halt next to a blackened building façade half its original height.

Stave followed her without asking permission. They took a straight street that led between mountains of rubble, from which here and there remnants of wall protruded, reminding Stave of a long-drawn-out cross on a grave.

The Nissen huts stood at a crossing in the shadow of the old flak bunker: tin barracks erected along all four streets. The chief inspector counted 20 of them, with here and there the yellowy flame of candlelight shining through windows cut in the barrel-like sides, while others just sat there in the dark. The air was filled with the acrid stench of wet wood burning. Blue smoke rose from thin, twisted tin chimneys and gusted amidst the lines strung between the huts and hung with washing, long frozen solid. There was a smell of cabbage soup and wet shoes, and here and there a well wrapped-up figure coming from the tram passed them, pushed open a door in one of the barracks and disappeared.

In those few seconds Stave got a glimpse of the interior; rough wooden tables, a tiny stove in the middle of the hut, made of black cast iron. Clothing or sheets in every colour hung from lines strung across the interior in every direction, either washing or as makeshift walls, so that families could have the minimum of privacy in these barracks with no rooms.

Stave wondered what it must be like for someone who had grown up in a grand mansion now to be living in a communal barracks in the midst of ruins. He wondered if Anna von Veckinhausen was ashamed. Or if she was just lucky still to be alive and have a roof over her head, even if it was made of corrugated iron.

Anna von Veckinhausen walked up to the door of the Nissen hut in the centre of the crossing, a crossing with a completely undamaged advertising column standing in the middle of it. Every day when she left the hut Anna von Veckinhausen would find herself staring at the photos of the murderer's victims. Maybe that was what led to her changing her statement, Stave thought in a moment of self-satisfaction.

A pair in dyed Wehrmacht greatcoats passed them, pushing a battered pram with a squeaking front axle. It didn't look as though there was a child in it, more like a lump of wood, the chief inspector thought. That reminded him of his own unheated apartment and then he wondered what it must be like at night in these thin-walled barracks.

Anna von Veckinhausen speeded up her pace.

She wants rid of me, the chief inspector thought, ever so slightly disappointed. She doesn't want to be seen with me here.

'Thanks you for accompanying me,' she said, as she reached the door in the front of the Nissen hut. 'Do you think I need a body-guard from now on?'

'Why do you say that?' Stave asked.

'Because the murderer saw me.'

The chief inspector thought back to his conversation with the journalist from *Die Zeit,* and with a feeling of pained guilt turned his eyes up to the grey sky. 'That is if the figure you saw was the killer. And if this figure did see you then he probably saw no more of you than you saw of him. He didn't see your face, and certainly doesn't know your name or address.'

'I'm sure you're right,' she replied, but it didn't sound as if she was convinced. She held out her hand. 'Good night, Chief Inspector.'

She waited until he had walked off a few paces, before opening the door. Stave didn't get the chance to look inside. He politely doffed his hat as a mark of farewell but the door had already closed with a tinny clang. He turned round slowly and set off on the long walk to Wandsbek, without limping. There was always the chance that she was watching him from one of the Nissen hut's tiny windows.

He strode along for few hundred metres, trying not to think of Anna von Veckinhausen, or his son, or his wife, but just the case. The goddamn case.

A Hamburg industrialist who had made military equipment for the old regime and the pretty conservative-minded aristocrat from East Prussia – could there be a connection? The word 'bottleneck' on a piece of paper, and looted antiques, sold to the Brits. Was there a connection to be made there? A shrouded figure amidst the rubble. A long coat. The smell of tobacco. If he could trust the statement of a single witness. And could he trust Anna von Veckinhausen? Don't think about her, not now. But then could he trust anybody? MacDonald – in the light of all the leads pointing to the British?

Maschke, after the orphan child had pointed to him, and who was obviously hiding something? Ehrlich, who might well be on a personal vendetta and not really interested in finding the killer at all?

He dragged himself up the staircase to his apartment, no longer trying to hide his limp. The stairwell was dark anyway. He was almost expecting to find Ruge or another uniformed policeman outside his door, with more, almost certainly, bad news. But the landing by his doorway was deserted. Stave unlocked the door, then carefully locked it behind him. He threw himself down on the tatty sofa, still wearing his coat and hat. It was freezing cold. He ought to go into the kitchen to get himself a bite to eat, but he was too exhausted. Anna. Don't think of her. The chief inspector fell asleep on the sofa, his last thought before slipping into oblivion was astonishment at how weary he really was.

Number Four

Wednesday, 12 February 1947

Hell, Stave thought to himself, isn't hot – it's cold.

When he looked out of his office window he saw houses that had been cleaned automatically, their roofs and north or east gable walls blasted by a wind that had sucked up Arctic ice and used it to sand the tiles and plaster like an invisible plane. In places sheltered from the blast of the wind there were still pockets of sheet ice and layers of powder snow on the guttering, window frames and in the empty door-frames of bombed-out houses. The temperature had been constant since January, but the light had changed: for eight hours a day now there was a blue-shimmering sun in a cloudless sky, bathing the world in an eerie brightness that highlighted even the smallest of details. The cracks in the façade of the Music Hall on the square opposite looked to the chief inspector like a Dürer engraving, each cracked capital on the columns casting grotesque shadows. Yet here I am typing in the dark, Stave mused; it was a bad joke.

Dr Czrisini's third autopsy report was lying in his in-tray. Assumed date of death: twentieth of January. No other significant details. Stave wondered how many other people had been killed on that day – and when they would find their bodies.

Kleensch had published his article in *Die Zeit*: a measured piece with no absurd speculation, no hysteria, no inflated suggestion of hope – just enough to indicate that the police were making progress. Stave had warned Cuddel Breuer and Ehrlich in advance so they would not feel they were hearing it for the first time from the press.

But apart from that, nothing.

He had posted men near the Lappenbergs Allee crime scene, a pretty grim job in this cold. And now a few deep-frozen, bored-stiff officers hated him for it, because nobody had turned up. No reaction on the part of the killer, no information from the public, no new leads. Nothing, nothing, nothing.

No news either from Anna von Veckinhausen. Had she seen the article? Was she furious at him? Stave had asked MacDonald to check out her story about the sale of the kitsch painting. It appeared to be true. MacDonald hadn't exactly identified which of his comrades-in-arms had bought the item of dubious value, but Anna von Veck-inhausen was, it turned out, known to many British officers, who appreciated the goods she sold. The lieutenant had let him know in the nicest possible way that many of his superior officers would be extremely unhappy if her supply chain was interrupted. The chief inspector had just nodded and muttered something incomprehensi-ble, but he had got the message.

He wouldn't be able to threaten Anna von Veckinhausen with charges for her looting or dealings on the black market. Either she cooperated voluntarily or she didn't. And if she did have something to do with the murders, then he had better have proper evidence before he arrested her.

As for 'Bottleneck', MacDonald had got nowhere. And Hellinger, the industrialist, was still missing.

Maschke had gone round all the older, retired doctors – it was his own idea and he had got their numbers from the medical council. He had asked all of them about the victims, the old man in particu-lar. In vain. It had been a good idea though, Stave reckoned. He should have thought of it himself. The vice squad man was getting better and better.

Stave sat and stared at the thin files he had placed carefully next to one another on his desk. Three investigation files. Three murder cases. Three single sheets of paper and a few photos. Could it be that the solution to the case lay in these sparse files? Could he have overlooked something?

It was exactly midday when his door flew open, and Maschke charged in.

'Ever heard of knocking first?' Stave asked.

'We have a new murder,' the vice squad man blurted.

'This time, I'll drive, ' Stave told him in no uncertain terms two minutes later as they climbed into the old Mercedes. 'What's the story?'

'We have a fresh corpse.'

'Who is it?'

'A man in a cellar, in Borgfelde, behind the Berliner Tor station. Just been found. It was reported to the local police station around 11.30.'

'In the east of the city again.'

'And another heavily bombed area.'

Stave put his foot down, racing down to the Alster and along the Jungfernstieg, pushing the old eight-cylinder as hard as it would go, and blaring his horn when a man in a Wehrmacht greatcoat didn't get out of the way quickly enough. Maschke's knuckles were white as he hung on for dear life to the passenger door handle.

'Don't worry, the police won't stop us,' the chief inspector assured him.

Four bodies: two men, one woman and one little girl. Three of the corpses found in the east of the city, this latest approximately halfway between where the body of the first, the young woman, had been found and where the girl had been found near the canal. Was there a pattern emerging?

'52 Anckelmann Strasse,' Maschke only just managed to tell him.

Stave took the corner into Glockengiesserwall, the Mercedes swerving wildly when one rear wheel hit a roof tile frozen to the road, but he got it back under control.

'A bit icy in patches,' Maschke gasped.

'I'm beginning to enjoy myself.'

Past the main station, then through St Georg. Black marketeers stared in their wake. When they reached Borgfelder Strasse, Stave put his foot down again. Half a kilometre, dead straight. Nobody around. Then two sharp right turns, and with a screech of brakes he brought the car to a halt.

'One dead body a day is more than enough,' Maschke muttered as he opened his door.

Stave climbed out too, leaning briefly against the vehicle's dented hood. The engine was ticking as it cooled down. For a few moments, Stave held his hands on the hood, enjoying the warmth as it flowed into his veins like a hot liquid.

'That feels good, doesn't it?'

'I'm quite hot enough,' Maschke answered drily.

The chief inspector looked around; behind them stood the steel supports for the elevated railway, every sixth or seventh twisted and bent, empty façades of burnt-out apartment blocks, four or five storeys high, bombed-out office buildings, half-demolished warehouses. The cobbled street had been partly cleared, but there wasn't a habitable building for at least 300 metres in any direction.

A pattern, Stave thought to himself, I'm starting to see a pattern.

A uniformed policeman emerged from between two half-height walls to their right, waved and came over. He was extremely young, little more than a kid. Stave had never seen him before. He gave them an almost military salute, looking as if he was about to stand to attention.

'As you were,' Stave said, introducing himself and Maschke. The lad had probably fought in the Wehrmacht. There were one or two habits he needed to lose. 'Where is the man?'

'It's a woman, Chief Inspector.'

Stave stared at the young policeman, embarrassing him.

'Two men found the body. In an unlit cellar. They ran out in panic and reported it to us. They thought it was a male corpse, but they obviously didn't look close enough. It's a woman.'

Stave was taken aback for a minute. Two women, an old man, a little girl – did that fit a pattern any better?

The uniform led the way. 'The building at 52 Anckelmann Strasse is completely in ruins,' he explained. 'We could get to the cellar by going through the ruins, but it's easier this way.'

He led Stave and Maschke some 50 metres along the street to a neighbouring building, which had only partly collapsed. A reinforced archway there led to several partly collapsed internal yards, through which they made their way back in the other direction.

Stave stopped outside the remains of a commercial storeroom. 'The Hanseatic Mica Import Company' was written in faded black letters against a red background. Someone was clambering though the ruins of number 52 Anckelmann Strasse. Dr Czrisini. The two detectives acknowledged the pathologist; the uniformed policeman nodded towards an entrance to a cellar.

'Watch the steps,' he warned them. 'They're loose.'

'No door,' Stave remarked as they walked down the fragile steps. Not much light. He took out his notebook and wrote down a description of the external aspect of the scene. The uniform fiddled with an old torch until finally it produced a weak yellow beam of light. A few other people appeared at the foot of the stairs. Stave could only make out their dirty shoes and the hems of long over-coats. He stared as if into a dark cave.

A room with a cement floor, a few fallen roof tiles, plaster fallen from the walls, a second room, dark because no light from the stairwell reached it. Plaster dust here too, but no rubble, no furniture.

Just a corpse.

Aged about 35, Stave reckoned, maybe a little younger. She was lying on the ground, naked. Frozen to the cement. There were blue-red blood settlement marks all over her body. Her mouth was slightly open, as were her eyes, her right hand on the floor, the left over her navel, fingers bent slightly. Without saying a word, Stave took the torch from the young policeman and shone it directly on the victim. The policeman looked as if he were about to be sick.

'You can wait outside,' the chief inspector told him.

Dr Czrisini took a large flashlight out of his doctor's bag. It was brighter. He touched the woman's face with a gloved hand. 'Thin, long face. Well nourished though,' he muttered. 'Dark brown eye-lashes, dyed, plucked eyebrows. Possibly remnants of face powder on her cheeks. Medium-blond hair, probably bleached. Ear lobes pierced. Nothing in the left ear. In the right…' he hesitated, then felt with his hand round the back of the head, pulled at her hair a bit. '…right earring came loose, but caught in her hair.' The pathologist handed Stave an earring.

The chief inspector looked at it closely, a pearl on a gold hanger. 'Unusual shape,' he mumbled. 'The gold worked into the shape of a starfish with the pearl in the middle.'

'I can't tell you anything about that,' Czrisini replied. 'Jewellery isn't exactly my specialty.'

The pathologist raised the corpse's eyelids. 'Grey-blue eyes.' Then he pulled her jaw open and shone the light into her mouth. 'Upper plate with two false teeth: the right inner incisor and the first right molar, and on the right two gold-filled molars.'

He began to examine her from the head down. 'Frozen solid. Rigor mortis not evident. Strangulation marks on the throat, reddish brown, two centimetres wide at the front and to the left. To the right and rear, three to five millimetres. Well looked-after fingernails, with red nail polish, the tips finished with a nail pencil. Pale bands on her left wrist and ring finger. Presumably traces of a watch and ring. Long surgical scar, some 14 centimetres long, from her navel to pubic mound. Probably from an abdominal operation. Well healed. Scar tissue.'

'No evidence in the dust on the cellar floor of the body having been dragged,' Stave added. 'No dirt on the body. Highly unlikely that she was killed here.'

'She was killed somewhere else and brought here post mortem,' Maschke said. 'To hide the body.'

'Maybe perhaps to undress and rob her without being disturbed,' the chief inspector added. 'One way or another, the killer must have come down those loose steps and left her here, carrying a torch at the same time.'

'Obviously a strong man,' the pathologist said.

'But was it planned beforehand?' Maschke interjected. 'Did he know about this cellar and decide in advance this would be a good place to hide the body? Or did he just look for the nearest hiding place after the murder and come across this place by chance?'

'He would have needed a torch.' Stave scratched his head. 'That suggests it was pre-planned. Unless of course he always carries one. Or else he knows the area so well that he could find his way to this cellar in the dark.'

'I'm wondering where she came from,' the pathologist mused.

'She was obviously well-to-do, possibly rich,' Stave said. 'Gold teeth, gold earrings, a watch, a ring, nail polish. Can't remember when I last saw a woman with a manicure.'

'The nail polish is too expensive, too modest and too well-applied for a lady of the night,' Maschke added. 'This was a proper lady.'

'And she almost certainly didn't live behind the station in Borgfelde,' Stave remarked, almost cheerfully. 'Winterhude maybe? Or Blankenese? Definitely a better part of town than here. Somewhere that survived undamaged. A neighbourhood that's still intact, which means somebody must know her.'

Czrisini pointed to her left ring finger then to her abdomen. 'Probably married too. In which case there's a husband. But with a scar like that, I doubt she'd have had children. On the other hand this could help the investigation. Operations like that are a lot less common than appendectomies or dental work. There has to be a surgeon or gynaecologist who remembers carrying it out.'

'Can we estimate a time of death?'

'Not here and now. I'll thaw the body out back at the institute. We'll know more once we've cut her open. I expect the brain will have started to rot.'

Stave's sudden moment of euphoria evaporated. 'So you think the body may have been here for some time?'

The pathologist nodded. 'For more than a day or two at least.'

It's unbelievable, Stave thought. A rich woman, with a husband, neighbours; if this woman was murdered days ago then surely some-body would have missed her by now. But he couldn't remember a single report over the past week or so that would fit the victim. I need a breath of fresh air, he thought.

'We'd better talk to the men who found her,' Stave said. 'Dr Czrisini, your people can take the corpse as soon as the photographer has done his work.'

August Hoffmann and his workman Heinrich Scharfenort were scrap metal dealers, both pale-faced and around Stave's age.

'You found the victim?' The chief inspector had deliberately chosen a neutral expression.

Even so Hoffmann gave him a guilty look. 'We really thought it was a man. I've only just heard that it's a woman down there.'

'The main thing is that you reported it,' Stave replied. 'Tell me what happened.'

The workman glanced at the ground, leaving his boss to answer.

'We were looking for baking trays.'

'Baking trays?'

'Up until '43 there used to be a major bakery here. I recently found a huge baking tray in the rubble. By chance,' he was quick to add, 'I thought to myself there might be some more lying around. So Herr Scharfenort and I came round today to…'

He hesitated.

The chief inspector nodded understandingly. 'Find more metal,' he finished the sentence. 'That's why you were down in the cellar.'

'Exactly. The ground level ruins have all been stripped long ago. We brought carbide lamps to illuminate the cellars.'

'And you took those down with you?'

The scrap metal man nodded, looking as if he wanted to go behind a wall and throw up, but in the end he managed to pull himself together.

'We came down the steps and lit up the first room, then the second. All of a sudden I spotted a naked foot.'

'What about you?' Stave turned to the workman.

He glanced up and said, 'I was behind the boss. I didn't see anything. Herr Hoffmann called out, "There's a body." And we got out of there.'

'Anything else unusual strike you?'

'That was unusual enough.'

'You didn't see anybody?'

Both of them shook their heads.

'Were you here over the previous few days? You said you'd found a baking tray here.'

'Three days ago I took a shortcut I'd not taken before. That was when I spotted it in a partly blocked cellar entrance, and then I got the idea to bring the carbide lamps. Apart from that I've never been here before.'

'Do you know if there's anyone here regularly? Somebody else who might take the same shortcut.'

Once again they shook their heads.

Stave nodded and dismissed the pair of them.

'Anything new?'

Stave was standing in front of his boss. Cuddel Breuer wasn't looking at him. He was staring at a sniffer dog wandering, half frozen and unenthusiastically, around the rubble. 'He can't find a scent,' he remarked.

Stave ditched the formalities too. 'Dr Czrisini reckons the body had been here for several days. Doesn't look like this was the scene of the crime.'

Breuer nodded silently, then dug deep into his broad overcoat and pulled out a big flashlight, and still without saying a word went down the steps into the cellar.

He doesn't trust me any more, Stave thought.

A few minutes later, Breuer came out again. 'You've got one damn difficult case on your hands, Stave. Come and see me when you're done here.' He turned around and left without saying goodbye.

At least you didn't find any more than I did, Stave said to himself, sombrely.

As Breuer turned round a remnant of wall twice the height of a man, he nearly collided with a figure stumbling through the ruins: Kleensch from *Die Zeit*.

'Looks like everything's about to hit the fan today,' Stave muttered. He dithered for a second. Should he just ignore the reporter? Dismiss him? But then he would nose around, ask questions. Cause trouble. Better to take things in hand. Stave went up to the reporter, shook his hand and led him down into the cellar.

'A new rubble murderer victim,' the journalist said, looking at the body in the yellowish light of the torch. Calmly.

He's already thinking about the article he's going to write, Stave realised. He told Kleensch everything they knew and indicated the clues that suggested the victim had been well-to-do.

'Nowadays it seems nobody notices when the rich go missing, just like the poor. That really is democracy,' Kleensch quipped.

'You're not going to write that?'

He smiled. 'I don't think my publisher would like to see that in print. And the British wouldn't like it either. I prefer to hold on to my job. Cigarette?'

'Please don't smoke at the crime scene,' the chief inspector replied, shaking his head at the same time. He waved a hand back towards the door.

'Nobody would want to read that,' he said when they were back outside, in a half-hearted attempt to stop the man writing his story.

Kleensch gave him a wry smile. 'I'm afraid you're wrong there, Chief Inspector. People enjoy reading murder stories. Horrible stories. The problem is nobody heeds the moral of the story. So I shall leave out the philosophical bit and concentrate on the details. If you know what I mean.'

Stave nodded in resignation. 'You do your job and I'll do mine.'

'People are going to be afraid even if I were to promise you to be economical with the truth. The rubble murderer is becoming a personification of evil, a bogeyman. It's as if he's given this vile cold a human face, even if nobody knows what it looks like. It could be anyone. Every figure walking along the street behind me, every shadow in the ruins, every taciturn new neighbour. People are starting to suspect one another. We could end up with more accusations than we had under Hitler. But there's not much to do about it. People are going to give you hell, I'm afraid. But sooner or later you'll catch the villain responsible. And then you'll be a hero.'

'I appreciate your optimism.'

'It's necessary. Especially in the face of death.' Kleensch doffed his hat and stumbled away.

At least he didn't talk to anybody else, Stave reflected. It wouldn't have been good news if he'd started annoying Breuer with his questions, or Stave would have had to explain himself.

A while later Stave drove back to the office in the Mercedes, alone. Maschke had declined a lift under the flimsiest of excuses – he preferred to walk to keep fit. Driving along Jungfernstieg the chief inspector suddenly stepped on the brakes. The car spluttered to a halt in a few metres. This is my opportunity, Stave thought.

For the past few days, despairing over his lack of leads, Stave had considered involving a psychologist, and had asked around as to who the best in Hamburg were. But then he had put the idea to one side. Partly because he was embarrassed about the idea; nobody much in the murder squad had high regard for psychologists. Partly because he was ashamed that doing so would show his colleagues how little confidence he had: going to a shrink. Who knows, maybe he should put himself on the couch.

Not on your life.

But here he was, purely by chance, on his own and as it happened one of Hamburg's best-known psychologists had his practice right here, on the Jungfernstieg. Professor Walter Bürger-Prinz.

Stave walked down the almost pristine, elegant street that led gradually to the glittering ice of the Alster on his right. To his left stood the colonnaded façades of the grand buildings that had survived the firestorms intact. Once again the chief inspector was overcome by a sense of rage at the injustice. Why had all this pomp and grandeur, based on greed and inequality, survived?

He pulled himself together. It was hardly a psychologist's fault that the British had preferred to wipe out the working-class districts rather than the grand boulevards.

He couldn't remember the number of the building where the practice was located, but as he walked along slowly he soon came across a large noticeboard with the professor's name on it. Fifth floor. The chief inspector pushed open a door nearly three metres high. Light-coloured marble and wrought-iron banisters, but no light bulbs left in the chandelier, he was pleased to see. The old-fashioned lift in the centre of the stairwell was out of order, because the electricity was off. Stave slowly began the long climb up the stairs.

When he finally reached the practice anteroom, however, he found himself up to his ankles in thick-piled carpets looking at an English club armchair, a desk and a teak bookshelf, which along with the scent of Earl Grey tea and furniture polish, made Stave, in his worn-out shoes, tatty suit and torn overcoat, feel grubby. Behind the desk sat a female receptionist in her fifties, with hair pulled back tight and wearing a pair of nickel glasses.

'May I help you?'

But it sounded more like, 'No dogs or beggars!'

Stave had intended to ask if the professor might see him, just for a few minutes. But the intimidating façade, the endless marble staircase, the heady scent in the air and now this dismissive receptionist had wound him up more than he could take. Angrily, he marched up to her desk and slammed his police ID down in front of her nose.

'CID. I need to speak to Professor Bürger-Prinz. Immediately.'

She recoiled in shock and distress as if nobody had ever spoken to her in that tone before. For a few moments the expression of disgust vanished from her face, then she got to her feet and disappeared behind a leather-upholstered door.

Stave didn't have long to wait. He was led through the door into another world, a big room with door-height windows looking out on to the Alster, a desk, three armchairs and an actual couch. None of it, however, was really English but it all looked somehow modern, and at the same time strangely old-fashioned, as if it dated back to before the war. Probably from the Bauhaus movement, Stave reckoned. The armchairs were cubes of chrome and black leather, the couch looking as if it had been poured out of the same materials. Probably very comfortable, the chief inspector thought, though on the other hand it looked a bit like the table Dr Czrisini used to dissect corpses on. But then this one was used for dissections too, in a manner of speaking.

The walls were white, a single painting hanging opposite the windows: oblique black streaks on an ochre background. Modern art, Stave supposed. The parquet floor was polished. On a sideboard by the middle window was a sculpture of a sitting man, Asian-looking. Buddha maybe? There were no certificates or diplomas hanging on the walls, no family photo on the desk. No telephone.

Once upon a time Stave had seen a photograph of Sigmund Freud in a book and was subconsciously expecting to see someone who looked like him. Instead the man approaching him looked like something from a recruiting poster for the SS. Professor Bürgen-Prinz was about 1.90 metres tall with short blond hair and the most luminous blue eyes Stave had ever seen, the colour of the water in a Norwegian fjord. The chief inspector felt they were looking straight through him.

'Why do you need to see me so urgently?' he said in the deep, perfectly modulated voice of a practised public speaker or singer. The psychologist held out his hand and took Stave's in a firm grip.

Stave felt relieved when Bürger-Prinz indicated they should use the armchairs rather than the couch. He apologised for the intrusion, then began to tell him about the victims, the places the bodies had been found, the few leads they had, the medallions with their strange symbols, about the missing person posters and the fact they had elicited no response. Dead people whom nobody missed. Strangulations. Bodies stripped bare. Ruins, charred walls. Thin layers of snow on cement.

The psychologist let him speak without interrupting. He just watched him with those irritating eyes, took no notes, just sat there in his armchair, relaxed and attentive at the same time. Maybe my tale has got to him, Stave thought, at least awakened his professional interest. Or maybe he just knows how to pose.

'I read the story about this rubble murderer,' the psychologist said eventually, when Stave dried up. 'In *Die Zeit*. And the photos of your victims are everywhere.'

'Can you see some kind of pattern in it?' Stave asked. 'Do the murders tell us anything about the murderer? Something we might have missed? What is there that links murders, apart from the method? I'm desperate for some sort of lead.'

'That's everything you know?'

'That's everything I know.'

Bürger-Prinz frowned. 'I hope you're not expecting me to give you an answer just like that to a case that an experienced criminologist such as yourself has been working on in vain?'

'Maybe you might recognise some sort of pattern,' Stave said. 'Maybe in the choice of the places our unknown perpetrator leaves his victims. Or maybe the victims he chooses themselves.'

The psychologist stood up, walked over to his desk, took a city map of Hamburg out of a drawer and studied it. 'Ruins, working-class districts, three of them east of the Alster, one west. Cellars, lift-shafts, bomb craters. Your killer is content just to hide the bodies. That's enough for him.'

'What do you mean?'

'He's not trying to get rid of them forever. Just for long enough for him not to be caught.'

'Hardly surprising. All of the victims, possibly except for the last – we're still waiting for the autopsy report – were killed on the same day, the twentieth of January.'

'But they might not all have been put where they were found on that day.'

Stave stared at him. 'You mean somebody kills all these people, then keeps their bodies somewhere and only disposes of them one by one?'

Bürger-Prinz gave him an indulgent smile. 'It's cold enough. And your unknown perpetrator wouldn't be the first killer to move bodies around days or weeks after their murder.'

'You think somebody's playing a sick joke on us?'

'Maybe. But there might also be practical reasons for it. He can only carry one body at a time. Maybe he does it every night.'

'Every night?' The chief inspector closed his eyes.

'One way or another, the killer is behaving rationally. He's thought it out. There is also something in common in each case. The bodies left in the east were all near the main station whereas the one left in the west was near Dammtor station.'

'You think the murderer chooses his victims in trains? Or at the stations?'

'Or kills them near a station. Then he hides the bodies in the ruins nearby.'

'But all of them on one day? Four bodies, two stations? The trains only run during the day. The stations are abandoned from eight in the evening. If our murderer kills someone during the day, how does he manage to move the bodies to the ruins where we found them without being noticed? And if he only hides them at night, how could he have met them earlier at the station? Does he kill them somewhere in the daytime, then wait for hours on end to hide them somewhere in the dark? Doesn't sound likely.'

'It would be possible if his victims were on the last train. A train arriving at 5.30 p.m. pulls into a station that is already dark. Very dark. And in this cold already empty. Let's imagine he killed the old man at Dammtor station, and the three females at the main station. It's not impossible.'

'You think he's an experienced killer?'

Bürger-Prinz thought for a moment. 'Maybe our murderer deliberately chooses weaker victims,' he mused.

Stave just looked at him blankly.

'Maybe he picks the person on the train he thinks will be easiest to deal with. A woman. A child. An old man.'

The chief inspector thought of the endless hours he had spent at the station, staring at the incoming carriages, the thousands of people pushing past him. He shook his head. 'Might have been the case with the girl, even the old man. But it doesn't work for the two women. There's no train these days where a woman would be the easiest victim. There are always children on the move, and old people and war wounded.'

Then he hesitated. Something had occurred to him. 'The old man was the only victim to have been beaten, badly beaten at that, as far as the pathologist could make out. But of the four victims he was in no way the strongest or most mobile. Both women would definitely have been able to put up more of a defence or been able to run away more easily.'

The psychologist smiled. 'I see what you're getting at: a family. Somebody has a vicious hatred of one family, possibly even his own. So they all have to die. But the old man, the patriarch, he deserves to suffer the most and so the murderer beats him before strangling him.'

Stave nodded. 'Obviously it could just be a coincidence. Maybe the murderer wanted to strangle them all without giving them any opportunity to defend themselves. Maybe he creeps up behind them. But in the case of the old man alone, something went wrong, something beyond his control. And so he had to lay into him. But even if we go with that, it's not chance that...'

'The beating could be an indicator of violent anger, a desire for revenge, punishment, getting even.'

'In which case the murderer already knows his victims. He's killing them for some reason we don't know. But in one case, he attacks in a particularly violent way.'

'As a punishment.'

'An old man, a woman in her mid-thirties, a woman of about twenty and a little girl of eight at most. Who could possibly have something against such a varied group of people? Some driven fanatic who wants to kill all his own family?'

'If all the victims were related.'

'Why else are there no missing person reports? Maybe the only relative who might report them missing is the killer himself.'

The psychologist looked out of the window. 'The old man might be the father of both women, and the grandfather of the little girl, or maybe the grandfather of both her and the younger woman. But was one of the women the mother of the little girl? The older one might have been but you tell me the pathologist doesn't think she'd ever been pregnant.'

'She'd had an abdominal operation. We don't know when. And until the autopsy we won't know what the operation was for.'

'If there was a 14-centimetre scar then it's unlikely there's too much intact down there,' the psychologist said.

'But she still might have been pregnant before the operation.'

'Okay, if we accept that hypothesis, then we have an old man who could be her father and the grandfather of the child, and another young female relation who just might be the much younger sister of the older woman.'

Stave smiled for the first time since he'd walked through the practice door. 'Let's also assume that the means of death and the witness statement suggest that the murderer is male. And let's assume he is a relative of the victims. Then the main suspect has to be the husband of the older woman and father of the child. That's who we're looking for.'

Bürger-Prinz looked at him almost sympathetically. 'Maybe you'll find him in the rubble too, frozen to the ground with strangulation marks on his neck.'

The chief inspector inhaled sharply. He had had a vision, in which from now on he would find a corpse in the ruins every day: a girl, a boy, a woman, a man … and when this eternal winter finally came to an end, bodies that had lain undiscovered for months in cellars would thaw and the stench of corruption would bring the curious. And then the police.

'If it really is some domestic drama we're witnessing,' the psychologist continued calmly, 'then we're missing a few characters. A grandmother. Another set of grandparents. The child's father and presumed husband of the older woman. Maybe more children. Brothers and sisters of the grown-ups. Not to mention more distant relatives. There are a lot of potential victims, or potential killers.'

Stave sighed. 'You mean, we're going to find another couple of victims who fit the theory? And that only then can we be sure it is a family thing.'

Bürger-Prinz shook his head. 'When you've found your twentieth victim, then we can be reasonably sure that it's not a family thing. But just a few more victims. A boy or a girl would fit as well as older people of either sex. A man or a woman. Think about it: you might assume a man between 35 and 50 could be the husband and father. A younger man could be the brother or even the husband of the younger woman. You can be sure of one thing. The next body you find will fit the theory. And the next. You'll still know no more than you know now.'

'What about the medallion?'

'Did the killer leave it there as a marker?'

'I doubt it. Too inconspicuous and not consistent. We've found two victims with no medallion, meaning that the killer didn't leave any marker near them. Or that he left it so discreetly that we didn't find it. Neither of those fits in with a murderer who leaves a marker with each of his victims. So the medallions must have belonged to the victims. To members of the same family. Maybe a family crest?'

'Not the crest of any Hamburg family I know,' the psychologist replied. 'But then it doesn't have to be a family crest.'

'What else?'

'Maybe some kind of religious symbol. A cross and two daggers, it's not hard to see a spiritual connection.'

'A sect of some sort? Like the Jehovah's Witnesses? The old man was circumcised.'

'Like the Jews. But the Muslims too.'

'Jews or Muslims would hardly be likely to wear a cross.'

'So Christians. Maybe all four of them belonged to the same religious community.'

'But no other member of that community reported them missing? No pastor? No sect leader?'

'Sects don't often relish the glare of publicity or the attention of the police. Particularly after the events of recent years.'

Stave thought of the Jehovah's Witnesses who had been reviled as 'bible bashers' and locked up in concentration camps. The past few minutes spent with the psychologist had taught him a lot, more than he had hoped for. But what was he to do with the theories and facts? How could he fit them in with the case? Were any of them even relevant? Or was he just on another dead-end trail?

'Thank you for your time,' he said with an air of resignation, and got to his feet.

Back at headquarters Stave strolled down the dimly lit corridor to his office but stopped when he reached the door. It was ajar, and he could make out two figures inside: MacDonald and Erna Berg. He made it his business to cough discreetly.

But neither of them turned round. His secretary was sitting at her desk, her face stained with tears. The young Brit was standing to one side behind her, bending over and whispering in her ear.

Stave was pleased that he didn't have a clue what he might be saying. Nothing to do with me, he told himself. They seemed already to be having a crisis in their relationship even though they'd only been a couple for a few days. Stave decided to leave them to it for the moment and instead of going into his own office, he went along the corridor to see the boss. After all that's what Cuddel Breuer had told him to do.

Stave went over their findings in his head again, coaxed himself to get on with it and told Breuer about his meeting with Bürger-Prinz.

'I have to admit you're trying everything.'

Stave stood there silently, not sure if it was meant seriously or sarcastically. 'I'm doing my best.'

'Tell that to the mayor,' Breuer said. 'He wants us to go and see him. He's not happy.'

Stave and Breuer took the Mercedes the few hundred metres to the city hall, even though Stave would have preferred to walk. It would have given him time to think.

The city hall with its impressive neo-Renaissance façade and its tall, tapering tower had not been damaged: a monument to the riches of trade and bourgeois pride standing there in a wasteland of rubble. A tram came round a corner and screeched to a stop. Tradesmen and postal workers climbed in. Passers-by rushed past as if they were heading for the nearest air-raid shelter, the sound of the sirens still in their ears.

The chief inspector followed his boss into the imposing building, down corridors half in darkness to the unheated office. Mayor Max Brauer greeted them. A massive, energetic man with a square jaw, grey hair brushed back and bright eyes. Sixty years old. Until 1933 he had been mayor of Altona, the Hamburg suburb that then had independent status, before being kicked out by the Nazis. He left for China then eventually the USA. He had returned a year ago and had been Hamburg's mayor for the past three months.

Stave knew him slightly, because in December 1946 he had worked on a knife-fight between Altona black marketeers and had been going round looking for witnesses at the scene, Palmaille, the broad promenade along the bank of the Elbe. It had been a Sunday morning and he was ringing doorbells. Number 49 had a nameplate that said 'Attic Apartment: Brauer', but it was a common name and he thought nothing of it. It had been a bit of shock when he found himself face-to-face with the mayor.

He recognised Stave again and shook his hand with a firm grip. 'Please excuse the fact that there's no heating,' the mayor said. He had his own overcoat on, but didn't seem to be frozen through.

Cuddel Breuer left it to Stave to bring him up to date with the state of affairs.

'We need to do something,' Brauer said after listening to Stave's report. 'Show we mean business.'

Cuddel Breuer nodded. Stave made do with staring expressionlessly into space.

'In all my years I have never experienced a winter as hard as this,' the mayor went on. 'Nobody has any idea when the frost will end. In another week? Or another month? Even two? How are we to get through this winter? Even in the best of times it would have been an enormous challenge. We have burst water pipes all over the city, electricity pylons falling down, coal ships that can't get into port, unusable country roads, I hardly need tell you. But in these extraordinary conditions...'

I hear what you're saying, Stave thought. You've just been mayor for three months. People have expectations. The chief inspector would have liked to help Brauer, he had voted for him in November 1946. But what was he to do? He felt like a failure and just stood there in silence.

'We'll get some more posters printed, warning people to be careful,' Cuddel Breuer said in his place.

'We've put as many officers on the case as we can,' Stave said, finally opening his mouth. 'The British are cooperating. We've gone down more avenues than in any other case since the collapse, even sending out requests to the Soviet zone. And we still don't even know the identity of the victims. I've never seen anything like it.'

The mayor nodded understandingly, smiled even, but remained persistent. 'Obviously we can't just go out and make an arrest, I know that. But I read the newspapers. And I hear what the ordinary people are saying. They write me letters. There's whispering going on, even amongst the city officials.

'Everybody is afraid, everybody is asking who the victims are – and who the murderer is. Everybody has their own theory, everybody suspects everybody else. There are nasty rumours going round.

It's as if all the misery, the deprivation and humiliations are stoking up a hatred that's looking for something to focus on. And this faceless murderer is becoming that focus. As long as it remains as cold as this and there is no arrest, that hate and anger will grow. Sooner or later people are going to accuse the police and the whole administration of incompetence. And sooner or later somebody is going to say what I am sure some people are already thinking, that things didn't used to be like this – under Adolf. I cannot sit here doing nothing while some crazy killer creates a situation where people start to get nostalgic for the Nazis!'

Stave had already heard the same story in one shape or form from Breuer, from public prosecutor Ehrlich, from MacDonald; even Kleensch from *Die Zeit* had said something of the sort. He stared at the mayor, who looked back at them still with a smile on his face, but the chief inspector realised that he was faced with something else here: an ultimatum. Either they produced something or the mayor himself would take over if only so as not to appear helpless. Stave got the message that what mattered was not necessarily catching the killer but at least making sure that the headlines on the story improved, or, better still, disappeared altogether. As long as people calmed down. As long as they forgot about it.

'I assume these posters have already been printed?' Brauer asked.

For the first time since Stave had known him, Cuddel Breuer looked embarrassed. 'We consider it necessary to try once more to find out the victims' identities. And to warn the public.'

'Go ahead, but Stave has told me that he has no great hopes that putting these grim photos up on advertising hoardings all round the city will help in their identification. I suggest that if there are no results this time, in future you conduct your investigation more discreetly.'

'With no headlines. I get the message,' Stave said.

Brauer gave a sad smile. 'My concerns are no longer limited to a few burst water pipes. The hospitals are stretched beyond capacity; they're seeing pulmonary infections, starvation, oedema, frostbite. Every day more people than our lunatic has killed are dying. Seen from a purely statistical point of view, he's a much more minor problem. But psychologically, it's another story. I cannot have this killer become a symbol of our failure. That is all I'm asking of you.'

Breuer and Stave said nothing as they walked back to the Mercedes. Only when the heavy car doors had closed did Stave dare to open his mouth, as if he was afraid they were listening to him in the city hall.

'What happens if the victims are never identified?' he asked. 'And if we never solve the case? If the killer gets away?'

'Then you'd better pray for a thaw soon,' Breuer grumbled, turning the key in the ignition, 'so we don't freeze our backsides off when we're put back into uniform and assigned to traffic duty.'

When Stave, hungry and dejected, finally got back to his office, the anteroom was empty. Erna Berg and MacDonald had gone. But as soon as he entered his own office, he stopped dead. Something was missing. It took him a second to realise what it was.

The murder files were gone.

He hurried over to his desk, certain that he had left them there this morning after Mashcke came in with the news of the fourth murder. He hadn't put them back in his filing cabinet; he'd just dashed out. Had his secretary been tidying up? It had been ages since she'd done anything of the sort. Nonetheless he pulled open the filing cabinet drawer.

It was empty.

Stave looked round in confusion. Don't panic, he told himself, pull yourself together.

He looked in the anteroom: no sign of them.

He slumped into his chair, breathing heavily. Had somebody stolen the files? Maschke? He'd been on his way back to HQ when Stave went off to see Bürger-Prinz. MacDonald, who'd been schmoozing with Erna Berg in the anteroom? Or Erna Berg herself, who had looked at the end of her tether? But why would anybody want to get rid of the murder files?

192 THE MURDERER IN RUINS

For a terrible moment, Stave imagined the rubble murderer himself had stolen into his rooms to erase the few traces of his deeds. Absurd, he told himself. Or was it? Somebody was sabotaging the investigation.

What was he to do? Go to Breuer? After the way the mayor had just hauled them over the coals, Breuer would immediately suspend him for incompetence. Ehrlich? The same. I can't trust anybody, Stave thought. Somebody has it in for me.

He stayed late in the office, going through his notebooks and writing down everything they knew about the four murder cases. He would ask Dr Czrisini to get him copies of the autopsy reports and new copies of the police crime scene photographs. If necessary he could re-interrogate the few witnesses they had. Anna von Veckinhausen. His thoughts turned to her for a moment, but he quickly forced himself to get back to the new development.

When at last he wearily got up from his desk, just before midnight, he knew he could carry on with the investigation, the official investigation into the rubble murderer – and his private investigation into the theft of the files. He would look discreetly for the individual pages, and he would check out the people who up until now he had considered colleagues, even friends.

And he would trust nobody from now on.

Between Colleagues

Ice-cold water on his skin and Sunlight soap the colour of clotted bile. Stave was well aware that the Sunlight soap factory in the suburb of Bahrenfeld boiled up bones. Last year he had done an investigation out there, because he suspected a killer had thrown the body of his victim into the vat. He hadn't been able to prove it, but what did that show?

He scrubbed himself until his skin was burning. He felt he needed to get rid of all the dirt, not just the dirt he could see, but the invisible dirt. And by now it was light enough for him to see his own face in the mirror that hung over the sink. Not that it exactly cheered him up.

Out on the street he was glad not to be in uniform. Nobody recognised him as a policeman. Everywhere he looked he saw the posters: the headline 'Does anyone recognise these people?' And then the photographs of four corpses. The text below was, if you read it properly, an obvious plea for someone to identify at least one of them. Cuddel Breuer had given permission for 60,000 of these posters to be printed. It seemed to Stave as if every wall, every advertising column was covered in them. They had been sent out by courier to the police in other cities, even in the Soviet zone.

I'm imagining this, Stave told himself, but it seemed people were walking more quickly, avoiding eye contact more than ever, wrapping themselves ever deeper in their scarves and overcoats. Nobody walked near the ruins. People avoided them as if they carried the plague. People preferred to walk down the middle of the road than in the shelter of an empty façade or a half-collapsed wall.

In the guts of a bombed-out apartment house somebody had set up a little booth, like an ulcer made out of planks and cardboard. A frozen-solid piece of cloth hung from a line outside it. A cellar window had been built into the front of this makeshift dwelling with torn curtains still twitching from the hand that pulled them to. Somebody is watching me, the chief inspector thought as he passed. Somebody is on the lookout. He felt as if unseen eyes were following him, and turned his head discreetly. There was nobody there. He walked faster, then slowed down, turned abruptly to the right, then took an oblique turn back towards the street he had come from. Nobody. Just the usual bundled figures rushing hither and thither.

You're driving yourself crazy, he thought.

When he got to the office he briefly hoped for a miracle, that the files would be lying back on his desk, that somebody had made a mistake. A harmless accident.

But the documents were still missing.

Stave wandered down the long corridors to find the police photographer. He couldn't send Erna Berg as she wasn't in yet, which was unusual in itself, he noted. He found the photographer in his lab and ordered new copies of the photos of the victims in the rubble murderer case. He paid no attention to the astonished look the request provoked.

When he got back to his office, Erna Berg was just opening the door, her face pale and puffy, her eyes red, but trying not to let any of it show.

The pangs of love, Stave guessed. If she doesn't want to talk to me about it, she doesn't have to. He said 'Good morning' in his usual voice as if there was nothing evidently wrong. 'Please call in Maschke,' he told her, and with just the slightest hint of reticence, 'and tell Lieutenant MacDonald to come over at 2 p.m. this afternoon.'

When Maschke got there, the two of them went together to see Dr Czrisini. Stave wanted to be there when the body was cut open. His colleague went pale when he heard where they were going, and said nothing the whole way.

It took them barely a quarter of an hour, along the embankment, past Dammtor station. If Bürger-Prinz is right, it struck Stave, then I'm walking through the rubble murderer's patch. White steam from a locomotive rose from the steel and glass ceiling of the station. People in overcoats, their heads covered with anything they could find, hundreds of them, just like everywhere else. I'm hardly the most vulnerable person amongst this lot, Stave told himself. The killer won't be lurking here waiting for me. He had no hope of spotting a suspect here.

They hurried on, across the wasteland around the university, turned into Neue Raben Strasse, a peaceful district in Rotherham, near the Alster where the pathology institute was located. Stave wondered how many owners of these privileged villas knew there had been corpses strewn all around the district.

A few minutes later the two of them were standing in the brightly lit room next to the dissecting table with the corpse laid out on it. Thawed now. Dr Czrisini greeted Stave, then Maschke, and introduced them to his young, bespectacled assistant who would take notes on the pathologist's findings during the autopsy.

Stave shook their hands and huddled ever deeper into his overcoat, earning a haughty glance from the assistant. Stave gave him a friendly smile in return. Don't get your hopes up, I'm not going to fall over. He wasn't so sure he could say the same about his vice squad colleague. Maschke had barely shaken hands and looked like he might throw up into one of their chrome basins at any moment. Stave was just cold. Even the two doctors were wearing overcoats under their white coats.

Czrisini started with the head, feeling it and examining it before taking up a scalpel and a bone saw. He proceeded methodically, dictating as he went along, much of it stuff Stave already knew. But then he stopped.

'Small reddish brown dried-up wounds on the left side of the forehead,' the pathologist said. 'Bleeding within the skin, the right side of the forehead swollen above the eyelid. Possibly the result of blows to the head.'

So it wasn't just the old man who'd been beaten before he'd been killed, Stave thought. At least one of the women had tried to defend herself – either that or the killer had been harbouring a deep-seated hatred of her too.

After a bit Czrisini sawed off the top of the skull. A heavy smell filled the room. The assistant glanced discreetly, or so he thought, over at Stave, who gave him a sardonic smile in return.

Maschke, however, gagged, put his right hand over his mouth and dashed for the door, to a scornful look from the assistant. Stave felt like kicking him. People should be glad that not everyone could be so blasé about poking around in corpses.

'Brain already substantially degraded,' Czrisini dictated imperturbably. Then he looked at the chief inspector and added, 'Indicator for a time of death approximately four weeks ago.'

'The twentieth of January then,' Stave murmured.

'Very possibly,' Czrisini said.

The assistant glanced at the pair of them, clearly wondering how on earth they could have come to such an exact date.

'Dental plate in the upper jaw,' said the pathologist. 'Two artificial molars in the lower jaw, gold. Right lingual bone and both upper laryngeal bones broken,' Czrisini noted as he began dealing with the throat. 'Typical in a strangulation case. Almost certainly the cause of death.'

The pathologist slowly made his way down the body, flayed it, and analysed the bones, nerves and internal organs.

'Substantial partially digested foodstuff in the stomach,' he noted. The smell did not improve. Czrisini's assistant glance at Stave again.

'Any idea what she might have eaten?' the chief inspector asked.

'Bread most likely. Or porridge. Enough at least for her not to be hungry.'

Eventually the doctor got to her lower abdomen. Stave came closer out of curiosity.

'No sign of vaginal injury,' Czrisini noted. He took up the scalpel again, sliced open the old scar, entering the woman's body the way a surgeon must once have done.

'Left fallopian tube missing.'

'The result of an operation?'

'Probably. The right-side tube has developed abnormally and the ovary is enlarged.' He stopped, then cut away some tissue which Stave couldn't identify as belonging to any organ.

'There,' the pathologist said, indicating something red in the ovary which the chief inspector didn't recognise. 'Something in the ovary. Saturated with blood. About the size of a cherry.'

Stave felt queasy for the first time. 'An embryo?' he wheezed.

'No, a tumour,' Czrisini replied.

'Cancer?'

'Whether it's benign or malignant, I can't tell easily. But it hardly makes any difference, does it?'

The chief inspector had pulled himself to. 'Could she have had children?'

The pathologist stared long and hard at the corpse's largely eviscerated abdomen, then at the organs he had removed, lying in the steel receptacles. Then he shook his head.

'I doubt it. This woman has growths and deformations in her abdomen and probably had for some time. That is probably why the left fallopian tube was removed. The one on the right is also abnormal. And then there's that tumour in her ovary. In any case there are no indications of a successful birth, no old vaginal scars. No, I would put money on her being childless.'

'When did this woman have her operation?'

'Hard to say. The scars are completely healed. Not in the last 12 months. But probably within the last ten years. Before that she would have been exceptionally young for an invasive procedure such as this.'

'Between 1937 and 1946. In a private surgery?'

Czrisini gave him a surprised look and shook his head. 'No, if it was all done properly it would have been in a hospital with a surgical ward.'

'Did many hospitals in the Reich carry out operations of this nature?'

'In the whole of the Reich? Hundreds.'

'Pity.'

Stave followed the rest of the autopsy in silence. There was nothing more that might have been of any use to him.

A man who was the only other victim to have been beaten defending himself; a woman who might have been the mother of the child. What had cropped up in Bürger-Prinz's practice the other day as an elegant family drama hypothesis had been ripped asunder by the pathologist's scalpel like some rotten internal organ. The woman lying on the dissecting table had never had children. And in all probability, she too had been beaten by the murderer prior to being strangled.

So, what was he left with? Four victims, all probably killed on the same day. Two medallions. The result of the autopsy. This woman was well-to-do. The earring shaped like a starfish. Delicate hands, not those of a manual worker. Nor were those of the old man, or the younger woman. That was too much of a coincidence to be chance, the chief inspector thought. All four victims belonged together.

Did the operation give him any other lead? If the dead woman wasn't from Hamburg – and nobody here had identified her – then where might the operation have been carried out. In the east? Königsberg? In the decimated capital, Berlin? It could have been anywhere from Flensburg to Garmisch. Who might remember her? Where might the surgeon live – if he was still alive, which in the circumstances was probably unlikely.

'I'll send you a report,' Czrisini said, washing his hands.

'Please send me copies of the other three autopsies too,' Stave said, ignoring the stare of the assistant.

'Sorry I brought you with me,' he said to Maschke outside the door of the institute. The vice squad man had been leaning against a wall, smoking, his face still pale and the hand holding the Lucky Strike still shaking slightly. 'I thought you would be interested in this part of working with the murder squad.'

'I'd prefer to stick with my ladies of the night,' Maschke said, not sounding in the least sarcastic.

MacDonald turned up in Stave's office at the agreed time. The lieutenant was pale-faced and shifty-looking. He avoided Erna Berg's eyes. And barely glanced at Stave. He was as nervous as a cat on a hot tin roof.

'Should I put up a notice saying, "Out of bounds for German civilians"?' the chief inspector muttered.

MacDonald stared at him in irritation for a second, as if he'd just been wakened from a dream, then shook his head apologetically.

'We don't even notice things like that, I'm afraid,' he said glibly. 'It's old colonial tradition. Don't let it get to you, old boy.'

'Barriers are still barriers, and I'm no coolie,' Stave replied.

'Nonetheless a sign like that is honest and open,' the lieutenant came back at him, with unexpected seriousness. 'I can assure you that in England we have worse barriers. Often invisible, retrospective barriers – Oxford, certain clubs, the officers' lounge. They somehow manage to make people ashamed of their background, their own family, their own name.'

Stave thought of his own, not exactly glorious career in the police. There had been trouble with the Nazis. Had he ever felt ashamed of his own background? Had he ever been shown the door because he had been born into the wrong family? He wondered what secret battles MacDonald had had to fight to get where he was today.

'I've got nothing against your family name,' he said.

'You even manage to pronounce it properly,' the lieutenant said with a smile.

Stave smiled too. Does no harm to be up to speed at times, he thought but didn't say.

Maschke came in. Following the autopsy, Stave had told him to take a break but he seemed to have recovered. We'll get this done, between the three of us, the inspector thought to himself.

He closed the office door and went over the results of the autopsy. He had sent a photo of the earring to Department S but had had nothing back from them. The other earring had not turned up on the black market yet. An officer had gone round every jeweller in the city that had reopened. Nothing. And nobody remembered having made anything like it. Stave didn't mention his visit to Bürger-Prinz the previous day.

'Anybody got any new ideas?' he asked at the end.

'We could send the photos and descriptions of the three adult victims to every CID department in all former parts of the Reich, or at least those where there are CID departments. Maybe one of them is not just a victim, but was also investigated by the police,' Maschke suggested.

Stave nodded, annoyed with himself. It was a simple idea, he should have thought of it himself. It's gradually getting on top of me, he thought. At least Maschke was still on the ball. 'We should assume that they were all members of one family, a well-to-do family and not from Hamburg.'

The three of them talked it over, although actually only two of them said anything. MacDonald just stared blankly out of the window. For Stave the discussion was more or less déjà vu because it was almost identical to the conversation he'd had with the psychologist. Except that this time there was no suggestion that the older of the two women might have been the child's mother.

'If this is all based on some domestic thing, then we're not likely to get any further as to the motives without some sort of lead,' Maschke concluded. He sounded weary. 'If somebody got mad at Daddy because he took his toy scooter away and as a result decided to exterminate the entire family, how likely are we to find that out? Or if some perverted old uncle attacks his niece? Or if some long-suffering housewife just decided to bump off all her relations? Any of those could be motive enough, but nobody might know anything about it. We don't have anything to go on.'

'Maybe it has something to do with an inheritance,' Stave suggested. The idea had just occurred to him: 'Somebody killing off the rest of the family so he alone can inherit? All the victims were well fed, so they weren't poor. That means there was something worth inheriting. There have always been people willing to murder for money. These days it might not be greed but need that prompts somebody to speed up their inheritance. A couple of old medallions or paintings to sell on the black market. For some people that could mean the difference between freezing to death or not. Starving or not. Although I don't think it's very probable given that the victims were stripped naked. Would somebody killing for an inheritance do that? Still, it's an avenue worth exploring.'

Maschke thought about it for a moment, then nodded. 'Okay, but what do we do next?'

'If we're writing to all the CID departments in the former Reich, then we should ask them for information about any suspicious inheritance claims. Meanwhile in Hamburg and Schleswig-Holstein we should talk to all the registry offices, cemetery administrators and funeral parlours: ask them if anyone matching the descriptions of any of our four victims matches someone reported dead, even under unsuspicious circumstances? Did all the funerals reported actually take place?'

The vice squad man stared at him in astonishment.

'Maybe somebody kills his wife, reports her death to the registrar, and arranges her funeral. He gets his inheritance, but he doesn't actually go ahead with the funeral, because he's afraid somebody will notice the strangulation marks. So he dumps the body in the rubble and doesn't bother with a funeral. No official will bother to find out if the funeral referred to on the death certificate actually took place. Certainly not the way things are at present. And an undertaker isn't necessarily going to run to the registrar or police because a funeral is cancelled. He'll just think the client got a cheaper offer.'

'I wouldn't want to be your rich uncle,' Maschke mumbled.

'We've got two big jobs to do,' Stave said. 'We've got to put together the letter to go out to all the CID offices, registrars and so forth. That means we're going to need dozens of copies of the photos, maybe even hundreds. Frau Berg can deal with that.'

He noticed MacDonald wince at her name. But nobody said anything.

'And we need to send a letter to all the surgeons who've carried out ovarian operations in the last ten years, with photographs of the older woman, both head and abdomen. We need to pay a visit in person to every doctor in a 200-kilometre radius of Hamburg. That will be quicker. You can do that, Maschke.'

'My lucky day,' the vice squad man said, though he didn't seem too unhappy with the task. 'As long as you don't ask me to attend another autopsy, I'm your man.'

He's glad to be out of here, Stave reckoned. Out of the firing line if the rubble murderer causes us any more grief. Maschke had no idea that for all that he seemed to be giving him a task that might be better for his career prospects, the chief inspector had his own reasons.

Stave got to his feet. 'To work.'

Stave hung back a few moments after his men had left the office before going out into the anteroom. Maybe MacDonald and Frau Berg would be grateful for a couple of minutes on their own. But when he finally opened the door, his secretary was sitting behind her desk alone. He told her what her needed her do, and she took a note, though her hand was shaking.

It had got to a point where he could no longer pretend not to have noticed anything. 'Is there something wrong?' he asked. A second too late, he realised how intimate that sounded. 'You of course don't have to tell me anything,' he added quickly, realising that that sounded even more awkward.

Erna Berg made a brave effort at a smile, then collapsed in tears. Stave stood there next to her, embarrassed as he watched the tears roll down her cheeks behind hands covering her eyes, ending in a puddle on the desk. He took out his handkerchief to wipe her face, but then decided that would be even more embarrassingly intimate, and instead just used it to wipe the desk. For what seemed like an eternity he stood there agonising, not knowing what to do, terrified that at any moment somebody would open the door and come in.

Eventually his secretary calmed down, took the handkerchief from his hand and wiped her eyes, sniffling.

'I can hardly give this back to you like this,' she mumbled, putting it in her pocket. 'I'll wash it and iron it and bring it back tomorrow.'

'Keep it,' Stave said.

'One thing less to worry about. I'm sorry for making a scene.'

'Take the rest of the day off.'

She glanced up at him in horror. 'Right now I'm better off here than at home.' She took a deep breath. 'I'm sure you've got wind of...'

'MacDonald?'

'James – Lieutenant MacDonald warned me that you were on to us.'

'You haven't done anything for me to be on to.'

'Thanks for the well-meant lie, but Herr MacDonald and I have become close over the past few weeks.'

'It's not a crime.'

'If you're a married woman, expecting a child and suddenly your husband turns up, now of all times, it's pretty close.'

Stave sat down on the visitor's chair in front of the desk. 'Turbulent times,' he mumbled.

'The thing is, I thought I was a widow. My husband was reported missing. No news, nothing to indicate he was still alive. You know how it is.' She blushed fiercely and turned her eyes to the floor. 'Then Lieutenant MacDonald arrives in your office. We talked together. We are both lonely, single, one thing led to another. It was never part of the plan that I would get pregnant so quickly. But we want the child. We've been dreaming of a future together. Including my son. Herr MacDonald wants to adopt him. We want to move to England, at some stage. To get away from all the rubble here.' She put her hands to her eyes. 'And then, two days ago, there's a knock on the door. I thought it was James. I was surprised, I opened the door and – there's my husband, standing there. A pale shadow of his former self. With just one leg. And that look in his eyes, lost, helpless and yet at the same time somehow brutal.'

She burst into tears again. Stave waited until she had recovered, relieved that she wasn't looking at him. His whole body was wracked with anger and envy. Envy that the husband she thought lost forever had returned, while there was still no trace of his son. And anger that she wasn't even pleased by the fact.

'Does your husband have any idea about your...' he tried to find a suitable word, but couldn't and ended up using the rather lame, '...little difficulty?'

She shook her head. 'For the time being James and I are not seeing one another outside work. It's been a shock for him too. But I can't keep my condition a secret forever. It's not as if I can pretend it's my husband's baby. I can't. You understand that.'

Stave understood only too well. A man who had left one of his legs somewhere in Russia and had returned to his young wife. A wife who looks at him with horror when he knocks on her door. A wife who pulls away from him in bed at night as if he had the plague. He wondered if even his little son didn't dare go near the man with the disability?

'What are you going to do?'

She pulled herself together all of a sudden, forced a smile. 'First of all, I'm going to deal with all these letters, Chief Inspector.'

'I'm sorry,' Stave said, getting to his feet. 'Obviously it's none of my business.'

Stave stood looking at the city map with the four red tacks. Three in the east, one in the west. The three crime scenes east of the Alster were barely 15 minutes' walk apart. But from there to Lappenbergs Allee was at least an hour on foot.

That means the killer had access to a car or a truck.

Stave thought about what that meant. It meant that the killer had to be one of the very few Germans who were allowed to drive. Or that he was British. On the other hand, motor vehicles were anything but inconspicuous. And none of the places where the bodies had been found were directly accessible by a vehicle – which meant that the bodies would have to be carried from the vehicle on the street to the spot where they were found. Hardly possible for that not to be noticed during the day. And at night, a vehicle of any sort would have been all the more noticeable because the British hardly ever drove at night and it was expressly forbidden for Germans.

Goddamnit, thought Stave. How come nothing fits? Every time some little detail messes up the theory. He thought back to the last autopsy. Why would a killer apparently so greedy that he even steals underclothes ignore a woman's gold teeth? Gold would buy you anything you wanted on the black market.

Was he just stripping them to cover his tracks? But if he wasn't killing them to rob them, if he didn't rape them, if he had no family grudge against them, why on earth did he kill them in the first place?

Stave was so angry he could have bashed his head against the wall. Angry with the murderer, but even more so with himself, and with his colleagues who weren't helping, and who were either obsessed with their own private dramas, or even sabotaging his efforts.

By now it was gone 6 p.m. The anteroom was empty, the corridor was deserted. Right, thought Stave, if I can't get anywhere with the main task, maybe I should investigate the other one. The private one.

He left his room and went quietly along the dimly lit corridor, glancing cautiously in the other offices where the doors were open. It was a quiet evening. Stave reached the stairwell, went down two floors and stopped. Up until that point, anybody who might have seen him would have thought he was just going home. But from here on he was in foreign territory. The chief inspector took a deep breath and entered the realm of the vice squad.

There was a corridor with offices on either side, just like upstairs in the homicide department. There were no lights on anywhere. Stave hurried down the corridor in the dark, taking stock of the nameplates on the doors.

Police Inspector Lothar Maschke.

He glanced around, then tried the door handle.

Not locked.

Stave slipped through the door silently and closed it behind him. His heart was pounding. He had never done anything forbidden in all his life, and yet here he was, breaking into a colleague's office.

He took his torch from his pocket, turned it on and looked round. There was no anteroom, just one tiny office. It looked messy, piles of reports and police mug shots, notebooks, empty Lucky Strike packets all over the desk. An overflowing ashtray. A chair carelessly pushed back from the desk rather than neatly tucked in. On the wall, held up with four rusty tacks at a bit of an angle, was a map of Hamburg with the places where the bodies were found marked with pencil crosses. On another wall was Maschke's police academy diploma. That wasn't straight either.

Stave walked over to the desk, taking care not to touch anything. A framed photo of a serious-looking elderly woman. The chief inspector recalled that his colleague still lived at home with his mother. Apart from that there was nothing personal. Just the pile of stuff on the desk, copies of the missing person posters, the autopsy reports, the police photographs, lists of surgeons and dentists.

But not the missing files.

Stave pulled on thin black leather gloves, then began sorting through the paper, taking care to leave it exactly as it had been. You never knew if the mess might be deliberate.

Nothing.

The desk drawers next. There were two on either side. Top left: cigarettes, lighters. Stave raised his eyebrows. A lot of them for somebody on a police salary. Either his colleague sent half his pay literally up in smoke or he had sources a detective ought not to.

The lower drawer was deep and contained index cards with photos. Stave pulled one out and studied it. It showed police mug shots, with names next to them. Notes on the other side, in Maschke's handwriting.

'Street name: Lena or the Dane.'

'Carries knife on each ankle.'

'Willy Warncke's girl (Fat Willy).'

'Yvonne Delluc. Has family here.'

'Note: Isabelle is favourite with British officers. Don't go hard on her.'

'Arrested 5.1.47 black marketing, one pair nylon stockings, 20 cigarettes.'

The chief inspector flicked through the pile. Whores. Pimps. Whores. Pimps. No punters. Astonishing how many of his targets Maschke had categorised in his brief time with the vice squad.

The index cards were in no recognisable order, but Stave reckoned Maschke would know where each was. There's definitely some sort of order in this apparent chaos, he thought to himself.

Right upper drawer: pencils, a broken sharpener, notebooks with pages torn out. There were one or two that were full but that Maschke clearly intended to use again. Next to them a couple of rubbers and two bent paperclips, a few rusty tacks and flakes of tobacco.

Lower right drawer as deep as that on the left: a dozen or so scraps of paper, mostly scrunched up, another three notebooks. Stave shone the pale milk beam from his torch in and glanced over the scraps of paper. Columns of figures. The pieces of paper were covered in scribbled numbers. Sometimes there were just a few on one sheet, sometimes there were lots. The notebooks were also stuffed with numbers. Telephone numbers? Safe combinations? There was nothing to give a clue as to what they meant. No names, not even a single letter.

Beneath the sheets of paper was a current Reichsbahn train timetable for all the occupation zones – not much use this winter when nobody had any idea when, or if, a train might depart.

Below that were topographical maps, the sort they had handed out in the Wehrmacht, large scale – Northern Germany, Lower Saxony, Denmark, the Netherlands, Belgium and Luxembourg, France, Bavaria and Austria, Switzerland.

Stave stared in amazement at the neatly folded maps. Obviously the area round Hamburg was of interest to a detective, but foreign countries? He drew up a map in his head: all the countries to the north, west and south of the old Reich borders. Maschke had been in the Wehrmacht, on the western front. But why had he kept all these maps? Why had a U-boat sailor even had them? Stave went through them again. They seemed pristine, except for the one of France. The lines along the folds were white. There were tears around the edges. He took it out and spread it carefully on the piled-high desk. The map covered all of France, and was the size of the desk.

There were pencil marks here and there, military signs, letters and numbers, probably abbreviations for units. Dates next to them. Several of the marks had been erased and written over, or sometimes just crossed out and something else scribbled in.

It painted the picture of a retreat.

The oldest note was from 1 June 1944, almost on the Atlantic coast to the north of Bordeaux. Then there was a line that went north to Normandy. The Allied invasion, Stave thought to himself. Then the line fell back to the east. The last entry was near Strasbourg, towards the end of November 1944.

As the chief inspector was folding the map up again, the beam fell on a faded official Reich stamp on the rear: an eagle and a swastika, with a few scribbles beneath. Stave was just about to put the map back with the others when he suddenly froze: in the midst of the stamp was writing, the double runes of the SS.

And underneath, barely legible, a name: 'Hans Herthge.' In Maschke's handwriting.

Stave was wondering what it might mean when he heard a noise in the corridor outside.

Footsteps.

The chief inspector had just seconds to think. Whoever it was would almost certainly walk straight past. But what if they didn't? What if they found him in here with a torch peering into the desk drawers of one of his colleagues? Should he hide? But where?

Brazen it out. He closed the drawer, turned off the torch, shoved the map of France and his leather gloves into his overcoat pocket and turned on the desk reading light. If somebody spotted him, then he would act as if he had nothing to hide.

The footsteps got louder, then stopped. Somebody was standing right outside the door. Stave bent his head over the desk as if he was looking for something.

The handle was turned. Quietly. Stave looked up. It was public prosecutor Ehrlich.

The two men stared at one another for a minute, both of them clearly awkward.

'Good evening,' Stave said, breaking the silence first. 'Can I help you?'

'Have I got the wrong floor? I thought this was Inspector Maschke's office.'

'Spot on, but I fear my colleague has already gone home for the day.'

'And you've been transferred to the vice squad?' The prosecutor looked puzzled.

Stave used the few moments to make up a story. 'Tomorrow Maschke is to go round all surgeons who might have carried out an operation like that undergone by the fourth victim. I've already sent him out to talk to medical people. The truss, the dentures, you remember? It occurred to me that there might be specialist doctors who deal with hernias in men and abdominal operations in women. If the victims belonged to the same family, that might be a lead. Given that Maschke had already left, I thought I'd look and see if I could find anything. But,' he nodded at the mess on the desk, 'I guess I'll have to wait and ask him tomorrow.'

Ehrlich looked at him sceptically for a moment, then smiled and said, 'I understand.' It didn't sound as if he understood anything. 'Then I will also just have to wait to speak to the inspector. Pity.'

The prosecutor made a little bow, then closed the door behind him. The steps receded down the corridor.

Stave took a deep breath. Cold sweat ran down the back of his neck. Had Ehrlich swallowed his story? Would he mention this unfortunate meeting to Maschke? At the very least he would now have to mention his idiotic idea about the surgeons to the vice squad man, if only to keep his story consistent.

He waited a few minutes more, until he was sure that Ehrlich was really gone, put the papers back as they were, wondered if he should replace the map of France but decided in the end to hold on to it. For the time being. Until he had worked out what the 'Hans Herthge' business was about.

He turned off the light, went out into the corridor, and left the dark building as quickly as possible. It was only when he was outside, on the cold and draughty square, that it occurred to Stave that Ehrlich hadn't told him what he was doing looking for Maschke so late in the day.

Dark streets. The ruins like ghostly castles. Somewhere the motor of a British jeep growled. A curtain, frozen solid, blown out from a load of fallen tiles, waving back and forth in the wind. Otherwise it was painfully quiet. Over the past few years Stave had got so used to the view of the city in ruins that he hardly noticed it any more. But now, hurrying home, he felt uncomfortable, insecure. Threatened.

Shadows haunted empty windows. Reflections of half-destroyed walls. Corpses? Or a killer lurking in wait for some nocturnal wanderer? I'm becoming paranoid, the chief inspector told himself, not for the first time.

He too now walked down the middle of streets, as far as possible from the ruined lots. He felt a tingle down his spine, as if somebody was watching him. Turned on his heel. Nobody there.

But still he felt he was not alone.

He reached for his gun, flicked off the safety on the FN22, began walking faster despite the pain in his left leg. It seemed to take forever.

When at last Stave got to his building, he took the steps two at a time and threw open the door to his apartment. His heart was pounding; he was covered in sweat and panting for breath.

I'm acting like an idiot, like a rookie, he told himself. If somebody had come up to me to ask the time I might have shot them. He waited until his hand stopped trembling then clicked the safety on his FN22 back on. I need to get more sleep, he thought, and I need to get warmed up properly for once. If only this bloody frost would come to an end. But at the same time, that was something else he was afraid of: the smell of stinking corpses thawing.

He got himself dinner: bread that tasted of paper, a thin slice of cheese, water, an old potato that needed heating for an hour on the stove before he could get it down his throat. Then he lay down on his back, waiting for sleep, like a dead man stretched out on a bed, motionless, under a ton of tiredness. Yet something else was weighing on his mind, holding him back from drifting off to dreamland.

Eventually his hand found the radio. The old box gave off a yellowish glow as it warmed up. He hadn't turned it on in months. In the 'brown days' all you got was endless Liszt, and then, 'The High Command of the Wehrmacht announces…' The shrill voices of Hitler or Goebbels interspersed with the cries of 'Heil!' from the devout in some sports arena, like a storm of hail on a window. Then Wagner. He was so fed up with it all that he preferred not to turn the radio on at all. He knew of colleagues and neighbours who secretly listened to the BBC, but he never dared.

But today there was supposed to be a new station starting up: *Nordwestdeutscher Rundfunk,* Northwest German Radio, run by British officers and young German journalists. A sort of BBC for Germans. Stave had heard about it but not shown much interest, although he had overheard colleagues now and then looking forward to it starting.

But now, as sleep wouldn't come, he gave it a go. At least it would give the illusion there was somebody else in the room. An announcer, then a whooshing sound, the crackle of static, complete silence and darkness for a few moments when the electricity gave up. And then he was listening to a play. Stave didn't get the name of the writer, and only half listened to the narrator; he just enjoyed having the sound and the glow of the radio, a splinter of normality.

He heard the story of a man returning from the war, rejected by everybody. Heard the man talking to the Elbe. Odd, he thought, how could anybody talk to the Elbe when it's under a metre of ice?

And gradually he drifts into a dream in which his son is talking to the Elbe and the waves have somehow taken on the contours of Margarethe. It's warm, the undamaged apartment buildings shine in the sun. Stave feels sad and lucky at the same time as he glides beyond the dream into the realm of deepest darkness where he sleeps as he has not done for years.

Discovery

Stave had been in his office on the telephone since 7 a.m. His fingertips had turned red from dialling so much and he was now using a pencil. He had tried on Friday to get hold of Maschke. He was desperate to speak to him before Ehrlich so that he could give him his version of their evening encounter in his office. But his efforts had been in vain. He had completely failed to reach his vice squad colleague in any hotel, police station or even hospital in the whole of northern Germany. On several occasions he had reached people who had seen Maschke recently, often just a few hours earlier. It's as if he was trying to avoid me, Stave thought. But that was absurd.

He had spent the weekend at the station – which gave him lots of time to think things over. The longer this awful winter lasted the less coal there was to deliver. And more and more locomotives were out of action due to burst pipes or frozen boilers. By now there were fewer trains in a day than there used to be in an hour.

Stave spent his time wandering up and down deserted platforms, if only to keep the cold from getting to his leg. He was worried because he had convinced himself that Ehrlich had wanted to talk to Maschke about him. Or that Maschke had unexpectedly come back for the weekend and gone into his office. Stave imagined Maschke coming into the room that appeared to be in such mess, maybe just to pick up a packet of cigarettes, and discovering that one particular piece of paper amidst the pile on his desk was not at the oblique angle he had left it. Then he imagined Maschke checking out the whole desktop and working out that his carefully arranged chaos had been disturbed. He would know that it had been thoroughly searched because he would open the lower right desk drawer, go through his maps and realise that one of them was missing. Then Ehrlich would call...

And when he wasn't thinking about Maschke, then his troubled thoughts would revolve around the rubble murderer. What if he was here at the station too, also looking out for someone? What if the murderer came across Stave's son before he did, found him clambering off a train exhausted and emaciated? A weakened veteran returning from the war would be easy prey. A beat officer would ring Stave up and say, 'We've got another body.' He would go out to some ruined lot and find the body of a naked young man ... approach it and then be horrified to recognise it.

The chief inspector had paced the vast station concourse aimlessly like a caged tiger, unsettled, angry. When the last train had spluttered out of the station in the evening he was exhausted, as always, frozen, disappointed and yet at the same time somehow relieved that nothing had happened. That another weekend had gone by uneventfully.

Suddenly Stave flinched as the phone rang. He grabbed the receiver.

'Maschke here.'

He heard crackling, swooping sounds, as if his colleague was calling from the North Pole.

'I've been trying to get through to you for an hour. What's going on? It's constantly engaged.'

Stave did his best not to allow any sign of relief into his voice.

'Had a few calls to make,' he replied. 'Nothing important. How about you?'

Maschke was calling from Travemünde, cursing the hoteliers as racketeers. Five hundred Reichsmarks per night for a room with a sea view. Breakfast with real coffee, marmalade, a bottle of whisky at night for 800 Reichsmarks.

'The hotel is full,' he shouted over the crackling line. 'It's just that the clientele has changed.'

'It sounds like business people on expenses, like it used to be.' Stave couldn't resist a tinge of *Schadenfreude*. Cynical old Maschke who hunted down pimps and hookers but deep down couldn't stop believing that people were basically good.

Or then again? He remembered the map of France with the SS stamp and the name Hans Herthge.

Should I just call him 'Herthge' in the middle of the call and see how he reacts, Stave wondered, but quickly jettisoned the idea. He would have too much to explain if he did. Instead he told Maschke to check out surgeons who had carried out both hernia and ovarian operations. He chose his words carefully, kept it vague, didn't say expressly that he'd been in Maschke's office the previous evening, but at least if he should find out from Ehrlich then he would be able to say that he'd mentioned the idea to him on the phone.

His vice squad colleague said nothing for a moment or two. Was he suspicious? Then he answered, 'Okay, I'll try that.'

Despite the crackling on the line Stave thought there was a sceptical tone to his voice. 'Hernias and ovarian operations. So far I've covered Hamburg to the Baltic coast. Now I'll take it as far as the Danish border. Then from the North Sea south. It'll take days. So far I've talked to some 20 surgeons. You wouldn't believe how many blokes muck about with women's down-under bits. But nobody admits to dealings with the woman we're talking about. And I asked every doctor I've spoken to if they thought she could have children after an operation like that, and they all said it was highly unlikely.'

'What about our other victims?'

'I've shown every doctor I've visited every damn police photo-graph of every victim, the old guy, the younger woman, the kid. It would appear that not one of our victims ever went to a doctor. They all seem to have been remarkably healthy. None of them can ever have suffered anything more than a sore throat.'

'Check in with headquarters every two days, even if you don't come up with anything. But be thorough. And check out older, retired doctors. I'd prefer you wasted an extra day rather than took an hour too few.'

At least that's got Maschke out of my hair, he thought as put the receiver down.

By now there was a constant rattle of keys on the typewriter in the outer office. Frau Berg had arrived.

'How are you?' Stave asked her, unnecessarily. She looked as if she hadn't slept for three days.

'Fine,' she lied. The clatter of the typewriter got louder.

'Get me a few more folders for my in-tray. I need to sort the files out.' Stave was just floating a theory.

But Erna Berg just nodded.

The word 'files' didn't seem to make her nervous. Of all his colleagues she had had the best opportunity to steal the murder files. But she had no obvious motive. She didn't react at all to the word. It was always possible, of course, that she was just a good actress. But in that case wouldn't she have done a better job in covering up the business with her husband and MacDonald?

'Anything else I can do for you?' she looked up at him.

Stave realised that he had been staring at her, reddened, and shook his head. Then he thought again. 'Yes, ask MacDonald to come in.'

She managed the faintest of smiles, then said, 'I'd love to but the lieutenant has disappeared.'

'Disappeared?'

'Gone. Vanished without trace. Nobody at his office can tell me where he is. I've been ringing regularly, and not just on business. Sometimes he disappears for a few hours, but sometimes for a day or more. And then suddenly James is back again. I have no idea what he's up to these days. Maybe he has another woman.'

'I doubt it,' the chief inspector said, although in reality he didn't know MacDonald well enough to say anything of the sort.

'Keep trying.'

'You don't have to tell me. I'll let you know as soon as I get hold of him. '

Stave went back into his office. Maschke was out of the way. MacDonald had disappeared. Erna Berg was preoccupied with her own problems. Cuddel Breuer and Ehrlich weren't on his heels – a weekend without finding a fresh victim had given him breathing space, a stay of execution before they started on at him again.

I'll go through everything all over again, on my own, thoroughly, he told himself. I shall interview all the most important witnesses once again. 'Check with the transport department if there's a car available,' he told his secretary.

'For the whole day?'

'Half a day. Or just an hour or two, if that's all they can let me have.'

'Where's is it to go to?'

'Out. On the trail of a murderer.' He didn't know what else to say.

Half an hour later, Stave screeched the old Mercedes round a tight corner on to the Elbe embankment. He'd wondered for a moment or two if he should have called first to tell them he was coming, but in the end decided against it. If they turned him away from the Warburg Children's Health Home then he could play it by the book and get MacDonald to help him if necessary, if he showed up again, that was. He wondered for a moment or two why MacDonald had gone missing, and if perhaps Erna Berg's suspicions were justified.

He had to stop at the gates of the Warburg building. They were locked and there was nobody around. Stave rang the bell. Eventually a teenager appeared on the other side and said, 'What do you want?'

Stave automatically began to fish in his overcoat pocket for his police ID, then changed his mind and simply gave his name, without mentioning any rank, and added, 'I need to speak to Madame Dubois.'

The boy disappeared. A minute passed. Then another. The chief inspector began to worry that he'd made a mistake. But eventually the slender figure of the villa's warden appeared, opened the gate and waved him in.

'It's a shame you haven't found your murderer yet,' Thérèse Dubois said.

'What makes you think I haven't already arrested him?'

'If you had, would you be here?'

Stave followed her into the villa's winter garden, wondering how much he ought to tell her.

'I'm not here about the rubble murderer,' he said, sitting down.

'Another investigation?'

'Maybe. I don't know yet. It's early days.'

'And you need my help?'

'I need a little girl's help.'

Thérèse Dubois smiled. A knowing smile, Stave reckoned.

'Anouk Magaldi. You asked me her name when you were last here. I wondered why, and wondered when you would come back and tell me.'

'Can I have a word with her?'

'Why?'

'She seemed to know one of my colleagues. It was as if she recognised him.'

Thérèse Dubois looked at him silently.

'My colleague knows nothing about this,' the chief inspector added. 'I have reason to doubt just who my colleague really is.'

'You think he might have been a Nazi?'

'Lots of people were Nazis. What I want to know is what sort of Nazi.'

'You mean if he might be somebody public prosecutor Ehrlich ought to be interested in?'

Stave dithered for a moment, then said, 'Yes.'

'I'll go and fetch her.'

A few minutes later the little girl was standing in front of him: skinny for her age, arms and legs like matchsticks, big eyes, long dark hair. Stave held out his hand for her to shake, but she paid no attention, just stood staring at him, cautiously.

'Do you speak German?' he asked.

She shook here head.

'I'll translate for her,' Thérèse Dubois said.

'When you saw my colleague, why did you do this?' Stave asked, making the throat-cutting gesture with his hand.

The warden had barely said two words before the little girl broke into a torrent of words, speaking as if she was out of breath, running, made a gesture as if she was throwing something, ducked down to avoid it, closed her eyes, looked terrified, made as if to run off.

Stave didn't understand a word of it, but even before Thérèse Dubois had begun to translate for him, he realised he was going to hear a story of some atrocity.

'Anouk is Jewish. She and her relatives lived in a little village northwest of Limoges,' the warden explained. 'So they had to be particularly discreet during the German occupation. In the summer of '44 soldiers came into their village and they hid in a cellar, something most of the other inhabitants didn't feel the need to do.'

'What sort of soldiers?'

'Germans. Waffen-SS. The invasion of Normandy had happened four days earlier. The soldiers were on their way to the front. Most of the French thought the German occupation would soon be over. The Resistance was launching ever more attacks. And the SS had decided to take their revenge. There and then.'

Stave said nothing, waited for her to continue.

'They took all the men and teenage boys, locked them in sheds or garages and shot them. They forced all the women and children into the church. Then they set fire to it, threw hand grenades in and fired into the blaze. By the end nearly everybody was dead, more than 600 people, a third of them children.'

Anouk's parents were discovered and shot. She only escaped by hiding behind a table overloaded with bits of wood and tools. The SS men didn't notice her. But she crept over to a window, looked out and saw it all. After the massacre the SS set fire to all the remaining houses. When it finally got too hot for her in the cellar, she sneaked out. Nobody spotted her, and the next day she bumped into a Resistance group. That was what saved her. Only a handful of others survived.'

Stave looked at the little girl and said, 'And the man I was with the other day was one of the soldiers?'

The warden translated. The little girl nodded. Then another torrent of words and gestures. She walked to one side and put her finger to her throat.

'He belonged to the troop that dragged her parents from the cellar and later she saw him firing into the church and laughing.'

Stave closed his eyes and tried to imagine Maschke as a tough young man in the black uniform with the peaked hat that came low over the eyes, with the death's head on it. Or more likely in his grey SS helmet with the twin lightning flashes on each side, a cigarette in his mouth.

'What was the name of the village?' he asked eventually.

'Oradour-sur-Glane.'

'When was the massacre?'

'10 June 1944.'

Stave pulled out the map of France he had taken from Maschke's drawer and laid it out on the floor. The girl stared at him silently.

'Can you point out on this map where the village is?'

The warden looked at it and finally picked a spot almost right in the middle of the country.

The chief inspector bent down and looked at the map. Exactly at the point she indicated was a pencil mark: '10 June '44.'

On the way back Stave drove unusually slowly. Lothar Maschke's real name was Hans Herthge, and he wasn't on a U-boat but was a soldier in the Waffen-SS. He was a murderer, jointly responsible for the deaths of more than 600 people.

And we're getting worked up over four deaths, but then corrected himself: we should be getting worked up – murder is murder.

What was he to do? He had the testimony of an eight-year-old. Thérèse Dubois promised him the little girl would testify in court, as if Stave might go there and then to the public prosecutor. But what could Ehrlich do? If he was found guilty, Maschke would face the death penalty. But was the testimony of an eight-year-old girl enough to sentence a police officer to death? And could it even be proved that Maschke was Hans Herthge? There was the map, but Stave had stolen it from his colleague's desk under questionable circumstances. What might a skilled defence lawyer do with that? The likely result was that Maschke would walk free for lack of evidence. And Stave would be a grass. The man who ratted on a colleague. He might as well pick up his hat and coat and leave the force.

I need to talk to Ehrlich, he thought to himself. In confidence. See what we can do. Get more proof. Then all of a sudden he slammed on the brakes, and the car came to a juddering halt.

Ehrlich had been in Maschke's office that evening. He hadn't told Stave why he wanted to talk to the vice squad man. Maybe he hadn't wanted to talk to him. Maybe the public prosecutor wanted to do the same as the chief inspector: to rummage round in Maschke's desk drawers, but for a different reason. Maybe Ehrlich knew something about Maschke's dark secret. What was it Thérèse Dubois had said? That Ehrlich was always digging up new cases. That he was out for revenge. Somebody who has a lot of accounts to settle with the Nazis.

Stave stared out of the dirty windscreen. A man pushing a bicycle with bent forks along the pavement stared at him suspiciously, then hurried on his way. The chief inspector ignored him. Who was playing what game here? No wonder Maschke hadn't wanted to be in the building when they had first come to the children's home. No wonder that he wasn't happy with their research into Displaced Persons. He must have been afraid somebody he had nearly killed might recognise him? Any Jew, any refugee who had survived something like that might have recognised him and blown his cover. No wonder Maschke had been so keen to suggest the killer was some black marketeer. No wonder he had used physical force to try to make the first possible suspect they had come across confess.

Was it Maschke who had stolen the files then? Was there something in them that might have given a clue to his SS past? If so, what was it? A shiver ran down Stave's spine and he knew it wasn't because of the cold wind blowing into the car.

His thoughts turned to the public prosecutor. Had Ehrlich ever been interested in the rubble murderer at all? Or had he already had his suspicions about Maschke/Herthge, and was just using the case to lure him into a trap? Had the public prosecutor been poking around late at night in Stave's own office, like he had attempted to do in Maschke's? Could it have been Ehrlich who had taken the case files? There again, Stave couldn't think of any reason to suspect him, any motive, anything he had said or done.

As he was leaving Thérèse Dubois had told him she didn't think the evidence of an eight-year-old would be enough to convict Maschke. She had said it with a sad smile. 'It's easier to kill 600 people in a single day than to bring a murderer to justice,' were her words.

'He'll end up in court, I promise you,' Stave had replied. 'I'll find the proof I need.'

Now he was wondering if that was a promise he could keep.

Back at the office he had to drag himself down the corridor, ignoring the pain in his leg and the fact that he was hungry. Erna Berg was just putting down the telephone receiver when he walked in.

'MacDonald?'

'He called. He's on his way here.'

'Anything else I ought to know about?'

'No. Nobody called. Nobody's been in.'

'No more dead bodies.'

Erna Berg gave a shy little smile and said, 'May I take the afternoon off? I'd like to go and see the gynaecologist.'

Stave gave her a look. Gynaecologist or abortionist? What do I care, he realised and nodded. 'Off you go. Doesn't look like there'll be much more to do here today.' He hesitated for a minute and then added, 'Good luck,' but so quietly that she almost certainly didn't hear him.

After his secretary had left Stave spent the next half-hour on the phone, ringing round hotels and police stations on the Baltic coast, but he couldn't track down Maschke. He's probably with some doctor, he thought to himself.

Should he call up Maschke's personnel file? Maybe he'd find some clue there as to his change of identity. A forged document? Some contradiction in his supposed CV? But what would he tell the personnel department he wanted the file for? That an old acquaintance had made some allegation against him? But why would he want the whole file? Better to leave it where it was. There was nothing for it. Stave would have to go and speak to the public prosecutor. Ehrlich would find it easier to get hold of the files discreetly.

But he felt better nonetheless. I'm getting somewhere, he thought to himself. I just have to deal with this my way. Maschke's real name is Herthge. That's a discovery in itself.

There was a knock on his door. It was MacDonald.

'I've finally managed to track down that story Anna von Veckinhausen told you,' the lieutenant said. 'On the day in question she did indeed sell a painting to a British officer outside the Garrison Theatre. I've even seen it. Best quality German kitsch. Price: 520 Reichsmarks.' Then he took a deep breath, and said, 'By the way, where's your secretary?' – trying hard and failing to sound casual about it.

'She's gone to see a gynaecologist,' Stave told him.

MacDonald put his head in his hands and began rubbing his temples. For the first time he struck the chief inspector as weary. 'It seems I don't have much luck with women,' he muttered.

'Frau Berg looks to me as if she's head over heels in love,' Stave said stiffly, not really knowing what to say to make the man feel better.

MacDonald smiled. 'Not exactly the way a married woman is

supposed to be in her situation. Believe me, I know what I'm talking about.' He lapsed into silence.

Stave said nothing, waiting to see what was coming next.

'Erna is the second woman to have meant something in my life,' the officer eventually added. 'The first was a wonderful, clever woman with a real lust for life but unfortunately married to one of my brother officers in the same regiment. The son of a lord. Heir to a stately home, a vast fortune and half a dozen noble titles.'

'Hardly a fair fight then.'

'More like a scandal. She might well have chosen me in the end. But then rumours about us began to circulate in the officers' club.'

'Those invisible barriers?' Stave said.

MacDonald gave a thin smile. 'An aristocratic English lady and a Scottish nobody. It would have been the end of her social life. Mine too. So she went back to her husband. Everything according to the rules.' The lieutenant waved his hand as if swatting an irritating fly. 'Good enough reason to volunteer for the front line, don't you think?'

'A good reason to stay here,' Stave told him with a smile. 'Frau Berg is certainly no aristocrat,' he said, encouragingly.

Speaking of aristocratic ladies, he thought to himself, time for me to interview a witness or two. Starting with Anna von Veckinhausen.

He took the tram, getting off at the stop near the charred wall. The street that still had street lamps. He was glad it was barely 3 p.m. The food shops had already closed so there were no queues outside their doors. Just a few children who'd had lessons in the morning playing out on the street despite the cold. Lots of children were still at school at that time, and their parents were either at work or out somewhere doing deals on the black market. The streets between the ruins were all but empty.

The ideal time to commit a murder, the chief inspector told himself. Why do I always assume they happened in the late afternoon or evening, he wondered. There'd be almost no likelihood of a witness to an early afternoon killing.

Could that fit in with Anna von Veckinhausen's story? It was already dusk when she had spotted the figure she mentioned. But by then, Stave reckoned, the old man they had found near Lappenbergs Allee was already dead. The murderer had hidden the body and stripped it. That took time. Maybe the witness had disturbed him, wandering through the rubble as it was getting dark.

The Nissen huts at the crossroads. Empty streets. The barracks, almost in the middle of the city, where Anna von Veckinhausen lived. Or to be more precise, where she had disappeared behind a door the evening he had been with her. He hadn't been able to see inside. So what now? He couldn't be sure that she was there. Maybe she was out looking for more antiques somewhere in the rubble? One way or the other, he could hardly ring up in advance to tell her he was coming. There were no telephones in the Nissen huts.

The chief inspector knocked on the door. It sounded as if he was banging an empty oil drum. An old man with no teeth opened the door instantly, as if he'd been lurking behind it waiting for him. His shirt was stained and he smelled of onions. Stave's stomach rumbled.

The chief inspector gave his name, but didn't mention any police rank, or show him his ID. He didn't want to embarrass Anna von Veckinhausen by revealing that he was a policemen. He asked for her by name.

'Never heard the name before,' the old man grumbled, giving him a suspicious look.

Had Stave's witness been leading him on? Maybe she didn't live here after all? He gave the old man a description of her.

'Oh, her,' he replied, stepping back to let Stave in.

He walked in. How long had this old boy been living in the same Nissen hut as Anna von Veckinhuasen without even knowing her name?

The cast-iron stove in the centre of the hut, smaller than a beer barrel, was burning, orange flames glowing through the rips in the ragged sheet hanging inside the door. There was a smell of rust in the stale air. The Nissen hut wasn't much larger than a weekend allotment shed. Within seconds Stave's face was glowing from the warmth of the stove, but his back, which faced the outside wall was still cold. If that stove were to go out, everybody in here would freeze, he thought. He wondered briefly if they took turns at night to tend the fire. Like people did back in the Stone Age.

Grey Wehrmacht blankets hanging from wires divided the Nissen hut into four separate areas, centred on the stove in the middle. The old man walked past the stove to the rear left partition and shouted out 'Visitor' as if he was on a parade ground.

It took just a few seconds before Anna von Veckinhausen appeared from behind the blanket. Stave got a glimpse of a camp bed and two wooden vegetable crates turned upside down, obviously serving as a stool and table, a trunk, and fixed to the hut wall a little oil painting of a church in winter.

She quickly pulled the blanket behind her to stop him seeing anything else. Maybe she has something she wants to hide, Stave thought. Or maybe she's just embarrassed by her circumstances. She looked exhausted and not exactly delighted to see him.

'I just wanted to ask you a few more questions,' he said.

'Does your newspaper friend need some more information for one of his stories?'

Before Stave could reply she had disappeared behind the blanket again. For a second or two, the chief inspector was afraid she would just leave him standing there like an awkward schoolboy. What was he to do? He could hardly force her to answer any more questions. At least not unless he requested a formal interview. But he had no real grounds to do so. What would he do if she went and complained to her British officer friends about him? To his relief, she appeared again after a few minutes, in an overcoat and headscarf.

The old man was still standing next to the stove, watching their every move.

'Shall we go for a walk?' Anna von Veckinhausen suggested, loud enough for him to hear.

Stave would have preferred to stay where he was, soaking up the heat from the stove, but he nodded, pleased that she was ready to talk to him at all.

They wandered through the ruins as far as the Wandse. Before the war it had been a river, squeezed in here and there, but with grassland or trees on either side, all of which had carved a green line through the eastern side of Hamburg, no more than a few hundred metres wide in places but several kilometres long. You would see children throwing breadcrumbs for ducks, herons perched on the bank, grey and motionless as a sculpture, waiting to spot a fish, butterflies, squirrels turning somersaults in the branches, rustling the leaves, molehills.

Now the Wandse was a strip of grey-black ice, frozen solid. The fish, ducks and herons had all vanished, or had been caught, cooked and eaten. The trees had been chopped down for firewood. All that remained were stumps, with bits of bomb shrapnel embedded in them. The green spaces had vanished under mountains of rubble, dumped there to clear the streets.

'You told a journalist I saw the rubble murderer,' Anna von Veckinhausen said accusingly when they had reached what remained of the river.

Relieved to be able to give his left leg a bit of a rest, Stave just shrugged and said, 'I told him a woman had possibly caught a glimpse of the killer. Kleensch would have found out sooner or later. Better to give him my side of the story than for him to make up his own.'

'But the rubble murderer now knows that there's a witness, a female witness. He might even know who it is because he might have seen me too that night.'

'If he did see you then he would in any case have worked out you would go to the police. And even if he read the piece in the newspaper, he still wouldn't have your name or know where you lived.'

This time it was Anna von Veckinhausen who shrugged.

'I had hoped the newspaper story would make the killer nervous,' the chief inspector admitted. 'Maybe so nervous that he would go back to the scene of his crime to remove clues or something. That sort of thing happens.'

'And? Did he?'

Stave shook his head. 'Maybe he's not bothered by our investigation. Maybe he feels he has nothing to worry about.'

'I can imagine,' Anna von Veckinhausen said, staring at the ice.

'Have you had somebody watching me?'

'No. Why do you ask?'

'I'm your only witness, aren't I? Don't you think the murderer might be out there looking for me? To shut me up?'

'He doesn't know anything about you. Would you prefer it if we kept an eye on you?'

She smiled briefly for the first time. 'Maybe not.'

'Do you feel as if you're being watched?'

She put her arm across her upper body, in that defensive position Stave had noticed before.

'Don't we all?' she asked.

She walks on, along the river, Stave following alongside. He's hungry, weary; his leg hurts. He'd like to ask her into a cafe, even if it is only for a cup of thin cabbage soup in a bombed-out building. But he doesn't dare even suggest the idea. He can't think of anything else to ask her. Stupid of me even to have come here, he thinks to himself. But it's nice, so very nice to have the company of a woman again. Even in this cold. Even in this desolate parkland, even if I have to be careful not to walk too close to her, making sure all the time there's at least half a metre between us. The elegant way she walks, despite the shabby overcoat covering most of her body and the heavy boots on her feet. The strands of long dark hair poking out from under the headscarf, strands she absently pushes back from her eyes, though never quite far enough to stop them falling down again. The vulnerability, when she puts her arm across her breast protectively. The smile she uses so rarely. Stave even thinks he catches a whiff of perfume, which is impossible especially in this cold.

Stop acting like an idiot, he tells himself.

Because he can't think of anything else, he asks her the same questions once more. She's happy to answer him. But there are no more contradictions, as far as he can tell. But then there is a part of him that's happy just to be there next to her, listening to the sound of her voice. At some stage, without discussion, they turn around and head back. It's getting dark but the frozen river gleams like a silver ribbon.

'You're not getting very far with your case,' Anna von Veckinhausen said. It was a statement, not a question, but not meant in a hostile way.

He smiled, embarrassed. 'I've never come across a case like this before, where we can't even identify the victims.'

'You're surprised?'

He stared at her, suddenly taken aback, and said, 'Yes.'

She shook her head. 'You still believe there's good in people? Despite all this?' and she waved a hand at the ruins around them.

'I can't see what identifying the bodies of four people has to do with believing there's good in people.'

Anna von Veckinhausen smiled at him, sympathetically, he thought. 'Take the old man who opened the door to you back at the Nissen hut. Johann Schwarzhuber. A widower, a refugee from Breslau, been in Hamburg eight months, used to be a carpenter, and a party member, now he's a pensioner with no relatives. I know all of that despite probably never having exchanged more than a few dozens words with him. But what does he know about me?'

'He didn't even know your name.'

'If I failed to return from our walk along the Wandse tonight, Chief Inspector, good old Johannn Schwarzhuber wouldn't even report me missing. And if a photo of me suddenly appeared on posters around the city, he wouldn't bother to go to the police to identify me. He would turn his head away and set to looting what little I have in the hut before somebody else did. For the last eight months, all there has been between him and me is a woollen blanket.

We have starved and frozen together. But Schwarzhuber wouldn't give a damn if I was dead. Or the two families with children who also share our hut. He wouldn't give a damn about them either. Or anyone else on the whole planet. He would help nobody but himself.

'Hamburg is full of Johann Schwarzhubers, thousands of them crawling about in the ruins, lurking in huts, staring out of frozen windowpanes. I bet you somebody out there knows your four victims, but is thinking, somebody else can take the trouble of going to the police.'

'Maybe there are lots of Johann Schwarzhubers out there,' the chief inspector argued, 'but not everybody in Hamburg is a Johann Schwarzhuber. If you were not to return from our walk tonight, he might not report you missing, but somebody else would.'

Anna von Veckinhausen looked long and hard at him, then shook her head with a weary smile. 'You're wrong,' she murmured, letting her voice fade away and staring at the ice on the river.

'Then it must be pure good luck that you at least made the effort to go to the police,' Stave said. Would nobody really miss Anna von Veckinhausen, he wondered? How sad – but deep down there was a part of him that was gladdened by the news: it meant she had no husband.

The all of a sudden something occurred to him. He took a photo out of his coat pocket, a photo of the earring that had belonged to the fourth victim. 'You're an expert on art and jewellery. Have you ever seen this before?'

Anna von Veckinhausen took the photo, handling it carefully as if it was a piece of art itself. 'René Lalique,' she said after studying it for a few brief seconds.

Stave stared at her. 'Who?'

She smiled charitably. 'A jeweller, who makes items a policeman could not afford to buy. Art nouveau. René Lalique was a Parisian fine jeweller. He produced pieces like this from 1870 until 1914. Does it have something to do with your murders?'

Stave took the photograph back. 'If and when I catch this bastard,

I may well owe it entirely to you.' Then he told her the circumstances in which the earring had been found. 'Where did this René Lalique sell his jewellery?'

'Only in Paris. But this earring is virtually an antique. It may have been handed on several times before it became the property of your victim.'

'But it could signify that the woman who wore it had been in France, possibly before the war, and that she was probably rich?'

'Whoever it belonged to was undoubtedly rich.'

Stave's thoughts turned to the medallions. 'Is there any religious meaning to starfish and pearls? Connected with some cult, or anything like that?'

She looked at him, slightly puzzled for a minute or two, and then shook her head.

'That's a shame,' the chief inspector said. 'It would have been nice if you could have done the whole job for me.'

Anna von Veckinhausen smiled again. When they reached the Nissen hut she held out her hand to him. Stave shook it, holding on just a second or two more than strictly necessary.

'Let me know if you want a painting to hang on those bare walls of your office.'

'I'll be in touch,' said Stave. 'That's a promise.'

Lost in his thoughts, Stave wandered through the ruins, exhausted by the amount of walking he'd done, but strangely happy. I'm finally getting somewhere, he thought. And he could not help adding mentally, and I just might be beginning to get somewhere with Anna von Veckinhausen, although he didn't dare ask himself where that 'somewhere' might be.

Given that he had to pass near to Marienthal on his way home – the electricity had been turned off by now so it was too late for the trams – and that this seemed to be his lucky day, he decided to stop by the Hellinger household. Maybe the industrialist had turned up again without his wife bothering to inform the police. Things like that happened. Or maybe his wife will have thought of something else that might be of interest. And apart from anything else, it was warm in her villa, and she had hot tea.

The street was lined with grand houses, each one as dark as a tomb. When he was close to the house, he had second thoughts for a moment. Then he spotted Frau Hellinger though the window, sitting at her kitchen table in tears. Stave hesitated for a minute, then knocked on the door anyway. It was a while before the door was opened. The industrialist's wife looked pale, but if he had not caught sight of her a few minutes ago he would have had no idea that she had been sobbing her heart out. She looked at him worriedly.

She must think I have bad news, Stave realised, and smiled quickly, telling her he had nothing new to report, but was just wondering if she had thought of anything more she might want to tell the police since he was last there.

To his relief she asked him in. Into the warmth, the scent of hot coal and tea.

'I'm not sure I have anything more I can tell you,' she mumbled. 'You know my husband was doing business with the English?'

Stave said nothing, just sipped at the tea she had poured him.

'You know also that he made navigation equipment for U-boats. What more is there to tell you?'

The chief inspector had an idea. 'Who was the last visitor your husband had before his disappearance?'

She thought for a moment. 'The day before...? Nobody called. But two days before an English officer was here. He used to come quite regularly to the house, or to my husband's office. They talked about technical stuff, I assumed, though I don't really know.'

'Do you know his name by any chance?'

'Oh yes, a charming young man. Not very military at all. Lieutenant MacDonald. James C. MacDonald.'

Signs of Life

Tuesday, 18 February 1947

It was the cold that came to Stave's rescue. He had tossed back and forth in his sleep, thrown the blanket off and lain there bathed in sweat on the crumpled sheet until the bitter cold chased away at the spectre of his nightmare. Fire. Bombs. Smoke. The stench of burning flesh. Margarethe's face. Always the same scenes from the same movie – and yet every time they seemed fresh. As if Stave had seen Margarethe in the flames, had stood there next to the flames, screaming. Yet she never heard him, because her body was frozen to the floor, despite the heat of the flames. With a small red line around her neck. Staring at him with open eyes, coated in ice.

I really need to solve this case, the chief inspector told himself, otherwise it's going to haunt the rest of my life. Once upon a time he had been able to leave his investigations at the door, the way he hung up his coat on a peg. As soon as he got home, that was it with work; he stopped thinking about it. His apartment was his little fortress of domestic happiness. Until the bombs fell.

Stave felt his way around the apartment. The ice on the window-panes obscured the early dawn sunlight. He felt as if he was groping his way through a thick barley soup just to get to the kitchen table. The grey glow obscured his view of the wonky table and the chair with one broken leg. He reached for the back of the chair, nearly knocking the enamel coffee cup over. Not that it mattered. He didn't have any coffee, and hot water was in as short supply as daylight,

Power cut.

Stave had forgotten that each district of the city had its power cut off for two hours a week, because there was not enough coal to fuel all of the power stations. This morning was Wandsbek's turn. Where was his candle?

He tried to build up his courage. I can still think, even in the twilight. MacDonald. The Englishman had been leading him up the garden path, not admitting his visits to the missing industrialist. But why? Did it have something to do with the murders? Was Hellinger the next corpse they would find in some cellar? Did he finally have a concrete lead to the killer? MacDonald? It seemed absurd.

He hadn't paid any attention to the lieutenant's alibis. Erna Berg had said he was often missing for hours on end. What had he been doing during this time? He might be the killer. But what would the motive have been? Looting was hardly likely. The occupation officers lived like colonial lords, just think of the business Anna von Veckinhausen did selling them antiques. And in any case, Frau Hellinger hadn't known any of the other victims – what could be the connection between those four and a missing industrialist? And how might MacDonald be involved in all of this?

What about the missing files? Was that part of it? They had mentioned Hellinger by name, a name that had merely been languishing in the records of the Search Office and in a police station somewhere. But there were readers for the murder files: Stave, Maschke, right up to Cuddel Breuer and public prosecutor Ehrlich. That increased the possibility of somebody at some time making the link between Hellinger and MacDonald. And then there was that puzzling English word on the piece of paper Hellinger had dropped: 'Bottleneck'. That had been in the files too. So maybe the lieutenant, who for some reason or other wanted to conceal his relationship with Hellinger, had got rid of the files. Obviously he would have known that he would get Stave's attention. But he would also have known that in the circumstances, it would hardly have sent Stave running to his superior officer. Here and now in his quiet little office he could imagine it: a way to stop inquisitive eyes taking another look at the files. It was certainly a motive.

Did he have the opportunity? MacDonald had been hanging around with Erna Berg frequently enough, including at times when Stave wasn't in his office. It would only have taken a second for the files to have disappeared into his greatcoat. Or maybe his secretary had been in on the act and had stolen the files for her lover. If she had had a bad conscience about it, Stave would hardly have noticed, given how distraught she had been about her other personal circumstances.

Then he turned his thoughts to the dead woman's earring. A Parisian jeweller. Very expensive. When might the victim have been in the French capital? Before the war? Ten, at most fifteen years ago? As a young adult? Would a woman in her early twenties have worn jewellery like that? He tried to think what Margarethe would have thought of it. But the idea was absurd; when they'd been young and in love, she'd dreamed of other things. A bigger apartment. New toys for Karl. Another child. In any case, Anna von Veckinhausen had said the earrings had been made before 1914. At that time the fourth victim would have been too young to buy them or have anybody buy them for her. So maybe she had inherited them? But who in Hamburg had French jewellery? Least of all these days? Rich families. But surely somebody would have made a robbery or missing persons report?

The investigation was getting somewhere, but Stave still didn't see where. He watched his breath in the cold air, little blue clouds rising from his lips like cigarette smoke.

Which brought him back to Maschke.

Yesterday, he had been happy to have him as far away as possible. Today was different. Up until now he had reckoned that he could have relied on MacDonald to find Maschke and bring him back whenever it suited him. But now he felt he couldn't trust the lieutenant any more either. So it would be better if he had the vice squad man back where he could keep an eye on him. He needed to get hold of him on the phone, and not give anything away, he realised. He would have to find an excuse to break off his questioning of the doctors and get him back to Hamburg as soon as possible.

He pulled his heavy overcoat on awkwardly. Overnight a fine layer of ice had formed on it and when he pulled it over his shoulders it fell to the ground in a glistening cloud. It was a size too big for him now anyway. I've got so thin, he thought. All the clothes I have are now a size too large.

Stave pulled on his hat, scarf, gloves, picked up his gun, his torch. Why do I even bother? Why do I go out into the cold, battle against the wind, spend my time with people like MacDonald, Ehrlich, Maschke or Erna Berg, who all have their own agendas? Agendas in which I'm nothing more than a nuisance?

But what else was there to do? Sit alone in his grey apartment, thinking about the wife who'd burned to death? Or his estranged son who might or might not one day come home? If he was even still alive?

I am 43 years old, Stave thought to himself, and I don't have a lot to show for my life. And then he left the flat, locked the door as carefully as always, walked down the stairs and out on to the street where the freezing wind hit him in the face like a fist. As it always did.

'How are things?' he asked Erna Berg, when he got to the office an hour later.

'The baby is doing well. The doctor says I'll begin to show in a week or two.'

So, no abortion. Stave wondered what decision she'd come to. Would she confess all to her husband? Would she break things off with MacDonald? But it was all personal stuff, not his business. He closed the door to his office behind him.

He spent his time on the phone, but still couldn't get hold of Maschke. It worried him that he couldn't find a hotel where Maschke might have spent the night. Don't let him have done a runner, he prayed, wondering if he might have given away that he was on to him. Eventually he got to his feet, left the police HQ and walked the few hundred metres to the public prosecutor's office.

Ehrlich ran a hand over his bald pate but seemed happy to see him. It smelled of tea in his office as always. Earl Grey, Stave reckoned.

'What can I do for you?'

You could arrest my colleagues, was what Stave would have liked to say. But he wasn't at that stage yet.

'I'm afraid I've got nothing more to report in the rubble murderer case. But I've been doing some other investigations for which I'd appreciate your support. In a few administrative matters. Discreetly.'

'Discretion lies at the heart of a public prosecutor's duty,' Ehrlich said, smiling.

'I need to see some files. I don't want to tell you just yet about the case they relate to because it might not even be a case. I'm at a very early stage in my investigations,' the chief inspector said, hoping his face didn't give away the fact that he was lying.

'You might give me at least some general idea of the direction your investigations are taking. Is this a political matter?'

Stave thought for a moment. 'Possibly, eventually. Primarily it requires me to make some discreet inquiries about my colleagues.'

Ehrlich looked at him with those pale bright eyes.

'Do you mean colleagues who are also involved in the rubble murderer investigation?'

'If I told you that, I would already be setting you after those involved. This needs to be discreet in the utmost.'

'Understood. What files do you need?'

'Oradour. A town in France where the SS committed a massacre in June 1944.'

'I've heard of it,' the prosecutor broke in. 'The massacre, that is.'

He stared long and hard at Stave. The chief inspector stood there, feeling like he was on trial himself. He squirmed uncomfortably in the chair while Ehrlich just sat there looking at him.

'The office next to mine is empty today,' the man said at last. 'I'll have the files brought to you there. You can study them as you will, but you can't take them away with you. There isn't a lot in any case.'

'Wasn't there an investigation?'

'Of course there was, but there were no suspects. Immediately after the massacre, Field Marshal Rommel tried to set up a court martial, but Hitler himself cancelled it. After that, the issue simply disappeared. The SS unit was in any case wiped out fighting the Allies at the end of June 1944. Wiped out completely.'

'No survivors?'

Ehrlich gave him a bleak smile. 'Up until a few minutes ago, I thought there had been no survivors. Now I'm not so sure.'

Stave smiled back. 'Thank you, prosecutor.'

'Keep me in the loop. If you find something, I want to know about it. And if you don't find anything, I'd like to know that too.'

Stave sat in the office next door, enjoying the quiet, the warmth. He could even take his overcoat off. Ehrlich had ordered tea for him and he sat there drinking it. Maybe life's not so bad after all, he thought to himself.

Eventually a bespectacled filing clerk in a grey coat brought him a Leitz box file. The chief inspector did his best not to be disappointed at how light it was.

It didn't take him long. He already knew the story of the massacre, and the testimony of the little girl in the Warburg children home's matched what was in the file. Then he scanned a mimeographed copy of the names of soldiers in the SS unit. It included 'Herthge, Hans', which hardly surprised him. Nor did the absence of anyone called Maschke.

There was a second list, much shorter. It was the names of the survivors. He ran his eyes down it: 'Desaux, Joseph; Delluc, Yvonne; Fourché, Roger; Magaldi, Anouk.' There were a few more. He made a list of all the names even though there was only one he needed: Anouk Magaldi. The fact that her name was on the list was enough to make her a credible witness in court.

There were also a few witness statements, including an extract from the War Log compiled by the Supreme Command of the Wehrmacht for 30 June 1944, which noted: '3 Company SS Panzer Grenadier Regiment 4 wiped out.'

The only other thing was a document in French which, thanks to his old school language lessons, Stave just about managed to translate: the public prosecutor's office in the city of Limoges had issued a warrant for the arrest of all members of the SS unit. But that was it. Nothing more. Not a single letter or document to suggest that any members of the SS unit had ever been brought to trial.

The chief inspector rubbed the back of his neck. At least he could now substantiate the little girl's story. Hans Herthge was a murderer. All he had to do was prove that Maschke was really Herthge. There was just one more line to cross and the matter was done and dusted. But he still felt he had missed something.

Stave set the box file down on Ehrlich's desk.

'Anything you want to share with me?' the prosecutor asked.

'Not right now, but soon. There is one other lead I need to track down. Then we need to talk.' Stave nodded at the box file and said, 'You'll be able to add a couple more documents in here.'

'That's my man,' Ehrlich replied.

Stave walked down Feld Strasse and through the backstreets of St Pauli until he reached Altona. He was walking fast, to keep the warmth of the office in his bones. He reached the Search Office building, pushed open the great door and looked at the endless lines of boxes in which the individual fates of human beings were catalogued. There was nobody to be seen in the gloomy corridors. It was as if even the search for the missing had been frozen solid. He knocked on Andreas Brems's door and walked in without waiting for a reply. It will already have been dealt with, he thought to himself.

Brems greeted him with a gentle but weary smile. 'Are you looking for your missing person or somebody else's?'

'Somebody else's. One Lothar Maschke.'

Brems indicated that he should sit down at his desk. He got up himself and went out, coming back a few minutes later with a yellow filing card.

'Maschke, Lothar, born 1916 in Flensburg, lived in Hamburg

from 1920, called up to the navy in September 1939, appointed leading seaman on board U-453. Reported missing on 2 June 1945 by his neighbour, Wilhelmine Herthge.'

'Got you!' Stave said under his breath.

That had to be his colleague's mother, Stave reckoned. She reports a neighbour missing, and at the same time her son returns from the war. Her son who's somehow survived the fighting in Normandy in which all his other SS comrades may have died. Her son who had committed cold-blooded murder in Oradour. A son who realises that the massacre could still be a threat to him. And who suddenly finds out that the next-door neighbour, who just happened to be about the same age, is missing. A neighbour with no living relatives left. If he had, why would it have been Frau Herthge who reported him missing, rather than his own mother or wife? How easy must it have been to break into his apartment, steal a few papers and take his name. He would only have to have persuaded his mother, but she was unlikely to betray her own son, who from now on would be living with her at home, and unlikely to stray too far. Nothing to stop his mother keeping her own name. Who would notice that mother and son had different surnames? And even if they did, people would think that his mother had probably been widowed after his birth, remarried and taken the name of her new husband. Not exactly unusual in a time when millions of women had lost their husbands. No funeral, no death certificate, no need to report anything to any bureaucratic office – the real Lothar Maschke had been declared missing, but not dead. And who in any case bothered to check the names of everyone in Hamburg against the vast number of index cards in the hands of the Search Office? Nobody. So Hans Herthge simply becomes the new Lothar Maschke. The new Maschke gets new personal documents – not hard in a city where tens of thousands of identity cards and birth certificates were destroyed in a firestorm of bombing. Who was going to check every application for a duplicate? So the new Maschke simply took over all the documents of the old one, even claimed his ration card. He was probably interviewed at some time by a British officer and asked about his relationship with the Nazi party, but U-boat crew were generally approved. And in the end this new Maschke is in the clear and feels so secure that he can even chat about his time in France. He settles down in his little nest, starts a new life and what better disguise than to apply for a job with the police, of all things?

'I'll need to take this card,' Stave told Brems, 'it's evidence.'

The researcher shrugged. 'Nobody has ever asked about him, or we'd have had a note on the file. But let me make a copy, just to keep things in order.'

He took a second card from a box and began copying the details with a fountain pen, though it was so cold that the ink was almost freezing and there were blank lines left on the new card.

Nobody will ever be able to read that, the chief inspector thought, but it doesn't matter any more.

Stave nodded in farewell, and was just about to open the door when Brems cleared his throat, and said: 'I don't want to give you any false hopes, by the way, but we are expecting a letter from the Red Cross today with a new list of prisoners-of-war in the Soviet Union. I know that there is not much chance of finding names on it that we don't already have. But we can't rule it out.'

'Just check names beginning with "St" for me,' the chief inspector said, hoping that the tremor in his voice wasn't too noticeable. Then he turned away quickly.

Don't get your hopes up. No unrealistic hopes.

On the way back Stave dropped into a cafe that had survived the war almost intact, apart from the fact that the four-storey building's façade had collapsed, as if some monster had ripped its face off. The front of the cafe had been boarded up and a couple of pieces of glass inserted with nails and putty to let light in. The chief inspector ordered a bowl of potato soup, which came with grey bread, butter and tea.

The soup was a pale yellow colour, but at least it was hot. The bread crumbled beneath his fingers, and he had no idea what the paste on it was, except that it certainly wasn't proper butter. The tea smelt of nettles. Supposed to be good for you, Stave told himself, and slurped at the bitter brew. He left the cafe feeling hungrier than ever.

When he got back to the office he was surprised to find MacDonald waiting for him.

'I need to talk to you,' the lieutenant said.

'My lucky day,' Stave answered, offering the officer a chair.

Erna Berg glanced through the outer door, seemingly calm, clearly with no idea what her lover had on his mind, Stave reckoned. So she wasn't in on it. He closed the door.

'You've been back to see Frau Hellinger,' MacDonald said bluntly. It was a statement, not a question.

'Are you having me watched?'

The Brit smiled apologetically. 'Not you. We're watching Frau Hellinger.'

'Who's "we"?'

'It's a long story.'

'Have you come to tell it to me?'

'I'm afraid there's no alternative,' MacDonald said with a sigh. Then he smiled again, one of those apologetic, charming Oxford smiles, and took a loose-leaf binder out of his briefcase.

It was the case files.

'I'm sorry for the inconvenience, old boy. I thought I could get away with it. But you're too good. I'm going to have to let you in on a secret.'

Stave looked down at the files, then at MacDonald, and then eventually said, 'What is it that you have to "let me in" on?'

'Operation Bottleneck,' the Brit answered, smiling yet again. He shrugged and raised his hands, then let them fall to his side. 'I should probably have done so earlier, at least when Hellinger's name first came up.'

MacDonald glanced briefly at the closed door, then at the files.

'The other story is actually a lot more complicated than Operation Bottleneck, but I think you're already in the picture there.'

'Is there something I can help you with?'

'Yes, you could take your service issue revolver and put a neat round hole in Frau Hellinger's husband's head,' the lieutenant replied, pulling a face. 'Only joking. This is my problem and mine alone – unlike the other one.'

'Operation Bottleneck. It was you there that morning that Martin Hellinger disappeared?'

'I abducted him.'

Stave leant back. 'Maybe you want to start at the beginning?'

'I am an officer in His Majesty's Army,' MacDonald began, 'but I also belong to another organisation, which recruited me back in my student days, the British Intelligence Objectives Sub-Committee. They used a good argument to convince me to sign up. They saw to it that the scandal surrounding my affair with a married lady from an aristocratic family just disappeared, like snuffing out a match.'

'Must be a very specific sort of organisation.'

'You could call it,' the lieutenant hesitated, 'a sort of secret service.'

'Like the Gestapo?'

For the first time, MacDonald seemed to lose control of himself, gave Stave a look of disgust and said, 'I hardly think so. We are a few dozen men, officers of His Majesty and a few officials in a couple of ministries in London, scientists and academics in universities and a few specially chosen companies. We answer directly to the government. Our task is to seek out scientists and technicians in occupied Germany who worked for the Nazi regime.'

'To punish them?'

'Personally that would be my preference. But no. Our job is not to punish these gentlemen. We are after men with all kinds of technical knowledge, aircraft engine manufacturers, physicists who developed bombs, U-boat developers. But also specialists who could be useful to our badly damaged economy: chemists who researched using excrement as fertiliser, steel industry and mining engineers, technicians who might have plans for new cars or better radios lying in their desk drawers.'

'Or precision timepieces?'

'And trigonometric calculators. Calculating machines are going to be big business in the future, and Dr Hellinger recognised that sooner than most people.'

'What do you do then?'

'We abduct the gentlemen concerned,' MacDonald replied, as if it was some student prank. 'We knock on their doors and take them away. A trip in a jeep to the nearest military airfield where a plane is already waiting, engines running – and before the gentlemen concerned know what's hit them, they are guests of His Majesty in a castle in the Scottish Highlands. Or in a laboratory outside London. Or a shipyard in Liverpool. They get milked; we drag all the knowledge we can out of these specialists, let them do their calculations, experiments, screw things together, until we know everything they know. Then we use what we've got out of them for our own research, either civilian or military.'

'And these gentlemen don't mind being milked? Is there no such thing as patent law?'

MacDonald laughed. 'Patent law, after a war which killed 20 million. What good is it winning the war? In the old days the temples would have been plundered, today it's knowledge we're stealing. Not an altogether unfair price for what your country inflicted on the world.'

'And these specialists are happy enough just to give away their knowledge?'

'The sooner they tell us all they know, the sooner they get to go home again. We're not monsters. We don't need to use Gestapo methods. We just wait for them to agree. Usually they're like show-off children, so proud of their inventions, they tell us everything we want to know on day one. Even if they're murderous weapons. In fact particularly so.'

'So does that mean Dr Hellinger is going to turn up again one day soon?'

'Of course. He's not exactly one of the most reluctant. Unfortunately this damn cold has hit my homeland too, and we have hardly any aircraft fuel. Many of our harbours too are frozen in. We simply have no way of getting Hellinger back at the moment, either by ship or plane. But as soon as the thaw sets in, he'll be on his way home. He'll make up some story to tell his wife to explain his absence. We'll help him with that and from now on he and his family will get heavy industrial worker ration cards in return for their silence. That is Operation Bottleneck. It's gone well up until now. Hellinger would have turned up again. His wife would have withdrawn the "missing person" report. And that would have been it. No questions and nobody would have noticed.

'But then the cold set in, and the murderer appeared on the scene. The Hellinger case has nothing to do with the rubble murderer. Pure coincidence. But then his name is listed in a murder file and who knows who might read it there? And the damn note Hellinger left. I had told him about the operation when I picked him up so that he wouldn't kick up a fuss. But then he does the dirty on me by leaving this note. No idea how he managed to write it in time. I had him out of the house in two minutes flat.'

'And then you simply stole the files?'

'I removed them. You would suddenly have come across them again, as soon as Hellinger was back. You would have taken Hellinger off the list of victims and that would have been that.'

'Stupid thing to do.'

MacDonald was taken aback for a minute, then he laughed. 'You're right. I hadn't thought it through. I just happened to be here to see Erna and spotted them lying there.'

'The two of you were in my office?'

'Don't blame Frau Berg. I persuaded her. We were alone and less likely to be disturbed than in the outer office, if you know what I mean.'

'You and my secretary … here in my office?' Stave didn't quite know how to complete the accusation.

'Good grief, old boy, were you never in love? We just suddenly found ourselves on our own together once again. It was a perfect opportunity.'

'A perfect opportunity for you to take my files at the same time. Opportunistic indeed.'

'Don't take offence. I swear it was purely amorous intentions that brought us into your office. And afterwards my head was possibly not as clear as it should have been.'

'Obviously.'

Stave closed his eyes and thought. 'I'll believe you, Lieutenant, if only because your story is so distasteful and your motive so badly thought through. I also believe that there's no connection between the Hellinger case and the rubble murderer. But his name was in the file, and I am going to have to explain why his disappearance is no longer relevant.'

'Who's likely to ask?'

'Nobody, probably. But I take pride in my investigations being thorough and properly documented.'

'Make an exception this time.'

'What if I choose not to?'

'One mention of Operation Bottleneck and you'll find yourself the next guest of His Majesty. We have just about enough aircraft fuel to see to that.'

'I thought as much,' Stave replied. 'There again I've always wanted to see a Scottish castle.'

'Not when it's minus 20 Celsius.'

'I suppose there is that argument.' Stave said nothing for a few moments, thinking the matter over. 'You have my word that I'll make no mention of Operation Bottleneck,' he eventually promised. 'There'll be nothing more about Hellinger in the files. Nor about the way the files went missing.'

MacDonald took a deep breath. 'Thank you for that. I would have found it deeply disagreeable to have to do something as unpleasant as kidnapping you. But I am obliged to do everything I can to keep this operation secret.'

'Do you find it equally unpleasant kidnapping people like Hellinger?'

'No,' the lieutenant replied without hesitation. 'The Nazis had their butchers to do their dirty work, in the Gestapo, in the concentration camps. I'm sure you know the type I mean. Brutal men, with no conscience, but not bright enough to do too much harm on their own. Hitler needed cleverer men for that. Like our good Dr Hellinger with his trigonometric calculators. They worked brilliantly, as 10,000 sailors' widows from Liverpool to Halifax will testify. No, he doesn't get my sympathy.'

'We have something in common there.'

'That's why I enjoy working with you so much, Chief Inspector.'

'Would you say the same for my colleague, Maschke?'

Suddenly MacDonald was cautious. 'Why do you ask?'

'How much do you know about him?'

The lieutenant shrugged his shoulders. 'When I was seconded to this investigation, obviously I read through the personnel files of those I would be working with.'

'Very thorough of you.'

'Just being professional. But I didn't see anything particularly interesting in Maschke's file. That's all I know about him.'

'Would you get the personnel files for me to look at?'

'Gladly, as thanks for your cooperation in the Operation Bottleneck business. But why were you asking about Maschke in particular?'

'Now I have a secret from you, Lieutenant. But I promise you I'll let you in on it before long. When the time is right.'

MacDonald nodded and got to his feet. 'Fair enough. Just let me know.'

When the lieutenant already had his hand on the door handle to leave, Stave cleared his throat. 'Just promise me you won't ask me to be godfather to your child,' he said. 'even if it might have been conceived in my office.'

'*Touché*,' said MacDonald, touching his cap to Stave as he left.

Stave stared out of the window for a long time after the lieutenant had left. He was relieved to have his files back again. I'm such an old stickler for doing things by the book, he thought to himself. Margarethe would have laughed. She would have told me not to make such a fuss.

But things were getting clearer. He could trust MacDonald after all, and, it seemed, Erna Berg too, even if he was still shocked at the idea that, despite being a married woman, she had offered herself to an officer of the army of occupation here in his office. On *this* desk.

The disappearance of the files had been cleared up. Hellinger was no longer part of the investigation. He was not a suspect, and, thank God, not another victim.

Stave now had enough witnesses and statements to take Maschke to court and charge him with being a former SS man involved in the Oradour massacre. He wondered if it might not be wiser to have Maschke arrested straight away. Or should he leave his former colleague in the dark, play him until he somehow gave himself away? I'm going to have to talk to Ehrlich again, he thought. The public prosecutor must have some idea that Maschke had a Nazi past. Why else had he bumped into him that night in Maschke's office? He was snooping after something. But he almost certainly had no idea that Maschke had been at Oradour. The Nazi-hunter would be grateful when Stave presented him with the evidence. He would have a new trial, maybe back in the Curio House.

His thoughts were interrupted by a knock on the door. Erna Berg popped her head in. 'You have a visitor.'

It was Andreas Brems from the Search Office.

Stave wanted to get up, as politeness demanded, but all of a sudden his leg went as limp as a deflated bicycle tube. He was about to say something but he couldn't get a word out.

The researcher, no doubt used to giving people bad news, smiled forgivingly, pulled up a chair, sat down and unfolded a sheet of paper, all without saying a word. Then he pointed down at what was a mimeographed sheet of paper with a list of names on it. Names, names and more names.

'We've found your son,' he said. And quickly added: 'Alive.'

Stave gripped the edges of his desk, his mind in a whirl. Karl, a 17-year-old in a Wehrmacht uniform far too big for him, a look of scorn and disgust on his face as he said farewell to his father. Stave forced himself to thank Brems formally, shook his hand across the desk, then bent his head over the list, lifted it in his hand, no longer caring that it was trembling so much it was making the sheet of paper rustle.

The one and only link to his son: 'Stave, Karl.'

And then one more word. Stave stopped and read it again, having no idea what it meant. 'What does this mean? Vorkuta.'

'It's where your son is at present.' Brems cleared his throat. 'A prisoner-of-war camp. In Siberia.'

'Siberia?'

Stave closed his eyes. People in Hamburg had been talking for months about 'Siberian temperatures'. And he'd seen the bodies of the murderer's victims, frozen to the ground. He'd heard of others frozen stiff too; victims not of a murderer but of the cold itself. If it was as cold as this in Hamburg, what must it be like out there?

'What can I do?' he heard himself say flatly, though his voice was filled with hope.

'Nothing. At least not for the moment. The Red Cross furnished us this list. It may be that at some stage a representative will gain access to the camp to talk to the prisoners or bring them post. We can't be certain of that, but we will do everything we can to improve conditions for the prisoners.'

'When will they let him go?'

'Ask Comrade Stalin. Nobody can say. When the trains were still running, prisoners did return from Siberia. At the moment it's still too cold, but the winter won't last forever.'

'Can I write to him at least?'

'We'll be happy to take a letter for you. But there's no rush. It will take weeks before we can get a representative to northern Russia. If at all. You're confused. Happy but confused. I understand that. I see it every day. For now just enjoy the good news. Give it time to sink in. Wait until then before writing a letter.'

'One way or another, at least he's been found.'

'And once we've found someone, we don't lose track of them.'

At last Stave managed to get up from his chair. 'Thank you very much,' he said. 'And for coming to tell me personally.'

'You came often enough to us,' said Brems, shaking his hand in farewell.

When he left the room, Stave stared out of the window again. Night was coming on, black as ink. In the outside office he heard a chair scrape over the linoleum floor: Erna Berg getting up from her desk to go home. An air bubble gurgled in a radiator that was little more than cold, the sound of footsteps down the corridor, and then nothing but the silence of an abandoned question.

I need to get myself a map of Russia, Stave thought to himself. Find out where Vorkuta is.

A Letter

Stave woke up and sensed something had changed. For a second he was afraid there was somebody else in the room. He sat up, looked around. Nobody there. It was only then that he realised what it was that had changed.

Outside a bird was singing. There was no hard sheet of ice across his window, just puddles on the window sill where the frozen patterns made by the frost had melted. He could no longer see his breath, his hands no longer ached, he didn't automatically shiver, not even when his bare feet touched the floor.

Carefully Stave got to his feet, still not trusting the temperature, made his way to the window and looked out. He could see sunlight. The wall opposite shone a warm yellow. Three or four people were walking along the street, still cautiously wrapped in coats and scarves. One of them dared to take his hat off. When did I last see that, Stave asked himself. An uncovered head in the open air.

He didn't bother with breakfast, just splashed some water on his face and dashed to the door. Should he take his coat or not? Let's not be overconfident, he thought and grabbed the heavy woollen thing. He took his gun, shoved it inside his jacket, along with his police ID. But he left his pocket torch lying on the shelf below the clothes hook. Why would he need a torch on such a bright and sunny day?

Out on the street, he felt as if his body was divided in two, with the border somewhere just above his knees. The ground was still frozen solid, and the cold crept up from it. Stave took a deep breath, hoping to inhale the promise of spring: flowers, leaves, grass. But it was still too early for that. The odour of dust, rust and decay still filled his nose, stronger than ever. He unbuttoned his coat, walking slowly, revelling in every footstep. At the street corner people queued in their dozens, tin buckets, jugs, old canisters in their hands, waiting patiently for their turn to fill up whatever container they had with water from a stand pump. These were the unlucky ones whose domestic water pipes had burst over the past few weeks and had since been obliged to get their water from pumps out on the streets. Stave walked past the queue; until yesterday it had been a silent wall of wrapped-up shapes, today he could see faces, hear people talking. From somewhere he even heard a laugh from behind him as he walked along the road. An old man walking towards him doffed his hat in greeting. When he glanced at a passing woman, she blushed and smiled shyly. A couple of schoolboys were kicking a broken cobblestone back and forth, before finally kicking it into the ruins. Survivors, thought Stave to himself, that's what we are: survivors.

He wondered if the thaw had set in out in Siberia. Or would it still be cold there? With Brems's help he had located Vorkuta after failing himself to find anywhere of that name on the map of the Soviet Union he had acquired. A dot at the northern end of the Ural Mountains. Far, far away from any town or railway line marked on the map. The chief inspector asked himself how his son might have got there, from Berlin to Vorkuta. He had written a letter to him, sitting over it by candlelight one long night. It had been difficult to find the words. 'You're no poet,' Anna von Veckinhuasen had teased him.

He had not mentioned her to his son. He was too ashamed. He didn't mention the rubble murderer either. Instead he wrote of Margarethe, memories, described Hamburg, but not in too much detail. He didn't want to worry his son. General stuff. Only at the end, when he had signed off with 'Your father', did he add, as a postscript: 'I love you and miss you.'

When had he last told his son that? Had he ever? He couldn't remember having done so.

Survivors, Stave thought to himself again, glancing discreetly at the passers-by on the street, walking as if they'd just been liberated from some camp. If we could survive this winter in Hamburg, why not in Vorkuta too? Karl was young and strong. He would survive. He had to.

It was four weeks since MacDonald had come clean to him about the stolen files, and revealed the existence of Operation Bottleneck. Four weeks since he had found out Maschke's true identity. Four tough weeks in which nothing else had happened.

But that in itself was something, the chief inspector told himself. There had been no more bodies. Every day with no new spectacular discovery saw the leash he was on lengthen a little. Stave felt he could act a little more freely, as if he had more room to manoeuvre. No new corpse meant no new headline. No popular panic. And no panic had meant no more awkward questions from the mayor, or Cuddel Breuer, or Ehrlich. And now overnight, like a miracle, it was spring. Before long everyone would have forgotten the rubble murderer.

Everyone but me, Stave thought. I won't.

When Stave got to the office, Erna Berg turned her head away while saying hello to him. The chief inspector stopped for a moment, bent down and looked her in the face. Her right eye was swollen and bruised.

'Your husband?' he asked.

She nodded towards her stomach, which was slightly but noticeably distended. 'I told him. I couldn't keep it a secret any longer.'

'I'll deal with it,' said MacDonald who had come in from the hallway without either of them noticing.

'Let's talk in my office, not out here,' Stave said.

'All three of us,' the lieutenant said, taking Erna Berg's arm.

'What do you want to do?' Stave asked, sitting down at his desk.

Erna Berg sat opposite, MacDonald standing behind with his hands on her shoulders.

'I want to get divorced,' the secretary answered.

'I have already got Frau Berg an apartment,' the lieutenant said. 'And when this sorry affair has been dealt with, we're going to get married.' He smiled.

'But you already have a son,' Stave said. He said no more. The way things stood, a judge would almost certainly give the father custody; it was the mother who had committed adultery.

'I'll deal with it,' MacDonald said. He sounded determined. 'The boy will grow up living with us.'

The chief inspector stared at him long and hard until he realised that the lieutenant was serious – and that the lieutenant would win. He should have felt sympathy for Erna Berg's husband, who had lost a leg in the war and now was going to lose his family too. But he had been shocked at the sight of his secretary's swollen eye. All of a sudden, without intending it, his sympathies had switched to this young British officer who was so polite, so self-confident, so nonchalant, everything that he, Stave, was not.

'You have my blessing,' he said.

'I wasn't aware you were a pastor,' MacDonald said.

Stave could see a twitch in the side of Erna Berg's face that wasn't swollen. Any minute now she's going to burst into tears, he realised.

'Any new developments in the case?' he asked, before they all went sentimental.

'No, Chief Inspector,' his secretary answered, taking a deep breath, pulling herself together and smiling shyly, almost conspiratorially. 'No new bodies. And no queries from Herr Breuer.'

'I'm not sure which I was dreading more,' Stave sighed with relief. Then he lifted his right hand as if he were trying to scare the pair of them away, but the gesture became part blessing, part friendly wave.

'Take some time off,' he said. 'You'll need time to sort out your new apartment. And I imagine there are one or two other things you need to deal with.'

Within 30 seconds they were gone.

Stave sat there looking at the thin files on the murder case, spread out neatly on his desk. He was beginning to realise that he wasn't going to get any further. And that he probably never would.

The fact that there was no new victim was on the one hand a good thing, but it could also mean that there was no opportunity for the killer to make a mistake. The murders could be at an end because he was afraid that a victim might fight back successfully, or that somebody would spot him in the act. Or that somebody in Hamburg would come forth to identify the victims. It might mean it was all over, without a proper ending.

Now that the thaw had set in, it would eventually rain. And rain would soak the posters on the streets and wash the photos to the ground, along with Stave's urgent pleas for help. There was no way he would get permission to print new ones, to worry people again.

What was he to do with these four cases? The paperwork was spread across his desk; he'd carried out every search imaginable, questioned every witness he could find, followed every lead. Maybe, at some stage, chance would come to his assistance. Maybe the killer would get drunk in some bar and give himself away; it had happened before. Maybe some newcomer to Hamburg would find one of the few posters to survive the winter and call in to say, 'I know who that is.'

But what if they didn't? Then the rubble murderer would get away with it, Stave was forced to admit. And I'll spend the rest of my life thinking about it, he thought. And I'll never stop asking myself: what might you have missed?

Feeling sorry for yourself isn't going to do any good, he told himself, carefully collecting the folders and putting them back in the filing cabinet. He got up from his chair and strode towards the door, another file under his arm: the personnel file on Lothar Maschke that MacDonald had procured for him. And another couple of interesting documents. It was time to go and talk to Ehrlich.

But as he walked down the corridor, he kept thinking to himself, what might I have missed? Missed? Down the staircase with the irritating pattern on the steps. Missed? Through the entrance hallway, past the little bronze elephant. Missed? Past the Mercedes outside in the street. Missed? Walking to Ehrlich's office. Missed? The sculpture of a woman. Ehrlich. Woman. Ehrlich.

'What an idiot I am!' he suddenly shouted aloud.

And he began running.

Names

Stave ran all the way back to the office. Damn his leg. He was running so fast that he stumbled. By the time he was back outside the grandiose building he was coughing for breath. The Mercedes was still standing there. The key was in the ignition. Stave pulled the door open, jumped into the driver's seat and sped off with the engine howling. To hell with traffic rules.

There were bicycles everywhere and people out walking, soaking up the sun. The chief inspector swore, parped the horn, held the steering wheel tight as he roared round the bends.

The answer had been lying on his desk for a month, but not in the files he had so worried about, but in his own notebook. *And I didn't see it.* He could have thumped himself in the face. *I just hope the witness is still alive,* he suddenly thought. *I just hope she isn't one of those who froze to death over the course of this long winter.*

Yvonne Delluc.

He had made a note of the name. Then struck it out. She was one of the survivors of Oradour. And he had seen the name before, in Maschke's card index. The card index in which the vice squad man had noted all the names of his ladies of the night and their pimps. He could see it in his mind's eye now as clearly as if he had just crept into his colleague's office an hour ago.

'Yvonne Delluc. Has family here.'

A Frenchwoman. And a survivor of Oradour. An earring from a Parisian jeweller. Stave had no idea what else she might have lost along the banks of the Elbe. But it was no wonder nobody had come forward to identify her. Not one of her neighbours. Not one of the British. None of the DPs – who were in any case former forced labour workers or former concentration camp inmates, whereas the survivors of Oradour were normal French citizens from the provinces. Nobody had dragged them to Hamburg.

'Has family here,' the note Maschke/Herthge had made. Somehow or other the Oradour survivor had bumped into the only surviving Oradour killer, and he had taken a note of her name. And the fact that she had other family here.

Could Yvonne Delluc have been the young woman? Or the older woman? Or even the child? Stave would find out. Maybe.

He put his foot down, the engine roared, the tyres squealed as he turned yet another bend.

How would he have come across Yvonne Delluc? By chance, when he had been looking for witnesses along the Reeperbahn, one of the hookers had mentioned that one of the vice squad men seemed a bit over-keen – to the extent that he accused ordinary harmless women of being prostitutes. Could that have been how he came across Yvonne Delluc? An elegant woman, not someone worn and haggard, a woman with a French name. Lots of prostitutes used French names, but in this case it happened to be her real name. Maschke might have thought he was checking out a whore and suddenly realised he was dealing with one of the witnesses of the massacre he had taken part in. At which point he kills her. And then, just to be sure, wipes out the rest of her family.

Then he volunteers to join the investigation, just to keep tabs on it. So that he can do what he has to if suspicion points to him: plant false evidence or at least know in advance when it was time to disappear.

'One Peter, One Peter, please call in.'

The voice over the radio caused Stave to flinch. Keeping his eyes on the road he thumped the radio furiously until it stopped.

The brakes screeched and the vehicle came to a shuddering halt. Stave leapt out of the car. There before him was the dark sinister bulk of the Eilbek bunker.

The chief inspector threw open the steel door and climbed the stairs to the first inhabited floor, dashing past the wooden partitions. The air was clammier than it had been on his first visit two months ago, warmer now, but mouldy and stuffy. The same ripped oilskin jackets hung at the entrance.

Stave sighed with relief: it meant Anton Thuman was still alive. He stomped into the man's little cubicle. The old seaman sprang to his feet and had put up his fists before recognising him.

'There are more polite ways of announcing one's presence, Herr Commissar,' he shouted at him, keeping his fists up.

The chief inspector managed, just, to control his anger. What angst he might have been spared if this man had just spoken up. One of the first witnesses he had spoken to, the day after they had discovered the first body! The young woman. He had mentioned a French family in the next cubicle who had been taken away by a policeman the day before. A policeman!

Stave reached into his jacket. Thuman's eyes opened wide.

'Don't shoot!' he called out.

The chief inspector ignored his pleas, and instead pulled out the photographs of the victims. Thuman, obviously relieved, put down his fists. Stave handed the photos to him, his hand shaking with anger.

'The people who lived next door,' the old seaman said indifferently. 'The French.'

The chief inspector closed his eyes for a moment. 'Why did you not report this to the police ages ago?' he said, trying hard to keep calm.

'Why should I have?'

'Did you not see the posters all over the city?' Stave asked, incredulously.

Thuman stared with empty eyes at the partition wall. 'I hardly ever leave here. And if I do, I don't look at stuff like that. In any case, I can't read. Never learned to. Never needed to.'

Stave leant back against the wooden planks and ran his hand over his eyes.

'Do you know what the family next door were called?'

'We were never introduced.'

'Delluc?'

'Maybe. Maybe not.'

'Can you describe the family to me? How many of them were there? Men, women, children?'

'An old guy who walked with a stick. Two women, ladies, if you know what I mean. One of them young and pretty but a bit cheeky. The other was also pretty, but a bit older. And a kid.'

'A little girl?'

'How old?'

'No idea. I don't have children. Small, though.'

The chief inspector sighed. Thuman's hardly going to be a great witness in court, he sighed.

'More like six? Or more like 14?'

'More like six.'

'Any more members of the family?'

'Just those four in the photographs. As far as I know.'

Stave pulled out one more photograph. From Maschke's personnel file.

'Is this the policeman who took the family away?'

'That's him. Filled the place with smoke, but didn't offer me a single Lucky Strike. Arrogant bastard.'

'Did the family go with him willingly?'

'Whoever goes willingly with the police?'

'What do you mean?'

'They both looked unhappy. But the policeman didn't have to act tough. No handcuffs, no truncheon. Didn't go around shouting at people.'

'Both?'

'The older woman and the little girl. Neither of the others were there at the time. But they never came back either.'

'Is their cubicle occupied again?'

'Yes, but I don't know their name.'

'Doesn't matter. But are any of the French family's possessions still there?'

Thuman looked at the ground. 'No, everything's gone,' he mumbled.

'Gone? Did the policeman take their stuff?'

'No, when the French lot didn't come back after a few days, a few lads from upstairs came down and snaffled all their stuff.'

'Go the police headquarters on Karl-Muck Platz, and ask for Inspector Müller. He'll take your statement.'

'Why aren't you coming with me?'

'Because I have other things to take care of.'

'And what if I don't go?'

'Then you'll end up in a hole that'll make this bunker look like a luxury hotel.'

Stave sped through the city. I just hope they're not already out looking for this car, he thought. And I hope there's enough fuel in the tank.

It took him more than an hour to get to the Warburg Children's Health Home. He screeched to a halt before the gates, almost crashing into them, and parped his horn. The young man who had opened the gates for him before came running out.

'What do you think you're doing? We have children here,' he remonstrated. But he opened the gates all the same.

'I know,' said Stave. 'It's one of them I'm here to see,' and he put his foot down, and roared off up the drive sending gravel flying on either side.

Thérèse Dubois had been standing by the window of the veranda watching him, and opened the door a few seconds later.

'You've caught him!' she said.

'I need to speak to Anouk Magaldi,' Stave replied.

Five minutes later he was showing the girl the photos of the four victims. On his last two visits he hadn't dared show the photos to the child.

And the warden had told him that the young children never left the villa grounds. So there would have been no way Anouk Magaldi could have seen the posters.

The little girl studied the photos, slowly, one by one. She looked sad but not particularly interested by the first three. Stave's pulse raced. When he showed her the fourth, she flinched, and stared at it with tears in her eyes. It was the photo of the younger woman.

'Mademoiselle Delluc,' the little girl whispered.

The chief inspector sighed with relief and leaned back in the wicker chair.

'An Oradour survivor?' Thérèse Dubois asked.

'Who finally met her murderer in Hamburg,' Stave replied.

'Your colleague?'

He nodded wearily. 'My colleague, who joined the police under a false name. My colleague, who used to be an SS man and was probably the only surviving member of the brigade that committed the massacre. And here in Hamburg he came across a victim of his crime. He strangled her to eliminate a witness who could have landed him in court. Then stripped her naked so that nobody could identify her.'

'What about the other three victims?'

Stave asked Anouk Magaldi, who told him that she had never seen any of Yvonne Delluc's three relatives before. The young woman herself had not even been from Oradour. She had just been staying with friends. Her family had lived elsewhere.

'Possibly in Paris,' Stave murmured, thinking of the earrings. Then he remembered the medallions and showed the little girl a photo of one. She beamed at him, put her hand to her neck and from under her jumper pulled out an identical one.

Stave looked at the girl, then down at the little medallion in her hand, and muttered: 'I was so close. So close, so often.'

Then he pulled himself together, and said, 'What does it mean, the cross and two daggers?'

She answered, speaking fast, with pride in her voice. Thérèse

Dubois translated. 'It's the coat of arms of Oradour. Don't ask me what the symbols stand for, but the few survivors all wear it, and their relatives too. In memory.'

'Their relatives too,' the chief inspector noted, with satisfaction. 'At last I have everything I need. Can she tell me anything more about Yvonne Delluc? If she had a job? If she was married? If she had children?'

Anouk Magaldi thought, then shook her head, smiled and said, '*Elle est Juive, comme moi.*'

'A Jew, like me,' the warden translated. 'Why would a Jew who had escaped a massacre come to the country of those who committed it?' she asked.

'I'm afraid I have no answer for that,' Stave said grimly. 'But be patient. In time all the details will come out. In the next trial at the Curio House.'

It was lunchtime. Stave hoped Erhlich wouldn't be out at some restaurant or in one of the British officers' clubs. He had a few interesting things to put before the public prosecutor. He was in luck and before long was sitting at the prosecutor's desk, the man's eyes behind his thick glasses upon him.

Stave recounted the previous life of Lothar Maschke, whose real name was Hans Herthge and who had been in an *SS Panzergrenadier* unit. He told him about the little orphan in the children's home in Warburg, and about the map he had found in Maschke's desk, without going into detail about how the map came to be in his hands.

Erhlich just nodded, clearly recalling that night they had bumped into one another in the vice squad man's office. Next to the map Stave laid the Search Office's index card with Maschke's name on it. He told him about the coat of arms of the village of Oradour and the medallions found on two of the victims, about the Paris jeweller, about the illiterate seaman in the bunker who paid no attention to posters because he couldn't read what was written on them, and wasn't surprised when a family living next door to him simply disappeared. A French family.

Ehrlich listened to him patiently, then smiled and polished his glasses. 'So what is your version of the chain of events?'

'Herthge alias Maschke bumps into Yvonne Delluc in Hamburg. I have no idea if he realised straight away that she was a survivor of Oradour. Or if it was her who recognised him and confronted him. Nor have I any idea what this young woman and the other members of her family were doing in our city. Nor do I know what relationship they bore to one another.

'But they meet, and Herthge/Maschke realises she could send him to the gallows, and so he kills her. Probably not when they first meet. Maybe he runs off. Or maybe she doesn't recognise him straight away. Or maybe he kidnaps her and holds her prisoner. Either way he has time enough to make a note of her name on his index card and the fact that she had relatives here. He obviously worked that out one way or another.

'He's also careful, methodical. He waits until he knows more about Yvonne Delluc's circumstances, then he strikes, mercilessly, eliminating all the evidence. He murders Yvonne Delluc somewhere in the city and hides her body in the ruins. How he got her body there I still don't know. Then he lies in wait for the old man and when he finds him, murders him on the spot. Maybe he found out he always took the same route. Then finally, on some pretext or other, he lures the other woman and child out of the bunker. They probably have no idea what's going on, they weren't in Oradour. Once they're out of the Eilbek bunker, he kills them and dumps their bodies. It's not impossible that he got hold of a police vehicle and used it to transport them to near where we later found them, and then dumped them in the ruins when the moment was right.

'What did he have to worry about? Yvonne Delluc and her family had only been living in the bunker for a few weeks. Bunker folk don't bother much with their neighbours. There's a good chance nobody in the bunker would remember them. And there didn't seem to be anybody else here in Hamburg who knew them. The little girl didn't go to school, which is why all our efforts to pursue that line of enquiry led nowhere. They weren't entitled to ration cards. There was no doctor here who had ever treated any of them, nor anywhere else in the former Reich. We should have been looking in France, but how could we have known that?

'As soon as we found the first body, Herthge/Maschke volunteered to join the investigation, so that he could keep an eye on things. He knew we would find the other victims and that it would make waves. What he didn't know was that in his haste to strip and loot his victims he had overlooked a couple of things. Nor did he know that there was another Oradour survivor living in Hamburg, one who would finally put me on his tail.'

'Does Herthge still have no idea, or does he suspect you're on to him?'

'Unfortunately,' Stave said, 'I've sent Maschke, alias Herthge, off on his travels, on the rubble murderer case. He's supposed to be going round the whole of northern Germany talking to doctors to find a lead. I only learned of his double identity after he was already on the road. Up until some four weeks or so ago, he had been calling the office intermittently. But not since then.'

'Have you sent out word to other police stations?' Ehrlich asked.

'Discreetly. Make it seem we're looking for Maschke because we're worried something's happened to him. Not that we want to arrest him.'

'Time to change that. Send out an arrest warrant for him.'

Ehrlich sat back in his chair, looking happily at the detective.

'You have had him under suspicion for some time?' Stave said.

The public prosecutor smiled. 'You think that was why I wanted to pay a visit to his office? Indeed, there had been hints: reports from other SS members who – faced with the gallows or a life sentence – were willing to grass on their former comrades. In circumstances like that, you can do yourself a bit of good. And there were always rumours when someone or other had gone under cover and taken a new identity. Maschke's name came up, and when I realised he was a policeman, my ears pricked up. But there was no SS man of this name in any of the files. I guessed, therefore, that Lothar Maschke had to be a false identity and that he had served in the SS under another name. I had no idea what that name might have been, nor in which unit he might have served. I can hardly wait to ask Herthge himself these questions. In court. I am deeply indebted to you.'

'Then perhaps you can do me two favours,' Stave replied.

The public prosecutor raised an eyebrow. 'What might they be?'

'First of all, call Cuddel Breuer and explain to him why I borrowed the Mercedes.'

'Borrowed,' Erhlich repeated, with a laugh. 'I would be willing to bet the Head of CID has never heard the public prosecutor use that word as a euphemism for car theft. My pleasure. And the second favour?'

'I want to know who the other victims were. It might not make any difference. When you're dead, you're dead. But I feel somehow better if there are names. Then at least their names survive.'

'I agree,' said Ehrlich.

A brief telephone call later and Ehrlich gave Stave a reassuring wink.

'Your boss just wants to know if you got any dents in his Mercedes. But he's very pleased with our news. He reckons that wrapping up the rubble murderer case is a good end to the winter.'

His next conversation took a lot longer. The public prosecutor spoke French fluently, albeit with a thick accent, Stave noted. He kept nodding, making notes, raised an eyebrow in surprise at one point. He's not liking what he's hearing, the chief inspector noted. I hope there are no problems. Not now.

Eventually Ehrlich put the phone down.

'The Dellucs were Jewish,' he said.

'I already know that.'

'Many members of the family were deported. The others went into hiding, three in Paris and one in Oradour.'

'Yvonne Delluc.'

'The grandfather of the family, René Delluc, had friends who stood by him, even in hard times. He went into hiding in Paris. He had a son and a daughter. The son was deported, but his daughter, Georgette, went into hiding with him.'

'The older woman, the one who had had the operation.'

Ehrlich nodded. 'She was the aunt of the little girl, Sarah. And also of Yvonne. Sarah and Yvonne were sisters, the daughters of the son who had been deported.'

'What brought them to Hamburg?'

'The desire to make it to Palestine, my French colleague assumes, although he has no proof. But there are hints. Apparently the Dellucs had been trying to get to the Holy Land since 1945, but as you know the British won't let any Jews in.'

Stave remembered that Thérèse Dubois had said the same thing. 'That's why they were trying to leave via the British zone of occupation, because the controls on ships leaving for Palestine are less strict here.'

'The port was badly damaged. Even the British are pleased when freighters are halfway able to load or unload. It's vital for the occupation zone. So who's checking all the paperwork? Who really checks whether a cargo shop that has just delivered a load of wheat is really bound for Cyprus next? Or might be heading for a port just that little bit further east? It's a long way round to get to the Holy Land, but after all that the Jews have been through over the past few years, it's a risk worth taking. There are more and more people being smuggled on board ships bound for Palestine. DPs and Jews who arrived after 1945.'

'Like the Dellucs.'

'Yes. Their misfortune was that they arrived too late. They disappeared from France around November 1946, but by then the Elbe had begun to freeze over. We were running short of coal. No further ships were departing. They sat tight, waiting for the thaw when they could be on the move again. They had no idea that they would be stuck here for weeks. And certainly no idea that they would run into one of the Oradour murderers.'

'Where do you think Herthge might be?'

Ehrlich raised his hands. 'Somehow or other he seems to have got wind that we're on his trail. He might not know for sure, but is being cautious, and when you sent him off round northern Germany, he took the opportunity to disappear. He wasn't going to get as good a chance again.

'Once we issue the warrant for his arrest, we obviously have to send an officer round to see his mother. But I doubt very much he'd be stupid enough to hide there. Maybe he's already on the way to South America: Argentina, Chile, Paraguay. It's no longer a secret that there are Nazi colonies out there.'

'It would be hard to get from northern Germany to South America. Even if he has comrades to help him.'

'The only port anywhere close from which ships leave for South America is Hamburg. But the ice is melting. In a week or two steamers will be sailing again.'

'You think he might hide around here that long?'

'He knows his way around the ruins. He's proved that. And now that the weather's getting warmer, he'll find it easier to get by.'

'Maybe he's shacked up with some whore or pimp. He knows that world well enough.'

'Or maybe with a former comrade. There're enough SS men still walking around free.'

'I hate putting up "wanted" posters,' the chief inspector said, getting up from his chair. 'It would make waves if people found out the police were after one of their own. On the other hand, I'd rather see Herthge's picture up on a wall than that of another strangled child.'

As Stave left, Ehrlich got up and shook his hand, a gesture he realised the prosecutor had previously avoided.

'We should go for a meal together occasionally,' Ehrlich said. Stave left his office and walked silently back to the CID headquarters.

When he entered his office, it looked somehow smaller and quieter than it used to, but also cleaner.

On his desk was a large, light-coloured envelope. From the Red Cross.

Life Goes On

Stave stared at the envelope, overcome all of a sudden. It took an enormous effort for him to walk the last two steps to his desk, stretch out and take the envelope in his hands. He ripped it open, his hands trembling. Inside was another envelope, much smaller, grey and rough, as if made from cheap toilet paper. It was addressed to him, care of Hamburg CID. In his son's handwriting.

Stave collapsed into his seat, stared out of the window, then back at the envelope. Karl was alive. And yet he felt a frisson of angst: what might he have written?

Eventually he summoned the courage to open this envelope too, slowly and carefully, as if it was a precious treasure. Inside was a small sheet of paper, not even the size of a page in an exercise book, ripped along the bottom, as if it had been torn from a larger sheet. The letters in pale blue pencil were barely legible, but the handwriting was unmistakable from all that homework, which Stave had once corrected so that the teacher wouldn't find any mistakes in it.

Father,
This scrap of paper is all I have, so this will have to be brief. I am fine, under the circumstances. I was taken prisoner in Berlin. A Soviet court sentenced me, why, I have no idea, to ten years in Vorkuta, but perhaps they'll reduce that. I'm still young. We help one another out here as best we can. Siberia is very cold, but the winter will be over in a month or two. I hope to be back in our apartment in Hamburg soon. Then we can talk about everything.
Karl

Stave laid it down carefully on his desk, though for a moment he had almost scrunched it up, even though it was so precious. He was disappointed, and at the same time ashamed of himself for being so. Nothing about life in the camp or about what his life had been like over the past two years. No personal message. It's your own damn self-pity at work again, he told himself. Read it again, carefully. Karl had only a scrap of paper. Were you expecting him to write a novel? And every word he wrote would be read by a Soviet censor out there in Vorkuta. Karl, your proud, so sensitive, lone wolf of a boy would not want some Soviet political officer reading anything personal. Maybe there was a message for him from his son in that cold factual language.

He read the letter again, and there it was: '*I hope to be back in our Hamburg apartment soon.*'

'*Our apartment.*'

That one word *our* – didn't that reflect a togetherness of father and son? Didn't it show that Karl wanted to come back? That this was still his home? Home, what did that mean if not togetherness, trust and, hopefully, love?

Stave could have cried if he hadn't feared that some colleague might burst in and find him slumped in tears on his desk. This was the first step of Karl's return. Nothing more, but nothing less. And Karl had a thousand steps at least to take. I have to handle this carefully, he told himself.

He left the building and walked the few hundred metres to the Hansaplatz. We're not about to carry out a raid today, he thought, and hopefully nobody will recognise me from the last time.

'*Siberia is very cold,*' Karl had written. Wasn't it possible to send parcels via the Red Cross? Stave would take the cigarettes he had saved up and the few Reichsmarks notes that he always carried with him for fear of burglars and visit the black market. What could he get? A coat, scarf, hat? Shoes, good heavy winter shoes or boots. Whatever.

The chief inspector pulled up the collar of his coat, even though the air wasn't cold. That way the collar and hat pulled down over his eyes would conceal his face, he hoped. Then he joined the throng of the shuffling figures wandering this way and that on the square. He stopped for a few minutes, displaying his wares from inside his overcoat, and whispering, 'Winter shoes, size 42, winter shoes.'

'Over here,' a careworn, elderly woman strolling nearby hissed. She looked vaguely familiar. She was probably arrested in the raid, he thought, but luckily he hadn't interviewed her himself. Hopefully she won't recognise me, he thought, but she gave him a shy smile. She probably thought she wouldn't be able to get rid of winter shoes, now that it's getting warm again.

She walks a bit faster and he follows her to the edge of the square. In the shadows of a house doorway she pulls out an old shopping bag with a pair of brown men's shoes in it. Thick soles, sturdy leather. They would do for winter shoes, even though the leather was scarred and the soles worn.

'Barely worn,' the woman lies.

'How much?' Stave asks, hoping they're the right size.

'500 Reichsmarks,' she replies.

Cheeky, especially now that the winter's over, he thinks.

'Done,' he says. What else can he do?

Furtive glances, two hasty movements, and the deal's done.

The woman disappears without a second glance.

'Was it a good deal?'

Stave spins round, shocked, desperately trying to think up an excuse in case it's one of his colleagues. But then he catches his breath.

Anna von Veckinhausen.

Stave feels himself redden.

Everything that enters his mind sounds stupid, so he stands there trying to think of something to say.

She comes over to him and nods at the pair of shoes. 'If I were you, I'd hide those under my coat, or else every policeman within

500 metres will arrest you. But if there's a raid, it's no good. Just drop them and play dumb.'

'I've had the experience,' he replies, quickly hiding his purchase.

'For you? Winter is finally over.'

'For my son. In Siberia. It's still cold there.'

The smile fades from Anna von Veckinhausen's face. 'He's a Soviet prisoner.' Not a question, a statement. 'That must be tough for you as a father.'

'To be honest, not really,' the chief inspector replies. 'Up until four weeks ago, I had no idea whether or not my son was still alive. In that respect the fact he is in a camp in Siberia is relatively good news.'

'What has happened to us, when something like that is good news?' she whispers. Then she takes his arm and says, 'Walk with me for a bit.'

Confused, Stave nods, stiffer than normal, feeling as awkward as some 14-year-old. Anna's hand is on his lower arm. Just the cloth and pullover wool keeping skin from skin. He hasn't been this close to a woman in ages.

'What was your business at the Hansaplatz?' he asks.

'The usual. A meeting with a British officer at the station. I got hold of a passable copy of Caspar David Friedrich's *The Monk by the Sea*, horrible frame, pseudo-baroque, gilded with lots of chips on it. But it's an oil and done by somebody who knew what he was doing.'

'Did you get a good deal?'

She smiles, but says nothing.

Stave wondered if she had palmed it off on the Brit as an original. American officers, according to popular wisdom, were so ignorant they'd buy any old rubbish. But the English? He didn't press her. Otherwise she'll just take me for a typical policeman, he told himself. Out loud he said, 'Do you fancy taking a look at some original Friedrichs? We could take a stroll through the Kunsthalle?'

It was only a short walk, just a few minutes from the station, where three trains with steam pouring from their funnels had pulled in. 'There must be coal supplies again,' said Stave. 'I can't remember the last time I saw more than one train in the station.'

'I guess that means they'll be starting domestic deliveries again; with any luck we'll be able to get warm by the time summer comes,' Anna von Veckinhuasen replied. 'I don't mean to be sarcastic. Everybody's doing what they can.'

They turned right past the station and 200 metres ahead of them the Kunsthalle loomed: a great grey box with a rotunda crowned by a dome, like a side of bacon with a musket ball stuck in it. The imposing façade of the old museum was dirty, but almost undamaged. A few scars caused by bomb shrapnel, streaks of smoke on the cornices. In front of the rotunda stood an ancient oak tree with a trunk thicker than the columns on the façade.

'Incredible that that tree's still unharmed,' Stave commented.

'There are always survivors, even in the plant world.'

In the shadow of the oak tree stood a tall bronze statue of a man on a horse, naked save for an antique helmet. 'Rider,' Stave read the inscription on the plaque below. 'I'd never have guessed.'

'There's another miracle for you,' Anna von Veckinhausen said. 'That the thing wasn't melted down.'

'Some Nazi obviously liked it, or at least preferred it to the church bells. They were all melted down to make hand-grenade casings.'

Stave bought two entrance tickets. His companion nodded gratefully.

'How did you know that the Kunsthalle was open again?'

'I didn't. We're just lucky,' Stave replied.

The museum had re-opened shortly after the end of the war. The collection had been housed either in bank safes or in the concrete bunker at Heiligengeistfeld, at least those works that the brownshirts had not declared to be *entartet*, unworthy to be considered art. The latter had all been sold off abroad, cheap. But in winter it had been impossible to heat the great galleries, not least because some of the roofs had been damaged and only partly patched up. So the museum had been closed and in fact this warm day was the first of the new season.

Most people, however, were out enjoying the sunshine, and hardly anybody thought of spending the precious daylight hours indoors. As a result Stave and Anna von Veckinhausen had the museum almost to themselves, and were able to wander leisurely from gallery to gallery. Some had black streaks down the walls from water coming in, and others were suspiciously empty, notably those that had been dedicated to modern art. Even so they enjoyed strolling slowly past the masterpieces. What is it that I like most, Stave asked himself, and answered: it's the colours. The oils and watercolours, the blues and reds, the yellows and greens, the gold of the old masters – it was a treat for the eye, in contrast to the grey and black of the ruins, the brown of people's clothing.

Anna von Veckinhausen was still on his arm. He wondered what she was thinking. They were both silent.

Eventually they reached the gallery with the works of Caspar David Friedrich. Stave stared at the fantastic landscapes and the tiny figures: women in bonnets, men in old-fashioned traditional dress, all of them with their backs to the spectator. He spent a long time over the painting entitled *Eismeer*, of a ship crushed between mighty ice floes. Once upon a time he had considered it surreal but after this winter it no longer seemed so. It was years since he had last been in here. With Margarethe. He quickly suppressed the memory.

Stave nodded at the paintings and said, 'It's funny to think that these are little more than 100 years old. To me, now, they seem like relics from the ancient world, on another continent.'

'That's what they are. Nothing Friedrich saw still exists, nothing he believed in is believed any more.'

'But the works are still displayed on the walls here. And people come to see them. Like us.'

'Because we long for those long-gone days. Because we feel we've lost something, but we don't know what it is.'

'There again, Caspar David Friedrich would have liked that.'

'But only that. He painted picturesque ruins into woods and mountains. If he were to see the ruins here today, he'd soon lose his taste for gaping windows and ruined walls.'

She put her free arm across her chest, and shuddered. 'I need to get out of here, back into the sunlight.'

From the museum it was only a short stroll across the broad pavements of the Glockengiesserwall to the Inner Alster. Before the war the river, turned into a giant square here by two dams, had reflected Hamburg's most famous façades – the Jungfernstieg. The psychologist's practice was just opposite the Glockengiesserwall. There were trees along the embankment, promenades, the offices of important shipping companies behind the façades, and the spires of the city's churches towering above the glistening tiled roofs. Before the war the citizens of Hamburg would stroll up and down here in their Sunday best, and now they were here again, trying to ignore the cracks in the façades and their own dowdy dress.

Stave and his companion made their way carefully over the temporarily repaired rail tracks to the Ballindamm, around two empty, long-abandoned wagons which up until the beginning of the winter workers had used to bring rubble from the town and tip it into the Alster. The ice on the river no longer glittered, but lay there white and watery in the sunlight, like spilt milk. Yet only on the surface. The ice below was still up to three metres thick. A few intrepid souls were skating in wide circles on it, sending little sprays of water up behind them. Most people stayed on the embankment, as if it were somehow unseemly to venture on to the ice.

Stave shivered. The cold rising from the Alster reminded him of the morgue. Maybe because he was taking a casual walk, something he was unused to doing. Going for a walk along the waterfront was an activity that was simultaneously pointless and an end in itself: you walk along the riverfront without following any particular route because no one route mattered more than any other; when you went for a walk you ended up where you started from. It was as if this casual walk, this feeling of doing something and at the same time doing nothing, was untying a knot in his soul.

And suddenly the chief inspector began to talk, unaware of how or why he started, but he talked about his son in Siberia and how they'd argued back in the summer of 1945 when he set out for the front. About his son's scorn for his father, and his youthful enthusiasm, so painfully genuine, so horribly misled. About Margarethe and the night she died in the bombing. About the rubble murderer, who turned out to be one of his colleagues. And a Jewish family fleeing to find a new home who got stranded amidst the ice in a hostile city. A city with a murderer at large, a murderer whose fate and theirs were inextricably linked. About Lothar Maschke, who was really Hans Herthge, about whom he now knew a lot but not everything – things he couldn't believe. But what was the point of knowing something if that knowledge had no consequence.

They reached the end of the Ballindamm, but instead of turning on to the Jungfernstieg and walking further along the Inner Alster, they turned around and went back the way they came. They didn't discuss it, but they could both see that there were hundreds of people walking along the Jungfernstieg, whereas the Ballindamm, with its abandoned wagons, was less crowded.

The other side of the street was emptier still, so they crossed the Lombardsbrücke Bridge separating the Inner and Outer Alster, which widened to become a lake, the shores lined with reeds. The caster-sugar white of the Atlantic Hotel was reflected in the film of water lying on top of the ice. Most of the houses just beyond the hotel had been bombed but the devastation ended a couple of hundred metres further on. To the north the greenery was sprinkled with villas, smaller than the grand establishments on the Inner Alster, but also more discreet, further back from the water and hidden behind trees and bushes: most of them had been commandeered by the British, who didn't need to chop down the trees in their own gardens for firewood.

They wander northwards, the sun sinking, its rays warm and golden. Exhausted and somewhat embarrassed, Stave stops. Anna von Veckinhausen now knows everything about him. But he knows next to nothing about her. She's walked silently at his side, but he feels her silence was well meant.

They stop briefly behind the Atlantic, concealed from the villas and the street by a screen of thin branches, like a ripped curtain. It was getting near the curfew hour, and the few casual strollers who had chosen the same path were disappearing between the houses. The Alster was wide and empty.

'Sorry for having rattled on like that,' Stave says. 'It's not like me.'

'Then it's been my lucky day,' she replies. 'I enjoyed listening.'

'I didn't know what to say to you.'

'When a man doesn't know what to say to a women, he should kiss her.'

Stave thinks he's misheard. But Anna von Veckinhausen puts both arms round his neck and pulls him towards her.

They ended the day in a flophouse. Somebody had scribbled Hotel Pension Rudolf Prem on a wooden board above the door of the one house still standing between the Atlantic and the villa quarter. They were too hungry for each other's bodies to make it all the way back to Stave's apartment. The Nissen hut with internal partitions that were no more than bits of cloth was hardly an option. And they couldn't afford the Atlantic.

Stave booked a room in the Pension Prem, throwing a few Reichsmarks down on the counter and signing in as Herr and Frau Schmidt, so obviously false that the elderly, half-blind landlord raisesd a sceptical eyebrow, mumbled something incomprehensible, but still handed them the key. The room was on the first floor, small but more or less clean, the interior glowing in the evening sun as if the windows were made of amber. They were in a hurry, slamming the door and locking it. They fell on to the narrow bed, starved of tenderness and intimacy. Only later, when the initial hunger had been satisfied, did they become calmer, gentler, more inquisitive.

At some stage Stave held Anna in his arms, her body shining like alabaster in the moonlight, feeling her pulse, her breath on his chest, her warmth. We're alive, he thought to himself. We're alive again.

Stave ran a fingertip gently down the long curve of her back: 'I still don't know anything about you.'

She sighed, not so much exasperation as irony in her voice: 'Are you still on duty, Chief Inspector?'

'I'm not asking you as a policeman, but as a lover.'

Anna shook her head. 'Give me time,' she said, then kissed him. 'We've both lost so much that we've almost nothing left to lose. But we have time, we have time enough.'

Stave reflected on her words. As a detective he had never enough time. He was always too late. That's what the job was all about at the end of the day: something had to have happened before he was called in. Always pressure to make an arrest before it happened again. But did he have to live his whole life as if it were a case?

'You're right,' he whispered to her, and suddenly felt as if a weight had slipped from his shoulders. 'We have all the time in the world.'

They crept out of the room after midnight, not wanting to be found together in the morning. The old porter was snoring behind the desk. Stave set the room key down quietly, next to the bell, then pushed open the door and they slipped out into the night.

Stave's police ID meant he didn't have to worry about the curfew. If a British patrol stopped him he could always say he was on a case. But could he offer Anna the same protection? Or would the British military police arrest her? It would be better not to test it. So he led her down the backstreets towards Eilbek. The moon lent the city a silvery sheen. Suddenly the cracked walls and empty windows took on the aura of ancient ruins. The vast expanses of ruins were transformed into a city of temples and forums, amphitheatres and palaces. The air was mild, but the cold stored in the ground still seeped forth. Stave had draped his overcoat around Anna's shoulders as they made their way, arms around one another, across narrow footpaths between remains of walls. Stave breathed in her aroma happily.

His son was alive. He had found new love. Winter was over. All of a sudden he felt as if he had been given a new beginning, a colossal, undeserved happiness at having got through it all. A happiness that almost overwhelmed him, that wanted to burst out of his body. He felt like singing and dancing like a lunatic, though in a silent city under curfew that might not be the cleverest thing to do. But the silence on the streets and the sheer exuberance flooding his soul inspired him to do something very different, albeit no less pleasurable. He stopped, pulled Anna towards him, and embraced her in a passionate kiss right there in the middle of the street.

When at last they dragged themselves apart, she smiled at him, surprised, breathless, but didn't ask him why.

Eventually they reached the Nissen huts, standing there at the crossroads, black like the shells of giant tortoises. They hardly dared breathe as they crossed the last few metres, trying to make no noise. Only a few millimetres of tin separated them from hundreds of eyes and ears. At the door of her hut they kissed farewell. Stave scribbled his address on a page from his notebook and handed it to her.

'I'll come round tomorrow,' Anna whispered. Then she slipped through the door silently and disappeared into the dark interior of the hut. Stave crept away until he was sure he was far enough from the row of barracks that nobody looking out of the windows would pay him any attention. Then he increased his pace and turned into the broad Wandsbek Strasse, almost running. He felt as if he was floating on air. Even his injured leg didn't hurt any more. Alive, he cried. I'm alive again.

Then, from behind, he felt a thin wire thrown around his neck. And drawn tight.

The Murderer in Ruins

Stave choked, tried to scream. Struggled for breath, tried to break free and run. To no avail. He was trapped in a fearsome vice that was squeezing tight on his neck. Scenes from the autopsy table flashed before his eyes: a crushed windpipe, reddish-brown line around the thread. He lashed out blindly in panic, his fists flailing in the air, occasionally making contact at best with some cloth behind his back. He's wearing a thick overcoat, Stave realised. The gun, in the holster underneath his own overcoat. But he had done it up after leaving the Nissen hut colony. He ripped at the buttons, but none of them came free. The choking sensation worsened by the second, his head was pounding as if it would explode, his legs were giving way. He fell to his knees. Any second now and I'm done for, he knew. He gave up trying to pull at the wire around his throat, began to flail behind him with his fists again. By now his attacker had to be standing above him – the perfect position. Stave's blind thrashing got weaker, more spasmodic.

He needed something hard. The winter shoes, for his son, in his overcoat. He shoved his hand into the outer pocket, felt the hard soles, yanked the shoes out and whacked them hard behind him.

He heard a dull grunt. He'd hit his attacker's knees, surprised him. The man stumbled, loosened his grip. Stave jumped up, throwing his weight in front of him. The wire cut into his throat, blood flowed down his collar – but the choking sensation lessened. He squeezed his left hand under the wire, pulled it further away. More blood, his hand was bleeding now. But he caught a breath of air, at long last. His right hand continued to flail behind him.

He tried to cry out, but managed only a squawk.

Breathe in. Lash out. Step backwards.

Then suddenly the attacker gave up. The pressure on his throat vanished. He could hear running footsteps, scattering stones.

A red mist descended over Stave's eyes as he spun round, the wire still around his throat. He spotted a shape against the remains of a wall, tore at his coat with trembling hands. Damn, damn, damn. Then the cold steel of the gun. He pulled the FN22 from its holster.

The gunshot rang in his ears, echoed far and wide through the ruins. Another and another. Half blind and mad with rage, Stave emptied the magazine, firing in the direction of the figure he had glimpsed.

Silence.

The chief inspector collapsed to the ground in the moonlight, pulled the loop of wire from around his neck, took a deep breath. In, out, in. His heart was pounding, his hands trembling. But his brain was working.

The rubble murderer.

Stave pulled himself up, stumbled towards the spot between two remnants of walls, half his height, where he had last glimpsed the figure. There was a spot of something on the ground. Stave bent down. Blood. I hit him, he gloated. He looked around, but all he could see were two fields of ruins, a mess of rubble, steel beams, tangled cables, shards of glass, nothing resembling a pathway.

But there was another drop of blood.

He's climbed over the rubble, Stave told himself. He followed the trail of blood, quietly cursing his wounded leg. He put the shoes back in his coat pocket, but kept the gun in his right hand. The magazine was empty, but the gun itself was a weapon, hard enough to smash down on somebody's head. Two tiles gave way beneath his feet, clattering down the pile of rubble, sending up a cloud of cement dust. His eyes watered.

Behind the two ruined street blocks was the remains of a bombed house which would have housed three or four families, 30 metres high, all the external walls charred, the window openings empty, no roof, no internal floors remaining. Just heaps of rubble. There was a sign next to the entrance where a door hung at an angle from just the upper hinge. 'No entry. Liable to collapse.'

But the trail of blood led inside.

I've got you, Stave thought, wading carefully through the doorway into the burnt-out building.

Darkness. The moonlight came in only through the gaping windows. Everywhere there were shadows and pitch-black areas. Stave held his breath. Heard nothing.

Or then again? Steps, scraping, as if someone were dragging something along. A wounded leg? A heavy burden? The chief inspector listened out. Somewhere in this ruin, the murderer was on the move. Stave felt in his overcoat pocket for his torch. Not there. Today of all days, he hadn't brought it with him. Because he didn't think he would be finding any more bodies in the rubble, because at last it was spring, and the evenings were getting light. Damnably negligent. He looked around him trying to make out details in the darkness. The building had no roof, no internal walls. Where could his attacker hide? Think. What do you know about the rubble murderer? He always hid his victims as deep as possible: a cellar, a bomb crater, the bottom of a lift shaft.

A cellar.

Stave ventured further in. The walls, towering above him, seemed to be trembling. It's your imagination, he told himself. Don't let yourself go crazy. He heard a cracking noise, somewhere amidst the piles of stone. Mortar fell to the ground behind his back. He heard a step, a second, then more. Somewhere towards the centre of the ruin. More steps, coming closer this time. He raised the gun.

There. A staircase. Leading down to the cellar. Everything above ground had been bombed to pieces. But the stairs, half hidden under the rubble, led down. The cellar might be undamaged. Now Stave thought he could hear someone breathing heavily, wheezing. Someone in pain, wounded.

Pitch darkness. Stave used his left hand to feel his way forwards, the FN22 still raised in his right. A corridor. Narrow, but possibly very long. He could feel a draught, could taste cement dust on his lips, splinters of wood. He reached out with his hand and felt: a support pillar, wedged in between the ground and the ceiling, an emergency support from the bombing raids. Slave workers were sent in by the local *Gauleiter* after the 'All Clear' was sounded to prop up cellars and walls with wooden beams. The idea was to keep larger ruins from collapsing so that the rubble could be cleared and allow access for the fire service.

He edged forwards a few paces further. The corridor took a turn. He could see light up ahead: a hole in the ceiling where silvery moonlight fell through on to the ground. And on the ground he glimpsed a figure, curled up in pain.

Lothar Maschke/Hans Herthge.

Stave moved towards him, cautiously. The man who had once been his colleague was lying on his side, his right hand pressed against his stomach. Blood was oozing between his fingers, spreading out over the tiled floor like oil. His left hand clenched the dust. His legs trembled.

A shot to the stomach, Stave told himself. He must be suffering like hell. He'll die. The chief inspector came closer, bent down carefully, still holding his gun in his hand.

Herthge's face glistened with sweat. His eyes were open wide.

'Can you hear me?' Stave asked.

'You won't give me any peace, will you?' Herthge wheezed between his teeth. 'You want to watch me croak.'

'It's not a pretty sight,' Stave replied. He had no sympathy for the murderer. In fact he was still afraid of him, even now, seeing him lying there in his own blood. Perhaps he hated him too, though Stave tried not to think about that. Professional curiosity came first: find out all he could about the killings, before it's too late.

'Tell me what I need to know,' he suggested to Herthge. 'Then I'll go, leave you here to die on your own. I'll send a few of my colleagues, but for your sake, I'll make sure they don't get here until after you're dead. On the other hand, if you don't talk to me now, I'm going to stay here and watch you die. Even if it takes hours.'

'Best deal I've ever been offered,' Herthge whispered, making a gruesome grimace.

'How did you bump into Yvonne Delluc?'

'I thought she was a streetwalker: young, well dressed, threw French words around,' the dying man gasped. 'She wasn't in my files, so I stopped her and checked her out.' He gasped for breath, beads of sweat glistening on his brow. 'In fact she was only going out to deal on the black market, to hack something or other. I didn't recognise her from Oradour. But she recognised me. Immediately began screaming at me, calling me a murderer and threatened to have me arrested. Happily she was only speaking French and nobody in the street understood.'

'So you strangled her then and there.'

Herthge pressed his lips together. His face was so pale now that Stave feared he might die before he told him everything. 'No,' he groaned. 'I didn't know how she got here, and if there might be any others in Hamburg. I denied everything, told her that she was making a mistake. Eventually I managed to persuade her. Then I let her go, but followed her discreetly.'

'As far as the Eilbek bunker.'

'Then I knew where she lived and who she lived with. The next day, when I saw her heading out for the black market again, I dragged her into the ruins and strangled her. I stripped her so that nobody could identify her. I burnt her clothes later in my stove at home. You could have raided the black marketeers as often as you liked and still found nothing, Chief Inspector.' Despite his agony, he grinned scornfully.

'Then I drove back to the bunker, in the CID Mercedes. I borrowed it quite legitimately. Unfortunately only the other woman and the girl were there. It wasn't difficult to invent a pretext to get them into the car. Then I tied them up, drove down a side street and silenced them forever. Just as I had with Yvonne Delluc. But beforehand I had to beat the woman until she told me where the old man was. He'd gone looting in the ruins on the other side of the Alster.'

'Why didn't you hide the two bodies in the same place?'

'I didn't want them to be found too quickly,' Herthge gasped. 'I didn't want to be disturbed for a couple of hours,' he managed to say. 'Then I went looking for the old man. It was getting dark by the time I found him. The rest was easy.'

'Easy,' Stave repeated with disgust. He thought for a moment, then asked, 'Why did you try to kill me? You must have known that it was too late. Whether you killed me or not didn't matter. They've put out a warrant for your arrest. Why didn't you go into hiding?'

Herthge gave a mirthless laugh. His breath was failing. By now the blood had formed a large pool all around his body and was still oozing from between his fingers.

'I wasn't sure,' he wheezed. 'Only guessed you had me in your sights. I thought the only one who posed a threat to me was the other witness, that woman who caught a glimpse of me in Lappenbergs Allee.'

'Anna von Veckinhausen.'

'It wasn't exactly hard to find out that it was her who had given you that bit of information. It was in the files. Wasn't hard either to find out where she lived. I thought that if I got her out of the way, then there would be no more witnesses. I was lying in wait for her.'

'Today?'

'Yes. But she was never alone. As you know only too well.'

Stave imagined Herthge following them, to the Kunsthalle, along the Alster, to the flophouse where he had made love to Anna. Imagined him sneaking after them through the rubble. It made him feel sick. He had to make an effort not to kick the dying man.

'And because you couldn't get your hands on your real target, you went for me instead.'

'I was angry that you'd got in the way. I wasn't thinking straight. Everybody makes a mistake.'

Herthge's breathing was fading fast. His legs no longer trembled. He was lying in a pool of blood.

'I'm cold,' he whispered.

'Hell's a cold place,' Stave said, then got to his feet, turned around and left.

A few hundred metres away, in an almost undamaged apartment block, lights glimmered behind boarded-up windows – candles, low-wattage light bulbs. Some of the windows were open. There was the sound of voices and gramophone music. Chief Inspector Frank Stave took one last look at the cellar where Herthge lay dying. He stood there for a long time, looking at the ruins, which in the merciful moonlight looked almost majestic. Then, in the shadow of a scarred and fractured wall, he limped away.

Notes

1. The 'One Peter' call reflects the Hamburg slang 'Peterwagen' for a police car. It remains in common use to this day, but is believed to have originated with the British occupation as a mispronunciation of 'patrol car', although there are some who believe it to have come from the Blue Peter naval flag, signalling 'All on Board'.
2. Then and now one of Hamburg's major shipbuilding and aircraft companies.
3. Galicia had been part of the Austro-Hungarian empire before 1918, when it was given to newly independent Poland. It was seized by the USSR in 1939 and made part of the Soviet Republic of Ukraine. Many of its people initially welcomed German armies in 1941. In 1945 it was reintegrated into Ukraine, which became independent in 1990. Galicia's capital was called Lemberg under the Austrians, Lwow under the Poles, Lvov in Soviet days and Lviv by the Ukrainians today.
4. The *Wilhelm Gustloff* was built in 1937 as a cruise liner for the Nazi party's labour organisation and used for holidays for workers and civil servants until 1939, when it was requisitioned by the *Kriegsmarine* to become naval accommodation. In October 1945 it was seconded to the evacuation of civilians fleeing the Russian invasion of East Prussia. Torpedoed by a Russian submarine, the overcrowded vessel sank within 40 minutes, unable to use most of its lifeboats because of frozen davits. German vessels managed to rescue 1,252 of those on board but the vast majority, 9,343, including some 5,000 children, perished in unseasonably icy waters with temperatures down to minus 18°C, the greatest loss of life in maritime history.

Afterword

There really was a 'rubble murderer' who claimed four victims in Hamburg in the terrible, cold winter of 1946–7. That was the name he was given at the time, a name that struck fear in people's minds. But who he really was remains a mystery.

This thriller is based on the original case. I have done my best to depict the bombed-out city as accurately as possible, from the food rationing to the radio play that was broadcast on the newly founded North West German Radio (NWDR). A few of the figures who feature in this book really existed, such as Mayor Max Brauer and CID chief 'Cuddel' Breuer – whose nickname was spelled by some contemporary writers as 'Kuddel'. In the case of the others I have allowed myself considerable artistic licence. There really was a police officer called Frank Stave, but my protagonist has nothing to do with this historical individual. Most of the other characters are invented, and any similarities with people alive at that time are pure chance.

The murders were played out just as described here: the details of the victims, the places where their bodies were found and many other details are based on the investigations carried out by the police and the pathologist's reports. The wording on the posters erected is authentic as is much of the other data from the autopsies. On the other hand I have inserted a few other, small but consequential, details to help Chief Inspector Frank Stave track down the killer – sadly only in this book.

In reality there were no such clues. The police tried long and hard over several years to solve the case, but never found anything that might help them identify the killer or reveal his motive. The series of killings ended, as abruptly as it began, with the fourth murder. All I can do is speculate as to the reason.

What remains even more shocking is that the detectives never identified the victims. Despite all the efforts, which I have described here – the posters and photographs put up, not just around the city of Hamburg but in all of occupied Germany – not one person ever came forward to identify the old man, either of the two women or the little girl. Whether or not they were related, whether there was any relationship at all between them and why they were marked out to die, remains to this day unknown.

In my research for this book I worked my way through mountains of literature, newspaper articles, letters and other documents. Particular thanks are due to Dr Ortwin Pelc from the Museum of Hamburg, Uwe Hanse from the city's police museum and Wolfgang Kopitsch, previously at the regional police academy in Hamburg, now council leader in the North Hamburg district, all of whom gave me important advice and information about the city at the time. Dr Uwe Heldt of Mohrbooks and Angela Tsakiris of DuMont did a critical read-through of the manuscript. My most sincere thanks to all of them – and of course to my wife Françoise, and our children Julie and Anouk for their tolerance during many long, often late, hours spent at my computer.